Lela May Wight grew up [with] sisters. Yes, it was noisy, [and she found escape] in romance books. She st[arted] to write them too! She ho[pes to give her] readers the same escapism when the world is a little too loud. Lela May lives in the UK, with her two sons and her very own hero, who never complains about her book addiction—he buys her more books! Check out what she's up to at lelamaywight.com.

Clare Connelly was raised in small-town Australia among a family of avid readers. She spent much of her childhood up a tree, Mills & Boon book in hand. Clare is married to her own real-life hero, and they live in a bungalow near the sea with their two children. She is frequently found staring into space—a surefire sign that she's in the world of her characters. She has a penchant for French food and ice-cold champagne, and Mills & Boon novels continue to be her favourite ever books. Writing for Modern is a long-held dream. Clare can be contacted via clareconnelly.com or at her Facebook page.

Also by Lela May Wight

His Desert Bride by Demand
Bound by a Sicilian Secret
The King She Shouldn't Crave
Italian Wife Wanted

Also by Clare Connelly

Pregnant Before the Proposal
Unwanted Royal Wife
Billion-Dollar Secret Between Them

Royally Tempted collection

Twins for His Majesty

Discover more at millsandboon.co.uk.

DARING CONFESSIONS

LELA MAY WIGHT

CLARE CONNELLY

MILLS & BOON

All rights reserved including the right of reproduction in whole or in part in any form. This edition is published by arrangement with Harlequin Enterprises ULC.

This is a work of fiction. Names, characters, places, locations and incidents are purely fictional and bear no relationship to any real life individuals, living or dead, or to any actual places, business establishments, locations, events or incidents. Any resemblance is entirely coincidental.

Without limiting the author's and publisher's exclusive rights, any unauthorised use of this publication to train generative artificial intelligence (AI) technologies is expressly prohibited. HarperCollins also exercise their rights under Article 4(3) of the Digital Single Market Directive 2019/790 and expressly reserve this publication from the text and data mining exception.

® and TM are trademarks owned and used by the trademark owner and/or its licensee. Trademarks marked with ® are registered with the United Kingdom Patent Office and/or the Office for Harmonisation in the Internal Market and in other countries.

First published in Great Britain 2025 by Mills & Boon, an imprint of HarperCollins*Publishers* Ltd, 1 London Bridge Street, London, SE1 9GF

www.harpercollins.co.uk

HarperCollins*Publishers*, Macken House, 39/40 Mayor Street Upper, Dublin 1, D01 C9W8, Ireland

Daring Confessions © 2025 Harlequin Enterprises ULC

Kidnapped for Her Secret © 2025 Lela May Wight

Billion-Dollar Dating Deception © 2025 Clare Connelly

ISBN: 978-0-263-34481-3

09/25

This book contains FSC™ certified paper and other controlled sources to ensure responsible forest management.

For more information visit www.harpercollins.co.uk/green.

Printed and Bound in the UK using 100% Renewable Electricity at CPI Group (UK) Ltd, Croydon, CR0 4YY

KIDNAPPED FOR HER SECRET

LELA MAY WIGHT

MILLS & BOON

CHAPTER ONE

IN A ROOM full of eyes watching her, only *his* made Aurora Arundel feel like an impostor.

She was projecting, she knew. She shouldn't be in New York. Not for this exclusive auction of a single piece of coveted artwork, or for the masquerade ball that followed.

It wasn't her invitation. It had been meant for her parents. But the dead couldn't forbid her from attending tonight.

The dead couldn't complain that she'd stolen their invitation.

Only she knew that the gold embossed invitation wasn't hers as she moved through the black iron gates and up the pebbled driveway to the columned entrance of Eachus House. Only she noticed her fingers trembling as she released the invitation from her sapphire-adorned fingers into the white-gloved hands of the man who stood beneath the cherub-topped entrance.

The prayer on her lips had been for her ears only, thanking whatever gods that be that she was able to keep her spine straight and her head held high as she was ushered her through the heavy oak doors and guided through hallways with painted ceilings and ornate walls, up the floating oak staircase, and finally to the green drawing room, transformed, only for tonight, only for the invited, into an auction room.

Gilded mirrors lined the vivid green walls. The velvet apple-green drapes were drawn against the night. An oak lectern displaying the name of a famous auction house was positioned in front of a marble fireplace of epic proportions, masterfully crafted with silver-accented winding vines.

Ball gown after ball gown moved around the room as everyone began to take their seats. Aurora had been handed a gold-etched paddle, and the auctioneer had taken her to her seat in front of a podium, where the wooden legs of the easel beside her peeked out from beneath a black cloth.

The room was heavy with tension. All eyes fastened on the easel's black cloth. All hands itched to reveal what lay beneath.

This was the appetiser for the night before the red ballroom opened its doors and they were all encouraged to indulge in champagne, music and the discretion their masks would afford them for the night.

Only the staff knew who was behind the masks, and only because they knew the names allotted to the numbered paddles.

And Aurora understood it to be one of those games the elite played. The night would start this way in order to build the anticipation, to fire the blood—*to heat it*.

The rich didn't care that tonight was supposed to be for charity. They didn't care about those the charity would support in their darkest hour.

Her parents had certainly never cared.

But *she* did.

Up and up Aurora drove the bid. The price rising to hundreds of thousands of dollars within minutes for a painting no one would see until the bidding war was over.

And *his* gaze intensified with every bid she placed.

His tilted head, his elegant, bow-tied neck, arched so he could stare at her from the front row of intricately carved antique white chairs. The curved gold leaf mask covering his cheeks, his nose, and his upper lip only sharpened his green-rimmed irises, making the inner amber of his eyes glow.

She was aware of how different her gown was from all the others around her. Her mother wouldn't have approved of her dress either. The colour or the cut. *The sequins.* How she shimmered under the chandelier hanging from the high ceiling. How it drew attention to her.

Her mother, Lady Arundel, wife of Lord Arundel, most definitely would not have approved of the mask she'd chosen. The dainty pearls rising in stalks from the blue-and-brushed gold mask. The shells clustered on the right-hand side, interlaced with the purest of diamonds and uniquely cut sapphires.

She knew what she looked like. A mermaid. She'd chosen the off-the-shoulder asymmetrical gown with its thigh-high slit to showcase she was, in fact, human, with legs. Each adornment she'd approved. On purpose. Because she liked them. She liked that tonight, she was daring. Uncompromising.

Yet under the onslaught of the man's gaze, the bow on her left shoulder felt too big. Her bare right shoulder felt too exposed. Too naked. She felt too bright. Too colourful. Too breathless.

The bodice of her aquamarine dress felt too tight. And she was all too conscious of the skin and muscle beneath it. Of her breasts tightening, her nipples hardening.

Aurora swallowed, readying herself to continue the bidding. For herself. For her brother.

Pain settled inside her chest. Still acute even after all this time. Still as visceral as the night she'd been told he was gone.

She straightened her spine, squared her shoulders. She would end this. Now. She would win for Michael. For all the times she'd let him down, for all the times she hadn't fought for him.

Her pulse raced. Her heart hammered hard inside her ribs. 'Fifty million,' she said. The crowded room gasped. But he didn't. The eyes holding hers hostage didn't blink.

'Where's fifty million and one?' The rhythmic auctioneer's chant trickled into her consciousness, but her eyes lowered to the subtle movement of his mouth.

Slowly, the pink tip of his tongue revealed itself to sweep across his full, blushed-pink bottom lip. And she felt it. The gentle stroke of his tongue on her.

A gasp leapt out from her parted lips in a hush of expelled air.

'Anyone?' the auctioneer continued from the front of the room.

She waited for the stranger's mouth to move. For him to bid against her.

She wanted to hear his voice, she realised. She wanted to know if it matched the intensity of his gaze. But he didn't speak. The set line of his bearded jaw was a sculpted thing. A *beautiful* thing defined by a thousand chestnut hairs interlaced with strings of red fire, kissed by shards of ice.

'Fifty million, and holding...'

Aurora raised her gaze from his jaw to his eyes to find him still staring at her.

'Are we all done?'

The silence pulsed.

'And selling at fifty million US dollars...' The gavel fell. *'Sold.'*

The stranger looked away, and Aurora released the breath she hadn't known she was holding. Only then did the tightness—*the burn*—in her chest ease. She had won.

He turned his back on her, revealing his chestnut hair

speckled with grey, pulled back at his nape in a low bun, sat on the crisp white collar of his shirt.

As he stood, her gaze swept over his magnificent stature. He was a giant. At least six-foot-five. A Viking ripped from an era long ago. His broad shoulders tense with a barely contained energy inside the sculpted fabric of his black tuxedo.

Without another glance in her direction, he walked out of an oak-panelled side door.

And he took the air with him. Stole it.

The room was suddenly too stifling, too thin yet too heavy at the same time. As if he'd ripped something from the very core of her existence—her ability to breathe, to inhale.

Aurora nipped at the inside of her cheek.

She was being ridiculous.

He was no one. Certainly no one she knew. A stranger.

'Thank you for your bids. And congratulations…?'

Aurora turned back to the auctioneer as she spoke and held up her paddle, showing him the number on the front.

'Congratulations, 265.'

The auctioneer, with her unmasked face and her long strands of black silken hair swishing on her shoulders, moved to the easel. She raised her slender brown fingers, her nails painted in a glittering gold, matching her own billowing gown. She gripped the black cloth, and everyone in the room held their breath in anticipation.

'I give you *Divinity*,' she said, and pulled the cloth free.

Applause boomed from everybody in the room.

Aurora settled her gaze on the single piece of artwork she'd won. It was lighted to perfection beside the auctioneer's lectern. The smallest details of the little boy's face, painted in heavy, bold lines in a medium she didn't recognise, were visible, right down to the smallest cluster of freckles on his right cheek. And she realised she knew the artist. Sebastian

Shard. She understood his uncouth methods and the use of an assortment of uncommon media had made him a household name, along with his inspirational flight to fame from the streets.

It was a beautiful piece. A haunting piece. Green-and-amber eyes looked out at their audience, asking for something she had seen in her brother's eyes the night he'd begged her parents not to disown him, pleaded for their help, not their disinheritance.

You should have helped him.

A tightness gripped her throat.

She looked over the masked crowd, dressed in their finery, the atmosphere buzzing with an adrenaline she didn't feel. Not yet. But surely she would, wouldn't she?

Tonight, the fifty million dollars she had paid for the piece of artwork before her would be donated to those without shelter, without a home. To those who lived on the streets. It was a cause her parents should have invested in long ago. They should have put aside their ugly views and done the right thing by their son as a way of making amends.

She waited for it. The exhilaration. But nothing came. No relief. Not redemption.

And Aurora began to understand that despite what she'd hoped, this one altruistic act didn't erase all the times she'd let her parents trample her moral consciousness. They never would have listened to her anyway, but she knew her silence went deeper.

Disgust crawled over her skin.

She had so desperately needed their love, their approval…

Golden girl, Michael had christened her, and she'd played her role impeccably. She'd been the perfect daughter, and still they'd withheld the love that should have been unconditional, should have been given to both children freely.

Her chest ached. She knew that tonight didn't redeem her. It wouldn't bring her brother back. Wouldn't stop the guilt she felt for remaining her parents' golden girl while Michael had died the black sheep.

But this was a start, right?

Tonight, she had broken free of their chains and paid an enormous sum to a charity that helped people like her brother. People who didn't have or weren't able to go home.

So why didn't it feel...*good*?

Because you're too late. You can't save him now.

The applause around her died.

And so too did something inside Aurora.

She clenched her hands into tight fists, the heavy handle of the gold paddle biting into her flesh.

What was the point of any of this? The dress? The shoes?

She never should have come here. Tonight meant nothing. Not to her brother. Not really to the people on the streets her money would support. Because this event, the people in this room, her parents, even Aurora herself, were so far removed from what her brother had lived through. What he had died enduring.

Taking a deep, pained breath, she gazed at the flamboyant bodies now being taken into the ballroom. Into a room where they would smile and nod, pleased with themselves for attending an event that would do good for people they would never see, never recognise as human.

In a minute, maybe an hour, they would forget why they had come here. Who tonight *should* be benefiting. They'd forget the people lining in queues to receive a bundle of fresh underwear and blankets so they could huddle, still cold, under a sky that would show them no mercy when the winter came.

A sky that had showed no mercy to Michael.

Did she really think a donation would make it all better? She was no better than any of them.

Aurora dropped the paddle. She needed out. Out of this room.

Blinded by grief and regret, she pushed herself through the crowd and through the doors, hurried along the wood-lined halls, and down the floating staircase. The bow on her hip, too big and obscene, she realised now, caught the vase standing in the alcove at the head of the staircase.

It fell. Smashed in to a thousand pieces of ceramic green. But on she ran without looking back. They could add it to her bill. She didn't care.

Her body urged her to go faster, as fast as her heels would allow. At the bottom of the oak stairs, she unhooked the silver straps around her ankles and slipped her heeled sandals free, one at a time.

Barefoot, she ran through the silk-lined corridor until she came to the first door that led outside.

She yanked down the silver handles and pushed open the French doors. Cool air greeted her flushed skin as she stared up at the starless sky. She dropped her shoes where she stood on the terrace. Eachus House was behind her, the grounds sprawled out before her, a perfectly manicured lawn, with trees on either side blocking out the skyline of New York.

And she did the only thing she could. She kept running.

It didn't matter which way. If she took the stairs leading down to the gardens on the right or the left. It didn't matter that shadows lay at the end of the lawn. It didn't matter that beyond the shadows were two hundred acres of woodlands, ponds, and landscaped meadows. It didn't matter where she went, only that she kept moving. As fast and as far as she could.

The bare soles of her feet tingled from the crush of the damp lawn, but she didn't stop. Not even when the grass turned to stone beneath her feet. She followed the softly lit path, through the man-made tunnel of tall firs, interlaced with swaying weeping willows, until she reached a dead end.

Black iron gates, bracketed by headed stone pillars, barred her way. She reached for the gold square in the centre, the key hole empty, and pushed.

Aurora stepped inside. Into an overgrown walled garden of wild flowers.

The trees outside the gates, and the high brick walls covered in ivy, hid this place from the windows of Eachus House.

The gate creaked as she closed it.

A rebellious mist of grief and guilt pressed down on her chest. It urged her to release the ugly truth threatening to consume her whole.

Her flesh goose pimpled. She shivered. How cold had her brother been? How scared had he been before the cold took him?

She'd never outrun it. Not her regret. Not her grief. Aurora's guilt was hers to carry forever, because she needed forgiveness from the one person who could never give it to her. She raised her face to the sky and closed her eyes. She wouldn't be worthy of it, even if he'd lived.

What she had done was undeniable. Unforgiveable. For twenty-one years, her silence, her complicity, her fear of standing up to her parents had killed him.

She didn't want to deny the truth anymore. The roar of it, so thick in her throat it was choking her.

Aurora opened her mouth, and she screamed.

Sebastian Shard watched her.

He stood under the domed roof, inside the walled garden, unseen in the shadows of the colonnade, but he saw her nestled in the wild flowers. He heard her. Not the woman who had been in the auction room, but the creature concealed within.

A creature in pain.

A mask of gold, and the perfect shade of oceanic blue, concealed her face and adorned it with shells and pearls of the sea.

She looked like a mermaid. A siren who'd lost her tail. Stranded on land, with two bare feet, coated in moisture and dirt. Her dress clung to her body like a second skin, and she shimmered.

Her elongated neck strained towards the sky. Towards the gods, begging them to hear her song. Calling to those who created her to collect her from where she stood and take her. But they wouldn't hear her. They never did. No matter how raw the prayer. How honest the roar.

The gods had forgotten them all.

He should know. He recognised the sound pulsing in his ears. And the sound unlocked the memory he'd buried deep—reminded him of a time long ago when he'd stood all alone in the dark, begging those same gods to take him too.

It was too intimate, too dangerous to listen to the rasp and curl of her voice, because it moved him. Enough that he stepped out from the shadows and into the soft light.

A dozen hidden lampposts discreetly placed in the foliage hugging the walls lit the space as if they were fireflies herding together inside the plants themselves.

He approached her on silent footfall. His leather shoes were cushioned by the vines spreading across the well-worn path of broken stone.

He did not want to get closer, he told himself.

He didn't want to watch her lips kiss the air.

He did not want to know why she sang to the dark sky.

He wanted her gone. Wanted to be gone from her presence.

But still he moved. Lured in by her siren's call. Its raw and uncensored melody.

He reached her. No more than two feet of distance between them. And she smelled of the night sky and the promise of a reckoning.

She stopped screaming then. But her breath came in short, ragged bursts. Her bodice pulled in tightly with each breath, pushing against her small breasts, making them strain against the fabric.

Black lashes swept upwards to reveal eyes too dark—*too deep*. Her eyes flew wide open beneath her mask. *'You!'*

'Me,' he agreed, owning who he was. The man who had stared at her in the auction room. Coveted her youthful grandeur, which reminded him of someone. Wishing she was that someone else. That his sister could take her place and be there with him. In a room of opulence, her every desire, his wish to grant.

She cleared her throat. 'You like to watch?' she asked, her voice a pained husk of too much air spent from her lungs.

'Yes,' he admitted, because he did. It was what he did. His only purpose. To watch, and transcribe what he saw to whatever canvas he had to hand, in whatever medium was closest. And he found no shame in watching her before. Or now.

She gasped. 'And who gave you permission to look?' Her eyes left his and scanned the space they shared.

'Do you not like to be looked at?'

'No.' Her gaze locked back on to his. 'Not the way you look at me.'

He inched closer, pulled by some invisible steel thread. But he resisted. Planted his feet. 'And how do I look at you?' he asked, but he knew the answer.

He knew his anger had been misplaced. *Illogical.* But still, he'd felt it, and she'd known it.

She'd understood his eyes, watching her in the auction room. The determined thrust of her chin, the frivolous wave of her hand as she'd bid on his artwork, had not been complimentary.

His sister would've been older than she clearly was. But his sister would never know the pleasure of waving one's hand and getting the object of her desire simply because she wanted it. She would never sit in a ball gown, or dance in a room full of people who would have once walked past her on the street and ignored her hardships. *Her suffering!*

This woman was not his sister.

Sebastian's sister was dead.

But this woman was alive. Breathing the same air he breathed.

'Like you know,' she whispered.

'Know what?'

'That I don't belong here.'

'You don't,' he agreed. He despised them all, but tonight, he'd despised *her* most. But he'd been wrong. She wasn't one of them. The masked elite who felt no pain or empathy. She was hurting.

'Is it so easy to tell?' she asked. 'So easy to see?'

'It is.' He swallowed. A mistake, because all he could taste was her.

'What gave it away?' She placed her hands on her hips, palms open, and his gaze followed the movement. 'The dress,' she concluded. 'My mother would have hated it, too. She'd never have let me choose it.'

He locked his jaw. He didn't hate it. It was a perfect choice. He liked it far too much.

'I wouldn't be here if she were alive.' Her hands waved at nothing in particular. 'I'd still be in the Cotswolds, smiling and nodding at things that did not make me want to smile.' The muscles in her throat tightened. 'They made me want to—'

'Scream?'

'Yes.' She flushed from the neck up, and he wanted to see beneath the mask. See the heat meet her cheeks and flood it.

'I thought screaming would make me feel better.'

'Did it?' he asked, because it had not made him feel better. It had drained him until he'd collapsed on the street and stayed there for a decade. But she was standing, and that intrigued him.

'It didn't.' She shook her head. The stalk of pearls rising from her mask danced. 'None of it has. Not coming here.' She reached up behind her mask, her fingers fumbling. 'Not this stupid mask!'

'Leave it on,' he commanded, because he would not give in to the temptation to see her face.

'*Why*?' she asked. 'When you can see straight through it? You know who my parents are, don't you? You know what they did? What *I* did?'

Questions he had no right to ask fought to be asked. He did not want to know her. Yet this creature fascinated him. And he couldn't help it. He asked, 'What did you do?'

Her nose twitched beneath her mask. 'I left my brother to die.'

His throat closed. Like he'd left his sister to die, too. Unprotected. Alone.

'I came here,' she continued when he didn't speak. Couldn't speak. 'Hoping, despite my parents' view of homelessness. Their ugly view that those who end up alone and on the streets somehow—' her slender shoulders rose and fell, drawing his attention to her taut collarbone and the hollow in its centre '—deserved it. Like my brother.'

'Your brother?' he asked. 'Was homeless?'

She nodded. 'I thought investing money—their money— would help.' She scraped perfectly white teeth across her bottom lip. 'But it's not enough. It's too late. My rebellion here, taking a stand against my parents' views on the world means nothing. Not for Michael.' She sucked in air through flaring nostrils. 'He's dead.'

'When did he die?' Sebastian asked. And it was raw in his throat. Not the question, but the similarity of their fates.

He'd donated the art tonight, and all the proceeds would be going back to the community he'd lived with for a decade. But she was right. It wasn't enough. Not for the people on the streets. Not for the dead.

'A year ago,' she confessed. 'And I left him there to die, on the streets, because my parents said it had to be that way. That he couldn't be saved. That they'd tried. But they hadn't tried, not really. They disinherited him. Turned their backs on him. And so did I.' Her slender throat convulsed. 'I... I should have been there for him.' Her black lashes swept down. Shutting him out. 'But I wasn't.'

His stomach dropped.

He hadn't been there for his sister either.

'Why not? Why weren't you there for him?' he asked, echoing the questions he'd asked himself too many times, over too many years, and always his answers were too weak—too selfish.

Her mouth grappled with what to say next.

'Why were you not there for your brother?' he pushed, because he wanted to hear it. Her justification for her failures. He'd never been able to justify his. His guilt was his punishment. A punishment he deserved. And he wanted no parole. No early release. This was his life sentence. To allow himself nothing but the pain, without reprieve.

'I wanted to believe them,' she admitted, and her eyes opened.

'Believe who?'

'My parents. I wanted to believe that their tough love—' she said, the word *love* in inverted commas '—would wake him up, bring him back, the old Michael. But it didn't. It brought him back in a coffin.'

His throat closed. Amelia never had a coffin. She didn't have a grave.

'He'd broken so many promises,' she continued, 'and the night my parents put him out on the streets, I didn't believe him when he said he'd change. I didn't believe *in* him. And I… I…if I'd stood up for him, if I'd sided with him, and he'd broken another promise to my parents, to me… My parents, they would have…' She expelled a heavy breath.

'Your parents would have what?'

'Taken me off the pedestal that they'd put me on,' she confessed. 'They would have kicked it out with both feet and left me on the floor too. And I was scared. I wasn't brave. I'm not brave. I'm still hiding behind this mask, in this hideous dress.'

'It isn't hideous.'

'It's not?'

'No.' He swallowed thickly. 'I don't know who your parents are. I do not know who *you* are. When I said you didn't belong here, I meant here, with me. Because I can't help you,' he said. 'I'm in no position to help you.'

'Who did you lose?' she asked.

He frowned. Was it so obvious?

'Everyone,' he confessed. The word was a heavy thing in his mouth. On his tongue.

'*Everyone*?' she husked.

He wouldn't tell her. He would not unload his burden onto her. The horrible thing he'd done. No. Besides, he'd held it close to his chest, kept it to himself, for so long, he didn't know how to tell it. The fire. The crib. *Amelia*.

'It was a long time ago,' he dismissed, but the words scraped against his throat. 'Twenty-five years ago. Tonight.'

'Does it still hurt?'

'Every day.'

'How do you survive it?'

'You don't,' he said honestly. 'You accept it.'

'Accept it?' she asked, and he heard the frown in her voice.

'You live with it until it becomes as much a part of you as the blood in your veins,' he told her, because her grief was brand new, and his was old. He knew how to navigate it. Whereas she… 'But you never forget. You keep your mask on. You armour yourself against your feelings. You never get attached to anyone again, and you never get hurt again.'

'That's terrible advice.' Her mouth turned down at the edges. 'I don't want to live like that. No one should have to.'

He shrugged. 'My advice stands,' he said. 'What you do with it is your choice.'

She dropped her gaze to her hands knotted at her middle. 'My choice?' she repeated softly. Carefully. 'I've spent my life making the wrong choices.' She swallowed, and his gaze locked to the motion. To the tendons stretching taut in her throat. 'Choices I didn't really want to make, choices my parents wanted me to make. And they made me believe if I made them, they would love me. But they didn't. They didn't love anything but themselves. They only pretended, called their cold presentation of affection, love, because I made myself the pinnacle of goodness—the golden child they only desired to display for public respectability.'

A roar built in Sebastian's chest.

Respectability. It was all the elite cared for in their gated communities, in their sky-high mansions. But it was all a lie, a cover-up, because the rot was already inside their communities, inside their mansions, in the very wood that held up their pretty homes, and yet they ignored it, until it all fell down.

And *she* was a damaged product of their selfishness to maintain a falsity.

Like you.

He stepped back. Heard the vines breaking beneath his feet.

He could not help her.

'Find your shoes and go back inside.'

Her hands dropped to her sides. 'What if I don't want to go back inside?'

The mask on his cheeks dug into his cheekbones. 'It isn't a choice.'

She stepped closer to him. *Too close.*

She stopped and lifted her gaze to his. 'I don't want to go back inside with them,' she said quietly. 'I don't want to stand in a room full of people who don't know me, don't care if I'm hurting.'

'I don't care either,' he told her, because he didn't care. At least, that's what he told himself, was convincing himself of. Not for her bare feet, not for her flesh covered in goose bumps. He did not want to carry her back inside to shelter, to warmth.

'Do you really want to be alone?' she asked. 'On the twenty-fifth anniversary of all you have lost?'

His spine stiffened. 'I do.'

She shook her head. Her high bun of twisted black silk loosened. His fingers itched to release it completely from its knot and watch it tumble to her shoulders. He curled his fingers into fists. 'Go.'

'You shouldn't be alone tonight. And I don't want to be alone,' she admitted. 'I've never had such a frank discussion with anyone. About anything. But we are talking. Connecting. And I—' She looked up at him. 'I don't want it to end.'

* * *

'Why would I care what *you* want?'

'If you really wanted to be alone,' she countered softly, 'you would have waited for me to leave without revealing you'd seen me.'

'But I did see you.'

'And here we are.' She inched closer until her scent, her softness, washed over him. 'Together.'

'Geography,' he said dismissively.

'Kiss me,' she said, and it snatched the breath from his lungs.

'Kiss you?'

'One kiss.' Her lips parted slowly, revealing the silken muscle in her mouth. 'And then if you still want to be alone, I'll leave.'

He didn't want to kiss her. And to prove it to his body, his brain, his neck dipped. Until the space between their lips became too close. And he said, 'No.'

'We don't even have to take our masks off.'

'No,' he said again, but the hard edge to his voice was lost.

'I want tonight to be more than a painful memory.' Her breath, warm and sweet, feathered his parted lips. 'I need it to be...*more*.'

He pulled away.

'*Please*,' she said, and the word, rasped from her lips, punched him in the solar plexus.

The gods hadn't heard him twenty-five years ago. But *if*, twenty-five years ago, someone had heard his cries, his plea, the night they'd all died, would he have stood up from his knees and walked out of that alley?

He'd never know. He was too old to change. Too scarred to heal. But she was young. She would know if a connection with a stranger could soothe. Change things for her.

And what was one kiss? There was no harm in giving her

that. A little help. A little softness, when her pain was still so new, so raw, and the world beyond tonight offered her nothing but loneliness.

This was not for him, he told himself. It was for her, and for the boy, who had not been given the same kindness.

His hands lifted from his sides, and he pushed the golden edge of his mask upwards with steady fingers. Just enough to reveal his lips.

'One kiss,' Sebastian agreed.

CHAPTER TWO

Aurora's heart raced, but she hesitated to step forward and embrace the electricity charging the small space between them. Embrace *him*.

It was too intimate. Too real. The space between their lips was too far and yet too close.

His mouth was beautiful. It was a mouth made for kissing.

What if she was wrong? What if this didn't make her feel better, either? What if she regretted her boldness? Her awareness of her body, of what it needed in this moment?

But what was one more regret?

She was full of them.

And wouldn't it be worse to have the opportunity to take something she truly wanted when it was within reach, but walk away?

Her gaze lifted to his, and her breath caught. If she balked, if she let doubt in, she'd never know if his kiss was as intense as his voice.

His eyes were not the same as they had been in Eachus House. Somehow, he looked deeper. *Saw more*. And her body liked it. Responded to it and to him. She liked his eyes on hers. Holding them captive with their intensity. And these feelings inside her were preferable to the pain he'd witnessed her scream into the trees.

She wasn't embarrassed he'd watched her, though. She didn't feel judged. She felt seen. Understood.

She swallowed and then stepped forward, the energy between them turning the air heavy and hot, making all the little hairs stand tall on her body.

It was only a kiss.

It would be fleeting.

She just needed it to ground her. Needed somewhere to channel the electricity coursing through her.

Aurora took in the slope of his gold nose, his uncovered upper lip. Her eyes locked on to the pout of his bottom lip, a stranger's lip that was waiting for her to kiss it.

A stranger she hadn't touched, and who had not touched her. Physically, at least. But he *had* touched her. Reached inside the twisted parts of her and loosened the knots making her lungs burn.

It would be more than a kiss, she knew. She wouldn't lie to herself tonight. His kiss would be the beginning. It would turn this night from a failure into something else, into something more. Something that was only hers. Something she'd chosen because it felt right, and *she* wanted it.

She wanted his lips on hers.

His hand slid to her lower back. He didn't apply pressure. Didn't pull her closer, but waited for her to lean in. Ready to welcome her body against his.

It had to be now. Otherwise, it would be a betrayal to herself, to the woman she wanted to be. A woman who made choices and stuck to her convictions.

A brave woman.

She placed her hands on his shoulders. Used the solid strength beneath her fingertips to keep herself steady and rose on the balls of her feet.

The tips of her braless breasts brushed against him. Aurora gasped as the touch of him, the feel of him teased her body, made her ache for a firmer, heavier embrace.

Her hands moved to stroke the back of his neck, then moved upwards over his hardened jaw.

She rose as high as she could on tiptoe, tilted her head and offered him her mouth. His hand pressed deeper into the dip at the base of her spine, lifting her slightly to meet him.

Aurora brushed her mouth over his. And it was powerful, intoxicating, the gentleness of it. His mouth on hers.

Aurora felt his breath quicken against her lips.

Her open palms cradled his jaw, and she pressed her mouth to his to finally taste him. To revel in the power, the control, he radiated.

Slowly, she pushed the tip of her tongue into his mouth. Feathered it against the inside of the warm, wet walls.

And he tasted of everything she didn't recognise, couldn't describe, but knew she wanted.

'*Ahh,*' she moaned into his mouth.

And he growled. It vibrated against her chest, inside her mouth.

Deeper she pushed her tongue. And there was his. Firmly it moved against hers. Danced to a tune only the two of them knew. And her body started to ache. Her skin. Her breasts. *Lower.*

Harder she pressed her mouth to his. Needing more. More pressure. More of him. But the lips against hers were unmoving now. His body against hers was rigid steel. Tight. *Wanting.*

She stopped. Opened her eyes. And there were his staring back at her. Vacant. Empty.

Aurora dropped her hand from his face and pulled away. She lowered onto the balls of her feet. His hand, so strong, so wide, fell from her back. And she felt rudderless.

'I've never kissed anyone,' she suddenly had the compulsion to explain. 'There's never been an opportunity. I've never longed for it. Until tonight. Until you.' She realised she was babbling. Overcorrecting a mistake that had made him stop. She wasn't sure what the mistake was, only that she'd made it.

Her skin was too hot. Her chest was too tight.

'Did I—' She inhaled, made her lungs suck in air. 'Did I do it wrong?'

A pulse flicked in the side of his cheek.

She stepped back. Away from the man watching her with an expression she didn't understand.

She swallowed. Took one last look at the masked stranger in the dark who had let her kiss him. And she felt too many things. Not success. Not failure. But something in the middle, where again she stood alone, regret so close to claiming her and this night as a disaster.

'Goodbye,' she said as she turned her back on him.

Fingers, firm but feather-light, caught her wrist. She halted. Turned. Raised her gaze to his. And what it was in his eyes, she didn't know, but it made her gasp with its visceral intensity as he said, 'Stay.'

Sebastian's eyes dropped to where he'd caught her. To where he'd wrapped his fingers around her small, delicate wrist and held her to him. And despite everything, every instinct telling him to let her go…he couldn't.

'Why?' she asked. 'You don't want me here.'

He lifted his eyes, watched her shoulders rise—*stiffen*. And then he met her gaze. Saw the tethered pain. The rejection she felt mirrored there. Something foreign spread over his skin. Something he didn't like.

'You didn't want to kiss me,' she said, and he felt the hurt in her words. 'I'm sorry I made you.'

'You made me do nothing.' He spoke through gritted teeth. 'You asked. Persisted,' he reminded her, reminded himself. 'But I said yes, because I wanted to.'

'The only reason you let me—let me kiss you,' she stuttered in an exhale, 'was because you pitied me. I don't need your pity kisses. I don't need you to pretend you liked it. I might be inexperienced, but even I know a man shouldn't react like that. Shouldn't freeze in response to a woman's touch.'

He could make her hate him, he knew. Make her feel worse. He could give her someone to blame for tonight. Could allow her to blame him for the hangover of regret and loss she'd wake up with tomorrow.

But he couldn't.

'I did like it,' he said, his voice rough, not his own. 'Too much.'

'Liar,' she whispered.

'I do not lie,' he said. It had been his choice to allow the kiss. It had also been his choice to place his hand in the dip at the base of her spine and lift her against him. And he had liked it. The taste of her. The heady moan she had made against him.

He should have let her run off into the night. Watched her as she went. But once upon a time he had been just like her. So alone, with no one to blame but himself for the failures of his mother and his stepfather, the man who was also his mother's pimp.

His stomach roiled. He had only himself to blame for Amelia's death. Only he could carry the burden of that. And this woman was burdened too.

Her load too heavy for someone so young. She was not to blame for the death she'd told him about. Her parents were, for not protecting their child from the drudgery of the streets. From the coldness, the loneliness. When they'd had every opportunity—every privilege—to save him.

'You're doing it right now,' she said, interrupting his thoughts. 'A man who wants to kiss a woman does not react the way you did.'

He swallowed thickly. Felt the drag of his Adam's apple inside his too dry throat. She was wrong. Their whole interaction had been honest. Too honest. He owed her that honesty now.

'I've had many opportunities to kiss…' he began,

'And mine just didn't compare.'

'I have no idea.'

'It was so bad—' she tugged her wrist free '—that there is no basis for comparison?'

He dropped his hands to his sides. Despite every bone in his body that demanded he recapture her, trap her here with him. To soothe her, to change the look of confusion in her eyes and bring back the heated look of pleasure she'd raked over him before.

'I don't need you to pretend. I don't need you to make me feel better,' she said. 'I don't feel better. I feel stupid for thinking—' She exhaled heavily. 'I feel so stupid for thinking I felt a connection to you. That I could have something that was mine, if only for a moment.' She straightened, her spine now ramrod-straight. 'I want to go back to England. I want to—'

'Do you want to know the truth?' he asked. 'Feel it? The truth of my desire?'

Their eyes locked. The silence pulsed for a beat too long.

'Yes,' she breathed.

He took her hand, and she let him claim it. Hers so small, delicate, and his so big, rough.

He didn't know why it was important for him to make her understand she was wanted. But it was. It was a truth he knew she needed. One *he* needed to prove.

He guided her hand towards his groin and released his hold of her.

'You want me to touch you?' she asked. *'There?'*

The length of him hardened even more then, and it stole his breath.

'I understand why you asked me to kiss you,' he said. 'Probably more than you do. And if you touch me, it's not my intention to seduce you, but to show you that you're not stupid, nor are you wrong.' He made himself breathe in and out. *Slowly*. 'I'm just the wrong man for you to kiss.' He straightened, planted his feet and waited.

He did not reach for her hand again. He didn't place her fingers on him. Although he wanted to do just that. Wanted to guide her to him. Instead, he waited for her to place her open palm on the heat of him. To touch him. Intimately.

And softly, tentatively, she did.

She gasped, and he pulsed. Everywhere.

Her eyes flew wide open. She withdrew the heat of her palm instantly. And its loss made the hard length of him ache in ways he'd forgotten were possible.

'My body enjoyed kissing you,' he admitted roughly.

She looked up at him from behind lowered lashes. 'But your brain didn't?' she asked.

'No.'

'So you froze,' she guessed. 'On purpose?'

'Yes.'

Her gaze narrowed. *'Why?'*

'Just because an opportunity arises to kiss someone doesn't mean you should,' he said. 'Kissing involves touching, feeling.'

'And you don't want to feel, do you? Emotionally or physically. You don't want to get attached,' she said, answering her own questions.

He nodded. He'd already told her these things. He didn't need to explain further.

'I made you feel, didn't I?'

He lifted his gaze to her face, to her mouth. And heat flooded him in places he hadn't thought could be heated.

He did not want to *need* her mouth.

But he did.

And the way she looked at him. All too knowing.

Tension flooded his jaw.

She said, 'I made you—'

'*Want*,' he growled. 'And I have wanted nothing, and no one, for longer than you have been alive.'

She frowned. 'You haven't wanted anyone?'

'No.'

'Haven't touched or kissed anyone?'

'No,' he answered. He would have shrugged his shoulders, but his body was so tight, held so rigid. 'I'm a virgin.'

She blinked rapidly. 'You're a virgin?'

'Yes,' he answered. He felt no shame. It had been necessary, was necessary. Besides, he knew the truth of it. His body might be untouched, but his mind had seen far too much, had been broken beyond repair before he'd even hit puberty. 'I'm as inexperienced as you.'

The silence that followed was not unpleasant or pleasant. It was...*thoughtful*. Her eyes were too gentle. She looked at him, and he let her look. He knew she would understand. He was a man with needs. He was inexperienced because he was a man who did not *want* to need such things. He did not want to feel the loss of them. Human contact. Touch. He had made the choice to abstain.

'Why did you come here?' she asked.

'The same reason as you,' he answered. 'To be alone.'

'But why the auction?' she asked. 'Why come here on the anniversary of your family's death?'

He had not told her he had lost his family. He'd said *everyone*. Because it had been. Everyone he'd cared for. Everyone he should have protected. But she knew all the same. Knew it was his own flesh and blood he'd failed, because she recognised in him what lived in her. The effects of severing a blood connection. Specifically with a sibling.

And he knew what it would ultimately do to her. That loss. It would hollow her out. And the fire he saw burn inside her would be extinguished. Her desire to shove all the pain, all the darkness into the night sky and fill that place where the pain had been, with hope, with light, would die inside her.

As it had died inside him.

'Why not here?' he asked.

'You came here so you didn't have to be alone, and you retreated to the gardens when it got too much. When you were surrounded by too many people who wouldn't understand. But I understand. I'm not the wrong person for you to be with tonight. You're not the wrong man for me to…kiss.'

His heart hammered.

'You understand me,' she said. 'And we found each other.'

'To find something means it was lost to you,' he told her harshly. Too harshly. 'I wasn't yours to find. I did not seek you out.'

His brain hiccupped, because he had, hadn't he? Revealed himself to her when he didn't have to?

He could have plugged his ears with his fingers. Shut his eyes. Turned away from the vision, this woman who was like a garden of wild flowers, calling to him, singing his name.

But he hadn't.

'We did not find each other,' he hissed, because she made it sound romantic. As if tonight had happened on purpose. As if their meeting had been fate.

'But we did,' she corrected him.

'This isn't a fairy tale,' he told her. 'This is not destiny.'

'Isn't it?'

A drop of rain fell then, a single splash on her blue-and-gold mask adorned cheek. Would her legs become a tail now as she got wet? Would the rain return her home? His thumb itched to swipe the drop away. To pretend the heavens wouldn't open tonight and take her.

He was too fanciful tonight. Too nostalgic. Too something akin to caring.

He was not himself.

'We are passing ships in the night. Nothing more,' he said, his voice too deep, too breathy, lacking in assurance. Beneath the words rang a question he didn't want to acknowledge, let alone hear the answer to.

He'd make them true. His words. She would not make a liar of him.

'But we haven't passed yet,' she said. 'We are still here, anchored. And tonight could be more than fleeting, for both of us. If we let it be,' she declared.

She teased him with what she held back, with what she *didn't* say.

'Explain,' he said.

He wanted to know why tonight he was here with her, and not face-down, drunk, from the bottles of alcohol he'd taken from a passing server and placed next to the stone bench inside the colonnade. They were untouched.

She knotted her hands, wrung them at her waist. 'We're both virgins,' she said quietly, and again the blush took her. Spread across her cheeks.

'What does that have to do with anything?'

'Everything,' she breathed.

She stood tall, all five feet of her, against the silence that hummed between them in this place of walls and weeds.

'I'm your awakening,' she declared. 'And you are mine.'

Laughter spilt from his lips. It was not to mock her, but himself, and the thoughts this creature took from his mind without his permission. Because so close were her words to what he knew she was now. A creature sent to taunt him tonight with all he'd denied himself for twenty-five years.

His laughter stopped. 'I am not asleep,' he said, but he questioned if he was. If this was a nightmare. If his mind had conjured her for him. To punish him.

'And neither am I,' she said, teasing him with the reality of her. Teasing him with all that was within reach. Connection. Understanding.

His heart stopped. 'I am not your awakening either.'

'But you are, don't you see?'

'No,' he said. He didn't want to see. 'You have mistaken a small kindest for more than it is. You misunderstand...*me*.'

'Make love to me,' she said, and her words were too loud. They boomed in his ears and echoed there until all he could hear was her on repeat.

'Let me make love to you,' she said, her voice so strong, so tempting.

'You,' he accused, 'have heard nothing I have said.'

'I've heard everything.' She placed her small hand on her chest. 'I know you've denied yourself everything.'

She moved closer, on silent feet, to stand in front of him. And his body recognised the shape of her. The heat of her. And it responded without his permission. It hardened again.

'You don't have to deny yourself me,' she said.

His body hummed. Temptation parted his lips, readying themselves for a kiss. For her.

He'd never touched a woman. He'd been attracted to others, but not so breathlessly. Never had a woman made him ache with a need to touch. To be touched.

What would it feel like to claim this night? To let his guard down and forget all that came before it?

She began to raise her hands, and he braced himself for

her touch. A touch he wanted more than air, he realised. More than any need to keep his vow…

Her palm cupped his cheek, and he couldn't help it. He leaned into it. Into her. And she was so soft. So warm.

Her hand moved. Her fingers stroked over the hair above his ears. And now her touch was too gentle. Too light.

He needed…*more*.

'Let me take it off.' Her fingers played with the string tying his mask in place.

He caught her wrist. 'No,' he rasped. 'I don't want to know your face, and I don't want you to know mine.' Here in the garden, masked, they were equal.

They were both inexperienced. Both alone and full of grief. But if he removed her mask, if she removed his, she'd know who he was. Despite his achievements, he was still the boy who had grown up on the streets.

'Okay. We'll leave them on,' she promised.

He released her wrist, and it fell weightlessly to her side. 'If we do this…' he started, and stopped.

He hadn't been a *we* for so long, it felt strange to let it roll off his tongue.

'If *we* do this?' she repeated, each word licking at his skin.

'It will only be this once,' he told her, because she needed to understand the rules.

'No names, no attachments,' he continued. 'I don't want a long-term lover. I don't want to care for anything or anyone. I will forever live my life alone. I won't care for you. Ever.'

Her big brown eyes locked onto his, and he knew he was lost to the night, to her, when she said, 'Only tonight. Only once.'

He was seduced. Lulled to his demise by a siren.

You are a fanciful idiot.

She had seduced him. This woman. With her plum lips. Her words. The song she sang, and he understood.

She'd made him a liar, and there was nothing he could do about it.

She made him need. Ache with it.

He lowered his head, and he accepted that this time, their kiss…

It was for him.

CHAPTER THREE

EXCITEMENT FEATHERED OVER Aurora's skin. His mouth was on hers.

And she wanted more. Wanted him to possess her, wanted him to claim her as his. Because she was his. In this stolen moment of time when they'd met, against all odds, both at an impasse in their lives.

The heavens opened.

Without a word, he tore his mouth from hers.

'Come.' He took her hand in his. Fire erupted in her palm, the blaze spreading up through her wrist, her forearm.

Using her other hand to stem the fat dollops of water as they fell onto her from the sky, she moved with him.

'Your feet,' he said as they ran, the rain so heavy it dripped from the flick of his nose.

She glanced down at her unpainted toes, covered in strands of wet grass. 'They're fine,' she said dismissively, but his hand was already releasing hers.

His arms circled her waist, and he lifted. She didn't think, didn't question. She clung to him with her thighs. Wrapped her arms around his long, thick neck. Dipped her head into his throat.

He was warm. Safe.

He strode up the stone path. Pink blooms and white flowers overcrowded by taller green reeds led their way forward.

He entered the terrace between two tall decorated stone columns, a balcony sheltering them from above.

She lifted her face. Met his eyes. His pupils were black disks pushing out the amber and green. She could feel his hammering heart. It mirrored hers.

She didn't need to remove his mask, know his face, or kiss his eyelids, the nose hidden to her, or his cheekbones. She recognised it by the feeling inside her.

It was *want*. The flare of desire burst inside her. In her chest. Her breasts, her nipples, hardened against the solid wall of his chest.

'Are you okay?' he asked.

'Yes.' She nodded.

She reached up to his face, and the air stilled. As did her heart. She tilted her neck, and he lowered his head. Lips met, mouths opened, and tongues mingled. Breathlessly.

How could he have wanted to deny himself, her, this? This connection between them.

It was more than skin-deep. It was fate. This awakening. Their awakening to the flesh. To feelings. To more…

Aurora didn't know exactly who she was, who she was becoming in this moment, but she knew who she didn't want to be anymore. A pinnacle of goodness. A golden girl.

Tomorrow, she knew, she would be changed.

Brand new.

Brave.

'Wait,' he said into her mouth, pulling away from her.

She followed him with her lips. *'Don't stop!'*

'I'm not,' he assured her, and his words, laced with tension, shook. 'I want to touch you,' he admitted.

She trembled. 'I want that, too.'

His nostrils flared. He stepped backwards until his legs met a stone bench. He lowered himself down, with her astride him.

She gasped as the intimate core of her came into contact with the hard length of him.

'I want *you*,' she said, and it felt powerful to say that. To speak the truth of her desire with words.

He swallowed, and she saw him struggle with the words stuck in his throat.

'I want…you,' he said, his voice a raw admission of desire. Of need. And she claimed it. The power he gave her in return.

He lifted his hand from her waist and stroked the seam of the asymmetrical sequins slashing across her chest. 'I want to taste you.'

And words were lost to her as she nodded. She watched his fingers, caught the slight tremble in them, as he pulled her dress down and revealed her naked breast.

'So beautiful.' His finger traced down her cheek, down the column of her throat, into the dip of her arched collarbone. 'Such smooth skin.'

He wrapped his palm over her breast, massaged.

And she felt beautiful.

'*Yes*!' she exclaimed. She couldn't help it. She tilted her head back. Offered him more of herself. And he didn't deny her. He pressed a kiss to her skin and tasted her.

He licked. He sucked. And the desire inside her built until she began to pant. She pushed her breast harder into his hand. Because it was what she needed.

She rocked instinctively against him. 'Oh…' she panted, and pressed her thighs together. Brought her core harder against him.

'More,' she demanded.

'*More*?' he asked.

'I want you,' she said, and swallowed, slickened her vocal cords. *'In me.'*

The pulse in his bristled cheek thundered. His mouth

opened, but she continued before he spoke. 'I don't want to go slowly. I don't want to wait. I want to feel you. All of you, inside me.'

His eyes turned black. His hands went to her hips. 'Brace yourself on your knees,' he told her, and she did.

Her knees pressed into stone, and she held herself above him. He reached for himself. Undid the silver buckle of his black belt, the button. And then slid down the zip and freed himself.

She gasped.

'If it hurts—if you want me to stop,' he husked, 'I will stop.'

'No,' she breathed. The word powerful on her lips, in the air pulsing between their faces. Their bodies. 'Don't stop.'

She chose this.

She chose *him*.

His hands went to the core of her. Stroked the seam between her thighs and pulled the scrap of material aside. He surged his hips upward, and he met her where she ached. Only the tip of him. The promise of him.

She made herself look at him, into his eyes, knowing it would be the same for him.

That tonight they were both shedding their old selves to have this moment together. Two virgins surrendering their selves to each other. To the desperate need to have this moment that couldn't be replicated. It could not be put on pause. Could not be denied.

They were two damaged souls, cowed by life but unable to hide from this. This honest connection. And it felt good. Almost *too* good.

Aurora understood that afterwards, after they'd taken what they wanted for themselves, she'd have to make her choice, to choose this path on her own. To feel everything the first twenty-one years of her life had denied her.

And she would.

She'd never go back to who she was before him.

'*Now,*' she pleaded. 'Do it now.'

His fingers went to her hips and pressed into her flesh. Into bone. Deeper.

She pushed against his fingers with her hips. Pushed them down. But he held her steady. Held her straddled above the heat, pressing at her core.

The tip of his swollen heat entered her. Slowly.

She would not let herself tense. She wouldn't hold back. But she felt the strain in his body. The pulse of his resistance.

'Is it hurting you?' she asked. She knew there was nothing to hurt him physically. But she felt it. His body expanding beneath her fingers, the bulge of his chest, and she understood his battle was internal.

'No,' he breathed through firmed lips, but she heard the lie.

Her voice as strained as his, she asked, 'Do you want to stop?'

'No.'

'Then don't.'

He thrust up inside her.

'*Ah!*' She threw her head back. It hurt. But it was a heated pain. She was so full. She shut her eyes against the intensity.

But he was...

Everywhere.

Sebastian knew he was going to come.

He held in the moan in his throat and gritted his teeth.

She was so warm. So soft. So tightly wrapped around him. As if she belonged there, and he belonged inside her. Their fit so perfect...

It was pain. It was pleasure. It was *everything*.

He bit the inside of his cheek. Locked his hips and fought the urge to push decades of denial into her body, without care.

Her eyes opened and found him. And only then did he move her. Lift her hips, ease the pressure sheathing him, promising oblivion, promising ecstasy.

She would find hers first.

He sank back inside her.

'Oh!' She ground her hips into him—clenched harder around him.

He reached between their bodies and pressed his thumb to the swollen nub of her.

Her mouth kissed the air. Sang a song neither of them had heard before. Neither had felt.

He was so hard inside her, it hurt. It wouldn't take long for his body to surrender to her, even if his mind didn't want to. Not yet.

He wanted to see her take her pleasure. Own it all. This night she'd demanded, and he'd given to her. Given her his hands, his mouth, his body. His surrender to fate. To her.

And he'd give her this.

He thrust up again.

Her head fell back. Her throat elongated, and he wanted to bury his face in her neck. Feast on her skin.

'Look at me,' he demanded, because he needed her eyes on him. He would to remember them as she came apart with him inside her.

Her eyes locked onto his. And there was no pain inside them anymore. No confusion. Only want. Only him.

He guided her hips, moved her, until he slid to her entrance and back in. And he concentrated on her eyes, and not on the need to spill himself that was so close to consuming him.

'I'm going to come!' she said, and so was he. But he fought against it. Enraptured, he watched her pleasure mount.

Her mask slipped.

His heart hammered. He should reach for it. Fix it into

place. But he couldn't move. If he did, if he changed the angle of his body, he would come too soon.

The mask fell. His breath halted as she came into view. Her face of ebony lines hued in yellow gold. Her small rounded nose, her plum lips, her big brown eyes, wide, shadowed by long black lashes.

Her face was everything he knew it would be.

Hauntingly beautiful.

She clenched so hard around him. He couldn't deny it anymore. His own release.

He growled. A roar so ferocious, his ears ached. He couldn't spill himself inside her. The risk was too great for both of them. However, much his body demanded he stay where he was.

He lifted her. But the heat of her body, the tightness of it, ripped his release from him. He lifted her higher. Spilt himself away from her on the ground.

Their eyes met, and hers were full of wonder and pleasure.

'I—'

'Shush.' He gathered her close, and she collapsed into his neck. Panting hard. As hard as he was.

He shrugged off his tux jacket and draped it over her shoulders. But his hands went inside to feel her.

He stroked her arched spine, and Sebastian let her softness wash over him. Let his body mould to hers. And oh, how delicate she was. How tenderly his arms held her, stroked her. Soothed her.

He closed his eyes. Pushed his nose into the escaped tendrils of hair resting at her nape.

And he drank her in.

She moved. Braced her hands on his shoulders and lifted her head.

'Again,' she husked, her breathing still erratic. She closed in on his mouth.

He gripped her face. Halted her. Smoothed the pads of his thumbs across her high sculpted cheekbones. Took in the warmth in her cheeks. Her swollen lips. Need overwhelmed him. To taste her again. To be with her again.

He pulled his mouth away. 'No more,' he said, but his body pulsed, seeking her out. He was still hard. Still wanting. It would be so easy to bury himself inside her again. His body was demanding it.

His lips twisted. Had he forgotten everything? He did not need. He should be sated. He should be anything but this.

He watched her eyes shutter. The wonder slip away.

'That's it?' she asked.

He nodded.

She scrambled off his lap and concealed her breast. He was grateful she did before he could pull her to him again. Bury his still hard flesh inside her body. Break his promise and have her again.

But his hands didn't release her. They guided her hips, steadying her as she found solid ground. Only then did he release her. And his hands ached with the absence of her.

'Thank you,' he rasped, the finality of his dismissal stinging his ears.

Her chest still rising and falling rapidly, she held his gaze. 'Thank you?' Her mouth grappled with what to say next. 'That's all you've got to say?'

He gritted his jaw. Nodded. And he looked away. It hurt. He wanted to learn every line of her face and commit them to memory. But he already had. She was seared into his retinas.

He tucked himself away. Zipped the fly. Fastened the button. Buckled his belt. And only then did he look at her again.

'It's time to go,' he said, and his body rebelled. He'd given her what he'd promised, taken what he'd needed.

A moment's reprieve.

'*Go?*' she repeated.

'Leave,' he told her with a voice too thick, laced heavily with a need he wouldn't recognise. A need to stay in her arms and press his forehead against hers. To listen to the husk of her breathing. To feel it, gentle and hot, feathering his skin.

'But I want to hold you,' she admitted. 'I want to be held.'

He ignored the hurt in her eyes. The confusion.

She was not his to hold.

'No,' he said. 'Once was promised, and it is done. It is finished. *Leave*,' he said again, and he did not answer the need of his hands to reach for her. To hold her gently.

He was not that man. He might have been, once. But he had nothing to give or to offer now. He didn't need anyone or anything.

He did not need her.

'*Please*,' he begged. 'Leave.'

Something caught in his chest.

He closed his eyes. Shut out what could have been. He shut her out. This creature sent to torture him with her softness. Her courage to change things. He was too old to learn anything new. To change who he'd made himself be. A man who was not gentle. A man who didn't care. A man who would not care now.

And so he did what he'd done for decades. He defaulted to what he knew. He closed down. Because this was too much. She made him feel too much.

She wasn't his to soothe.

She was not his to protect.

He heard her move. The pads of her feet scraping over stone as she did what he'd asked. And only when he heard her no more did he open his eyes. They searched for her, found her at the bottom of the broken stone path. On she ran through the black gates, and out of sight.

He leant forward and claimed her mask. His hands trembled violently.

The rain had taken her back to where she belonged.

Far away from him.

CHAPTER FOUR

Six Months Later...

THE PHONE PULSED in Sebastian's back pocket.

He wiped his hands on his thighs, the Technicolor of paints spreading into hued streaks of black against the dark material.

He withdrew the phone and sighed. He considered ending the call, but it would only ring again, until there was a knock on the front door instead. And if he didn't answer that, she'd climb through an open window or an unlocked door.

He placed the phone to his ear. 'Esther.'

'Have you looked at it yet?' his agent asked. 'I know it was delivered this morning.'

His lips lifted. No small talk. No softening of her irritated tone. Always straight to the point.

'No.'

She huffed, and he imagined her in her glass office in London, the skyscrapers behind her as she sat at her desk, small and formidable, in the largest and tallest art gallery the world had seen.

He'd only been there once, but he remembered the determined line of her mouth, daring those who entered to defy her.

Sabastian had dared to enter—and refuse her. What felt like a lifetime ago, in his fingerless gloves and woolly hat, he'd walked up to her desk and returned the cheque she'd handed him. He'd slid it, smudged from his dirty fingers, across her antique oak desk with embossed green leather, and walked away.

'Have you looked at *any* of them?' she asked, pulling him back into the present.

He didn't answer. He glanced at the small pile of newspapers stacked in the corner of his studio. Each was paper-clipped with a note from Esther, demanding that he call her once he'd looked at them.

He hadn't looked, and he hadn't called.

His gaze travelled over the walls of his studio. It had seemed the ideal place to work when he'd purchased the castle. The outer wall had crumbled, so he'd restored it, replacing the wall with glass, and now it looked as if nothing stood between him and the Scottish Highlands.

So much light flooded into the dark space. And it taunted him. A light he could never quite catch in the right position to tempt his artist's eye.

Easels sat in every available space, unfinished. The studio was chaos. Every medium he'd tried. Clay, spray foam, paint. He'd even gone out into the moors, walked knee-deep into the lowlands, collected heather and mud to build a sculpture.

Nothing was working.

Nothing *had* worked.

Until he'd gone back to the cheap spray-paint he'd started with, the kind that was so readily available from anywhere. And even then, the work felt old. Something he'd done before. A different picture with the same old media and the same canvas. The same street wall where he'd let himself first be what and who he was.

An artist.

Was he still one when he couldn't work? Couldn't come up with anything new, fresh?

He swallowed thickly. 'I haven't.'

'I know it's you.'

'And if it is?' he asked, walking over to the newspaper on top of the pile and picking it up.

'They've set up specialist teams to track them—to track you down,' she added, ignoring his question, and he snarled. His privacy was his own. They had no right.

'If any more pop up, without me knowing… They will take them before they hit the newspapers,' she continued. 'They will take them before the local councils can tape them off and keep them safe. And even then—' She sighed heavily.

Anger fizzed under his skin. It was for them. The public. The ordinary. The unseen. His work was not for the eyes of the rich.

'What have you done to stop this?' he asked.

'Nothing!' she hissed. 'I can't do anything if you don't tell me where they are.'

He unfolded the newspaper. The clip and Esther's note slid free and tinkled to the bare floorboards.

The front page, and there was his name. *Sebastian Shard or Copycat?*

And there was a map of the United Kingdom on the front cover beneath his name, with every place he'd visited over the last six months circled in bold red. As if he were a criminal.

He guessed he was. Defacing public property was a crime. But he knew first hand that when the poor didn't have an outlet—a canvas to release the worry—they found a way. As he had. Even though he wasn't poor anymore, even though he was richer than he'd ever dreamed he could be.

Are you worried?

He was not. He hadn't compromised her. He had not put

her at risk. He had not been too late. He'd pulled himself free in time.

His body pulsed.

This was not about *her*.

He'd only wished to return to something familiar. To find a way back to what had always come naturally to him. His art. But it had been lost to him. Since that night. Since her.

She'd thrown him into hell. Since he'd put his hands on her, used them in ways he never had before, shouldn't have used them at all, his hands didn't work anymore. Now he was broken.

He'd had no choice but to go back to the streets and do what he hadn't for so long, without a plan or protection for the pieces he'd left behind.

He'd painted a series of creatures. Mythical creatures, like her, throughout the United Kingdom on walls as tall as the castle he lived in, and floors as cracked as the broken stone path she had run down on bare feet. Ran away from him.

You sent her away.

He didn't want to remember her, but every time he closed his eyes, there she was. His siren. Her big brown eyes hurt and confused.

Shame gripped him by the throat and squeezed. He'd been cruel. Unnecessarily so. She was an innocent, and he'd taken that away from her. Used her and discarded her.

'Are you looking at them now?' Esther guessed. 'Look at today's. Page ten. It's a whole spread.'

He flipped to the pages she was referring to.

'Sebastian, your work is worth millions,' she said. 'And everyone knows it.'

His eyes scanned the corner of the newspaper. Page ten. He held it high in front of him. His stomach dropped. They had found it already and cut the brick from the wall itself from the side of a local convenience store, in the poorest estate he could find.

They'd taken it.

Left a hole in the community where beauty should have shone. He knew how his work made people feel. Knew it made them feel what he couldn't. *Hope.*

'You should have come to me,' she said. 'I could have protected it, protected them all. We could have made it into a spectacle. A treasure hunt for the public. But you didn't come to me. I didn't know where they'd show up. You haven't claimed them as yours, and without your name—'

'They are not mine,' he growled. 'They belong to them, to the people.'

'I know,' she said, and he heard the dip in her voice. A softness he didn't deserve.

He knew she loved him. In a maternal type of way, because she had found him. Discovered him.

Esther had seen him create a sculpture on a street behind the theatre she had been attending one evening. She'd watched him create art from soft spray foam, sculpting it into a face with a penknife.

The only face he'd drawn or made back then. Amelia's. Through his art, she had lived. Survived.

Esther had taken it and sold it. And then she had found him under the bridge, climbed into his tent, forever fearless, given him a cheque and her business card, and left.

He'd returned her cheque the next day and told her he had no use for a slip of paper with numbers on it, however obscene the figure was. He didn't have a bank account. He didn't have ID to cash it. He had little use for her, a woman who thought it her right to take his work. He had not made it for her, or people like her. Then he'd walked away.

The day after, she had come back with a bag full of cash. Real money.

He had refused it, but she had left it anyway. It was his. Payment for his work. And he had stared at it for days.

Of course, he needed the money. But that bag…

His chest tightened at the memory. It had been everything he didn't want. Didn't deserve. But desperately needed.

Esther had come back again a week later. This time with food. She had intrigued him, and so he had let her stay. He'd watched her as she'd placed a meal in front of him. A cheap white takeaway bag filled with hot foil tins. She'd eaten hers beside him, silently, and left.

She did that every day, even though he never ate with her. He simply watched her eat with her little white plastic fork, sitting comfortably inside *his* tent. And he wouldn't have admitted it then, probably not even now, but he had come to crave her company.

On the tenth day, she asked him a question. Several. Why hadn't he touched the money? Why hadn't he used it to move into a hotel or a hostel? But he hadn't answered her questions, any of them. It was not for her to know that he deserved his concrete bed. Except her final question.

She'd asked him who he painted for, if not for people like her. If not for the money.

Sebastian had told her the truth.

He painted for those who needed to see hope—to feel it. He made art for the people who felt invisible.

She'd promised, if he worked with her, she'd help him to bring his art, and the proceeds, to those who needed it.

And so they had begun.

Esther Mahoti, renowned agent, had plucked a homeless nobody from the streets, and he had risen to heights unseen before by any modern-day artist.

'If you're planning to do any more,' she said now, 'I'll protect them.'

And he knew she would. Esther kept her promises. She had every day for fifteen years.

He did not love her. He loved nothing anymore. But he liked her. Respected her.

'I will stop,' he said, and closed the paper.

'Sebastian…'

He heard nothing else.

His gaze locked on the small article on the left-hand side of the front page of the newspaper.

He scanned the blurred photo. Noted the way the beige collar of the woman's coat was turned up. The way her hair was in a high bun, wisps of black having broken free and kissing her cheeks. One hand was raised to tuck them away, her lips thinned, as her eyes stared at the photographer.

His gaze fell to her other hand, pressed to the rounded swell of her stomach bulging beneath the white shirt she wore.

His lungs forgot to inhale.

It was her. The woman who had made him want. Made him ache until he'd forgotten every vow he'd made to himself.

He read the title: *Heiress, Lady Aurora Arundel: pregnant. Who's the father?*

Sebastian closed his eyes.

The flashback that burst in his mind was a physical assault on his senses. His blood heated instantly. The memory was visceral. The scent of her, the softness of her against him, her tightness ripping a short-lived ecstasy from his body.

He opened his eyes and found her picture again. Her big, wide eyes…

Then his blood ran cold.

He was the father.

His mind roared with the truth, the certainty. They had both been virgins. They had not used protection.

Of course, it was possible that he wasn't the father. It had been six months. She could have met someone—

Bile rose in his throat.

He wouldn't, couldn't, think of that. He would not examine how the idea of another's hands on her flesh made him want to rage, made him want to break things.

She was not his, after all.

But the baby inside her...

A memory gripped him by the heart in a tight fist.

How he'd softly stroked Amelia's forehead, tucked the blanket around her small body, kissed her good-night, and closed the door behind him. Turned the key to keep her safe.

Only he hadn't kept her safe.

Death had taken her in his absence.

And now he had a choice to made.

Would she and his child be better off without him?

Had he learnt nothing? That doing things just because he wanted to had consequences. He'd left his sister all alone in a house of depravity to sneak out into the night and paint, and she'd died.

And his selfishness had come at a cost once again. He'd wanted a night, a moment six months ago, with a woman who'd heated his blood. And now she was pregnant, and alone. *His* baby growing inside her.

Maybe.

He had to know for sure. And if she was carrying his child, he wouldn't make the same mistake again. *He couldn't.* He'd protect them. The way he hadn't protected Amelia.

'Esther?' he croaked.

'Have you been listening?'

He ignored her.

'The auction,' he said, and images flooded his mind again, and made his body tighten in ways he swore it never would again.

But he'd keep his promise.
Only once.
This wasn't about her or him.
It was about the baby inside her.

'Eachus House, six months ago,' he growled, and charged out of his studio. 'I want the address of the winning bid. *Now.*'

If he was the father of her baby…

He'd stop at nothing to make sure they were safe.

Pride filled Aurora.

She fingered the green leaves of the cabbage, still wet from the morning downpour. It was so big, so ready. She'd grown nothing before. She'd never been allowed to push her hands into the dirt and dig a hole. Never been allowed to let a little seed flourish into life because she willed it so, and prepared the earth so it could flourish.

But here was the fruit of her labour. Several of them.

'Shall I cut them back, Miss Aurora?' the gardener asked.

She turned to him, looked at the wild bush of holly intertwined with vines of thorns and clusters of black and red fruit behind him.

'Mrs Arundel would be furious I've let them spread so far,' he said, his shears at the ready to take them down to the root.

She placed her hand on the damp, soft grass and pushed herself up from her knees.

'Let me help.' The gardener dropped his shears beside him and stooped toward her.

'I'm okay, Dennis.' She smiled, because she was. For the first time in so long, she was…okay. More than okay. She was flourishing like her little seeds.

Dennis released her elbow.

'Thank you,' she said, and stroked the swell of her stomach.

Together they stood, looking at the wild bush.

'Leave them,' she said.

'Leave them?'

'The holly, the brambles. Build a trellis,' she said. 'We will contain them, but we'll let them grow.'

'A good idea.' He nodded, and his eyes smiled. 'The student becomes the teacher.'

'Hardly!' She chuckled softly. She did that often these days. Laughed, because she could. Because she felt like it. Because it felt good to do so.

'I will build it,' he said. 'Do you want help to get into the house?'

'I'm pregnant, not an invalid,' she rebuked him lightly.

'It will be good to have a young one here.' His eyes moved over the manor standing tall at the edge of the grounds. Arundel Manor. A house, but never a home. At least, it hadn't been before.

'It will,' she agreed.

Dennis smiled. Waving, he left her alone in the garden of cabbages and wild blackberries.

She walked over to the wall of invasive fruit. Pinched the top of a juicy one, picked it. It was almost black. Ready and ripe. And she felt the urge to put it into her mouth, clamp her teeth through it and lick the juice from her fingers. But she knew she shouldn't. Not because her mother would have been appalled, but because it should be washed first.

She was ready to do the hard work. The preparation was done for the life growing inside her.

She gathered her skirt into a mock bowl and stared at the bump she couldn't hide beneath the green cotton. Didn't *want* to hide.

It was her little seed.

Finding out she was pregnant, she'd known she had to take charge of her life, learn how to be independent, live for herself. And so she had. The cook was teaching her how to prepare food, the gardener how to grow food.

It was something primal, she knew, and she embraced it. The need to have the skills to give her baby everything she hadn't. Freedom to dig a hole in the earth.

She reached for another blackberry and dropped it into her skirt. It would stain, *probably*. But she'd bought so many new dresses, dresses with jangly and dangling bits. Dresses her mother would have hated, but *she* adored.

He adored your dress.

She should not think of him.

But she did. Often. Too often.

She remembered in moments like these, when the world felt so right, that it wasn't because of her she'd changed. Not entirely. It was because of him. And she remembered too, late at night, when her hand, her fingers, found their way between her thighs, and she began to crave the fullness she'd felt with him.

He was the reason she had this gift inside her.

A baby.

A baby conceived of her desperation for more.

And now she had more.

A slither of embarrassment heated her cheeks, but she squashed it. The why or the how, it didn't matter anymore. She was pregnant. She was going to be a mother. But she couldn't squash it. Not completely.

Their night, her words, her desperate need to be close to a stranger, were embarrassing. How hard she'd persisted. How he'd discarded her before she'd had chance to catch her breath. When she could still feel him inside her.

Heat gathered in her abdomen as she plucked another berry, pricking her finger as she did so.

She hadn't gone back inside Eachus House that night. She'd run barefoot to the car park and found her driver.

She'd given him the shock of his life as she'd climbed inside, sealed herself in the cocoon of the limousine, in a man's jacket, drenched and barefoot.

She had been embarrassed then. And it had taken weeks for her not to cringe at the memory. For her heart to heal from such a devastating rejection. But she had healed. And so had her feet.

She picked more berries. A punnet's worth. That should be enough for a pie, or a crumble. She would ask her cook to show her how. Cooking didn't come naturally to Aurora, but she was getting better.

Aurora walked up the path to the house, bypassing the entrance into the main hall, and opened the French doors to the lounge.

She walked through the doorway, the sheer white silk of the curtains billowing around her as she did.

How she'd liked to pretend when she was younger, hiding behind these very drapes, that they were her veil and she was wearing a wedding dress. That her groom was waiting just beyond. A fanciful notion. She couldn't imagine being tied to another now. Couldn't imagine being held accountable to anyone but herself.

She was alone, and she was content to be so. For her baby. For the family she would make.

'Aurora.'

She swivelled on her heel to the call of her name. Shock wrapped itself around her.

A man stood in front of the fireplace in dark jeans. He wore a long-sleeved black T-shirt, sunglasses nestled in the V-neck, a curl of hair poking out. Then her gaze rose to take him all in. His chestnut hair falling around his shoulders, his thick neck, his green-and-amber eyes. Eyes she knew, intimately.

Recognition flared inside her.

It was *him*.

She gasped. Released her skirts. The blackberries fell to her feet.

'You.'

'Me,' he confirmed.

Her heart hammered in her ears in the deafening beat of a bass drum. 'How did you get in?'

'The door was unlocked,' he stated simply before walking toward her with long, stealthy strides.

She felt the urge to retreat. To run. But Aurora was done running.

She told herself to calm down, to breathe evenly, to stand tall.

He stopped, looked down at her as she turned her face to look up at him. Her heart continued to hammer and her breathing quickened as she remembered all too well how a moment like this had unfolded between them so many months ago.

Heated images stole her breath. But she would not soften under his gaze. She wouldn't let herself remember how good it had felt. She would only let herself remember the hurt of his rejection. Remember how much it still hurt.

A flash of anger burnt in her chest.

Her narrowed gaze returned to his. 'What do you want?'

'The baby, Aurora,' he growled, 'is it mine?'

He knew her name.

Reality returned in swift blows of anxiety. He shouldn't be here. This wasn't part of her plan. She was going to do this alone. Parenthood.

She did not need him.

'The baby is no one's but mine.'

He moved closer until her neck ached from looking up so high. 'Answer me.'

She placed both hands on her stomach. Held it. Protected it.

'Why would you care if it was yours?'

'Because if it is, you should have told me,' he said through gritted teeth. 'You should have found a way to tell me that you are carrying my child.'

She stiffened her spine. 'You made it clear you didn't share your life with anyone,' she reminded him. 'Not even a lover who had only moments ago trembled with the force of everything you shared. You didn't want to share your life for a moment longer than you had to. You didn't care that I needed to be held.'

She noted the way his pulse hammered in his bristled cheek.

'You care for nothing, and no one, remember?'

'I remember,' he answered.

She did too. She remembered everything. The feel of him. How good it was. How beautifully it could have ended between them. How he'd sent her away with her flesh still burning. Her lungs still panting. Her body, her mind, still *needing*.

She'd made the right choice for her baby. To not even attempt to seek him out. To try her best to forget him.

'So why would I tell you I was pregnant?' she asked, wanting to hear his response. Why he thought it was okay to stand here, in her house, asking if he was the father of her child, when he didn't care? 'Why would I think you'd care?' she continued. 'Why would a baby be any different?'

His eyes searched hers. 'So it *is* my child?'

She couldn't lie.

'Yes.'

His eyes dropped to her stomach. 'My baby,' he husked, and placed his hand on her stomach.

The possessive rasp of his voice, his touch, curled around Aurora. Her body responded to it, wanted to lean into it. Into him.

But why would she do that? He'd only push her away again.

She stepped back, and his hand fell away from her stomach, but his eyes did not leave hers.

'Were you ever going to try and find me?' he asked, his voice a low growl of accusation. 'Have you even tried to figure out who the man was who took your virginity and put a baby inside you?'

'No,' she admitted tightly. She wouldn't let herself feel guilty for her choice. 'I was never going to tell you, even if I could have found you,' she said honestly, and squared her shoulders. But still, she felt so small in front of him. His eyes watching her from up there with all that hair her fingers yearned to touch.

'But now I know.'

She clenched her fists. 'It changes nothing.'

'It changes everything, Aurora.'

She swallowed, trying desperately to moisten her throat. Her name in his mouth did things to her, the way his tongue caressed it so gently, so smoothly.

She shook her head. 'Not for me.'

She wouldn't let it change anything.

She tore her gaze from his, no longer able to stand the intensity.

Looking down, she saw that the blackberries she had been carrying had been crushed. All save a few.

She reached down for a survivor.

'They are ruined,' he said, and then he was on his knees, catching her wrist.

Her heart thundered, but she made herself look up into the face. It was too close to hers.

'Like us?' she accused. 'You…that night…you ruined it.'

'I did,' he admitted, swiping his thumb against the delicate skin on the inside of her wrist. And it zinged.

'Do you think of that night?' She swallowed. 'Do you think of me?'

She watched the heavy drag of his Adam's apple.

She didn't know why she needed to know. But she did.

She wouldn't let herself regret the question. He was here when she thought she'd never see his face again. Never lay eyes on the defined structure of his noble nose, his sculpted cheekbones, sharpened by the lines of his chestnut beard.

Her stomach somersaulted. Her body was taut with too many conflicting emotions.

'I think about that night,' she admitted, filling the too heavy silence. 'I think about you all the time, and...'

'And what?'

Heat bloomed in all the places it shouldn't.

'If you could change it?' Her skin hummed too loudly beneath his gentle, but firm, hold. 'If you could change the way *you* ended us, would you?'

Something flashed in his eyes. And she recognised it. It was need. Want.

She'd imagined all the ways their night could have ended, and she'd longed for every one of those alternative endings. To be taken in his arms. Taken to his bed, where they would have explored each other. She'd craved it. A different end, as she'd lain on her bed feeling rejected. Broken.

'No.' His fingers tightened around her wrist, pinching deeply. 'I wouldn't change it.'

She stood, none too elegantly. 'Why not?' she asked, unable to mask the hurt and vulnerability in her voice.

'There are no redos in life,' he said, and stood tall in one fluid motion. Swallowed the space that surrounded them until there was only him. 'I am not here for a repeat performance. I am here because of the child,' he declared.

Heat flushed her cheeks and spread down her throat. What

was wrong with her? Why did she still want a man who obviously did not want her?

Was it pregnancy hormones? Pheromones? Or was it something more basic? Something more primal that flooded her body with a need to be closer to him because the baby inside her was his?

She didn't know the reason, and she didn't want to know.

'The child,' she hissed, 'is growing inside me.' She curled her fingers into her palms until her nails pierced into flesh. 'We are a goddamn package!'

His eyes blazed. 'Then *you* and the baby will come with me. Now.'

The possessive demand made her toes curl. She ignored her traitorous feet.

'No,' she refused. 'We won't.'

'It is no longer a choice.'

'Who do you think you are?' she spat. 'Coming into my home and demanding things from me? I don't even know your name.'

She took in his chin, squared and sculpted with determination.

She did know him, though, she realised.

'At least, I didn't. I know who you are now,' she said.

His soft, pink lips thinned into a colourless line.

She nodded to herself. 'You're Sebastian Shard.'

His gaze narrowed. 'Does knowing who I am change things?' His lips twisted into something ugly. 'Because I'm rich? Because I'm famous?'

'*I'm* rich,' she countered. 'Probably not as rich as you, but... Of course it changes things.'

'Why? It will not change the facts. You are coming,' he said, his voice low and deep, 'with me.'

'Sebastian,' she tested it, rolled the syllables on her tongue.

Understanding formed in her consciousness.

'You are Sebastian Shard. A man who gives his art freely. A man who donates works worth millions to causes that will help thousands.'

'Knowing public facts about me,' he snarled, 'means nothing.'

'But it does.' She nodded to herself. 'You're the idol of the underdogs. A homeless man turned billionaire. An artist. A…recluse.'

Maybe she understood him a little more now. His actions, his words… He hid himself away from the world. And yet on the anniversary of a death that hurt him still twenty-five years later, he'd sought company and found her.

She'd made him want and need things he'd denied himself for a lifetime.

She remembered the bulge of tension in his body. The moment she'd thought being with her caused him physical pain.

The intensity of their connection had overwhelmed him. So much so that he'd withdrawn from her and retreated into himself. Back into his reclusive life.

But what did it mean? That he was here now when he could have stayed away… And Aurora would never have known who he was. Never have known he was the father of her baby. Did he deserve a chance to prove he could be the father her baby needed? She'd lived most of her life without choices. Could she really deny him that?

'We leave now.' His hands went to her waist, and he drew her in.

Sebastian was unconventional. His arrival, his demands. But a part of her liked it.

Hadn't she sworn to live her life fully? No half measures? Hadn't she vowed to herself, after New York, to accept nothing less than what she wanted?

And she wanted to go with him. Some part of her was

pleased he wanted to be a part of her child's life, to be involved. She'd prefer that...

'I'll come with you,' she decided, because he deserved a chance to prove he could be the father their child needed. And if she went with him, it would give her the opportunity to figure out if his determination to be part of his child's life was true.

His hands tightened on her waist. 'It was never a choice, Aurora.' He lifted her, and on silent feet, he carried her out of the door.

Maybe he was right.

Maybe neither of them had a choice in any of this.

Maybe fate had already chosen for them.

CHAPTER FIVE

As the helicopter flew above the tree line, Sebastian found it. The light that had been lost to him for months.

It was in her eyes.

Aurora, his brain hummed.

The pilot chased the afternoon sun atop the mountains, and Sebastian saw it shimmering in her eyes. There were no shadows lingering in their brown depths anymore. They were bright, and her light flowed through him in waves.

His hands itched to do what they hadn't been able to do for months without being forced. To work. He wanted to map the contours of her face in clay. To sculpt every line and create a version of her he could keep, touch, whenever he felt like it, because he would not touch *her*.

He flattened his palms on his knees. Refused to clench his fingers.

He would control it. These new, and unwanted, impulses that had flooded through him the moment she'd appeared in the doorway of her house, from beneath white silk. Rounded. Vibrant with the seed he'd put inside her. The seed growing now with the swell of him.

Sebastian had not meant to take her. He had not planned to take her in his arms and carry her away from all she'd known. But the confession that she was not over their one-night stand, that she thought about it, about him…

The moment she'd asked him whether he would have

changed how their night had ended if he could have, he'd known he would take her.

She was too naive, too vulnerable, with her romantic notions to be alone without him in this cruel and ugly world.

Dispassionate duty. That was all he could give. All he would give to keep them safe.

His home came into view.

'Sebastian.' Eyes wide, she turned from the window and looked at him. 'It's a castle.'

He nodded.

'It's beautiful,' she said.

So was she. She sat regally, suiting her inherited title. Lady Aurora Arundel.

Her brown skin shimmered beneath the loose-fitting green dress. Beads sat in an array of earthy colours on the cuffs and hem of her dress. Sewn in spirals on the seams outlining her body. Her planted feet were buckled in tan block heels. He yearned to remove them.

He wanted to see her feet. Inspect them. The soles that had run barefoot in the dark. To see if she was injured. If she'd healed.

'It is,' he agreed. Every muscle in his body urged him to close the distance between them. Rush to her, place his mouth upon hers, and crush her lips against his.

Control yourself.

Taking the sunglasses hanging from his T-shirt, Sebastian slipped them on.

She turned back to the view, and he watched her take it all in. The artillery walls. The high turrets. The foreboding black stone walls.

The helicopter descended to the dedicated landing pad just outside the castle walls. The pilot shut off the engine, and the blades slowed.

Sebastian unclipped his seat belt and stood, preparing to

reach across and unbuckle her seat belt, too. But she beat him to it. And the movement caused a rush of her warmth, her scent, to hit him square in the nostrils. He felt dizzy at the assault on his senses.

'Ready?' She smiled as she spoke.

He didn't return her smile. He was ready to do his duty. 'I am.'

The pilot opened the door, and she didn't hesitate. She took the pilot's outstretched hand and left Sebastian to catch up to her. Across the low grass, she moved to the gated entrance, ready to receive them.

She stopped when she reached it and shielded her eyes from the sun. Her neck arched upwards, her rounded stomach pressed forward. He wanted to rush to the swell of her. Feel it again. His baby inside her. But he made himself go slow. He wouldn't rush.

Unhurriedly, he walked to her and stopped beside her. He slipped his glasses off and held them out. 'Take these.'

She turned to him, a deep crease knitting her brows 'Why?'

'To shield your eyes from the sun,' he said.

She took them, pushed them onto the bridge of her nose. And he was grateful they blunted the force of her gaze on him.

'How long have you lived here?'

He hadn't expected her curiosity, didn't know quite what answer to give her. How much he wanted to share. 'Since... *after*,' he said simply, hoping she'd understand.

Her hand fell to her side, and he resisted the urge to take it. To hold it. Show her inside. Bring her into a place he'd invited no one else. Not his pilot. Not Esther. Only him.

He swallowed it down. The thrill tickling across his skin at the idea of being alone with her.

But he would not weaken.

'After your time on the streets?' she asked.

'Yes,' he replied.

'And you chose a castle in the Scottish Highlands?' she asked. 'Far away from any city? Away from people?'

He did not enjoy people. The night they had met, the only night he'd ever attended an event where his work was being sold, Esther had arranged it all. All so that he would be anonymous within the crowd. Would be asked no questions. He didn't like questions. And yet Aurora had asked more than anyone.

He nodded. It felt too intimate to tell her why he'd chosen this place when it had been decrepit and unwanted, its roof leaking with every storm. He didn't want to tell her that he'd hoped rebuilding this place, piece by piece, stone by stone, would fix something in him.

It was restored to its former glory now. Beyond it. But it hadn't fixed him.

'How many staff do you have?' she asked, looking over every grey stone distorted to black with history and age, lined with moss.

'None.'

'*None?* But it's huge.'

'The pantries are stocked monthly,' he said. 'It's all I need.'

'That's not very much,' she said.

'I am a man of little need,' he reminded her. 'I only take what is necessary to survive. To create my art.'

'Why would you live like that?' she asked. 'You're rich?'

'Because I want to,' he answered shortly. His riches allowed him luxuries, he knew. But he used only what he needed. Employed the staff he required as a necessity. And his team on the ground was only himself and his pilot.

'But that will change now you are here,' he assured her. He'd change it for her. The baby. 'I'll employ a team to cater to your and the baby's every physical need.'

What about her other needs? Her wants and desires.
He swallowed thickly.
He would not meet *those* needs.
'A team?' she asked.
'A chef, a cook—whatever else you want, Lady Aurora Arundel.' Her name felt exactly how he knew it would. It crowded his mouth. Heated his blood.
'It's a title, passed down from generation to generation. It has no real meaning anymore.'
'It means everything,' he corrected her. 'A name of nobility. A rich history of wealth and privilege.'
'You can talk.' She chuckled. 'Staff or no staff, you still live in a castle.'
'It was not always so,' he reminded her, and he didn't know why. Why it was important for her to know he was not one of them. The rich. The elite. The privileged. The ignorant.
'I know.' She scraped perfectly white teeth against the lushness of her bottom lip. 'I'm sorry. It must have been so hard for you,' she said. 'Out there.'
'I have known harder.'
'When your family died?'
He stiffened.
She removed her borrowed sunglasses and looked up into his face with wide brown eyes. 'The press never talks about the before.'
'The before?' he croaked. She couldn't know. No one did. No one except Esther ever would. And even she didn't know it all.
'Before your time on the streets,' she clarified.
'There is nothing else for the press to talk about,' he dismissed her tightly. 'There is nothing to know about the... *before*.'
'I'd like to know,' she said.
'There is *nothing* else,' he repeated. 'I am Sebastian

Shard. Street artist. Homeless man turned billionaire.' He used the words she'd said to him earlier to sum up who he was in a few sentences that revealed nothing.

'And who are you beneath the headlines?' she asked quietly.

'I am the father of your child. That is all that matters now,' he said, ending this, whatever *this* was, because he didn't want her questions. That part of his life was for no one. It was not a story for Esther to use to increase the worth of his art. It was his story. His burden. And he'd tell no one. Not even Aurora.

Her brown eyes searched his too deeply. 'Do you want to know if it's a boy or a girl?'

His gaze dropped to her stomach. 'Do you know?'

'I do.' Her hands tenderly moved to where his eyes lingered.

The image of a fat fist reaching for his cheek, pudgy fingers touching him with love, hit him squarely in the ribs. A memory of giving love freely in return. Without question. Without exception.

And you left her to die.

Sebastian's throat closed. He shook his head. The sex didn't matter. He looked back up at Aurora.

'Is it healthy?' he asked.

She smiled tightly. '*It's* perfect.'

'That is all I need to know.'

Her mouth firmed. She slipped the glasses back on and moved in front of him. Through the pillared entrance without him. Down the path of earth, until it turned to stone. She didn't stop. She didn't hesitate in her steps. She walked through the stone courtyard and met the stone steps. One step after the other, she took them to stand beneath the arched entrance.

She fingered the black iron handles to the heavy wooden doors. 'In here?' she called behind her.

'Yes,' he called back.

She pushed at the door and stepped inside. She slipped off his glasses and placed them on the small round table holding a basket of long reeds he'd pulled from the ground himself.

Hands knotted at her waist, she turned to him.

His heart hammered. There she stood in his sanctuary on the grey slate floor of the octagonal entrance to his lair. Waiting for him. And she was an array of earthy colours. Her dress. Her skin…

She wasn't scared, was she? But *he* was. Scared of her proximity, and his body's determination to get closer. But still he moved forward. He stepped inside the ruby-red entrance, which was now filled with the scent of her.

A reckoning was coming, he knew. He'd let her inside his home, his sanctuary…

She tilted her head, and he watched the heavy drag of her swallow.

'What now?' she asked.

Sebastian closed the door and turned the key.

He understood what they must do now.

He'd taken her. He'd brought her here. To keep her safe. To protect her from the monsters who lived out there.

And there was only one way to do it.

He'd give Aurora and their child what his mother and his sister had never known.

Commitment.

His commitment to protect her, to become her protector.

'You will stay here, with me.' He turned back to her and met the determined thrust of her chin. 'Forever.'

'Forever?' A chill feathered down Aurora's spine. 'What does that mean?'

'What is it you don't understand?' He stepped closer. The intensity of his eyes pinned her to the spot. 'The definition of *forever* is for all future time,' he said, and the tiny hairs on her body stood to attention. 'For always, you will stay with me, and I will protect you and the baby inside you.'

Her body responded to the possessive statement. To the undeniable truth of what grew inside her. A part of him. But...

She looked at the closed door, at the key still in the lock. All she needed to do was twist it, open it, and walk through it. But *he* had locked it. He wanted to keep her inside with him. *Forever.* And the commitment of his words, the confidence from him that she wouldn't object, that she'd stay with him, *always*, lit a coil of longing inside her to do just that.

She lifted her gaze to his. 'I'm to be your prisoner?' she asked, and her heart raced.

Despite the meaning of the word *prisoner*, her body hummed with the definition her mind conjured for her. It was not of bars and locked doors, but to always be in the presence of a man who looked at her with such power, and made her feel things she shouldn't.

But why shouldn't she?

He was the father of her child.

He was a man proposing forever.

'You are to be the mother of my child,' he countered. 'You are no prisoner.'

She flushed. 'So what do you mean to do with me?'

A pulse tattooed frantically on his cheek. 'I will do my duty to you, and the child.'

She frowned. 'Your duty?'

'I will give you both shelter. I will provide food. I will keep the fires burning. I will keep you both warm, and the cold world outside. I *will* keep you, and the baby I put inside you, safe, by whatever means necessary.'

'I've never been unsafe.'

'In New York, you were reckless.'

'So were you,' she countered. 'But *that* isn't my life. That night was different. It was…'

It flashed in her mind. The night that changed everything. The warmth of him. The hardness. The fullness of him inside her. But also, she remembered the softness of his hand claiming her wrist. She remembered the swipe of his open palm on her spine as she sat astride him, unravelling. The warmth of his jacket, being cocooned in his scent as he draped it over her shoulders.

'Life-altering,' he finished for her.

'Yes.' Heat gathered in her abdomen. 'But I've never been cold, Sebastian. I've always had food,' she told him. 'I have shelter. *Safety.* I can provide all of those things for the baby. On my own. So these things you offer…' She shrugged. 'They mean nothing to me.'

'And yet these things mean *everything*,' he growled, 'to me.'

The image of Michael, all alone under a winter's sky, hungry, cold and alone, kicked Aurora in the ribs.

'Was it so very hard to be without those things?' she asked. 'How did you survive out there? All alone? Without food? Shelter?' She shivered. 'Warmth?'

His eyes deepened with dark shadows. 'How is not important. I'm here.' He dipped a broad shoulder. 'I survived. But I will never allow the hardships of life—' he breathed heavily '—to harm a child of mine.'

And she understood a little of his determination to make sure the baby would never know such hardships.

'I'll never allow those things to harm my child either.'

'How can you protect a child from dangers you can't see?' he countered. 'Dangers you'll never understand because you haven't experienced them?'

'I don't need to experience a fire to understand it's hot,'

she responded. 'I don't need to experience falling on a sharp corner to understand it must be baby-proofed.'

'There is more to raising a baby than rounded edges.'

'I know what's important.'

'And what is it, Aurora, that you believe is important?' he asked.

'I'll never let them feel unwanted,' she answered. 'I will never ask them to be anything other than what they are. I will never throw them out simply because they upset or disappoint me. I will not disregard them, throw them away, when they find life hard, or when they make the wrong choices.'

'All these things you tell me are about sentiment and feelings. Feelings won't protect our child.'

'I've been protected all my life,' she summarised. 'Fed. Clothed. Sheltered. And those things weren't—aren't—enough.'

His chest swelled. And she wanted to touch it. The power barely contained beneath the thin fabric moulded to every contoured muscle of his chest.

'But that is all the baby needs.'

'It's not,' she said quietly. 'I've always had those needs met. But I always wanted—needed—more.'

The memory of the last time she'd demanded more was inescapable. She didn't want to escape it. She didn't regret her boldness six months ago, and she wouldn't regret it now.

'And what is it you think this *more* is?'

'I don't know,' she confessed. 'But it isn't dispassionate duty.'

His eyes held hers for a beat too long. 'Love,' he said, and the word *love* was a heavy, dirty thing he spat out of his mouth. 'Will not protect the baby.'

'I didn't mention love.'

'You implied it. But I will never love you,' he said, and it sounded like a threat to his very existence.

'I didn't ask you to love me,' she said, but her heart squeezed as she imagined what it could be like to be loved by a man, loved by *this* man, completely. Unconditionally.

All her life she'd asked for love, begged for it. And where had that gotten her? Playing a part in a family where she was merely a moving mouth, saying all the right words. The words they wanted to hear. No. Never again would she say words that weren't her thoughts. Her feelings. Her truth. Never again would she beg for love. *Ever*.

'Good,' he replied. 'Love isn't a precursor to doing what's needed. Dispassionate duty is all we can rely on.'

She bit her lip. Maybe he was right. She'd loved Michael, and that hadn't been enough to keep him safe from harm. Her need to be loved by her parents had blinded her to the duty she had to her brother.

'Your room is at the end of the corridor,' he informed her, and she understood the negotiations were over. For now. But she needed a minute too. To think, to acclimatise to her new surroundings, her new life.

'The chef will arrive at four, along with your belongings from Arundel Manor.'

Her brows knitted. 'How have you managed that?'

He shrugged. 'I am Sebastian Shard,' he replied without ego.

But who was Sebastian Shard? Who was the man beneath the headlines? Didn't she have a duty to her child to find out? She'd got a glimpse of him in New York, hadn't she? He was a man of empathy. Passion. And today, he was a man of uncompromising duty.

'She'll meet with you and discuss your dietary requirements. A personal maid and a housekeeper will also be at your disposal. Explore the grounds,' he said. 'Make a list of any changes you require or anything you need, and I'll provide it. Any other staff you need that I have overlooked, I'll employ.'

Shame heated her cheeks. He was willing to change his whole life, the way he'd lived inside these walls, for her and their baby.

It was humbling.

Sebastian's life had been hard. He'd lived on the fringes of society looking in. All he knew was how to survive. He'd built walls so high around him that they were endless. But life was about more than survival. She'd lived safely inside too high walls, and still she'd been alone, and sheltered from the life she wanted to live now. One without compromise.

But Sebastian had been alone too, living a life no one should live by choice.

Aurora watched him walk away without a backward glance.

And the truth hit her.

She'd let him take her because she didn't want to be alone.

And he'd locked her inside, because neither did he.

CHAPTER SIX

THE CASTLE WALLS hummed with noises Sebastian had forgotten.

Chatter and whispers of the new staff he'd employed floated into his ears. The drag of unopened boxes slid across floors. The shuffle of feet moving in and out of rooms he hadn't opened in years got louder and louder, until the single definable noises became too loud to distinguish individually.

And the scent of *her* lingered in every corridor. In every room that had remained closed and untouched, she'd opened every door, and parted all the curtains, lifted every dust sheet.

For seven days, he'd watched her invade his home and fill it with...*life*. And it was too bright. Too loud. Too interesting. Because his feet took him closer to the hum.

Closer to *her*.

He knew why he didn't command his feet to stop, to turn around and stay away, keep watching her from a distance. It was because of the compulsion to see her, watch her. And because for two days she'd stayed inside a room, far away from her own bedroom, and claimed it. He wanted to know why she'd locked herself in there and what the noises he could not define were coming from.

On silent feet, he approached the oak door. He stopped outside it, listening. But the noise from within was too soft, too gentle for him to hear right now.

As he reached for the handle, another memory hit him. The memory of a younger him with a smaller hand, reaching for a handle, and opening a door to find his mother.

His chest tightened at the recollection of what he'd found.

He had not looked for his mother again.

He'd stayed in the basement with the others.

He swallowed down the memory of the taste, too real now on his tongue, too hot and bitter. He closed his senses to the past infiltrating his present with the lewd sounds his tiny ears should never have heard. Of sights he never should have seen.

The handle he was holding now was tugged free from his grasp.

The door opened.

And she stole the air in his lungs.

Her plum lips parted to reveal perfectly white squared teeth.

'Sebastian,' she acknowledged, and her smile was too wide, too innocent, to greet a man who had brought her to his castle and then left her to fend for herself.

And yet she'd chosen to stay.

She'd found her way without him anyway. Claimed her place in a world far away from her own and made herself at home.

Would you have let her go if she'd asked?

No.

His gaze lifted from her smiling mouth to her eyes, bright and staring into his.

He'd been right to take her.

She was too small, too delicate, too innocent with her wide eyes and warm smile.

She wouldn't survive without him. She was too sentimental. She was too focused on the things that didn't matter. Feelings. Someone would take advantage of what she offered. Her riches, her softness.

'Aurora,' he said, and her smile spread wider. Even brighter than before.

He didn't smile. He frowned. Did he remember how?

Did you want to remember?

He did not. His face ached at the thought of trying to lift muscles atrophied by inaction.

'What are you doing in there?' he asked, too harshly.

She pushed the door wide. The hem of her blue dress skimmed across her ankles, revealing her naked feet sinking into the thick pile of the cream carpet as she stepped backward.

'Come see,' she said, and her invitation was too warm, too tempting, Never had a door been opened to him so quickly, or had anyone been so eager to invite him inside.

He hesitated. But wasn't that why he was here? To see what had kept her occupied?

He stepped forward and she took another step back until she stood in the centre of a room. He didn't remember ever having set foot inside. And his body urged him to quicken his step.

She spread her arms wide, palms upward. 'What do you think?'

He knew he should lift his gaze to the room she indicated with her gesture. But his eyes locked on her. Her hands moved to her midriff, cradled her bump, her fingers clasped together.

'Well?'

He finally looked around the room.

'It's yellow,' he said, because it was. But not just yellow. The walls were the shades of sunbeams. Hues of deeper yellows and oranges tinged with pink.

She nodded, the black silk loose at her shoulders swishing. 'Gender-neutral.'

His eyes moved over the white units lining the walls, some with shelves, another topped with a spongy mat. A changing mat, he recognised. Just like the one he'd used for Amelia, only the plastic had been split on that one, repaired with duct tape. He ignored the pain that flashed in his chest.

It felt warm, new.

He took in another unit with a small removable bath atop it. And in another corner, there was a rug with colourful shapes, a basket of soft toys.

His chest caved in.

He understood a baby was coming. He understood he was to be a father. But…

He swallowed, trying to loosen the grip of something too tight closing his windpipe. But it didn't help. The hold didn't loosen.

She turned her back on him and walked to the windows to retrieve something.

She turned back to him—her hands outstretched. 'It's so tiny,' she said, indicating the small outfit she held in her hands.

And he could not breathe.

He stepped back, but with each step he took, she followed him.

Her smile fell. 'Are you okay?'

He was not okay, but he nodded, and she nodded once in return.

'They've all been washed now.' She brought the white romper with its silver clasps up to her nose and inhaled. Her chest inflated. Her eyes closed. 'It smells so good.'

His heart, it hammered. The scent of a newborn's head beneath his nose was too visceral in his nostrils. A smell that was undefinable, yet defined by belonging only to the innocent. Innocents like Amelia. He remembered pressing his mouth to her wrinkled forehead as he held her close to whisper, *'Happy birthday.'*

'Do you want to help me fold them?' Aurora asked.

'Help you?' he choked.

He hadn't been asked to help when his mother had been pregnant with Amelia. Life had continued as it always had. There had been no new rompers bought. The hand-me-downs of his siblings were still in drawers. No small baths were readied for Amelia's arrival, when the sink would do just as well. He should know. He'd washed her many times after his mother had placed Amelia in his arms and told him to take her. She hadn't cared his arms were too long and gangly to be confident he could hold her safely. His mother only cared that he held her far away from her. Out of sight.

'The books say you can never have too many changes of clothes,' she said, though he was still lost in the memory of long ago.

She smiled again. But it was smaller. More tentative. 'I have lots to fold away,' she continued, 'in these tiny drawers, for a tiny person.' Her perfectly arched thick dark brows lifted, a request for help.

He looked at the open body suit in her hands. The tiny mittened hands...

It was all too real.

The baby was coming, and his lungs stuttered with the realization that he wasn't ready to meet it.

His eyes lifted to Aurora's watchful gaze.

'Why didn't you ask someone else to do this for you?' he asked.

'There's lots I have asked others to do,' she said. 'I didn't decorate this room or the one at home. I chose the colours, the furniture, and the clothes, and they all arrived and were put into place, prepared by people I'd paid to do it.'

'And so why choose to do this task yourself?' he asked. 'It's menial.'

She dipped her slender shoulder. The tilt of her head fell slightly to the right with her shrug. Her neck elongated, stretching the skin, exposing it to his eyes, and they followed the unconscious sensuality she oozed. The natural fluidity of her body.

'It feels important,' she said.

It was an explosion in his mind, the realization she wanted to fold these things with her small, elegant fingers. She hadn't instructed someone to fold them for her. She didn't abuse her wealth, her privilege, or ignore the need to be prepared.

She didn't care for his wealth either, did she? Not his name or his stardom. And neither did she need his privileges to ease her life.

She only wanted to fold clothes for the baby, and she wanted him to do it with her.

He needed to leave, to turn around and walk away. But she desired him to stay…

His feet felt like lead, but he made his body move towards her. Towards the woman waiting for him, holding the little romper.

His heart raged. Told him to turn around and run from the reality of her. From the reality of the baby inside her who would soon be here.

But what could be the harm? he asked himself. *Why not lend a hand? Why not help her?*

You tried to help her six months ago, too.

His body pulsed.

He would not *help* her that way again, he told himself, but his body called him a liar. He wanted to. He wanted to reach for the strands of hair kissing her left cheek and push them behind the curve of her ear. He wanted to cup her face, cradle it, and draw her towards him.

His mouth dried. His lips parted.

It would be a reprieve from the conflict in his chest to taste her again, wouldn't it? To lose himself in the heat of her?

He could. How easy it would be to reach for her, and ignore the agony of the past, and possess her mouth. Thrust his tongue between her lips until she moaned into his mouth as she had in the gardens of Eachus House.

He stiffened. Did he not remember? These urges, these impulses would not protect them.

He wouldn't lose himself again.

He would not let himself...*feel*.

'I'll help you,' he said, and forced himself to reach for the romper in her hands instead of her.

'Thank you,' she said, and released the romper to him.

She was right. It was as soft as brushed velvet. Nothing like the over-washed ones handed down to Amelia that were too thin, too worn.

Agony flooded his chest.

But he would not examine his pain in front of her.

He refused to feel it.

He would feel nothing.

For a millisecond before the shutters came down, Aurora had seen it written all over his face. Etched into every sculpted bone. *Fear*.

And she understood it.

She had known it.

She turned back to the windows overlooking the green- and autumn-tinged forests and valleys of the highlands. And with the view in front of her, she set about folding.

'Like this,' she said, and reached for a romper from the

pile. She folded the arms in first, and then the legs, before putting the two halves together. And his eyes watched every pull and push of her fingers with intent.

She started a new pile in front of the unfolded ones.

'Your turn,' she said, and she didn't know why she felt so breathless as he spread the romper in his hand, flat on the surface beside her, and copied what she'd done. But he did it faster, with the precision of practised hands. As if by rote...

She frowned. Maybe she'd been wrong...

Her eyes lingered on the tightness in his shoulders beneath his black jumper. His thick, corded neck.

No. She wasn't wrong.

She collected another.

Side by side, they folded.

The silence was thick with something domesticated, but somehow it wasn't a task performed for duty. It didn't feel cold.

A closeness, a vulnerability, pulsed in the air between them.

She swallowed. 'I was scared the first time I saw them,' she whispered.

'Saw what?'

'How small they are.'

'The baby's clothes?'

'These suits are so small. So delicate,' she explained.

His hands halted in their task. Only a momentary pause before he continued, but she saw it. And her hands itched to reach for his. Too smooth her fingertips over the veins on the backs.

'Babies come in all sizes,' he said dismissively. 'Why would you be scared of slips of cotton?'

'I've never held a baby.'

He didn't respond.

'It sounds stupid, but when I found out I was pregnant...'

She exhaled heavily. 'I was in a such a bubble. The life growing inside me felt so permanent.'

He placed a suit of the palest blue-and-white stripes onto her little pile. 'The baby will be permanent.'

'No.' She bit her lip. 'It's hard to explain,' she said. 'In my head, I knew that my pregnancy would end, but the moment I held that little suit, I laid it on my stomach, trying to imagine—trying to make it make sense that it would be a real baby with needs, Sebastian. And…'

She swallowed down the confession in her throat, not sure she wanted to admit that she'd wanted someone with her when the reality of the baby hit her. But she hadn't had anyone. Her family was dead. Her parents were not like the parents in books or TV shows who rubbed their daughter's back and told her everything would be okay. But she didn't want to be alone anymore, and he didn't have to be either.

'And?' he pressed gently.

'I was scared when I realised the baby would come and I had no experience of something so small, so precious. But then I remembered I didn't need the experience. I *was* a child once. An unhappy child. And I—'

'Will do things differently?'

'It's all I can do.' She waved at the room she'd readied for their baby. 'My brother and I had a room like this. A nursery. It was a cold room full of disapproving looks. *This* room will never be like the one I shared with Michael, with nannies who did their job. They kept us clean, fed us and kept us quiet.'

She swallowed tightly. 'But my parents, they wouldn't have known where to start if they'd had to change our clothes or give us a bath. We didn't exist in their worlds. We were barely seen, and God forbid we were heard. But I will know where things are, because I'll have put them there myself.

I'll know which toy the baby likes to play with in the bath. What their favourite comforter is at bedtime.'

The pulse in his cheek throbbed.

'What I'm saying is,' she started again, realizing she wasn't explaining herself very well, 'it's okay to be scared.'

'What makes you think *I'm* afraid?'

'Because I saw it in your eyes.'

'We are not the same. We have not lived the same lives,' he told her. 'We do not feel the same fear.'

'But you *do* feel it?' she asked.

He didn't respond.

'We could make up the crib together. It will help. The more things I ready for the baby, the more confident I feel,' she explained. 'And I have ducks. Duck comforters, duck sheets. Lots of ducks.'

His gaze narrowed. 'Where is the crib?'

'It hasn't arrived yet, but it should soon.' She waved at the empty space set aside for the antique one she'd fallen in love with online. 'It will go there.'

'You mean the baby is to sleep in here?' His eyes darkened. 'Away from you?'

'Not initially, but—'

'The baby should be with you at all times. It's your job to watch them. To make sure they sleep on their backs and not their sides. It is your responsibility not to close them in another room and forget them.'

His Adam's apple dragged up and down his throat. He turned on his heel.

'Sebastian?' she called after him. Confused.

'Play with your ducks, Aurora,' he called over his shoulder.

She wouldn't go back to the cold existence of doing what everyone else thought she should be doing. She wouldn't be seen and not heard. She needed no one's approval on how she chose to do things. How she chose to live her life. But—

'Why are you so upset I'm putting a crib in here? It's a nursery!'

'I'm not upset.'

'Then why are you leaving?'

He stopped in the doorway but didn't answer.

It made no sense.

He made no sense to her.

'I don't want to be alone anymore,' she confessed raggedly to his back.

His step faltered.

'You kidnapped me,' she said, standing taller, making her voice clearer. 'You took me from the life I was readying to live with the baby and put me in your world instead.' She moved closer to him. Invaded his space. 'And still I'm alone. Lonely. When you are right there.'

She'd known he needed time initially, as she had, to acclimatise. To settle. And she had settled. She'd opened all the doors, looked in every room, threw off sheets over furniture so beautiful, she'd marvelled it had been hidden, the dust-cloths collecting years of dust.

'I shouldn't have to be alone, Sebastian,' she said, her voice raw, because she knew what she wanted now. What that *more* was that had been so elusive when he'd asked her about it.

She wanted a companion to be by her side through the small tasks and the big ones to come. She wanted to be there for him too… So why not use the time they had before the baby arrived to cultivate something they both so obviously needed?

Friendship.

He turned to face her, his eyes falling to her stomach. 'In time, you will never be alone again.'

'I want *your* time, Sebastian.'

His eyes lifted to hers.

A low hum of heat gathered in her abdomen.

They could be more than friends.

They could be lovers.

She ached for it. His hands on her body. The fullness of him inside her.

A heated shiver licked at her skin.

'Have dinner with me?' she pushed.

His jaw was a throbbing line of stone, and the silence lasted too long.

It was too full, too intense.

'At eight,' he said abruptly, and nodded, a single deep dip. He walked out the door without a backward glance. Again.

He was as broken as she was, wasn't he? They'd both lost so much.

She wrapped her arms around herself, but still she shivered.

If they couldn't at least be friends…

She'd leave.

CHAPTER SEVEN

SEBASTIAN HADN'T BEEN back inside the nursery.

Aurora's admission of loneliness that day had been too raw to ignore or dismiss.

He'd been lonely in the early years of his self-imposed solitude. Now he was used to it. But she wasn't. And didn't he have a duty to provide some sort of company for her? To make sure she wasn't lonely. At least not until the baby.

He did.

Every evening since that afternoon, he had waited for her in a room he'd never used before she'd arrived. The table had never been set. The ornate chairs and wine-coloured velvet padded seats had never been sat in. But the candles were lit now. And they flickered in a line down the centre of the table in their silver candlesticks.

The clock chimed eight.

The door opened.

Tonight she wore gold. On her skin. In her hair. At her ears in dangling hoops. The material of her dress strained across her breasts. His fingers itched to touch her. To travel down the outline of her body to her waist, where the material flared out, softly caressing the swell of her.

He'd never dressed for dinner before. He usually ate in his studio. But she dressed for dinner. Made it a spectacle of colours and diamonds that sparkled in the light of all the candles in the room. And she had asked him to make a spectacle of it, too. To make their evening meals together an event. Something to look forward to.

And so he'd agreed. He'd ordered a wardrobe solely for her eyes. And every night he thought of her as he took his clothes off and dressed for her.

He shifted in his seat. Ignored the heat at his back. Tonight, the black iron fireplace was stoked, and it smouldered. Adding a heat he didn't need. He didn't want it lit. But every night, something was added. Changed by her.

Including him.

'Aurora,' he greeted her, his voice a heavy husk he did not recognise.

'Sebastian,' she greeted him.

He dipped his head. But he did not stand at the head of the table. He waited and watched.

Every night, the ritual was the same.

With unadorned fingers, the gold sleeves of her dress kissing her wrists, she collected her plate from the opposite end of the table, picked up her cutlery, and set it down beside him.

'That's better,' she said, and her smile didn't falter as she held his gaze.

Every night, she ordered them to be seated together. And every night he ordered the staff to change it back, only for her to move the place setting herself.

He stood now, pushing back his chair, and moved beside her.

'Is it?' he asked, and pulled out the chair she wasn't supposed to sit in and watched her take it regardless.

'It's perfect,' she said.

He tucked her in. And he didn't hold his tongue. 'Gold is the perfect colour for you.' He swallowed. 'You look beautiful.'

He took his own seat.

Her hand rose. 'I like this,' she said, and stroked the suede of his brown dinner jacket.

He caught her wrist and gently removed her fingers from his body.

How easily she touched him. As if it were a normal thing to do. But it wasn't natural to him. Her touch was anything but casual. His body strained beneath his jacket and open collared white shirt to press against her perfectly manicured fingertips.

'Thank you,' he husked and released her wrist. Trapped his hands on his thighs beneath the table.

'The cot arrived today,' she said. 'Would you like to see it?'

The blood stopped flowing to his vital organs. He hadn't seen a cot since that fateful night he'd settled Amelia, tucked the blanket beneath her chin, kissed her forehead and walked out of the house one last time.

'No,' he replied, and his answer was a weighted thing in his mouth.

Her eyes pleaded with him to continue the conversation she'd left on hold last week. But he'd buried it down deep, and he wouldn't dig it up. His reaction to her putting a cot in the nursery she was preparing for their child had been unfair, he knew.

He would not react now.

He'd known eventually he'd have to see where his baby would sleep. But right now was too much.

He blinked. Broke the intensity of her gaze and looked down at his plate, zeroing in on the birds painted in a circle onto the plate. He'd never seen these before.

Another Aurora addition. They must be.

He exhaled quietly through his nostrils. The cot meant nothing. He didn't need to see it. He did not want to.

He looked up, and he shuttered his gaze against the probing intensity of hers.

'I would not like to see it,' he said, and the light dimmed in her eyes.

His body revolted, urged him to take the words back, claim her hand where he'd abandoned it on the table and bring it back.

The light in her eyes.

His fingers clenched beneath the table.

'Not yet.'

Aurora felt it. The arrow of space Sebastian had left open for her.

'Tomorrow?' she pressed.

'No,' he said.

'The next day?' she asked, pushing him.

His lips compressed. He shook his head. The chestnut hair swept across his cheek, grazing the collar of his jacket, and she longed to push the hair out of his face, hold his cheeks, and ask him why. Why not yet?

'Then when?' she demanded, but she kept her voice soft, when everything inside her wanted to push him to tell her everything he wouldn't. Why the crib was such a trigger for him…

'Soon,' he promised, and butted her from the entrance to the fortress that he was. He slammed the doors of possibility closed, with her on the outside, looking in. And there was nothing for her to see but the shadows darkening the green in his eyes.

Soon was too long.

She dipped her head. Looked down to the dinner setting she'd moved to be closer to him.

It wasn't close enough.

All week she'd been subtle. Executed her plan to show him small intimacies, show him what their life could become. Sharing nightly meals together was a start, but there was more.

She'd been too subtle, perhaps.

Impatience made her skin tight. Her hands burned with the itch to clench her fists, slam them on the table, and demand to know who had hurt him. To promise she would not do the same. That their baby was coming. Soon. Time wasn't on their side. But she understood that was he needed.

Time.

Time to get used to her being here, in his space. To crave her when she wasn't with him. To look forward to the time when they would meet and she would sit beside him.

The doors to her right opened.

Her neck snapped towards the staff entering the room with the feast she'd asked them to prepare. Delicacies that could be held between two fingers and examined, could tantalise the tongue, the senses. Food fit to be talked about that could induce conversation.

But all week, regardless of her attempts to encourage him, the conversation between them had been one-sided. She wanted in. Into his head. She wanted the same honesty she'd seen the night they'd met. The passion.

She swallowed, looked down at the nested pastry set before her, layered with flavours and texture and complexity.

The staff left them alone.

'Shall we begin?' he asked.

Aurora looked at the pastry. Picked up her spoon and splatted it open. The layers merged and spread over the plate.

That was what she wanted. To merge with him. To get inside his mind and explore his complexities. His layers.

But he wouldn't let her in.

She dropped her spoon into the mess she'd created.

'I've lost my appetite.' She stood, pushed back the chair with her thighs.

'Aurora…'

And there it was. Every time he said her name, she felt

her whole body tighten with the need to feel his breath on her, speaking her name against her skin.

'You must eat,' he said. 'For the baby.'

She scowled, met his gaze, and thrust out her chin. 'The baby is fine.'

'But you're not?' he asked.

Her scowl fell. Did he care? Did he just not know how to do this? Them? Or was he humouring her?

She felt petulant. Impatient. She felt young and restless. And for once she wanted to allow herself to be all those things. To fight against Sebastian's calm exterior. He made her want to be all the things she had never been allowed to be.

She wanted everything, and she wanted it now.

Meeting him, making love to him, carrying their baby inside her, it had all changed her.

He'd changed her. Made her understand, recognise all the moments she'd let go when she could have reached out and claimed them. Made herself heard. Made it meaningful.

For Michael.

For herself.

'I'm fine,' she lied, because regardless of what she wanted, of how she wanted to act in this moment, he needed her to take things slower.

He needed time.

She advanced a step toward him and dipped her head to his ear. His hair whispered across her forehead. And she did what she longed to do. She touched the chestnut silk and pushed the hair behind his ear.

'Good night,' she husked and dipped her head further. Pressed her lips to his bristled cheek and kissed him.

A low moan vibrated in his chest.

She lifted her lips from his cheek, just enough to claim his face and turn it to her. And the long bristles of his beard pricked at her fingers. Made her skin tingle from her fingertips to her gold-sheathed toes.

Their eyes clashed and locked.

His eyes were an amber blaze, and they mirrored the hum in her body demanding she get closer. Taste his lips. His mouth.

She leaned in—

'What are you doing?' he said quietly, but so dangerously it hit her straight in the chest.

She inhaled heavily through lips that trembled. 'Kissing you good-night.'

'Why would you do that?'

Colour heated her cheeks.

'It's what people do.'

He stood—backing away from her. 'It's not what *we* will do.'

'Why not?'

'Aurora,' he warned darkly.

'My parents ate dinner together,' she said. 'They dressed up every night. But we were never allowed to join them. Not when we were younger. It was only when we got older that we were allowed in, and I realised it was all a show.'

He frowned. 'A show?'

'On the outside, they looked like the perfect couple.' She nodded. 'They sat together in the same room, but my parents avoided all meaningful contact. They barely spoke. They avoided the tough discussions that would make them uncomfortable. They never touched. Or kissed. They didn't even sleep in the same room.'

Her gut curdled at the visceral reaction to the memory. The uncomfortableness every time she was in the room with her parents. The silence. The expectation to nod. To smile. To comply with their clipped instructions or their dismissals. But Aurora need to talk. She needed the hard conversations.

'I have put on this show at your request.' His chest deflated as if she'd punched him in the ribs. 'I have done these things. Eaten with you, dressed for dinner to make you comfortable. To prove to you that you won't be alone. I will be beside you through this. Our pregnancy, and the arrival of our child. I have done this to show you what it means to stay with me. I am here for you. Both of you,' he told her.

'I don't want a show,' she said. 'I want no part of a relationship that is nothing more than a shell of respectability. I want nothing lukewarm. I want honesty and warmth. Passion. I want—'

'We are not in a relationship,' he told her.

'But we could be,' she said. 'I want us to do all the things my parents didn't,' she insisted. 'I want us to respect each other. I want us to talk. To touch.' Her gaze slid down the length of the noble nose and halted at his lips. Hairs feathered the softness of his pink mouth. 'To kiss.'

'No.'

'Admit it,' she pushed. 'Admit you enjoy spending time with me. That you think of me all day, waiting for dinner time. I think of you,' she confessed. 'All day. Every day. And I know you like it when we meet here in the evenings.'

She waved her hands around the room, at the flowers she'd made them put in here, the fire she'd insisted on being lit to warm the dark edges.

'You wait for me to sit beside you. You like it when I move my plate and get closer to you,' she told him, admitting what he wouldn't, but she knew. 'You want me closer, so let me get closer, Sebastian. Let me in. Tell me why you don't want to see the crib.'

The pulse in his cheek was an erratic drum, but his mouth remained sealed.

'I don't want to do this alone,' she told him. 'I want to raise our child together. But that means we need to be a team.'

'I will do my duty,' he replied, his tone too neutral, too calm. 'But that's all I have to give, Aurora. My protection.'

Fire flamed inside her ribs. 'I don't need your protection. I have my own money, my own house. If I wanted to, I could employ a team of guards. But I don't want a team of guards. I don't need a security detail. Our baby needs you. I need you.'

She placed a hand on her ever-growing stomach. His gaze fell to her belly. And she would not examine the expression in his eyes. She needed action from him. Not looks she couldn't decipher, however much they made her long.

It wasn't enough.

'We could be something special, Sebastian, but if we can't at least talk…'

She didn't want to force him.

She wanted him to want this.

And she knew he did. Knew he needed it as desperately as she did. To exploit this connection between them and make their lives together full. For themselves, and for the child in her belly. For the family they could become.

She turned on her heel. Walked out of the room and made herself keep her eyes forward. She wasn't playing games. She'd put her cards on the table. Again.

He wanted her, she knew. She could feel it. All the things she'd offered him freely, he needed. He wanted her to stay. He wanted them to be a family. But he wasn't ready to admit it. She had to give him the time to figure that out on his own.

And so she would.

Aurora walked out on him. And only when she was out of sight did she run to her room, close the door, and throw herself on the bed.

And she wailed.

CHAPTER EIGHT

One Month Later...

SEBASTIAN'S HANDS WERE still broken. No, it was worse. They didn't function anymore. Didn't bend to his will.

He held them out in front of him. His nails covered in the grey clay he'd pushed them into while trying to create something. *Anything.*

He noted the bulge of the veins on the hands he'd always relied on. The muscles he'd overworked and strained in his forearms. He'd pushed them too hard. And they ached. His wrists. His knuckles.

He looked at the monstrosity before him. It was still a lump of clay. Moulded into nothing recognizable with unskilled hands.

His hands.

He pushed his hand into it, flexed his aching fingers and gripped a fistful. He yanked it free and threw it.

It smashed to the floor at the foot of the window. A stream of light from the morning sun caressed its newly flattened form. Teased it with the warmth of what it could become when softened and moulded with care.

He padded across the wooden floor to the window. He stood in the beam of light, raised his head, and begged it to infiltrate his skin. To warm him. But it only teased him, too.

He couldn't be moulded by the heat in her eyes, her words,

her fleeting touch. But the temptation of them, of what he could become if he let her in, hummed beneath his skin.

They urged him to say *yes*, to all the things she wanted. All the things he'd never had, and neither had she. The warmth of a family not bound to a narrative of lies. A show performed to hide what was beneath fake smiles and pretty clothes.

He'd never worn pretty clothes for dinner. But his life had been a show for those on the outside. He'd had to lie to keep the veneer of respectability intact. Perhaps if he hadn't lied, hadn't tried so hard to protect himself, protect Amelia, she would still be alive. Twenty-five years later he still felt as though his heart had been cut from his chest. She'd been ripped away from him in an instant. Taken. If he hadn't allowed himself to care, to love her so much, he'd done the unthinkable to keep her safe, maybe she'd still be alive. If he'd taken the emotion out of it. Done his duty.

He'd do his duty now. Guard Aurora, and their child, from afar.

He'd keep them safe.

He opened his eyes, scanned the treetops, the leaves browning with the death of the summer season.

A single leaf fell, and he watched it. Followed it with his eyes.

His heart thundered.

He'd avoided her for days. *Weeks.*

He lifted his hand to his cheek. Where it burned still. It would have been so easy to lie to her that night, to turn his head and accept her offered mouth. To kiss her as she knew he wanted to. Push his tongue between her warm, wet lips and taste her.

And he had wanted to. It was visceral. The reaction of his body.

It was more than want.

It was *need*.

And he could not let himself need her. He wouldn't allow it. However much his body denied his command to stay still, to not react to her—he reacted.

He understood what she wanted. She had been clear, but he could not do it. And so he'd stayed away. Watched her grow from afar. And she'd grown in the weeks she'd been here. The baby inside her bigger. Almost here. Almost real.

His breath caught.

And there she was now, in the undergrowth beneath the window he was looking out of. *Real.*

He wanted air—wanted to breathe her air. His fist clenched, demanding he smash through the foot-thick glass and reach for her.

Her black hair hung loose on her shoulders, whispered across her bare arms. With one hand splayed forward in case she needed it for balance, her other hand held the swell of her beneath her thin cotton dress. And it was barely there. The dress. Its burnt amber tones sat on her brown skin as if it were part of her. A perfect colour match.

She took a step. Lifted her bare foot, and he saw what was on the ground beneath her.

Instinctually he reached into his back pocket. Gripped his mobile, opened the camera app and aimed it at her.

Her toes made contact first. Softly they pressed down on the dandelion. The only one in a field of green. The white feathered wishes separated from the flower. They flew up all around her. And he couldn't stop. He took shot after shot. Programmed to capture bursts of inspiration where he saw it.

And he saw it now.

He saw her.

Her hands lifted and played with a hundred wishes surrounding her. Her hands were delicate. Smooth.

She was young. Too young for him. He knew that. And

yet he had risked everything for her. Now everything had changed. *She* changed daily with the consequences of his choice to let his guard down.

He never should have done so.

But how could he regret it when she bloomed so vibrantly with the life inside her?

The life he had put there. Inside her body.

She caught a wish. Closed her fingers gently around it and brought it to her lips. They moved, whispering words he couldn't hear, and then she let it go. Allowed her wish to fly.

He could not make her wishes come true.

He could not be the man she wanted.

He was not ready to try. He didn't want to try. He didn't know how to do as she asked and not let himself get attached.

Brown eyes framed by long lashes looked up.

And she saw him, too.

Everything tightened. Every muscle jerked under the restraint of his will to not move. To not break through the glass.

He dipped his head. Acknowledged her. And then stepped back. Away from her. Until the shadows hid him from her. Hid her from him. He turned his back to the view, the only view his eyes wanted to see, and pushed his phone into his pocket.

He walked into the centre of the room. Far away from temptation. From the window. He closed his eyes and stood there. Paralysed. For only the gods knew for how long. Minutes. Hours.

His skin hummed and tingled. His mind reeled with incoherent thoughts. His body felt empty, malnourished. Deprived of her.

He'd missed her, he knew. Missed having her close. He thought of her every minute of every day...

He thrust his hands into his hair and dragged it back away from his face.

What the hell was happening to him?

He closed his eyes more tightly. Commanded his brain to tell his body to breathe deeply. In and out. But still his heart hammered. Still his body ached.

'So this is where you've been hiding?'

His eyes flew open. Found the source of the question. Of the voice.

'Aurora.'

She rested against the door frame casually, her breasts rising and falling with each breath.

His eyes fell lower to her feet, her ankles.

'Why do you refuse to wear shoes?' he asked.

'I like the feel of the earth beneath my feet,' she said without reaction to his reproach, and she moved into the room.

'So, have you?' she asked, as she cast her eyes around the room. To the art unseen by all but him.

'Have I what?'

Her head snapped forward, and she halted. 'Have you been hiding?' she repeated. 'From me?'

They both knew he had been, but Sebastian shrugged, feigning a nonchalance he didn't feel.

'Have you been searching for me?' he asked, because he could not stop the question.

'The castle has many rooms,' she answered, and looked again at the walls. To the art. 'And I have been in every one.'

'And now you have found me.'

'Yes,' she acknowledged, but she didn't glance at him. Did not smile in victory. 'And here you are in the tallest tower, in the highest room.'

'You should not have come up all those stairs,' he said. The image of her, heavy with his child, ascending the spiralling stone staircase, so narrow, so dangerous, made his blood turn molten.

'But I did,' she dismissed his concern softly.

He couldn't protect her, not even from the stairs. From putting herself in unnecessary danger. Because she didn't see the risk with her naive eyes. She did not understand it was a risk to be here. With him.

Like that night?

He hardened everywhere he shouldn't.

'None of the rest of the rooms are like this,' she said. 'This room feels like you.'

'And none of the others did?'

'No.' She reached up, splayed her fingers and let them hover above a face in the picture frame. And then she moved again. Her footfalls slow, the heels of her bare soles making contact first, and then her toes. Tiny and perfect, unscarred toes.

His breath snagged. 'And what do I feel like?' he asked, his voice gruff. Low.

Her fingers feathered one of the hooded floor-length fur coats he wore in winter on the moors. They hung on antlers he'd found in the forest, and they came out of the brick as if they were part of it now. Belonged there.

She stroked the coat, caressed it, allowed the brown fur to move through the spaces between her fingers. She turned to him. And she stole the minimal air he had in his lungs.

'You feel endless.'

'Endless?'

'You are a fortress,' she explained. 'You have lots of doors. Some are open. Some let people inside, but they are not where you live.'

She continued to walk, circled him like a predator, until she came to the window. She turned to him, and he faced her.

The light danced in the wisps of her hair. It kissed her skin. It made her shimmer. Like a goddess in the sun. She extended her arms wide.

'But I've found it,' she said.

'Found what?'

'The heart of you,' she said, gesturing to the walls, to the clay, to the splodge splattered on the floor at her feet. 'This is where you live.' She dropped her hand to her sides slowly. Gracefully. 'Your art… It—this—is your heart.'

'There is no heart here anymore,' he growled.

'It's everywhere,' she corrected him.

He looked at the studio. Tried to see it through her eyes. How the space looked active and alive with unfinished thoughts. The art on the walls was from long ago. A time when he'd accepted his art was all he was. All he had to give. But now…unfinished pieces littered every corner. The mound of clay he couldn't sculpt mocked him from its spot on the floor.

He turned to her. And there she waited for him to respond. Silently she stood in his space. With her naivety. Because so naive was she, she'd stumbled on the truth. His art was how he breathed. It was his life. How he gave back to those who were forgotten.

And she'd taken it from him.

He held out his clay-covered hands to her because he wanted her to see. *To know.*

'My hands are broken.'

Her lips parted, her eyes dropping to his hands. 'What do you mean, they're broken?'

'They do not work.'

She stepped closer. The pads of her naked feet warned him to move away. To drop his hands. But he couldn't. He was rooted to the spot.

'Why not?' she asked, and he saw her hands rise, saw them inch towards his, raised between them. Softly she took each of his hands in hers. She smoothed the clean pads of her thumbs over his dirty knuckles.

And it was everything. Softness, he knew he didn't deserve. But knew he had missed it. The feel of her on him, her touch, having her close, it was everything he had missed every day she had been here. Every day she had been away from him.

'Aurora...' He tried to tug his hands away.

She held on, drew his hands closer, until they hovered above the baby inside her.

'Let me see,' she said.

Her eyes moved over his clay-covered knuckles. And he let her look.

She took his right hand, turned it over, gently ran the tips of her fingers over his palm.

It was agony.

It was pleasure.

It was everything he should not allow himself to be feeling. But he couldn't pull away. He did not *want* to.

She took his left hand and did the same, and the trembling in his core changed. It burst inside his veins. His adrenaline spiked, flooded his chest.

'Come with me,' she said, and then she was leading him by the hand across the wooden floor, their bare feet padding in unison, toward the deep porcelain sink on the far left wall.

And he let her lead him there. Because he could not speak. He could not breathe for the fire eating his flesh alive from the inside out.

'Here.' She twisted the tap, but still she held his hand. Still she held on to him as the water gushed into the sink.

She reached for the soap on the waterlogged dish and placed it in his palm. And then she reached for his other hand and put it on the top of the soap.

And then...

He could not breathe.

She closed her hands over his, wrapped them in her much smaller ones. She pulled their joined hands beneath the water and slid them together. Lathered the soap and worked the suds between his fingers.

Aurora cleaned him. His hands. His knuckles. His skin.

And his lungs squeezed. Until nothing remained. Never had anyone cleaned him. Never had anyone wiped away the dirt from his skin. Even when he was younger, as young as he could remember, he had cared for himself. And when Amelia had arrived, he had cared for her.

But no one. not even his mother, had taken care of him.

'There,' she said, and turned off the tap, pulled his dripping hands closer. 'They're not broken. They were just dirty.'

She looked around the sink's edge. Looking for what, he did not know, and did not have the words to ask. He was rendered speechless by her naive assumption the dirt on his skin didn't go beyond the surface.

'It's more than that,' he said eventually.

She lifted the loose fabric at her waist and patted at his hands dry.

'More than what?' she asked.

'It's more than dirt. The reason they won't work,' he admitted.

Her dress, crumpled with moisture, fell back down to her thighs. She raised her head, looked up into his face with her brown eyes and asked, 'Then what is it?' Her brow creased. Lines deepened in her smooth, flawless skin. 'Why do your hands not work?'

He didn't deserve her concern. Her kindness.

'Tell me,' she urged. 'Why do you think your hands are broken?'

She'd always been honest with him. Since their very first meeting in New York. In her home. Here.

She slammed her truth against him, without apology, every time she could.

He'd offer her the same now.

'Because of you.'

* * *

Aurora saw it. Felt it. How hard it was for him admit.

'Because of me?' she repeated.

'I—' His body strained. Every muscle beneath his cream clay-covered T-shirt buzzed with a restrained energy. 'I haven't…'

He swallowed thickly. And she swallowed, too. Knowing this time she wouldn't get it wrong. She wouldn't demand. She wouldn't push him too hard, too fast, until he thought there was no other choice but to retreat.

'You haven't what?' She let her fingers press into his skin and clasped his hands gently between them.

'Since New York, since you, I have made nothing new.' His hands tensed in hers, and she saw the fight he had with himself not to close them into fists. 'My hands, they will not let me. They refuse me.'

'I saw your work in the paper.' She frowned. 'Wasn't that after…me?'

'That was not new.' He shook his head. His hair glided against the strained muscles in his throat. Over the pulse hammering there. 'It was nothing but a stencil of something I had created before. It was paint by numbers.'

'It was beautiful.'

The pulse hammered in his bristled jaw. 'You do not understand.'

'I don't.' She shook her head. 'I'm not an artist. So tell me. Explain it to me,' she said, and waited for the doors to close. To shut her out.

They didn't.

'Since I touched you…' he breathed, and she felt the heaviness of it. His exhale. His confession. 'My hands do not work the same. They do not *feel* the same.'

Her heart raced. But she kept her lips sealed. Waited. For him.

'I have tried everything,' he rasped. 'All my life, my hands…they are everything. They are what I am. All I have to give. But they do not feel right, Aurora. And I cannot fix them.'

They both looked down at his hands. To the source of his pain.

'You are more than your hands,' she breathed.

'*I am not!*' he roared. The pain in each word ricocheted through her chest until it landed inside her heart. And she hurt for him. Desperately.

And she did what she knew she shouldn't. She brought his hand to her mouth and kissed his knuckles.

'Aurora…' he husked deeply. But he didn't tell her to stop, so she didn't. She did the same to his other hand. Kissed each knuckle, each joint that wouldn't work for him the way he wanted them to. The way he knew they used to work.

She was no artist. But she was human. A woman who had to learn to change, to adapt, to her growing body. To teach her mind to think differently, to react differently, because she had changed, *was* changing, physically, emotionally, all the time…

She raised her eyes to his and said the only thing she could.

'If they do not work the same, if your hands do not *feel* the same,' she said, 'then they are changed, Sebastian. Listen to them.'

'They are not changed,' he said, rejected her idea. 'They are my hands. The same hands I have always had for forty years. I will always have them, as they are.'

'No,' she replied. 'New York, it happened to us both. I'm changed because of it.' Her gaze dropped to his lips. 'I am changed because of you. Perhaps you are changed because of me, too.'

'It is not the same,' he said. 'You are pregnant.'

'I'm not talking about the baby.' She released his right hand. 'I'm talking about in here,' she said, and brought his left hand to her chest. She held it flat against the drum of her heart.

'After…after we were together,' she continued. 'I knew I could never go back. I could never go back to the Aurora who said "please" and "thank you" for all the things I didn't want. I would never again hold my tongue in fear of offending someone else with my opinion. Or be someone I'm not.

'I listened to my body—to my mind,' she continued, wanting him to understand he wasn't broken. He was never broken. He was changing. 'I let the changes happen. I am letting them happen right now, here, with you.'

'I do not want to change. I can't.'

'You can.'

'No. I can't.' He pulled his hand from her chest, and she felt hollow without it. Her skin, her breasts ached for his touch.

But she let him go. She let him retreat.

'I'll call someone to escort you back down the tower staircase.'

'I'm not going anywhere!' she said. She wouldn't leave. Not yet.

'Fine. *I* will take you down myself,' he said.

'I won't let you send me away again,' she said. Even though his need to see her safe, the fact he cared about her, touched her deeply.

'Talk to me,' she urged. 'Tell me, why? Why won't you embrace change? Your body wants it. Your hands need it,' she told him, a tremble taking hold of her core. She suppressed it.

'I won't let it happen,' he said. 'I will not change. Not for my hands. Not for you.'

'Why is it so difficult for you to spend time with me?'

she asked, forgetting everything she'd promised herself she wouldn't do, forgetting the pep talk she'd given herself about not pushing him too hard. But he needed to be pushed. 'Why do you keep fighting my attempts to build a bond between us? Why are you fighting the chemistry between us? You don't have to.'

'I do,' he growled, not with just his chest but his whole body.

'Because you don't want to get hurt again,' she concluded for him. 'Because your family died? People die, Sebastian. My brother and my parents are dead. Death doesn't mean you have to push people away. You don't have to push me away.'

His chest swelled. 'But I must,' he said roughly, and his fists clenched at his sides. His body turning into solid, immovable stone.

'Why?'

His nostrils flared. His jaw squared.

'Tell me,' she pleaded. 'Make me understand why you can't let us be what I know we could. Together, in all the ways couples can be together. Why are you fighting this so hard?'

And she fought with every fibre of her being not to lean into him. To keep her distance.

'I have to, because if I don't, I cannot keep you safe, you or the baby. I couldn't keep *her* safe."

'Who?'

'Amelia.'

'Who is Amelia?'

'My sister.' He nodded, and she knew he was remembering everything he'd said the night they'd met.

'So badly did I want to paint,' he continued, 'so badly did I need an outlet for my pain that I left her. I left her at home. I locked her in her room to keep her safe, and then I snuck out. I thought she would be safe if I locked the door. If I kept them out.'

'Who out?' she asked, but he didn't hear.

'I thought... I promised myself I would only be out for an hour, and I was. But when I returned...she was gone. The fire has taken everything. I could have stopped it. I could have protected her if I'd have been there. If I hadn't been so selfish.'

'Your sister died in a fire?'

'She did,' he confirmed, and Aurora's heart broke for him.

Losing her parents had been hard. She had grieved. But losing Michael had been a different kind of a grief. A deeper pain.

'Sebastian...'

He dropped his hands to his sides and looked at her. The mist was gone, but the shadows lurked in his eyes.

'My hands do what I tell them to now,' he said. 'I create to please others now. I create for the people who need to see the light beyond their own darkness. I do not make art for me anymore. It is for them. For her.'

'For Amelia?' she asked.

'Yes!' he hissed. 'However unnatural it feels, I will keep my hands under control. Under my control.'

'You're punishing yourself?'

'I deserve it,' he said. 'My whole family is dead because I failed to protect them. And I failed you, too. I pushed you away in New York. I left you all alone and pregnant.'

'You didn't fail me,' she said. 'You are a gift.'

'I am no one's *gift*,' he snarled. 'But I will not fail again. I will not fail you. I will not make the same mistake.' He stepped back, away from her. 'I will keep my distance from you. I will keep my hands away. I will keep my head. Danger will never find you or our child.'

'Why would danger find us?' She stepped forward. Followed him. 'We're safe. You have made us safe. There's no one here but us. No one wants to hurt us…' Her body trembled, and her hand shook, but she made herself lift it. She pressed it to his chest, to the solid, unmoving muscle. 'I am here. Safe.' He inhaled deeply, and she felt it beneath his skin. He trembled too.

Aurora reached for his hand, and he let her claim it. Let her place it on the evidence of what they had made together.

Something beautiful.

Life.

'The baby is safe,' she assured him. 'There is no danger here. It is only us. Only what we could be. A family. A mother and father who are here for their child and each other. Friends. *More.*'

'Do you think because I live in a house, with a bed, I am civilised?' Sebastian murmured. 'You believe I'm safe? I was raised on the streets since I was fifteen. I'm not civilised. *I* am not safe.'

'Is that when it happened?' she asked. 'The fire?'

'It doesn't matter when it happened, it happened. I am still that man. That boy born into depravity, raised on the streets. You do not know me, Aurora. You do not know what I'm capable of. You do not want me to be your friend. Or lover. I am not capable of being either.'

'I think you are,' she countered, and her voice shook. 'I know you're a man of duty. A man who pretends not to care, but you care, deeply. You cared enough in the garden the night we met to help me through my grief. You are the man who cared about his unborn child enough to kidnap me. A man who donates the vast proceeds from his art to charity. You care whether or not you like it.'

'You are wrong.'

'I'm not,' she said. 'I've never been more right. So why not embrace it, Sebastian? Embrace this change? Embrace us?'

'Please go, Aurora,' he begged, but his hand remained on her stomach. All five tense digits curved around their baby.

He needed more time to accept this change that was happening between them.

'Okay.' She stood tall on the balls of her feet and leaned past the bump between them. 'One kiss and I'll go. If you still want me to.'

And she knew her words were an echo of that night. They both remembered how one kiss had not been enough.

He said nothing, but he didn't stop her as she leaned in. As she braced herself on his shoulders. And this time, she didn't aim for his cheek. She aimed for his mouth. For the kiss she needed to take. To give. To him.

She closed her eyes, and she kissed him with everything she had. She let him know she was here. With him.

She broke the seal of their mouths. Opened her eyes and met his.

'Listen to them,' she husked. 'Your hands, your body. Trust them and touch me the way you want to touch me. Kiss me the way you want to kiss me.'

He closed his eyes. His face contorted into a thousand lines of resistance. And she wanted to reach for each one, smooth them with her fingers. Her kisses.

'I do not know how,' he rasped, and pressed his forehead against hers. 'I do not trust myself to take only enough. I do not trust myself not to hurt you.'

'I trust you. All of you,' she told him. And she did. In ways she'd trusted no one.

Not only with her body, or her desires, but with her vulnerabilities, with the truth. However scared it made her feel, he'd allowed her to speak her truth from the moment they'd met. He'd allowed her to be honest with him about her wants, her needs.

She needed him now

And he needed her.

'Trust yourself, Sebastian,' she breathed. 'And—'

When she paused, he raised his head and stared into her eyes.

'Kiss me,' she demanded. 'Kiss me now.'

'It will be more than one kiss,' he admitted, voice raw.

'I know.'

'It will be...*more*.'

'I *want* more.'

He released a roar of both victory and defeat, and pressed his lips to hers.

And Aurora opened for him, took his pain and swallowed it whole. And she recognised the taste. It was an echo of her scream given back to her. The scream that had come from her when she'd thought she was all alone in the gardens the night they'd met. But she hadn't been alone. Just as he was not alone now. And she heard him, not only with her ears, not only with her body.

But with her heart.

CHAPTER NINE

Aurora's heart raged.

'Sebastian,' she breathed into his mouth, against the lips that were kissing her how she'd wanted to be kissed for weeks, months. Without hesitation. Without resistance.

His hands cradled her face, angled it softly, gently, as his tongue swept into her mouth. And she mewed for him as he tasted her. She pushed her tongue against his.

'*Oh*,' she moaned as he possessed her mouth. Claimed it as his. And it was his. It had only ever known his tongue. His taste. It was what she craved. What she'd yearned for since that night.

Him. *Only him.*

His hands moved. He swept the hair from her face, trailed his fingertips down the column of her throat, over her bare shoulders, down her arms, and she tingled. *Everywhere.*

His hands went to her waist. His lips pulled away from hers. But she knew this time he would come back to her without prompt or persuasion.

He was hers. As she was his.

This, them, it was fated.

Destiny.

'It will not be like last time,' he promised, and swept her into his arms. She knew she was safe with him.

He moved back towards the window. To the sun now throwing gentle rays onto the dark floor.

'I know,' she said, and touched his cheek. Stroked it.

His step faltered. He looked down into her upturned face. His cheeks were flushed. His pink lips parted enough for her to feel the shallow exhale of his breath touch her skin.

'I want to look,' he said. 'I want to see all of you.'

'Then look.'

He nodded. A single dip.

Gently he placed her on her feet before the window. Positioned her directly in the sun's warmth. And turned his back on her.

She didn't speak. She watched him. He moved to the sink with stealth and yanked free a felt tapestry from the wall beside it. But he didn't come back to her. He moved to the other wall and tore free the brown fur hanging there.

His eyes were black as he came towards her.

Her stomach somersaulted. A deep ache settled between her thighs. She reached for the tops of the spaghetti straps of her dress and pushed them off her shoulders.

'*No*,' he gritted out. 'Not yet.'

Her hands fell to her sides. Her heart raced harder, faster, as he knelt at her feet and spread out the tapestry. She now realised it was a pelt of soft, short fur.

'Here,' he said, and turned to her, held out his hand. 'Sit with me.'

She allowed his hand, warm and big, to close around hers, as he helped her down onto the floor with him.

They sat in front of each other on the makeshift bed.

The sunlight danced in his hair, which framed his face and fell to his shoulders. Her breath caught as she took in every line of his sculpted face.

'You're beautiful,' she husked, because it was true.

'No.' His hair moved forward as he shook his head. And she touched it. His chestnut hair was highlighted with grey and red. And it was like silk in her fingers. Feather-soft.

'Yes,' she corrected him. 'You are.'

His hand reached for her, and he stroked her own hair in return.

'The night I saw you in the gardens,' he said, 'I thought you weren't real, but a vision sent to torture me.'

'Torture you?'

'With your beauty,' he rasped. 'You lured me out because I wanted to see you, get closer to you. A siren calling me to my doom. My reckoning. I came willingly. And still you torture me. Because I want to see more. I want to touch all of you.'

'Then end it. This torture.' She sucked in a trembling breath. 'And touch me.'

'It will never end. I know this now.' He raised himself up on his knees until she looked up at him, and he down at her. 'I will only ever want more. More of your presence. Of your touch.' He pressed her down until her head met the pillow he'd made using the long furs. 'As I have every day, *every moment*, since we met.' And he leaned down, caught her lips and kissed her.

'*More*,' she demanded. 'I want more.'

His mouth moved, whispering kisses across the tip of her chin, her cheeks, the lids of her eyes.

He sat up on his knees, gazed down at her and tore the T-shirt from over his head. And she looked at him. At the broad shoulders, taut with strength. Power pulsed in his heaving, muscular chest. Her throat turned dry. Her mouth opened, her tongue seeking his tight pink nipples. Her eyes roved down to the prominent V leading down from his hips, lightly scattered with dark hair, and disappearing into his jeans.

'I will give you more.' He undid the button of his jeans, slid down the zip, and pushed them off with his boxers. Until he was naked at her feet. Proud and pulsing. '*Slowly*,' he promised thickly.

With unhurried hands, he undressed her. Pulled the lightweight stretchy dress down and over the bump protruding between them. Down over her thighs.

He gripped her ankles, one after the other, and pulled the dress free from her body until all she had on was her white knickers.

'I want to see all of you,' he growled, and reached for the white material sitting low on her hips. And slowly, agonizingly slowly, he took them down. His knuckles grazed the skin on her outer thighs.

'*Oh*,' she moaned, electrified.

He didn't pause. Didn't falter. He kept pulling the cotton down against her knees, down the tender flesh of her calves to her feet.

'Bend your knees,' he commanded, and she did just that. She bent her knees and planted her feet. Presented herself to him.

'Aurora,' he growled, his eyes moving over every naked inch of her skin. Her breasts, her darkened aureoles, her tight nipples. And down. Across her wide hips, her round stomach. His eyes rested on the dark triangle of curls between her legs. And she slickened. Felt the moisture coat her intimate lips.

'You are beauty itself,' he told her.

And she felt it. She felt precious. An artwork created just for his eyes. For his body. His hands.

Only for him.

He positioned himself between her knees. And ducked. Pressed his lips to the bone in her ankle and licked her.

'Sebastian!'

He didn't answer. He moved. Kissing upwards. Up her calf, her knee. Her inner thigh.

And then he kissed her there. At her core.

She squealed. Tried to lock her hips.

'I want to taste you.' He gripped her hips, pulled her onto his mouth and laved her with his tongue.

'Yes,' she panted, closing her eyes to encourage the intensity, or to diminish it, she didn't know. But the pleasure was overwhelming. Having his mouth on her. Kissing. Licking.

'Ahh!' She reached down and thrust her fingers into his hair as he caught the swollen nub at the centre of her and brought it between his lips. But he didn't relent as she pushed his head harder against her. He flicked his tongue and sucked until all she became was heat and trembling desire.

She didn't feel his hand leave her hip, but she knew it had when his finger pushed inside her. She clenched intimately around him. Rocked herself on the welcome digit. He pushed another inside her as his mouth worked her flesh.

And she was frantic. She clawed at him, tugging hair. Until all she could do was hold her breath and let it take over her. The warmth. So hot, so intoxicating was the illicit heat he dragged from inside her. It drugged her. And she was helpless as the light burst in her abdomen. Behind her eyes.

She locked her thighs around his head.

And Aurora screamed.

Pressure unravelled in her every muscle. Loosened her, until her legs fell, her fingers unclenched. And she was breathless. Panting. She felt—

'Wonderful!' She opened her eyes, and they found him high above her. Watching her, with his eyes on fire. 'You are a gift!' she said, a light, breathless chuckle leaving her lips.

'Again?' he rasped, and she heard the question. Recognised it.

'Again,' she said, and gave him the permission to take what he needed. What they both desired.

More.

She lifted her legs to his waist and wrapped them as best she could around him.

'I want you,' she husked her truth. 'I need you inside me. Now.'

His eyes darkened.

He positioned the silken length of him at her core.

'I want you again, and again, until you have nothing left to give,' she told him. 'And I will take it all from you.'

'I will hurt you.'

'I can take it,' she said. 'I want it. All of you. And I will give you the same. All of me,' she promised, and waited. Watched him fight the fight he'd been battling since the gardens. Since the first time he'd let her kiss him and he'd kissed her in return.

But it was a fight he couldn't win.

There was only surrender.

Their surrender.

To each other.

'Aurora,' he growled, and he pushed inside her to the hilt. She was so full. Complete.

And she surrendered to it. Surrendered everything she was, and all she would become, to him.

And she felt him do the same. Surrender all he was. All he would become.

To her.

Her tightness wrapped around Sebastian in a silken fist.

He understood it now.

This pain.

This pleasure.

It was his punishment.

And he would bear it. Endure it. For her.

He gripped her hips and thrust.

'Sebastian!' She gasped his name, and he gritted his teeth. Watched her eyes widen. Watched the pleasure bleed into them. The pleasure he was giving her.

Endless pleasure.

It was a just punishment for his crime. For taking her into his arms, for using her, taking what he needed, and discarding her roughly with his seed inside her.

His eyes fell to the swell of her between them.

He'd left her vulnerable and alone.

He'd never leave her alone again.

She'd never be lonely.

'Deeper,' she urged. 'I need you deeper.'

Gently he took hold of her ankles resting on his hips and lifted them. 'If it is uncomfortable,' he said, and swallowed, attempting to wash the roughness from his voice, 'tell me.'

'What?' she panted.

He placed her legs on his shoulders. 'This.'

He moved his hips forward.

'Wow.' Her neck elongated, the muscles stretching long and taut. She squirmed into the makeshift pillow. 'Oh, wow.'

And his body strained. He hardened inside her until the agony had no end. He was so deep. Deeper than he'd ever wished to be inside another human being. And it was… *everything.* To be this deep inside her. To give her this. To give her what she wanted. When he had already taken so much from her.

He would take no more.

'Please,' she cried. 'Move.'

And he did. He moved inside her. Pulled himself out to the entrance of her core and thrust back in. He slid in and out of her, again and again, until his chest was on fire. His erection was so hard, so deep, it hurt.

And he accepted the pain.

'Oh, Sebastian!' Her breasts rose and fell rapidly. Heat deepened the red undertones of her skin.

She was a goddess, and he would worship her as such.

'Oh, please. *Oh, please!*'

She would never beg him again. Not for company. Not for his kiss. Not for pleasure. She deserved everything she'd asked for, and he'd give it to her. But he would always hold himself back. Restrain himself. Never hurt her with the force of his desire. He'd never take. Only give.

It was his compromise. It was the only way to keep her safe. To protect her and his child. To be with her. To use his arms and his body to hold her, to keep her close, but to never let her in. He would never get attached. He would never feel anything but *this*. A physical need he would sate in her body.

She clenched around him intimately.

He closed his eyes. It was so intense. Almost too much.

'Aurora!' He roared her name as she squeezed his pleasure from him and found her own.

And he was flying.

Pure euphoria made him feel weightless.

It was a pleasure he had never known, never knew could exist, and it lifted him higher and higher.

'Sebastian!'

He opened his eyes, and there she was beneath him as he soared above her, calling him back to her with open arms. To cushion his fall.

And he knew he'd let him himself fly too high. If he fell now, into her softness, into her arms, he would crush her with the force, the impact of him.

He would pull himself free, roll off her. Fall on his own.

'Again,' she said. 'I'm—'

'Aurora!' She arched her hips, took him deeper still. Massaged him tightly with the heart of her.

And he couldn't help it.

He fell.

Aurora caught him up in her arms.

And all he could do was breathe. Breathe her in. Her scent.

'That was amazing!' she sighed after minutes, hours. God only knew.

He raised himself on his elbows, prayed for the strength to return to him.

But he was weak.

How could this be a punishment when it felt so right? When *he* felt so right here in her arms?

It swept through him. Despite his bold words of punishment. Temptation teased at him. In his mind. Somewhere in his chest, it stroked. Her words, her promise of having what he never had. A family. That he didn't have to be alone.

But she did not know him.

She only knew this. The chemistry they shared. She didn't understand that he couldn't give her the type of family she wanted. Couldn't be the man she needed.

'Thank you,' she said, and smiled at him. Reached up and stroked his cheek.

And he knew he had only one response. He had more to say this time. More than a pitiful thank-you in return for what she had given him.

'We will try it your way,' he husked. 'We will be together as you want. In all the ways you suggested.'

'In what ways?'

'We will talk.' He leaned down and stopped a whisper from her lips. 'We will touch.'

She tilted her mouth. 'And kiss?' she added for him, and closed the distance between their lips until it was nothing but millimetres. Their heated breath mingled. And he yearned for the gap to close completely.

'Yes,' he breathed. 'We will kiss.'

Her lips feathered his. And he longed for more.

'We will do all the things a real couple do,' she said against his mouth.

'We will,' he said, and pushed his promise into her mouth with the tip of his tongue.

He'd give her everything she wanted. Everything but love. He had none to give. He did not deserve hers. But everything else.

This…

He deepened their kiss, and she moaned into his mouth. His body pulsed, swelled, with the pleasure he was giving to her. The pleasure he'd continue to give until he couldn't.

Sebastian would embrace…change.

And he'd do it for her.

CHAPTER TEN

THUNDER BOOMED.

Aurora's sleep-heavy eyes flew wide open.

Yellow-white light crackled and lit up the sky outside. Water ran in a river down the panelled glass. The heavy drapes were open, and the next streak of lightning illuminated the room through the two large windows. Everything inside the room remained still, undisturbed by the storm.

The room dimmed as the lightning receded, but Aurora's restlessness remained. And it wasn't the wind or the thunder that disturbed her.

It was…

Slowly she turned her head on the once plump white pillow now indented from her head, from the pressure of her straining body after Sebastian had crept into bed that night. Slid beneath the heavy white linen, pressed his naked body against hers, and given her release. Again and again, until her listless body had clung to his, and she'd fallen into a deep, dreamless sleep.

She wasn't clinging to him now.

She wasn't asleep.

And it wasn't the storm that had woken her.

It was *him*.

'No…' he mumbled, his restless head arched, his thick neck straining. 'Please… *No!*'

'*Shush*,' she soothed, and reached between them, under

the sheets, and placed her hand on his chest. It was solid. His muscles were so taut.

'Amelia…' Sweat beaded on his forehead. His chestnut hair streaked across his furrowed forehead was black from the moisture soaking his body.

She pushed it back, cleared his forehead with a gentle swipe of her palm. 'You're dreaming,' she said in a hushed whisper.

'I'm sorry…' Tremors raked through his body. 'I'm so sorry…' he croaked on a barely contained sob, and that broke something inside her.

When Michael had died, she'd had so many dreams. Dreams of all the things she should have done and hadn't. She'd woken tear-drenched and raked with guilt. All alone.

He wasn't alone now.

She couldn't see what was doing it. Hurting him. But she could stop whatever was invading his sleep. She could make it go away.

'Sebastian.' She sat up beside him, stroked his broad bare shoulders. 'Wake up.'

Lightning crackled.

His eyes opened, wide and haunted. He looked up at her but he didn't speak. His face haggard, he stared at her, his breathing deep and uneven.

Emotion bubbled in her chest. Her eyes crowded with tears.

'What was she like?'

'Who?' he rasped roughly.

She couldn't help it. A tear slipped free.

He cleared his throat. 'Why are you crying?' His hand lifted to her cheek. The pad of his big thumb caught the tear. Wiped it away.

'For you,' she said. 'And Amelia.'

His hand fell to his side. Focus returned to his glazed eyes with sharp intensity. 'What did I say?'

'You were dreaming,' she explained.

His brow furrowed. 'I haven't dreamt of her for over a decade.'

He threw a hand over his eyes. Hid the shadows that had entered his eyes with the sound of his sister's name.

And she wouldn't let him do it again. Hide from her.

For two weeks, they had been together. They'd shared every meal. They had touched. Kissed. Every night, he'd climbed into her bed beside her, learnt her body and she his with a famished, ravenous intensity.

But talk? They'd shared words, talked about the baby, shared pleasantries about their meals…but she had still not passed the surface level of Sebastian.

And she wanted in. She wanted in desperately.

'Don't,' she said, and reached for his hand, pulled it away from his eyes and drew it towards her. Held it.

His eyes shuttered. 'Don't what?'

'Don't hide from me.'

'I'm right here.' He dragged his free hand through his hair. 'Where I have been every day, every night, for two weeks? With you.'

He pulled his hand free from her grasp, shifted his hips backwards and sat up against the intricately designed wooden headboard spanning the width of the bed and reaching to the ceiling.

He turned to her, opened his arms wide. 'Come,' he said. 'Come here.'

Thunder rumbled. More quietly now. The storm was moving. But Aurora understood she had a choice. She could crawl between his legs, sit on his lap and let him stir her tired body to life.

Or she could invite the storm inside.

Ignoring the heat stirring in her pelvis, she made a choice.

'No,' she said.

He turned from her, flipped on the beside lamp. The room filled with a soft amber artificial light. But he didn't reach for her again. He dropped his hands into his lap covered by the white sheet, low on his lips.

He arched a brow. 'No?'

She inhaled deeply, straightened her spine, and said more firmly, 'No.'

'Why not?'

'Because you're hurting.'

'I am not in pain.'

'But you were,' she pointed out. 'And your body remembers it, even if you don't want to acknowledge it. You *still* hurt enough for it to infiltrate your dreams.'

'It's only a dream.' He dismissed her with a flippant wave of his hand.

'It's your mind, consciously or subconsciously,' she said tightly, 'and it's telling you—'

'It tells me nothing I don't already know.'

'But I don't know,' she reminded him. 'And I want to. I want to know what your sister was like?'

'What does it matter what she was like?' he snarled, baring perfectly white teeth. 'She's dead.'

'But you're not.' She swallowed. 'And your sister lives inside you. In your dreams…' She blew out a breath, wanting him to understand, to let him know she understood, even if she didn't know all the facts, but she didn't know how to do it. How to show him.

'Do you talk about her?' she asked. *'Ever?'*

'No.'

'I don't talk about Michael either. I thought it would hurt too much. It *did* hurt in the gardens when I told you a little of him, of our relationship, and what happened to him. But I didn't tell you everything, and I… I think it hurts more not tell it. To not talk about him. All of him. Not just his death.'

'You want to talk about him now?'

She nodded.

'Tell me,' he said. 'Tell me about Michael.'

'He was…' She sucked in a lungful of fortifying breath. 'He was my big brother, and I loved him. I looked up to him. I envied him in the earlier days.'

'Why would you envy him?'

'He was always so…*free*.'

'Free?'

'He never put on a show. He never pretended to be anything other than what he was. Cheeky, naughty. Innocent things when we were young. Speaking out of turn. Playing pranks.' She swallowed. 'Harmless things, really.'

'Did you play pranks, too?' he asked gently.

Her chest tightened. 'Once.'

'And what happened?'

'It was silly,' she said, remembering. 'I collected worms from the garden and put them in the new nanny's bed. I didn't like her. She was mean.'

'She hurt you?'

'Only with words. But our parents assumed it was Michael, and I let them believe it. I let him take the blame, and he did. Not once did he tell them it wasn't him. And I started to lean into that. I wanted them to love me,' she confessed roughly. 'I pretended to be the golden child that day, and it became my role. I dedicated myself to it. To being perfect.'

'You are perfect.'

'I'm not,' she said. 'I wasn't. I leaned into Michael's misbehaviour to amplify my own goodness, because I wanted their approval, but they always withheld it anyway. Michael's behaviour grew worse…'

'How?' he pressed softly. 'How did it get worse?'

'It was light stuff at first,' she said. 'Parties. Smoking. Cannabis.' She swallowed, remembering finding him in the gazebo, reeking. 'He said it was a one-off. Then he promised he only did it when he needed to relax. When he had to come home to *them*. He was lying. He smoked it all the time. I could smell it. But I believed him. I believed it was harmless. That his habit wouldn't progress.'

'But it did?'

'He took harder stuff, until I couldn't see him behind his bleary red eyes.' Aurora scrunched up her nose to stem the burn there. 'My parents put so much pressure on us. On Michael, and he escaped it, them, with gambling highs and drugs. But the Michael I grew up with, who protected me from our parents' put-downs and took them all for himself, was gone, long before my parents abandoned him. Before I did. He was gone before he died. I realise that now.'

Pain lanced her through the chest. 'But the night my parents threw him out, he begged me to believe he could change, would change.' A tear fell, and she let it fall. 'I didn't believe him. I let him go off on his own because I didn't want to risk my parents' wrath, their displeasure. I wanted to be good. To be loved. To be the golden child. And then Michael died. *Alone*, because I had been manipulated into being the daughter they wanted.' She hissed, disgusted at what she'd let herself become to please her parents. Who, she realised now, would never have been pleased with her. Not obedient Aurora. Not rebellious Aurora.

'Don't cry.'

'How can I not?' she said. 'I didn't believe him. I didn't give him a chance, not even one last chance to change, because I was too afraid to stand by his side and fail with him. And what did I achieve not lobbying for him one last time? Nothing. I became the heiress to the Arundel name and fortune because I was the only one left. And they thought I'd look after it when they were dead, how they wanted it to be looked after. But after you…after New York, I realised

I didn't have to do it their way. I could live my life how I chose to.'

'And what choices did you make for your life?'

'I chose to continue being the person I became the night I met you,' she confessed. 'To be brave and bold in the choices I make now.'

She searched his eyes, and she saw nothing but shadows.

If he wouldn't let her in, she'd climb inside herself. Talk to the shadows he wouldn't recognise still took up too much space in his mind. *His dreams.*

She moved her body until she was on her knees. Her blue dotted nightgown rose to her thighs as she crawled onto his naked lap.

'Aurora…' He held up his hands in the air as she settled herself, her thighs on either side of his. The baby was big and round between them. 'What are you doing?'

'You need to talk about them, like I did,' she said. 'You need to talk about her. Amelia. You need to face your demons, and—'

'My demons are my own.'

'You can't control them.'

'I can.'

'No, not until you face them,' she said, realizing now it was the truth. 'Or they will own you. Mind, body and soul. Forever.'

She could almost touch it, see it, standing between them. A real-life demon blocking the connection between them that could be so much stronger if he allowed it to flow freely.

If only he talked to her.

Really talked.

'No. Aurora, I can't give you this. I have given you everything else, but I can't give you this.' His hands moved, and he stroked her hair. He coiled his fingers in it and tugged, not enough to hurt, but enough for her to feel the tension, the strength, in his hands. 'I will not put the images that haunt my dreams into your pretty little head. I won't dump my trauma into your innocent mind. I don't want you to know it.'

'But I want to know you, and whatever has happened is a part of you.'

'It's not a part you need.'

'So you'll keep it all to yourself?' she asked, undeterred. 'You'll continue to lock yourself away? I could have done that,' she almost shouted, but she didn't. 'I could have done what you did. Locked myself away in Arundel Manor with my grief and my guilt. But I didn't. I am here, with you, because *I* didn't.'

'We are not the same. You don't know—'

His jaw locked.

She searched his eyes. Those amber-and-green-filled depths. And she wanted to break down the walls surrounding him, but only he could do that.

'Then tell me,' she urged. 'Tell me everything.'

And she waited…

Hadn't she just revealed her own wound? Her own guilt? Hadn't they both tried to be something they weren't, something they shouldn't have had to be, for other people?

Their stories were so similar and yet so different.

His throat squeezed tightly.

She made it sound so easy to make a different choice. There were no different choices for him. But she was here, so soft, so determined to…help him.

No one had ever wanted to help him. Esther… He was money for her, pure and simple. Over time, she'd grown loyal. Loved him. *Maybe*. But Aurora… She had no reason to demand this of him, other than that she naively thought this would change something in him.

It wouldn't change anything. So why not tell her?

It might make her leave.

His stomach tensed. If he didn't tell her, she might leave too. Either way, it was a chance. A risk he wouldn't take.

It was only a story...

'There is no official story of my life before...' He was unsure where to begin.

'Tell me the unofficial one.'

'I have told no one about it,' he said. 'No one knows about the before.'

'No one?'

He shook his head. 'As far as the world knows, I'm Sebastian Shard, born the moment my agent Esther discovered me on the streets. Already a man.'

'But that isn't true.'

'No,' he said honestly. 'I was young, once. But I never really had a childhood, was never allowed one. I was never allowed to play with any other children. I was locked in a basement.'

He felt Aurora's gaze narrow. 'A basement?'

He nodded stiffly. 'I decorated it. I drew, I painted, on any surface I could from the moment I knew how. I turned it into our secret place,' he said, remembering the mural of a never-ending horizon of deep reds and burnt oranges. He swallowed thickly. 'Mine and Amelia's. Until the basement was gone, until we moved into a house with a man. A man who told me to call him Daddy.'

'Your stepfather?'

'He was never a father to me.' His necked corded. 'He was barely a man.' His hands clenched on the bedspread. 'He was my mother's pimp,' he spat.

'Your mother was a prostitute?'

'Yes,' he admitted, and it hurt to tell her. For her to know the shame he felt. 'We always lived in a shared house before... There were women everywhere. *I* knew what it was when I was seven, maybe eight. Maybe younger... Those women weren't my aunts. It wasn't a shared house. It was a brothel. Run by my mother.'

Her eyes flew wide open. 'She was a *madam*?'

'Yes.'

'Surely someone knew? A teacher? A doctor? Someone who could have taken you out of there? Put you into foster care? A family home?'

'It *was* a family, of sorts.' His blood heated. 'Before him.'

'Someone had to know there were children inside of a brothel!'

'There is no record of me. My home birth was undocumented, as was Amelia's. There was no one to know. We didn't exist officially.'

'But a midwife?' she asked. 'Surely a midwife was there to help your mum give birth?'

'When I was a child, there were always women around in various stages of dress,' he explained. 'There was enough of a collective of experience that there was no need for outside help.'

'How is that possible?' She frowned. 'This isn't the dark ages. Children aren't... Their existence isn't...unknown.'

'Children are missing to the system all the time, Aurora. And their existence is obsolete because it isn't on some computer,' he said too harshly.

He couldn't help it. He was angry at her for pushing him, angry at himself for telling. But it pulsed through him. A small part of him itched to tell the story he never had told anyone. To her. To have her understand him.

'It's not a pretty story. I don't know how to tell it without the ugly bits. I don't want the ugly bits in your head... I don't want to talk about it while you are on my lap.' His hands moved of their own volition. Touched her soft upper arms, and he stroked them. Soothed the ache in his fingers against her silky skin. 'You are so soft,' he said. 'So innocent.'

'Then tell me the pretty bits first.'

'There were no pretty things about my life,' he said. 'Until you.'

She smiled, but it didn't reach her eyes. 'Tell me about Amelia.'

'She died,' he said thickly. 'When she was three.'

'What about the three years she lived?'

'She…' Emotion clogged his throat.

Fingers, feather-light, stroked his cheek. 'It's okay to remember her.'

Was it? Was it okay to think of her tiny fingers? Fingers that had clung to him, trusted him. He had left her alone to die.

He closed his eyes. Shut out the trusting eyes clinging to his. He would not fail the trust Aurora placed in him. *Never.*

Lips, so smooth and soft, kissed his cheek. 'It's going to hurt,' she breathed against his skin as her lips moved to the tip of his nose and over to his other cheek.

'It will hurt to remember her happy,' she continued, and Aurora kissed him again. 'It'll hurt to know that, however happy she was, she died. But you have to remember more than her death, Sebastian.'

She kissed his eyelids now. His right one, then his left. And Sebastian trembled.

'You have to remember.' Her lips feathered his forehead. 'Remember how she lived. How she was part of your life. How she still is. Face whatever guilt it is you feel, and let yourself move on. Forgive yourself.'

His eyes flew open. He caught the wrists moving from his chest to hold his face. He wouldn't let her cradle his cheeks and push her innocence inside his skin with her gentle fingers.

He was not innocent.

He released her wrists and caught her waist.

'Sebastian!'

He ignored her. He could not have her on his lap. He could not feel her warmth when his blood ran so cold.

He lifted her, made his hands be careful, and placed her on the bed beside him.

'Sebastian,' she said. *'Please.'*

And it hurt him for her to beg. For him to break his promise to never to let her beg for anything from him. But this time, she was wrong. *This*...he could not change. He couldn't undo what he'd done.

'I will never forgive myself,' he hissed. His chest was so tight. 'She was beautiful. Innocence personified. She was the definition of it, with her curly black hair, her little button nose that squinched with her squinting big blue eyes when she laughed. And she laughed all the time. In our room we shared. A room with everything we needed, a kitchen. A bathroom. And I fed her. I burped her. *I loved her!*'

'I know,' she breathed heavily.

'You do not know. You do not know what it is like to have something precious given to you. Something so innocent you cannot help but love it.'

'I'm pregnant,' she said. 'Soon we'll both be given something precious. Something we will both love.' She placed her hand on her belly. 'I feel the baby all the time. Its tiny hands. Its feet. *I* understand that kind of love. The consuming nature of it. I understand how much you loved her.'

He dragged his hands through his too long hair. Pushed it back away from the skin that crawled with self-hate. *Self-disgust*.

He closed his eyes. Shut out Aurora. Her misted big brown eyes. He didn't deserve her compassion. And he'd tell her why. And then he'd open his eyes. Watch her tears disappear. Watch the shame he felt reflected in her eyes with the ugly images he'd now put into her beautiful, determined, naive, and stubborn mind.

He was not naive.

'Love is never enough,' he hissed, his eyes still closed. 'I was given a responsibility. To take care of her. And I did. I held her. I provided for her every need from the moment she was born. Because in the rooms beyond ours…the other rooms, filled with women. With men. Drinking. Having sex. Doing drugs. It wasn't safe for her there. But we were safe in our room. She was safe with *me*.'

'How old were you?'

He squeezed the bridge of his nose. 'I was twelve, and she was brand new. And she'd relied on me. And for three years, I kept her safe. I protected her. Until one night, while she was asleep in her crib beside my bed, I—'

He would tell her. However hard it was to admit. To thrust the words into her ears and have her know.

She had a right to know who she had made love to in New York.

She had a right to know who the man was she shared her bed with now.

He opened his eyes, and he hid nothing from her. He let her look into his eyes and see the man he was.

Unworthy.

'The house was full. All the rooms were occupied, and the others who didn't have rooms spilt into the lounge, the kitchen,' he told her, and he let the images bloom to life in his head. The open sex. *The depravity.*

'Our room was at the top of the house this time,' he continued. 'It was a beautiful house. In a neighbourhood where no one would ever expect such ugliness to live. Unlittered and privileged, the neighbourhood was picturesque. All of it was. All but our house. But our room had a lock. And

I wanted to get out. I wanted to breathe the night's air… Needed to paint, to draw, do something with my hands.'

He looked down at them. The hands trembling before him. 'To create the images I never found in life. Images of softness, of hope. And so I left her. I left Amelia sleeping in our room. I locked the door so no one would hurt her. I locked the door to keep her safe. I left, and I took the key…'

'Sebastian…' She cried openly now. Big, rolling tears dripped from the tip of her beautiful chin.

He had to stop her tears.

In the end, she would not pity him.

'I stayed out for an hour, no more…'

'The fire,' she said, and faster her tears fell.

His blood turned to ice. It ran into his bones. Threatened to shatter them to nothing but dust.

'When I came back… The house was gone. It was nothing but smoke and ash. Some survived. They stood with firemen or sat inside ambulances. But Amelia was gone. The top of the house… It was still smoking. She was…*dead*.'

Aurora swiped at her cheeks with the backs of her hands. And then she looked at him, her chest moving up and down as rapidly as his own. She lifted her arms and held them wide. 'Come to me,' she said.

'I will not.'

'Come to me,' she demanded again, and his body ached with his resistance to fall into her arms.

'I do not want your pity,' he growled. 'I do not deserve it.'

'You deserve everything,' she corrected him.

'Have you heard *nothing*?'

'I heard every word,' she said, still holding those dainty arms open for him.

'You were a child taking care of his sister in a house that should never have existed with children inside it. But you existed. Both of you did. And you made that existence bearable for your sister because you loved her. And you wanted a moment for yourself, and you did what you thought was right. You tried to keep her safe.'

'And I failed.'

'Your mother failed you. From the moment you were born, from the moment she thrust Amelia into your arms. It wasn't your fault. Forgive yourself, Sebastian.'

'Never.'

She rose on her knees. 'I'm going to hold you.'

'I do not want you to.'

'But I'm going to,' she said. 'I'm going to hold the little boy who needed someone to hold him. I'm going to hold you, the man who needs to be held because he has been alone for far too long. He has locked himself away for years because he blamed himself for something that was never his fault—' Her voice broke.

Something tore inside him. In his chest.

'It *was* my fault.'

'It wasn't,' she said, and she sat in front of him on her knees. 'But you've punished yourself enough.'

'It will never be enough.'

She brushed the tears away, but her eyes pleaded. 'Let me hold you.'

'I do not want your arms around me,' he lied, because all his body craved was her.

'Turn the light off.'

His gaze narrowed. 'Why?'

She gripped the hem of her nighty, tore it over her head and threw it on the ground.

'What are you doing?' he growled.

'I'm getting into bed.'

And she did.

He looked at her lying beside him.

'Hold me,' she said. But she kept her head where it was.

Her head on the pillow. Her eyes pointing at the wall. 'I need you to hold *us*.'

His body roared.

How could he deny her? He'd promised to meet all her needs. Physically at least.

He couldn't help it. His body wouldn't listen to his demand to stay still. To keep his hands away from her.

He flipped the light off. Slipped his hips down the bed and turned. Moulded his body to the shape of her.

She grabbed his wrists, his hands, and wrapped them around her. Around *them*.

He closed his eyes. 'Aurora—'

'Don't talk. You don't have to say anything else,' she told him. 'Just hold me and know I'm right here with you. *We* are.'

Tears filled his eyes.

He wouldn't shed them.

'Tomorrow, we'll find a way to honour the boy you were. The children like you,' she whispered. 'Tomorrow, we'll find a way to honour Amelia.'

'There is no honour to be found.'

'Sleep, Sebastian.'

And with his heart hammering, Sebastian closed his eyes. Let his mind only hear her. Her breathing. He did not examine the intimacy of the moment she was giving to him. But he knew it was the most intimate moment he'd ever had.

In this moment, he was closer to her than he'd ever been to anyone.

She understood he would not let her soothe him, and so she had asked him to soothe her. And she knew he wouldn't refuse her request, because…

She knew *him*.

She knew what he was, what he'd done, and still she wanted him here.

The knowledge shattered him. He felt raw. Broken open,

and all that kept him together was her. Her body pressed against his. The rhythmic lull of her soft exchange of air calmed something inside him. Her soft, small hands on top of his. She was holding their baby *with* him.

It was everything he shouldn't have.

Everything he didn't deserve.

But here it was.

Here they were.

His family.

And he held them both in his big, greedy hands. Because he was a glutton. *Selfish.*

But he couldn't let go of her.

He would never let them go.

A fatigue, so heavy, blanketed his mind.

He was so tired…

Darkness claimed him. And Sebastian slept a dreamless sleep, holding on to Aurora.

And she held him right back.

CHAPTER ELEVEN

THE KITCHENS HUMMED with activity and a thousand scents.

Aurora walked, one red silk pump after the other, through the white shirts and black waistcoats of the staff working diligently away in the smaller kitchen preparing the silver serving trays. The champagne glasses sparkled as the bubbles rose to the top. The canapés were the perfect size for the guests who were beginning to enter the great dining hall.

'Mind your backs,' a chef called as she stepped into the bigger second kitchen.

She stopped at the roasting trays, pulled from the ovens by the team of chefs in their whites. The trays steamed. The smell of tiny quails, smothered in herbs and butter, assaulted her airways, but she resisted the urge to stick her fingers in the juices and lick them.

She'd eat them soon enough at the head table with Sebastian.

'Miss Arundel?' She turned her back to the chefs, ignored the grumble of her stomach, and focused on the bright blue eyes of the event coordinator, Tina.

She was a godsend. Without her and Esther, she couldn't have pulled it off in a week. But together they had pulled it off in an afternoon.

Her stomach twinged. She was right to rush this—to rush him. Their time was almost up. The baby would be here in three weeks…

'What's wrong?' Aurora asked when those blue eyes, wide with worry, stared at her unblinkingly.

Tina pushed the microphone of her headset away from her lips. 'Nothing.' She smiled. A perfect smile. But Aurora wasn't fooled. It was brittle.

'Something's wrong,' Aurora said. 'The hall isn't ready, is it?'

She shook her head. 'The dining hall's ready,' she said. 'The guests are arriving and are being shown in.' She waved to the staff exiting the outer kitchen. 'The staff are taking the canapés out now…'

'So, then, what is it?'

'Esther Mahoti is here.'

'Is she?'

Aurora couldn't wait to meet her in person. A no-nonsense woman who had supplied everything Aurora needed to make today a success. She'd curated the perfect guest list, deployed the teams of staff to ready the castle. She'd planned, with her team, the transport for the guests, organised the art team to install Sebastian's pieces in the dining hall, and personally sent Aurora the silk pumps on her feet.

'She is.' Tina swallowed. 'And she's demanding to see Mr Shard.'

'Then show her to him.'

'I can't find him.' Panic tightened the slender throat inside the baby-pink necktie. 'I'm supposed to know where he is. Where *everyone* is. And Esther—'

'Will be fine,' she soothed, but her throat was tightening too.

'She'll never use our event company again if I lose the star of the show.'

'Bring Esther into the hall. Let her see what you've accomplished in such short notice.'

'It won't be enough. If I can't deliver Mr—'

'I'll deliver him.' Aurora tucked Tina's arm in hers and walked her back out the way she'd come.

Her stomach flipped. Was he ready? Had she demanded too much? Too quickly. Too fast.

'Do what you do best.' She smiled tightly. 'We'll be with you soon,' she promised.

Tina flipped her headset back into place and walked off, talking into it in hushed whispers.

Aurora watched her leave, turned on her heel, and pushed through the side door to the back of the courtyard.

Her heart raced. This morning Sebastian had kissed her forehead and told her he was going for a walk. Alone. It wasn't unusual. Since the night he'd told her about Amelia, he'd claimed more and more moments for himself. But he'd always returned to her by nightfall and climbed into bed beside her.

Aurora moved out of the side gate. She looked up at the skies. A helicopter whirred. It descended the mountains lined with trees. More guests.

She dropped her gaze to the trees standing guard at the entrance of the forest. She moved towards them, over the field of short green grass.

She'd find him.

Aurora stepped into the forest. Twigs broke underfoot as she took herself deeper into the overlapping trees.

'Sebastian?' she called, but all that answered her were the birds she'd startled, flying upwards to higher branches.

White beams of light shone through the branches overhead, scattered with drooping leaves.

She closed her eyes and listened.

She could hear running water.

She opened her eyes, listening, finding the right direction…

She moved toward the sound of rippling water, and it got closer with her every step.

Her feet halted at the top of an incline. A slow-flowing river moved below. A natural stairway of roots led the way down through the trees. She took them, step after step, down to the river. As she did, the trees parted.

And the view stole her breath.

'*There* you are. I found you,' she husked, stopping still.

He stood from where he knelt next to the river. And she watched him rise. Watched the sun play with the wisps of his hair hanging loose at his shoulders. His open-collared white shirt revealed the thick hair-covered throat. And up her eyes went. To the tip of his bristled chin, to linger on his plump pink lower lip. Up the length of his noble nose. To his eyes. Green-and-amber depths staring straight at her.

'I wasn't lost,' he said deeply.

She moved towards him. Her heart racing. Her body tightening, urging her closer. *Nearer.*

He had been lost. They both had in New York.

Would he tell her the same now as he had then? That he wasn't hers to find.

She cleared her throat. 'What are you doing down here?'

'Thinking.'

'And what have you been thinking about all morning?' she asked, her lips moving into a smile. But her lips were too heavy, her lungs too breathless to perform the ease she wanted to portray.

She wasn't at ease. The air hummed with it. A restlessness. And it made the hairs rise beneath her red-silk-covered arms.

'You,' he said, and his eyes dropped to her stomach. Rounded and obvious beneath the folds of her red sparkly gown. 'And the baby.'

She stopped before him. The moss-covered ground was soft beneath her shoes. 'What about us?'

'They have breached the walls,' he said. 'The doors are wide open. And in they go. Into my house.' His eyes rose to meet hers. 'You invited them inside.'

His eyes were not accusing. His voice was soft, and yet she felt like a traitor.

'We talked about this.' She exhaled heavily. They had talked about it the morning after he'd told her about Amelia. Lay in bed together. Naked. Holding each other. 'We decided to do it together for Amelia,' she reminded him. 'And we are doing it. *Today.*'

'I'm no speechmaker, Aurora,' he said. 'I don't stand in great halls, or on podiums, in front of people like them and talk. I do not talk about myself.'

'This isn't about you,' she said, knowing it was a half truth. It was the only part he would hear. The only reason he would do this was for her. But she understood he needed it far more than Amelia did now.

'They don't care,' he scoffed. 'They want what my hands create. They want my work. They don't care what Amelia endured. People like them, privileged and elite, ignore what happens in houses like the one I grew up in, houses next door to their own. They pretend that what happens inside those houses doesn't happen. But they know, Aurora. How could they not?' he said, his top lip lifting to expose gritted white teeth. 'They fear what lives in the dark, so they choose to be ignorant. To ignore it. They ignored Amelia's suffering.'

She wanted to touch him. Reach out and hold his hand. But he had to trust her enough to take it.

'I wish I'd stood on a podium,' she said. 'I wish I'd made my parents listen one last time. Made them realise Michael needed help. He needed love. Unconditional love...'

Her heart raced.

Love. There it was in her mind. On her tongue. And it didn't feel wrong to think it. To feel it.

She was in love with him.

She pushed it down. Today wasn't about her.

'I wish,' she breathed, 'I had used my voice before now. I wish I'd realised sooner the shame they made me feel about Michael, his condition, his addictions… It was nothing to be shameful about. It was an opportunity to expose the awful atrocities not only the rich experience, but the less fortunate.'

'They don't care, Aurora.'

'Then make them care.' She puffed out air. 'Stand in front of them as Sebastian Shard and tell them the causes they are donating to are worthy. The people that experience these awful things are worthy.'

That you *are worthy*, she added silently, because he wouldn't want to hear it. Nor would he accept it.

He had to believe today was for Amelia.

His lips firmed into a flat line. 'How am I supposed to do that?' he asked.

'Without shame,' she said, swallowing all the emotion in her chest that was threatening to clog her throat. 'You, Amelia…the children who have experienced, are still experiencing, the same things that you did…they have nothing to be embarrassed about. It isn't their fault the world is ugly sometimes, that it exposes them to unspeakable things.'

'But it was my fault that she died,' he corrected her. 'Am I supposed to tell them that? That I locked her in?'

'Yes,' she said. 'If you want to tell them your and Amelia's story, tell them. You did nothing wrong.'

'And what?' he snarled. Baring his perfectly white teeth. 'Stand up there and shame you. Tell the world that the baby inside you was put there by a man who abandoned his family. Left them to—'

'You abandoned no one,' she interjected sharply. 'You haven't abandoned us.'

His cheek pulsed. 'I want them to know you will be my wife.'

'Sebastian...' Her heart danced. She wanted to be that. To be his wife. She wanted to be his.

But not like this.

He thrust his hand into his pocket. He withdrew his hand, clenched in a fist, and held it out between them.

'Marry me.' He opened his hand, and there in his palm sat a ring of twisted silver, at its centre the bluest stone she'd ever seen.

'It is the same colour as your dress the night we met,' he said. 'Siren's blue.'

Her hand lifted. She couldn't stop it. She touched this ring that would bind her to him.

In name.

Her heart smashed against her ribs. She wanted more than twisted silver.

She dropped her hand, raised her eyes to his.

She wanted...

Her eyes filled with unwanted tears.

She wanted his heart. To *be* his heart. To be loved as intensely as he loved his art. As he had loved Amelia.

'Wear it, Aurora,' he urged. 'Our baby will not be undocumented. It will never be lost in the dark. Let them know I am your protector. Let them know Sebastian Shard, the enigma that creeps around in the dark and creates images that haunts them, protects you and our child.'

She wanted more. More than protection.

She wanted everything.

Everything he wasn't ready to give.

She reached for his fingers and closed them around the ring. 'Let's not talk of marriage today,' she said. 'But... I'll stand there beside you, whatever you choose to say, and I'll be proud to have them know you're the father of my child. You don't have to hide in the dark anymore, Sebastian.'

'Aurora...' His Adam's apple danced. 'They fear the dark. They fear the noises that come out of the shadows,' he told her fiercely. 'I am the dark, and they will fear me.'

'No.' She dropped her hands to her sides. 'You and Amelia were made to stay in the shadows. To hide. Don't make Amelia hide anymore.'

'She is dead, Aurora,' he said without venom, only acceptance. 'I understand what you have tried to do today, but opening the doors makes me weak.'

'You are not weak,' she corrected him quietly. 'You and Amelia deserve to exist. To be seen. Stand in front of them, Sebastian,' she urged, 'and tell them what you think is right.' She knew she was pushing him hard, but... 'Stand in front of them and tell them Amelia's story. Make them know *her* story. Make them see her. Make her death mean something. Something that can change things for other undocumented—*invisible*—children.'

His nostrils flared.

'You have an opportunity to not only donate your art to causes you believe in, but to be the face of it. Your face, without a mask, without hiding behind the art you make.' She swallowed. 'Today they are all here. So stand in front of them as yourself. For Amelia. Don't hide anymore, Sebastian. Make them see—'

'Me?'

'Yes,' she agreed, and she waited. Even though their time was almost up. The afternoon gala was ready to proceed... but he needed time, and she'd give him a little more.

He nodded and pocketed the ring. Then he did it. He pushed his fingers between hers. Entwined them until the pads of his fingers pressed against her knuckles.

'For Amelia,' he said, 'and after…' His throat bulged.

'After?'

'You will wear my ring,' he said, and pulled her into step beside him.

Aurora's heart swelled.

She knew the truth.

Today, it was for him.

She squeezed his hand tighter and let him lead her up the stairs of wood.

And after…

Her heart soared.

She'd marry him for herself. But only for the right reason. *For love.*

Sebastian guided Aurora out of the forest. *Slowly.*

He swallowed the urge to lift her, to tell her off again for taking stairs too steep and uneven, to find him. She wouldn't listen.

She'd delight in telling him that despite his vows, despite his decision not to care for her too deeply, to care about anything or anyone, he did. He cared.

And she was right. He did not want her to be. But he… cared. *Deeply.*

He'd shared himself with her, not only physically, but in ways he'd never shared himself before. He hadn't used pretty pictures he created to express himself. With her, he'd used words, given her ugly images that haunted him, voiced his thoughts, and confessed his crimes. He'd revealed to her the man he was beneath his name.

Yet still she held his hand.

And despite himself, he enjoyed, craved even, her ability to prove him wrong.

She'd shown him that he could change.

They stepped out of the forest, and the trees shook with

the wind, pushing them forward. He stopped, bringing them to a halt on the edge of the tree line. He watched the air lift the black silk kissing her shoulders.

'You are stunning, Aurora,' he growled, his voice raw.

'Thank you' she responded. 'I feel beautiful.' The edges of her painted plum lips curved upwards, and he couldn't help it. So did his. He smiled. Until the muscles he hadn't used in such a long time ached.

'Very, *very* beautiful,' he agreed.

The wind swept through the trees again. *Harder.* Red, brown and orange leaves left their branches. They scattered and fell around them like confetti.

And he knew it. In this moment, he wasn't the only one to embrace change. She *had* changed. No longer was she the broken creature screaming into the trees. She was vibrant. Confident. And it was so easy to feed from her youth, from her unbreakable confidence that her way was the right way.

Clarity cleared the last remaining doubts from his mind. The fog lifted, and so did something inside him.

She was right, *had* been right, before she'd known his name, his face...

She had known him the moment their eyes had met.

She'd known their worlds colliding was the beginning.

The beginning of something special.

She *was* his awakening.

This goddess in red silk, sparkling with stardust, was his reckoning.

His redemption.

She cocked her head to the side. 'Ready?'

He nodded.

He was.

Because of her.

His Aurora...

They both stepped forward, toward the castle, and he realised neither led the other. They walked together. Side by side. Hand in hand, out of the shadows, and into the full beam of a too bright sun.

He was not alone.

And it did not feel like weakness to have her beside him.

It was power.

She was his power, and she fortified him. Strengthened him in this choice to claim this opportunity she'd given to him with her small hand holding his. An opportunity to stand as himself and bring Amelia with him out of the shadows. To give his name and his face to a charity he would found to support children like her. Forgotten children.

And he would do it. Today.

He would no longer let the rich and the privileged elite remain ignorant.

He would make them look.

He would make them see more than his pretty art.

And they would acknowledge what they feared.

They would acknowledge *him*. All that he was, and all that he had become despite them.

Together, he and Aurora crossed the courtyard and entered the castle. Together, they walked down the corridor lined with a thousand windows. Long, heavy black drapes hung from the walls, tied with gold twine that held them open, let the light in. And on they went until they came to the two tall doors made of oak and iron. But neither stopped as Sebastian dipped his head and the staff on either side of the doors opened them.

Sebastian and Aurora swept into the great hall.

Together.

Hand in hand, they strode down the white carpeted central aisle between the circular oak tables of white cloth and silver cutlery to the front of the room.

They took to the stage, but she did not release his hand

as he turned. As he looked at the guests Aurora had invited. She squeezed it.

He didn't look at her. He kept his eyes on them. On the ball gowns and tiaras. The diamonds dripping from throats and fingers. On the eyes staring at him, wide with anticipation.

But he felt *her*. More than her hand holding his. *Inside* him. He squeezed her hand back and knew she felt him too. That she recognised him. And all that he was about to say wouldn't shock or appal her. He knew she had already accepted him. As he was.

And he couldn't let himself examine it any more deeply. How this realization made the ache inside him pulse with something foreign. Something he did not want to acknowledge.

He took what she offered.

Her acceptance.

That was all he wanted, not these impostors in his house.

He did not need *them* to accept him. He needed them only to know of him. Know he existed, *would exist*, with or without them. And so had Amelia.

'I am Sebastian Shard,' he said, and waited a breath too long for them to feel the weight of his name. The power of it.

His name mattered now.

He'd risen above them all from the dark places he'd called home. And he stood unflinchingly before them now as the man the forgotten boy had become.

'I am Sebastian Shard,' he said again, louder. Clearer. He would make them look now at the dirty secret they'd once preferred to ignore. 'And my mother was a prostitute. A *madam*. A pleasure provider to all those who entered her home and her body.'

The crowd gasped, and he let their shock feed him.

'I was, am, the children in your neighbourhood, and in

your gated communities,' he told them, opening their ignorant eyes. 'I was nothing more than a boy, living inside a house of depravity hidden beneath your respectable veneer,' he told them. For the first time, he did not feel shamed by his past. He felt…strong.

'There are many children like the boy I was. Living in dark spaces. Seeing unspeakable things. Ugly things. And we cannot forget them. I will not forget them.'

He inhaled deeply through flaring nostrils.

It was enough. He had said enough, told them enough.

He waved his free hand to the team of staff waiting beside the stage. He beckoned them to him with a flick of his wrist. They came. Gathered around the white cloth ten feet high behind him, concealing what he would now reveal.

He nodded, and dozens of hands pulled the cloth free until it revealed the twisted metal in all its glory. It was too tall to house in his studio, so he'd built it in the forest surrounding his home.

'It's me…' Aurora said, and he felt, heard the awe in her voice. And when he looked at her, everything, everyone else vanished.

'It is you,' he confirmed. His hands had wanted to build nothing else since the morning he'd seen her beneath his studio window. With a thousand wishes at her feet.

'Oh, Sebastian…' Her mouth parted, her eyes darting to his, then back to his creation. Metal bent to his will. He had moulded a moment. A private moment only he had seen.

'I built a thousand wishes at your feet,' he said to her. Only to her. 'Because I know, I understand, if Amelia had one wish, she would have wished for you, Aurora. Your spirit, your determination to live, to be who you are unashamed to be… Amelia would have wished for you to make me understand what was necessary. I understand now,' he said deeply. 'With your face, this sculpture, you will be the face of our new foundation to support children like her.' His throat clogged. 'Children like the boy I was.'

He turned back to the crowd, his heart raging. He raised his free hand to the walls that had been expertly lighted to showcase his art in all its forms.

'The art on the surrounding walls is yours to purchase,' he said, because he would take their money. He would take it all. 'But this—' he waved behind him '—is the symbol of our new charity. And it is called Amelia's Wish.'

He couldn't help it. His voice dried up in his throat. Something pushed it down…something he could not describe. It was light and heavy at the same time.

'Enjoy your meals,' he croaked. And pulled Aurora back the way they'd come. Down between the tables. And their eyes followed them.

Sebastian's feet faltered. Only slightly, only a tiny misstep, but Aurora's hold on him firmed as they…

Clapped.

Applauded his crude and ugly speech.

Applauded what he was and what he would now do.

For Amelia.

Hand in hand, Aurora and Sebastian made their exit out of the great hall.

He did not need their validation.

'Close the doors,' he said roughly. Shutting out their eyes, eyes he did not want on him.

He wanted her eyes.

He wanted her.

Only her.

'Aurora,' he said as the oak-and-iron doors closed behind them, the staff disappearing behind black drapes and through a side door.

'Why are we not in there?' she husked. 'You were amazing. Amelia…'

'I do not need to be in there now. I said all that had to be said.'

She swallowed thickly. 'She would be so proud of you. *I* am proud of you.' She smiled, but it quivered. Wavered.

He lifted his thumb to her lip, smoothed it across the plump softness. 'Thank you,' he said, because he knew this time, those two simple and unprofound words were enough. For her.

She kissed the tip of his thumb. Met his gaze and held it prisoner. And he was willing, he realised. A willing prisoner to her guard. He would be her captive. He would be with her. Always. Protect her with his name. His strength. The power she had unleashed within him to stand in front of them unashamed.

He dropped his thumb from her lip.

'Come to bed with me, Aurora.'

'Why?' she asked, and still her lip quivered.

'I want to take you to bed,' he said. 'I need to be with you. Naked. I want to hold you. Only you,' he said roughly. His truth. His needs. His wants.

'I was wrong,' he admitted. 'We have something special, Aurora. This, we, can work,' he said, and the word *we* did not feel stolen. It was theirs to have. 'We can be intimate. We can be friends. We can be lovers. Husband and wife. We can be a team and raise a family. The family we both want and never had before.'

They could do this.

This could work.

He knew it.

'I was wrong too,' she admitted.

He scowled. 'About what?'

'Us.'

'What about us?'

The delicate tendons in her throat tightened. 'We deserve everything.'

'I am offering you everything you asked for,' he said. 'You will never be alone or lonely. We'll be friends. We'll be intimate. We will be a family.'

'I want more.'

'There is no more.'

'There is,' she said, and her shoulders rose. Her spine straightened. 'There is love.'

'Aurora—'

She shook her head. 'I love you, Sebastian.'

Her eyes misted.

'And I need you to love me back.'

CHAPTER TWELVE

THE GROUND OPENED beneath Sebastian's feet. One step in the wrong direction, one step closer to her, and he knew he'd fall. Straight back into hell.

He released her hand.

It hurt, everywhere, to know he'd never take her hand again. Never hold it. Never feel the softness of her flawless skin press into his much rougher callused palms.

Because he had to let go.

He had to let *her* go.

'Don't.' Her grip tightened on his splayed fingers.

He would not close them.

'Don't shut me out,' she said. 'Don't... *Please.* Sebastian...'

Another broken promise.

He'd sworn never again would she beg. But here she begged him. With her big brown eyes. With her fingers holding on tightly to his.

His heart hurt. Its erratic thump was a raging beast inside him. Because here she was, begging for his love, and he couldn't give it to her. He would not. The type of love she spoke of had lived within him once, lived in his core. Love had been his purpose. And he'd needed it so much that it had destroyed him.

He wasn't so naive. He felt it again. Now. Love.

But saying it aloud, acknowledging, was different.

And he loved her too much. Too hard.

It was the same and yet different. It was a rush of warmth,

of want, of need. And his hands itched to wrap themselves around it, grasp it and not let go. But he knew if he did, he would squeeze too tightly. Crush it, crush her.

He would not crush her.

'Talk to me,' she demanded. 'Scream at me. Tell me this isn't what we agreed to. This isn't what either of us wanted. But it has happened. Love. This is love,' she whispered, and it fell over his skin, draped over his shoulders. It was a heavy thing. A comforting weight.

A lie.

His love was dangerous, and to accept hers... To give her his in return, his love...

It would be a curse.

'Please, don't close me out.'

He never should have let her in.

'This was a mistake, Aurora.' Bile rose in his throat. 'I never should have listened to you scream. I never should have come out of the shadows. I never should have shown—'

'Shown me who you are?' she interrupted. 'You never should have shown me the man beneath that mask? You never should have brought me here and shown me the man inside these castle walls is a man who deserves to be loved? You deserve to be cherished, Sebastian. You deserve to be loved, and I love—'

'Stop,' he said, but the demand sounded hollow, flimsy.

'I will not stop,' she said, her other hand locking around his wrist. 'We both deserved to be loved. We were made for each other. You were made for me to love you.'

His chest caved in on itself.

If she was meant for him, if he was meant for her, then why did it hurt so much?

Because love was pain.

His love was agony.

And he would not give it to her. All this love inside him. He would not drown her in his feelings, his attachment.

He would not kill her, too.

'Aurora, release me.'

'No.'

He had to make her, didn't he? He had to make her hate him. Run from him and never look back. It was the only way to keep her safe, because now she had named it, the love they both felt, he could not protect her. Life, love, could be ripped away in an instant. It would devastate her as it had him.

It would kill him to lose her love. To lose her to the same hands of fate that had taken Amelia. But better to lose her now than fall deeper.

He moved. Stepped forward into her air. Her scent. So warm, so pure. So *innocent*. And those deep brown eyes looked up at him.

He had brought her here and locked her inside. Shut her away from the world and made her his prisoner because he thought it was the only way to keep her safe.

But he had not been keeping her safe. He had not been protecting her.

He had been protecting himself.

The world sat in the room behind them, in a great hall, and he had dragged her outside. Closed the doors on the people inside.

If he kept her here, she would always be lonely, because he did not belong with people. He did not belong in great halls.

But she did.

He had to make himself do it. *For her.* He lifted his hand and cradled her cheek. Stroked the pad of his thumb across her sculpted cheekbone.

'Sebastian...'

He leaned in until her dark lashes fluttered closed and her lips parted.

It would be so easy to close his eyes, too. To lean in those few last millimetres and claim her kiss. Claim her. Keep her here with him. But he couldn't. He knew this now.

She deserved everything.

Everything he couldn't give her.

What kind of life would she have with him? If he put his ring on her finger, what kind of life would his child have?

They deserved to live their life fully. Free. And he'd only shackle them. Keep them on the fringes, on the outside of life. Where he belonged.

But they didn't.

She didn't.

He would set her free.

'I will never love you,' he breathed, the words between her parted lips.

Her eyes flew open.

'Sebastian—'

He tightened his fingers, held her face, made her look at him.

'You think this is love?' He laced his voice with mockery, but he was only mocking himself. Because he loved her. Needed her like air.

'It was never love. It could never be love. Not between us. I brought you here to imprison you because of my baby. Never for you. Only the child. You mean nothing to me.'

'*Liar*!' she spat into his mouth.

He was a liar. It was never all about the baby. It had always been about her. But he would tell a thousand lies to save her from a life with him. He now knew it wouldn't be a life at all.

Not the life she deserved.

'I do not love you,' he said again, each word raw in his throat, his body, his mind, rejecting them as false.

It would be the only truth she knew. The only truth he would give her.

'All you are to me,' he said, and his heart raged in protest, 'is an incubator for my heir.'

She gasped, and he felt the agony in it. But it was nothing compared to the agony she'd experience if he told her his truth. That his love would suffocate her.

She loosened her hold. Released his hand. And he felt the loss of her grip deep in his bones, as if her small, delicate fingers were the only thing holding him on his feet. But he did the same. He dropped his hand from her face. He stepped back. Away from her.

He would not take her with him.

'It was all a game to you?' she said, her eyes weeping angry tears. She swiped them away with a stiff wrist. 'You played me to get the baby?'

'Yes,' he said, his body urging him to drop to his knees and beg her forgiveness. To tell her he wasn't worthy. He was sorry.

But he couldn't.

'Was it *all* a lie?' she asked.

And the answer in his mouth was instant.

That she was the only real truth he'd ever known.

She was all he wanted.

But instead of telling her that, he took another step away from her, and he knew what waited behind him as he readied himself to tell another lie.

The only lie that would protect her from *him*.

'Yes,' he said.

The hole opened wider behind him.

'It was all a lie.' he confessed the lie she needed to hear, and Sebastian took the final step.

He plunged.

Straight into hell.

And he took his love with him.

Aurora trembled. A shudder spread from deep in her abdomen until her whole body throbbed with it. With rage and confusion.

She swiped at her traitorous eyes. But she knew they revealed the truth. That beneath it all, beneath the anger heating her cheeks, it was sadness that overwhelmed her A bone-deep sadness.

It had felt so natural to tell him, to confess her love. It was the next logical step. The natural progression in their relationship. And yet…

She looked at him. Standing so close and yet feeling so far away from her.

She swallowed. Tried to stem the tremble.

He stood before her, as himself, but he was not himself.

He was cold, detached.

He was not the Sebastian she was in love with.

'It doesn't make sense,' she said out loud to herself, but he answered.

'What have I not made clear, Aurora?' he asked. 'What do you not understand?' His jaw pulsed. 'I made a mistake. We were doomed from the start. I…we…are too different. It was an error on my part. A fatal mistake to let my guard down in New York. To let you…*this* happen.' His neck corded. He shook his head. 'I was wrong. We cannot work. And I cannot pretend any longer. I can no longer perform this…*show*.'

She searched his eyes. Vacant but for the colour of his green-and-amber irises.

And suddenly it clicked.

'You were the boy in the painting, weren't you?' she asked. 'In New York. *Divinity*.'

He frowned deeply. 'What has that got to do with anything?'

'I see you.'

'I am standing right here.'

'No,' she corrected him. 'You're not. This—' she waved at the entirety of him '—is not you.'

'There is no one here but you and I.'

'It was only you and I in New York. In your studio. In my bed,' she told him. 'In the forest, by the river...' She waved at the closed doors. 'On that stage...*that* was you.' She pointed at him with trembling hands. 'This person standing in front of me is nothing more than a shell of the man I love. It is a copy of you. Wearing a mask made to deceive. But I am not deceived.'

'You deceive yourself, Aurora,' he said. 'You do not know me. You only know what I have allowed you to know.'

'I know you. I know this. These cruel words you've said to me, are...' She waved at the walls, looking for a way to explain that she knew what he was doing and she wouldn't accept it. 'Your words are nothing but a defence. Arrows you're choosing to fire at me,' she summarised for him and for herself. 'But you have missed. They have only nicked the surface. They have only inflicted flesh wounds. I am not scared. I will not run away.'

'Then you are more naive than I thought.'

'I am not naive,' she said. 'I see you.'

She would not accept this fake Sebastian when the real one, the real Sebastian, was just beneath this cruel exterior of detachment.

He was not detached. And he loved, she knew, deeply. Intensely. Desperately.

She knew he loved her. Knew it as true as she knew his baby grew inside her.

'The painting in New York... A boy in rags, his skin covered in grime... But his eyes shone. So bright. *Vivid.* They hid nothing. They let all who looked at him understand what he wanted. What he needed. If only they could look beneath their initial reaction to his condition. If they could look past the bruises beneath his tired eyes. Beneath the filth. It was there for anyone to see. For anyone to give to him. They didn't see it. But I did. I recognised it.'

'There was nothing to see in that painting. There was

nothing to decode,' he said roughly. 'Nothing other than what it offered. *A painting!*'

'You're scared, aren't you?' she asked, a path clearing between all those conflicting emotions inside her that had been fogging her thoughts. 'You know I know, don't you?'

'You know nothing.'

'I do. I understand everything now. You need it still, the same thing that poor boy did, but you're scared to admit it. That the boy you were still lives inside you. And he still aches for it. Yearns for it more than anything else. He is searching for it. Begging for it. Something divine... I saw it in his eyes. And I see it in yours.'

'What are you talking about, Aurora?' he hissed. 'You are talking in riddles I do not want to understand. I do not need you to understand what the painting meant to me. *It means nothing!*'

'It's standing right in front of you,' she said, ignoring him. She knew it. Understood him more in this moment than she ever had. His search had been the same as hers. The want beneath the facade of her smiles. Her silenced voice. They both wanted it. And they could have it. They could have it all.

'I'm standing right in front of you. All you have to do is reach out and claim it. And it is yours. I am yours.'

'I have had you already, and taken all you had to give me.'

'Not this.'

'Not what?' he growled.

'Acceptance,' she husked.

'I do not need your acceptance.'

'You have it.'

'I do not want it.'

'Reach out, Sebastian. I am giving it to you. Acceptance. Love. Unconditional love.'

'Love is never enough.'

'It will be enough for us. We will have love. We will have everything we have never had before.'

'I do not...' He swallowed, and she watched the heavy drag of his Adam's apple in his throat. 'I do not love you. I do not want your love. What do I have to do to make you understand?'

'I won't let you do this, Sebastian.' She trembled. 'I won't let you stand there and pretend you don't care. I won't let you pretend—'

'It was all a pretence,' he said. 'I do not care. I do not love you.'

'You do,' she countered breathlessly. 'You care. You love. You love me.'

'No.' He swept past her. 'It is done,' he concluded. 'We are over. It's finished.'

And her hands, her body, her heart yearned to reach out, grab him, hold him to her, until he understood she was right here with him.

She knew him.

She loved him.

But he was already walking away. Down the corridor. He was leaving her behind.

'*Sebastian*!' she called, but he didn't turn, didn't stop.

And she couldn't help it. She kicked off her pumps and gave chase.

She watched him walk through the pillared entrance to the castle and down the stone steps. And still she chased after him.

He kept going. Across the field of green. Through the artillery walls.

The pilot greeted him. Sebastian's mouth moved. She couldn't hear him. But she felt the words leave his mouth. A harsh husk of demands.

He swung open the helicopter door.

The same helicopter she'd arrived in with him.

And then he turned. Waited for her. His body was stone. His eyes dark. His jaw set.

She slowed. Breathless and panting, she tried to ground herself, to feel the short grass beneath her bare feet. But she felt nothing but a hole in her chest. And it was spreading. Hollowing her from the inside out.

She arrived in front of him, her breathing ragged and fast.

'The pilot will take you back to Arundel Manor.'

'Sebastian, please.'

'Get inside, Aurora.'

'I won't.'

'There is nothing here for you anymore,' he said. 'It was a mistake to bring you here. And now you will go back. Back to where you belong.' He didn't touch her, didn't kiss her. He simply walked away. Turned his back on her. On everything they could have.

'I belong with you,' she said to his back. 'And you belong with me.'

He halted. 'All that belongs to you,' he said, 'will be returned to you. But I will not be among your possessions. I am not something to have. I am not yours to belong to. I belong to nothing and no one.'

'And the baby?'

'Will be safer with you,' he rasped, and she heard it. The break in his voice. 'It will be happier with you.'

'There is no danger here. You are not a danger to the baby,' she said. Something broke inside her. Snapped. He was still punishing himself for a mistake he'd made when he'd been nothing but a child. 'You can't keep punishing yourself.'

He stiffened. 'My punishment is not for you to decide,' he said, and he kept walking.

'I'm not afraid of you.'

'You should be.'

'I'm not afraid to get in this helicopter,' she shouted. 'I'm not afraid to walk away.'

'Then get in,' he called back.

'You'll miss me,' she told his retreating back.

He didn't falter. 'I won't,' he said, his voice quieter now, drifting to her ears only by the grace of the wind.

'You'll come for me,' she said, but he was too far away to hear. Her voice was too weak. Unsure…

She couldn't reach him anymore.

He didn't want to be reached.

He didn't want to hear.

He didn't want to be loved.

The pilot guided her inside the helicopter, and she let him, let him buckle her in and close the door.

The helicopter's blades came to life. And up and up they went. Above the tree line. Above the castle.

She saw him. Walking up the stone steps.

She waited for him to look up. To see her.

But he didn't.

He closed the doors. Shut himself inside without her.

Her chest seized. Her lungs locked.

He'd rather be inside, locked in *with them*, than with her.

The helicopter turned. Flew away from the castle. Away from him.

A tear slipped free. She didn't brush it away. She let it slide down her cheek. Let it drip to her dress. And she acknowledged her sadness. Acknowledged his last arrow had sliced through her ribs and entered her heart.

And it was bleeding.

Her heart was shredded.

Broken.

Their time was up.

And whatever they'd had together was over.

CHAPTER THIRTEEN

Two Weeks Later...

AURORA FINGERED THE delicate yellow crib bedding tied around the antique oak bars. She pinched the soft casing that would cushion the baby from the hardwood. The tiny ducks, dancing with their open beaks sewn by hand into the bedding, taunted her with their happiness.

She turned away from it. But it was useless. In every corner of her peach bedroom, he was there. Inside the little vases. In the boxes she hadn't let them put into storage, full of the birds of prey dining set.

He'd been true to his word.

The trucks had arrived the next day.

He'd returned...*everything*. The smallest vase. The largest dining set. Her silk pumps she'd kicked off outside the great dining hall.

He'd sent it all back.

The last box had arrived today.

She looked down at her hand, at the twisted strings of silver forming the band around her middle finger.

The note had said it had been made for her, that it belonged to her, and he didn't want it.

Her heart ached. *Still*.

He didn't want her.

She splayed her fingers, flexed them. The weight felt foreign. Wrong. And she supposed it was. It was on the wrong hand. It didn't belong on that finger. It was too tight. But she couldn't bear to wear it on the right finger. The silver clawed feet holding the blue stone in the centre pinched, indented her flesh like a branding iron.

His brand.

She knew that ran deeper than the mark that would disappear when she took the ring off.

He'd changed her. Marked her as his from the first night they'd met.

And still she was his. She ached for him. In every way...

Her stomach twinged. She stroked it. But still it ached. Tightened.

'Not yet, little one,' she whispered. 'A few more days, please.'

The baby was ready, she knew. But still she held on. Still she gave him time he hadn't requested. Time she didn't have to give him.

But he wasn't coming.

Not today. Not tomorrow. Not ever.

'Ouch!' She doubled over, her hands clutched to her stomach. The Braxton Hicks contraction was tighter than usual. So tight it stole her breath.

It was only a practice contraction. It would pass. It *had* to pass. She wasn't ready. Not without him.

He *would* come. He had to.

They were not over.

They were having a baby.

They were in love.

He doesn't love you.

Pain tore through her pelvis. *'Ahh!'*

She gritted her teeth and breathed through it.

He loved her.

He loved the baby inside her.

So why isn't he here?

The pain eased. But a pressure built in her back. A weighted thing on her spine.

She sat down on the edge of the bed.

Every day, the conversation was the same. A battle of her heart and her mind. He didn't want her. He'd sent her away... And what had she done? She'd let him push her into a helicopter. She'd let him end them. Without a fight.

She closed her eyes.

She wanted *him* to fight. *For them.*

She wanted him to walk into her room, as he had all those weeks ago, and take her.

She opened her eyes, looked above the crib where she'd made them hang the painting of Sebastian. His eyes watching. When the baby was born, when their baby slept in a crib beneath it, it would remind her what was important.

Love.

Unconditional love.

A sharp pain shot up her spine.

'*Oh, oh!*' she panted. Hard and deep. The pressure was so intense in her back, her temples throbbed. Her gaze misted.

The painting wobbled.

Who had ever fought for him? For the boy longing for acceptance, for love. For support.

She wished she had a time machine. She wished she could break down the doors of the basement and save him before Amelia's birth, before he'd known such pain. And regret. And guilt.

Who had ever fought for the man?

No one.

He was still all alone in his castle, in the highest room, in the highest tower...

There they were again. Those tears she didn't want, hot on her flushed cheeks. And she knew she had a choice.

She could wail. She could scream. Or she could accept it. The end of them. She could move on. Raise her child on her own. She would live, she'd exist with or without Sebastian.

She couldn't make him make the right choice.

She couldn't make him love her.

She couldn't make him accept her love.

But *she* could fight. She could fight the demons he still battled for him. She could protect him with her love. She could love him. Harder than he had ever known love.

A moan slipped from her lips. And it wasn't the physical pain crushing her hips in a vice grip. It was the pain of realizing her stupidity.

She was stupid. Blind.

She didn't need to be rescued.

He did.

All her life, she'd accepted things. The way she was supposed to behave. The choices she'd had to agree to. And all her life, she'd been on the outside of her own life. Waiting. Waiting for her parents' love and acceptance. She'd smiled through her pain, nodded when she'd disagreed with the ugly choices she'd been made to accept because she'd been too afraid to fight for what she believed in.

But she believed in her and Sebastian.

In their love.

What was she waiting for? For permission to love him?

He'd never give it to her without a fight.

She'd been fighting for them, she realised, since the night they met. Fighting for all they could be together. In the gardens. In the castle. And all the little fights that had led to this. The final battle she would need to win.

What weapons did she have?

Only herself.

Only her love.

He was sleeping beauty.

And she would wake him.

She reached for her phone next to the bed.

She couldn't even call him—she didn't have his number.

But Esther would. Esther would help her.

She rang the number she'd rung so many times during the week of the gala.

And she waited.

'Aurora.'

'Can you get me a helicopter?'

'Why are you so breathless?' Esther asked.

Was she?

'I need to go to him…' Her head swam. 'Now.'

The line went silent, and Aurora's heart throbbed.

She could get herself a helicopter. She'd never used one for herself. She didn't have one in the garden. Esther could arrange it faster.

'Please,' Aurora sobbed. 'He's all alone. He shouldn't be alone.'

'No, he shouldn't,' Esther agreed. 'I can get one for you. Are you at home? At the manor?'

The tears were back, but her smile was new. And it felt good to smile. To know that soon she would be with him. Where she belonged.

'Yes.'

'Stay on the line,' Esther said. 'I'll tell you how long it will be.'

'Make it soon,' she said.

'As soon as I can,' she promised, and Aurora almost jumped for joy, but she was too tired, too swollen and pregnant to do so.

She needed to get ready. She put her hand on the side of the bed and pushed—

Aurora's blood ran cold.

'Esther…'

'I'm still here.'

She sat back down on the bed. Reached for the part of her light blue dress now stained a deep red.

She lifted her fingers to her face. 'I'm bleeding.'

'*Bleeding*?' Esther demanded. 'Where from?'

She couldn't breathe. Her head was fuzzy. A deep fog was falling over her, making everything heavy. Everything weak.

'The baby,' she breathed, and it trembled from her lips. 'The baby, Esther...'

And then she could speak no more words.

The phone fell.

And so too did Aurora.

Sebastian was cold.

He knew he'd never be warm again.

He deserved to be cold. To sit here in the abandoned great dining hall, all alone, and freeze.

He probably would.

He turned up the collar on his brown winter fur. The same one he'd laid Aurora's head upon as he'd kissed her. Found pleasure in her, made love to her.

He closed his eyes. Shut out the empty tables. The empty room.

He'd sent them all away. And they had gone. Esther had taken all his art. All of it had sold the minute he'd left the stage with Aurora.

She'd taken his sculpture, too. It was placed inside the entrance to the building Esther had acquired for him for the headquarters of the charity he was now the face of. And *her* face would be the symbol for it. A symbol of hope for all those who needed it.

Amelia's Wish would be a success. A charity he should have set up the moment he'd been able to. He realised that now.

He realized it because of *her*.

Aurora.

It didn't matter how tightly he squeezed his eyes shut. She was always there. Burnt onto his retinas since the first time he'd turned his head and laid his gaze upon her.

She did not bring him hope.

She was his torment. His endless torture. His punishment.

And this was hell.

His heart hurt. It had not stopped hurting since she'd left. Since he'd forced her to go.

And he endured the hurt, because it was his to endure.

He'd spared her from sharing his fate. He'd saved her, and their child, from living this life with him. They did not deserve to share in his life sentence in this desolate place where nothing lived but pain.

It was the one good thing he'd ever done.

He had not done what he'd wanted to. He had had not crushed her with his love. Suffocated her with his greed to have her, hold her, always.

He had set her free.

And he could barely breathe. The air was too thin without her. His lungs strained for just a single breath of her. His skin ached for her softness. *Her closeness.*

He'd never be close to her again. He'd never touch her. He'd never again breathe in her scent.

The reckoning was over.

Her job was done.

She had made him acknowledge all of his misdeeds. Brought them back into his present, and he had faced them. And now he would pay for what he'd done.

She had woken him from a deep, dark slumber of self-pity.

But now he was always awake. Would always be aware of what he'd done.

What he had almost done to her too. Locked her away,

like he'd locked himself away. Kept her in the dark with him. But she deserved the light. So much of it.

He deserved the dark. He did not know how to live amongst other people with her.

His back pocket pulsed, vibrated furiously.

Again and again.

Sebastian pulled his phone free of his pocket.

'Esther,' he said, holding the phone to his ear.

'Don't panic,' she said.

'Why would I panic?' he replied. 'I do not panic.'

'She's okay,' she said, ignoring him. 'Or she will be. She was bleeding heavily. She's at the hospital. I'm on my way now.'

His blood roared. 'Where is she?'

'Cirencester. Private Hospital.'

He stood, his body moving on instinct to get to her. To be with her.

'I am on my way,' he said, and his voice was tight, weak.

He had been too weak, hadn't he?

Too afraid to fight for her.

For *her* love.

And now…

His throat squeezed. Threatening to crush his airways.

He burst through the entrance doors. They banged open. And he left them that way. Wide open as ran down the stone steps.

'The helicopter should be landing now,' Esther said. 'Can you see it?'

He could.

He could see it all.

His fear. Her strength. Their love. Rare and divine. She was everything he'd ever wanted.

And now he could lose it all.

He could lose her.

CHAPTER FOURTEEN

SEBASTIAN BURST THROUGH the hospital doors in his long brown fur coat and big black boots.

He steeled his spine, broadened his shoulders, and readied himself for the smoke. For the flames. For the chaos. His heart gushed. He could not ready himself for that. For loss.

He could not lose Aurora.

His breath snagged in his lungs. All was still. All was quiet. People sat on cream sofas, and they smiled and talked in gentle whispers. Others walked through the flowerpotted corridor as if nothing was happening. As if his Aurora was not bleeding. As if his love, his only love, was not dying. Without him.

'Aurora!' It was bellow, a scream, louder, rawer than the one he had screamed to the skies, to the gods, the morning Amelia had died.

Aurora would not die.

He would not allow it.

He would forsake the gods.

He would make them bring her back.

All eyes turned to him. Mouths dropped. A man in black walked towards him. His shoulders squared.

A guard wouldn't stop him.

'Where is she?' Sebastian demanded.

'He's with me.' Esther suddenly appeared behind the man. Her perfect black bob cut slashed across her determined brown-skinned jaw. She walked toward him. Looked up into his face, which was still staring down the man who barred his way to Aurora. But she was here. In one of these rooms. And he would find her.

She gripped his elbow. 'He's with me,' she said again, and he could not examine it. He could not think clearly. He could only think of Aurora. She needed him. And he was too late. But it meant something. Esther holding his elbow, claiming him as hers. Protecting him from confrontation.

'He's the father,' she continued. 'Aurora Arundel,' she explained. 'She's in recovery.'

The rage that filled his vision, aimed at this stranger, this man who meant him no harm, whose job it was to protect those in the hospital, dissipated.

Sebastian's shoulders sagged. He dropped his gaze to Esther's wide brown eyes. Bruises sat beneath her usually immaculately made-up eyes. Tightness bracketed her colourless mouth.

'Recovery?' he asked, and it was a prayer on his lips. 'She's…she's alive?'

She nodded. 'She's alive.'

Alive… She wasn't dead. She was not lost to him.

'Take me to her.'

Esther shook her head. 'She needs a little time.'

There was no time. He was already late. She was hurting. He'd sent her away to protect her, but he hadn't, he couldn't…

He could not breathe.

He'd failed her.

'Take me to her,' he demanded. *'Now.'*

He needed to see her. To know she was alive. To hold her. Breathe her in and fall to his knees, and beg for her forgiveness.

He had been wrong. So very wrong to send her away.

He would follow her everywhere she went now.

He would follow her into the light and let the sun flay the skin from his flesh, if that is what it took to be with her.

Esther's fingers tightened on his elbow. 'There's someone you should meet first.'

'Who?' he growled.

A tear slipped from the corner of her eye.

'Your son.'

'My son?' he repeated, and he couldn't fight it.

Amelia, clear as the day she was born, formed in his mind. Her tiny fingers. Her innocent eyes. He'd loved her instantly. And he couldn't ignore it. The fear in his gut. What if he couldn't give his baby the same?

What if he could not love his son?

'This way,' Esther said, and she led him down the corridor.

'He's in here,' she said, stopping.

She held the door open for him. The bed was empty, but beside it sat a crib on wheels. A hand, so small, fingers so tiny, peeped out at him over the rim.

He rushed to the crib and peered inside…

His heart burst.

He was perfection. He was… He had Aurora's black hair, thick and too long for a newborn. He had a little button nose, plum lips. But his eyes, they were just like Sebastian's.

And he vowed right there and then, his little eyes would never see the horrors his father had.

He dipped his hands inside, and he picked up his son. Claimed him. He brought him to his chest. Cradled him, kept him warm beneath the brown furs he wore.

It was instant.

The love.

The unconditional love.

Sebastian turned to Esther. Tears filled his eyes. 'I have a son.'

'You do.' She smiled, flaunted all of her perfectly square teeth as her eyes cried. 'Congratulations, Sebastian. You're a father.'

Sebastian closed his eyes.

And he wept.

All the tears he hadn't before been able to. For the boy he had been. For Amelia. For his son. For Aurora. And he cried, too, for love.

The love in his heart. The love all around him, in the touch of his son, in Esther's eyes. And they offered him nothing but warmth. Acceptance.

He knew he would never be cold again.

He was loved.

He loved them all, he realised.

Had she lifted the curse?

Had Aurora set him free?

Aurora opened her eyes. Soft amber lights lit the space. A room as big as any hotel room. A blue vertical tunnel sat in the room's corner.

She watched the bubbles rise in the softly swirling water. Let her eyes adjust to being here. To still being alive. To surviving. She breathed in deeply. Felt her lungs rise and fall. Her fingers gripped something too soft, too familiar. A brown blanket of the softest fur covered her body.

She was alive. But…

Her chest thumping, she turned her head to the side of the bed, to where the crib should be. Where her baby should be.

And her heart, it swelled.

There was her son. On his father's chest. His black-capped head cradled in a big, wide hand. A hand holding him so carefully, so gently, against his heart.

The heart he wouldn't let her have.

Sebastian's head lay back against the green leather of the

high-backed armchair, his hair cushioning his cheek, and it fell to his shoulder.

They both slept so peacefully together.

His eyes opened. His green-rimmed irises made the inner amber of his eyes glow.

'Forgive me,' he growled.

'You're here,' she said, her heart aching for him. He had punished himself enough. 'You found us. There is nothing to forgive.'

His gaze sharpened. 'There is *everything* to forgive.'

He went to stand.

'Don't,' she said. 'You'll wake him,'

'I won't.' He stood, moved to her bedside, and he did not wake the baby as he placed him in Aurora's arms. 'He should be in your arms. Where he is safe.'

And her heart, it could not take it. How could she make him understand he wasn't a danger? To either of them?

'He's so small,' she said. 'So precious.' And she held him close. Her son. The baby she had carried inside her for all those months. The baby that had brought Sebastian back to her. The baby that would make them a family. She pressed her lips to his head. Kissed him with all the love she had saved for him. Only the baby. But she had more love to give. More love to share with Sebastian. Her true love.

She raised her eyes to his. 'But he *is* safe with you,' she told him. 'We both are.'

He nodded. 'I know.'

'You do?'

'I know many things,' he replied. 'Because of you.'

'What else do you know?' she asked.

He sat down on the edge of the bed. And Aurora wanted to yell at him, to scream at him to choose everything. Now. With her. But she didn't scream. She didn't yell. She waited for him. Gave him time to tell her.

Because she would wait for him to be ready.

She'd wait for him for what felt like forever.

'I lied,' he said, and held her gaze. 'Amelia didn't wish for you. *I did.* Twenty-five years ago, I asked the gods, *I begged them*, for you, and they delivered my wish. They delivered you for me.'

Her heart broke for him. For all those years he'd spent alone. Waiting for…her.

'I'm sorry I was late.'

'I wasn't ready.' He shook his head. 'But I am ready now. I'm ready to change. For you. For our son.'

'I don't want you to change.'

'But I will,' he said. 'I will open the doors. I will let love in, and I will not suffocate it. I will not kill it. I will cherish it.'

'I need more than softness, Sebastian,' she said. 'I need your love.' She swallowed. 'I want your heart.'

'And it is yours. It was always yours,' he confessed. 'I knew it from the moment I saw you. I know that now. I understand I was too afraid to call it love. To name it. Claim it. I was scared that if I loved you as I loved Amelia, I would have to forever lock you inside a room to protect you. I would suffocate you with my love. So I sent you away. Both of you.' His nostrils flared. 'But I love you, Aurora. More than the air in my lungs. I am sorry I sent you away. I am sorry I pushed you away so many times when you only wanted to hold me. Let me hold you now, Aurora,' he begged. 'Let me love you.'

Her heart bloomed as she held the baby against her breast with one hand, and she held the other open for him to join them.

'Come to me,' she said, and his eyes glistened as he did just that. Leaned into her. Moved his mouth until it sat a hair's breadth away from hers. He breathed, 'I will always love you, Aurora. You were made for me to love. And I will love you with everything I am for the rest of my life.'

Gently he feathered his lips against hers. 'If you still want me to?' he asked roughly. His voice raw. 'If you can still love me?'

'I'll always love you, Sebastian.' She reached up to his face, and the air stilled. As did her heart. 'You were made for me to love. I was made for you to love.'

'Aurora…'

She didn't know who moved first. And she held his face, cradled it, as he gave to her all that was inside him.

His love.

His heart.

'I love you,' he breathed into her mouth.

And she understood time had reset.

Theirs was just beginning.

EPILOGUE

Six Months Later...

BLACK PILLAR LAMPPOSTS of knotted metal with glass tops lit the space. Dew clung to the leaves. Newly emerging buds lifted upwards to meet the sun. And the fireflies danced on the walls.

He'd replicated it perfectly. And yet it was different. They would not meet in the dark. He had all the lights on. There was no key in the gold lock. The black iron gates, bracketed by headed stone pillars, were wide open.

He was not hiding in the shadows of the colonnade.

He stood on the stone path, and he waited for her.

He would see her. She would see him. And they would meet here, in the gardens, where it had all begun.

Sebastian let his gaze wander over the walled garden of wild flowers. They had been trimmed and harnessed to allow for the small gathering of white chairs tied with silver bows. For the arch of wild flowers they'd meet beneath. But it was still wild. And he recognised it now, saw it. Its beauty. Because in all things wild, there was a stillness. A harmony.

Aurora was his stillness. She was his harmony. He was calm. He wore no other skin than his own. And he did not feel wild or tamed. He felt...*whole*. Seen.

His throat tightened.

His eyes fell on Esther and her wife. Their only guests.

Together, they held his son for him. Protected him with their love for him, their love for each other, and their love for... *Sebastian*. And he accepted it. Esther's loyalty. Her love. And he gave it back tenfold. She was...*they* were... his family.

He was loved, and he loved. Deeply. He accepted that now. Accepted what he hadn't been able to accept for twenty-five years—that he was not cursed to kill with his love. He was not blinded by feelings. His feelings made him stronger. His love was the precursor to everything he'd never had, but all he would have now with Aurora. A family.

All the air left his lungs in a hiss.

Through the iron gates, she came to him.

And Sebastian watched her. Pearls dotted her black hair, which was tied in a loose knot at the side of her head. A few silken locks fell forward to kiss her cheeks. Strands of smaller pearls hung from her ears. The white fur cape hanging from her shoulders moved in time with her white satin shoes. Her dress, sculpted to her body, was made of the iridescent pearls of the sea.

His siren had returned, and he would go with her willingly.

Because wherever she was, he was home.

She was his home.

She was his family.

Aurora *was* love.

His love.

He was born to love her. Made only for her. All he had been through, all he had endured, was to prepare him for how hard he could love.

And it was so very intensely. So very hard that he loved her.

She was his. She belonged to him, and he belonged to her.

And there on the broken stone path where they had met, they shared their vows and joined their hands in matrimony.
In love.
Unconditional love.
Forever.

* * * * *

Did you fall head over heels for
Kidnapped for Her Secret?
Then don't miss these other dazzlingly dramatic stories by Lela May Wight!

His Desert Bride by Demand
Bound by a Sicilian Secret
The King She Shouldn't Crave
Italian Wife Wanted

Available now!

BILLION-DOLLAR DATING DECEPTION

CLARE CONNELLY

MILLS & BOON

To Kel, a bestie I would do anything for.
The Lottie to my Jane, and my forever SLSM.

PROLOGUE

Zeus Papandreo had always loved the way the moonlight hit the dark timber floors of his father's study. As a young boy, he'd stood in this very same spot, looking out on the distant ocean, imagining that instead of being confined to an office, he was on a boat, at sea, free and wild, king of the ocean—king of everything.

Power had throbbed through him, even then.

Power, strength, determination.

In contrast, on this night he felt impotent. Robbed not only of his sense of power, but also of breath.

'She's twenty-three.'

Zeus closed his eyes against that, wishing his father had chosen another way to deliver this news. In writing? Over the phone? Anything that would have given him a little longer to absorb the body-blow-like information before responding.

'Her name is Charlotte.'

He wanted to punch something. To shake something, or someone. His father. He whirled around, obsidian eyes sparkling with ruthless distaste as he quickly did the requisite calculations.

'You are telling me you cheated on my mother, while she was in chemotherapy?'

Aristotle Papandreo paled perceptibly. 'It was not... Yes. I cheated.' The confession seemed to sap the older man of strength completely. He dropped his head forward, chin connecting to his chest.

A muscle jerked in Zeus's jaw. Three months ago his mother had died, after a decades-long struggle with cancer. A fight she'd taken head-on, waged countless battles against, determined to eke out as much of her life as she could, even when that life caused her so much pain in the end. Her courage and strength had been monumental, and Zeus couldn't help but draw his own strength from her.

Zeus swore loudly, the word satisfyingly crisp in the darkness of the office.

Aristotle flinched.

'And the *woman*,' he infused the word with disgust, 'that you slept with conceived a child.'

'Your sister.'

'Don't!' Zeus cursed once more. 'Don't call her that.'

'She is your sister, Zeus. She should know that.'

A muscle throbbed in Zeus's jaw as he clenched his teeth together. He strode to his father's liquor cabinet and poured a generous measure of Scotch.

'I couldn't tell you this while your mother—'

'She never knew?'

'Of course not.' Now it was Aristotle's turn to mutter something dark. 'I could never have put her through that.'

Zeus's eyes glittered. 'But sleeping with anything in a skirt was fine?'

'There was only one,' Aristotle corrected, holding up his finger.

'Oh, well, in that case, it's totally fine.'

'You do not know what it was like back then, Zeus.'

'Don't I?' He threw back a handy swig of Scotch, continuing to stare down his father. 'I was nine, but I remember.'

Aristotle glanced down at his hands. 'Mariah—Charlotte's mother… It wasn't planned.'

'I do not want to hear about it.'

'She is your sister,' Aristotle said again, more firmly. 'And it's time for her to become a part of this family.'

Zeus held the Scotch glass so firmly he was surprised it didn't shatter. 'Not my family.'

'I am meeting with my lawyers next week to go over things. I want to ensure she has what is owed to her.'

Zeus straightened.

'You're talking about leaving money to her?' Money, he didn't care about. Money, they had more than enough of.

'She is a Papandreo,' Aristotle insisted. 'This is her birthright, too.' Aristotle waved around the room, but they both knew he wasn't talking about the mansion in which they stood, but rather, the company that had been in their family for generations.

'You've got to be kidding me.' Zeus expelled a slow, angry breath. 'This is *my* birthright. Not hers. Mine.'

'She is your—'

'Don't. Just because you couldn't keep it in your pants twenty-three years ago, does not mean you can foist her on me now.'

'Oh, and you're one to talk?' Aristotle demanded sharply, for Zeus's dating history was littered with a string of short-term affairs. The older man expelled a rough sigh, dragged a hand through his hair, as if to reset himself. 'Have you forgotten the terms of company ownership, Zeus?'

Zeus squared his shoulders, meeting his father's gaze without hesitation. The antiquated term of company ownership was something he had never given much thought to, for the simple reason there'd never been anyone else in contention to inherit it. At sixty-five, his father was still young, and fit, and though Zeus had taken over the role of CEO some five years earlier, his father remained active in the company.

So the fact that some ancient Papandreo forebear, hundreds of years earlier, had had it written into the legal documentation of the company that the sole owner of Papandreo Group, as it was now known, had to be married had been neither here nor there to Zeus. For one thing, he had many years to find someone he could be bothered marrying. For another, there was no one else with a legal claim on the business who might challenge his inheritance.

At least, there hadn't been.

'That is an ancient, stupid term,' he muttered. 'No way would it stand up in court today.'

'I have tried to change it,' Aristotle said. 'It cannot be done.'

'I don't believe you.'

'Then do your best. Change it. Either way, Charlotte is my daughter, and I owe it to her to explain all of this.'

'You are saying that if she were to marry before me, you would be happy for her to inherit this? To run it, rather than me?'

'My preference would be for you to work together,' Aristotle contradicted.

'Impossible,' Zeus spat. 'She is nothing to me.' He slashed his hand angrily through the air. 'Nothing but proof of your infidelity.'

'You are angry—'

'No kidding.'

'I understand. I'm angry, too. I have been angry with myself for a long time, for that weakness of character. I did everything I could to hide Charlotte away, to spare your mother the pain of knowing what I'd done. But she's gone now, Zeus, and Charlotte deserves to come home.'

A muscle jerked low in his jaw.

'As for the company…' Aristotle looked at his son with something like sadness. 'If you are determined to be the one to inherit it, then you know what you must do.'

Zeus was very still as the reality of that splintered through him, shocking him to the core with a visceral sense of rejection.

'Marry someone?'

'Before she does,' Aristotle confirmed.

'She's twenty-three.'

'Yes, true. But who knows what she'll think when presented with the chance of stepping into a multibillion-dollar business…'

Zeus felt as though the wind had been knocked from his sails. Wasn't it highly likely that she'd jump through whatever damned hoops were necessary to secure the company? Who wouldn't? It was like winning the lottery a million times over. He closed his eyes on a wave of disgust.

'You should have told me this sooner.'

'I couldn't. Not until—'

'My mother died,' Zeus said, crossing his arms over his

chest, refusing to feel sympathy for his father. A man he had, until ten minutes ago, loved with every fibre of his being. A man Zeus would have said and done anything for, even laid down his own life. 'You disgust me,' he said, shaking his head, and with that, he stormed from the room, slamming the door behind him for good measure.

But he could not so easily box away the tangle of thoughts his father's pronouncement had given him, nor the sense of vulnerability that was tugging at his previously unassailable world view.

He was Zeus Papandreo, born to step into his father's shoes. His father, who had been almost godlike to Zeus until this night, when he learned he was mortal, after all.

He'd cheated.

Had another child with the woman he'd bedded.

You're one to talk.

After all, it wasn't as though Zeus lived like a monk. Far from it. If he'd bothered keeping the phone numbers of all the women he'd slept with, his phone would have run out of memory long ago. Which made the whole idea of marriage even less palatable. It was absurd.

Even when it was absolutely, utterly necessary. And suddenly, it wasn't just about stepping into his birthright; it was about keeping it from his father's love child; it was about hurting his father. It was about being king of the world, king of this empire and calling the shots.

He was Zeus Papandreo and in this, he would be unstoppable.

'Lottie, you can't do it,' Jane groaned, shaking her head from side to side so her long blond hair fluffed around her pretty, heart-shaped face. 'You can't marry someone you don't know.'

'Why not?' Lottie whirled around, hands on slender hips. 'Do you have any idea what that company's worth?'

'I know it's worth a *lot*,' Jane admitted. 'But so what? You have money.'

'I have some money,' Lottie muttered. 'But not *that* kind of money.'

Jane looked at her childhood best friend with a sinking feeling, because the expression on Lottie's face was nothing short of determined. And she knew from experience that when Lottie looked like that, there was simply no talking her down. Only, something about this wasn't adding up.

'What's going on? You've *never* wanted anything from him. You live *here*, in my tiny second bedroom, borrow my clothes, freeload off my streaming services, rather than digging into that ample trust fund and buying your own place or paying for any of that stuff yourself.'

Lottie's green eyes glittered with something more familiar to Jane, a look of impishness that reminded her of the time they'd crept out of their dormitories and into the kitchen of their prestigious boarding school, to steal all the ice cream for their dorm. They'd been fourteen years old, and it had earned them the adoration of every girl in that wing for the rest of their school careers.

'Maybe it's not about the money,' Lottie said with a lift of her shoulders and a crease of her brow.

'So, what is it, then?'

Lottie pursed her wide red lips, before reaching for her coffee and taking a sip. Though she'd been raised by her English mother, and was the quintessential English rose with her pale skin, wide-set green eyes and chestnut-red hair, there was no escaping the fact that certain traits in Lottie were pure Greek. Like her predilection for strong, tar-like coffee at all hours of the day.

'All my life, they've ignored me,' she said, the words blanked of emotion, but Jane heard it, regardless. Or perhaps it was echoes of the past. Of the way she knew that rejection had shaped Lottie, had wounded her. It was something they shared. Though Jane had two parents who acknowledged her in their lives, they had barely any time to give her, other than a few perfunctory holidays each year. They had paid for a nanny to watch her graduate high school and send them photographs. Though outwardly, both Charlotte and Jane had always projected an image of untouchable contentment to the world, to one another, they were honest. Each knew the truth. Rejection was awful, and they'd both suffered through more than enough of it.

'I know,' Jane murmured, sympathetically.

'And now he's telling me I can have the family business, if I want it. That I'm just as entitled to it as Zeus.' She layered the word with contempt, and Jane could well understand it. Where Lottie had been forced to live her life in hiding, never telling anyone who her father was—courtesy of the nondisclosure agreement Aristotle Papandreo had forced Lottie's mother to sign, in exchange for a huge payoff—Zeus had been in the spotlight as the much-adored sole son and heir to the Papandreo fortune.

'I never wanted it,' she said with a twist of her lips and a flash of those sea-green eyes. 'I would have said I hated the thought of it, until I realised I could reach out and take it, after all.'

'But why do you want it?' Jane pushed.

'Think of what we could do with that thing,' Lottie murmured, crossing the room and crouching in front of her oldest, closest friend. Lottie's hands closed over Jane's, who sighed softly. 'Think of the *good* we could do with it.'

Jane gnawed on her lower lip, as thousands of late-night conversations flooded her brain. All the ideas they'd had over the years, for ways to help the less advantaged. Neither had ever really felt as though they belonged in the elite school community they'd attended. They were different to the other girls, and their strong sense of social conscience had driven both to pursue careers in the charity and not-for-profit sector, upon leaving school.

'With you and me at the helm of the Papandreo Group, we could turn it on its head. Instead of seeking a gross amount of profits, we could make it our mission to divest. *Everything.*'

Jane gasped. 'You're talking about destroying it.'

'Yes.' Lottie's face tightened with renewed determination. 'It's obscene for anyone to have that kind of money.'

Jane didn't disagree.

'But not just to be spiteful,' Lottie promised. 'Don't get me wrong. I would enjoy every damned minute of pulling apart that business and selling it off and seeing the expressions on their faces as I did so,' she said, cheeks flushed now at the very idea. 'Mostly, though, it's about the good we could do. This is everything we've always said we wanted, Jane. Everything.'

And it was. A thousand of their plans suddenly seemed viable and within reach. Jane's breath came a little faster.

'Okay.' She squeezed Lottie's hand. Because, when

it came down to it, there was nothing she wouldn't do for her very best friend in the whole world. They'd been through too much together, knew too much about one another's lives, pains, weaknesses, to ever walk away in a moment of need. 'How can I help?'

'I'm glad you asked, because actually, I *do* need your help…'

CHAPTER ONE

JANE'S LEGS WERE wobbling a week later, as she strode into the sleekly glamorous bar in the expensive business district of central Athens. Not from nerves, but from the experience of wearing sky-high heels for the first time in years. In fact, the whole outfit was well and truly outside of Jane's comfort zone. She'd borrowed the whole ensemble from Lottie—who was far more at home in the latest fashions and had an eye for snatching things up from thrift shops, to meet her self-imposed budgetary restraints. At first, she'd thought she would be overdressed in the silky gold camisole top tucked into a white miniskirt, with strappy leather stilettos and a chunky golden necklace, but two steps into the bar and she saw that Lottie had chosen the perfect outfit.

This was not like their local Clapham pub, that was for sure. This place screamed highbrow, from the leather banquettes to the classy art on the walls and the subdued lighting.

She fought an urge to bite onto her lip, the gesture one of uncertainty that didn't belong with this persona. Tonight she was Jane Fisher, confident daughter of one of the world's most renowned human rights lawyers, graduate of an elite British public school and university, ready to take on the world.

Or rather, Zeus Papandreo.

'I just need you to flirt with him a bit,' Lottie had explained. 'Make him, you know, fall in love with you.'

Jane had immediately balked. 'I can't just make him fall in love with me!'

Lottie snorted then. 'Tell me the last time you looked at a guy twice who didn't immediately want you to have his babies?'

Jane's cheeks had flushed at her friend's description. For Jane, who hated attention, she'd cursed the fact, many times over, that she'd inherited her socialite mother's looks. Especially after Steven. 'You know I don't do serious.'

'I know that, but he doesn't. And he'll be just as fallible to your charms as everyone else, I promise.'

'How long do I need to do this for?'

'Until I'm married,' Lottie promised. 'And believe me, I plan to work fast.'

Jane's jaw had dropped. 'You're serious?'

'Don't worry. I'll find someone suitable.'

'Suitable? In weeks?'

'How hard can it be? You get proposed to all the time,' Lottie teased, then winced, because Jane had been proposed to twice, and both times had been disastrous—for Jane, who hated hurting anybody. 'Sorry.'

She shook her head. 'So, I just have to...'

'Well, the way I see it, he's going to be looking to get married, too,' Lottie explained. 'So, you just need to make him think you're swallowing his act. He'll probably be

super charming, move quickly, so it won't be hard. Just get him to think you're buying it, that you're keen to get married, but keep coming up with reasons to put it off—wanting your parents to meet him, that kind of thing. Basically, stall. Stall, stall, stall.'

And Jane had nodded, because how hard would that be? She just had to stop him from trying to hook up with anyone else and get them to marry him. Surely, she could do that?

'You'll have him eating out of the palm of your hand within hours—right where I need him. And I'll owe you forever. I am sorry to ask this of you, Jane. I know... I know it will be hard for you. But you're the only person I can trust. The only person who loves me enough to help me.'

Surreptitiously, Jane scanned the bar, looking for a glimpse of the man she now knew like the back of her hand, courtesy of Lottie and her wine-fuelled internet searching. They knew this bar was around the corner from his office, and that he'd been photographed leaving here with many beautiful women over the past few years, since he'd taken over as CEO of the Papandreo Group.

Unseating him from that role was the first thing on Lottie's list, and Jane couldn't say she blamed her friend. For the more she'd read about Zeus Papandreo, the less she liked him. While she was motivated primarily by helping her friend, she also couldn't resist the idea of taking him down a peg or two, for the sake of womankind. Men like him, who went through women as though they were worthless and good for one thing only, definitely deserved to have the tables turned from time to time. Out of nowhere, she thought of Steven—damn it, the last man she wanted to think of here and now—and her heart gave a familiar twist of pain, as sharp as it had been back then, as a seventeen-year-old, when he'd shattered it—and her—into a million pieces.

There was that old adage about time healing all wounds, but that was certainly not the case for Jane.

That particular emotional bruise was as tender now as it had been six years earlier. So, too, the pain her parents had inflicted over the years.

In her experience, some hurts just couldn't be eased. It was better to accept that than try to fight it.

A low whistle caught her attention, and she glanced towards the bar, where two suited men were looking at her as though they'd just fronted up to a buffet and she was the main attraction. 'Can we buy you a drink?'

'No, thank you.' She glanced beyond them. No sign of Zeus, so far. She strode beyond the men, not looking at them again, and found an empty spot down the other end. She ordered a mineral water—all the better to keep her wits about her. She opened up one of the news apps on her phone and began to read a long article on an overseas war, her gut rolling as the atrocities were described, and she felt that same yearning she'd known all her life to help.

'You're just like your father,' her mother had cooed once, and Jane had shied away from the comparison, even when it had, on some level, pleased her. Because her father had definitely wanted to help the world. He had taken cases all over, fighting for the underprivileged, doing everything he could to make their lives better. But his calling for justice was so strong that he'd forgotten all about the daughter he was leaving to be raised in utter luxury—by nannies, household staff and boarding-school mothers.

It wasn't much later when something made the hairs on the back of Jane's neck stand on end. Though the crowd in the bar didn't actually stop talking, she felt an eerie sense of silence descend, or her ears grew woolly, and she glanced up towards the door and saw the moment Zeus Papandreo strode in, every bit as world-owning as she had expected. Only, in that moment of crossing the threshold, before entering the bar, she saw something else, too. Something she was perhaps projecting onto him.

A look of burden.

A sense that he was carrying more than his fair share of worries.

A sense of brokenness.

It was gone in an instant, so thoroughly replaced by a look of arrogant command, that she thought she must have imagined it. He strode to the bar, easily clearing the way despite how crowded it was, gesturing towards the top of the shelves at a bottle of Scotch.

The barman, dressed in a white button-up shirt and vest turned, retrieved the bottle and poured a measure, sliding it across to Zeus with a polite nod.

Zeus took it, rested one elbow on the bar top and began to survey the room, just as Jane had done when she'd entered. She watched as he took notice of a group of women in the corner dressed in corporate clothes, so she presumed they'd come straight from the office. She saw the way his eyes lingered there a moment, one corner of his mouth lifting appreciatively, and her heart skipped a beat.

Showtime.

She straightened a little, pulling her silky blond hair over one shoulder, and positioning herself so the generous curve of her breasts against the silk of her camisole would be easily noticeable. Sure enough, the two men who'd offered to buy her a drink earlier glanced her way and she felt heat infuse her cheeks. For all she was willing to play the part of the vixen for Lottie, it was not a role Jane was particularly comfortable with.

She ran a finger down the side of her mineral water, making a show of tracing the condensation, then lifting her moist finger towards her mouth at the exact moment Zeus's glance shifted over her. And back again. Their eyes met, but she didn't slow her finger's progress, even when the charge of realisation was akin to an electric shock.

His eyes.

His eyes were so...intense.

Dark and brooding, and beautifully shaped, with the kind of lashes she thought only existed in romance novels and movies, thick and dark and curling, giving the impression that he wore eyeliner.

They bore into her as though with just one look he could see the finer points of her soul.

She pressed her fingertip to her lips, let it hover there a moment before dropping it to the bar and offering a slightly dismissive smile. Coming on too strong with a man like Zeus wouldn't work, she guessed. He was someone who liked to be in charge, who liked to do the chasing, and she somehow just knew that he would have been prey to enough money-hungry gold diggers in his time to spot one a mile off.

Play it cool, Lottie had advised, echoing Jane's own

judgement. *Let him think he has to work for you. It will kill him. And he's so damned stubborn, he won't give up until he thinks he's got you right where he wants you.*

Jane sipped her mineral water, manicured nails curved around the cut-crystal glass, as the nearest bartender uncorked a bottle of expensive champagne and placed it in a cooler with two glasses. Jane returned her attention to her phone, but it didn't last long. A moment later, the champagne ice bucket was placed directly in front of her. 'Compliments of the gentleman over there,' the barman said, nodding towards Zeus.

Her pulse flickered to life as she made a point of slowly, oh, so slowly, scanning the guests assembled at the bar before letting her gaze land on his face. One of his brows quirked upwards in a silent, flirtatious question. She responded in kind, offering a wry half smile and a 'please explain' expression.

No need to ask twice.

He strolled through the busy bar easily, but the bar itself was busy enough that in order to be next to her, he had to slide in close. So close she could feel his warmth and smell his tangy aftershave. So close she could see those magnificent eyes up close and marvel at the obsidian darkness of them. For a moment, she felt a rush of guilt for the deception she was about to try to perpetrate. But only a moment. Because wasn't he doing exactly the same thing?

Lottie had explained the arcane inheritance clause very carefully. It wasn't just Lottie who needed to get married in order to legally inherit the Papandreo Group, but Zeus as well. Meaning he was out here, no doubt looking for some poor woman he could con into agreeing to marry him, never mind how that might end up breaking her heart. If anything, Jane was doing her sisters a solid by foiling those plans. Because it would be much more devastating for a woman to be used by Zeus Papandreo than it could ever be for a man to be disappointed by Jane.

'I haven't seen you here before,' he said, voice lightly accented, deep and husky. The hairs on her arms stood on end and she bit back a shiver, as he reached across her and took the champagne from the cooler, along with one of the glasses. 'May I?'

Her pulse was strangely throbbing—courtesy of the plan, she assured herself. It didn't matter *why* she felt all lightheaded, though. She could make him believe the reason was his proximity, his masculine strength, his obvious attractiveness.

'Thank you,' she agreed, nodding once.

'So,' he asked, pouring the glass, 'who are you?'

'Isn't that a little direct?' she asked, a half smile on her lips as he finished pouring the champagne and held it towards her. She stared at the glass for a moment, working out how she could take it without touching his hands, but they were *big* hands, and they gripped almost the entire fragile glass.

In the end, she stopped hesitating and reached out, ignoring the frisson of shock that ran through her veins when her flesh connected with his. Her eyes, though, lifted, and her mouth went dry. His smile was knowing and arrogant. The perfect antidote to her natural, genuine reactions.

He thought he'd already won her over. He was used to this—walking into the bar, being all suave and gorgeous and getting whatever the hell he wanted from whomever he met. Well, he was about to meet his match.

'I happen to like direct,' he said, lifting one shoulder. 'Don't you—?' He let the sentence hang, midconstruction, in the air between them, and when she didn't fill the gap, he asked, 'What is your name?'

She pulled her lips to the side, thinking how commanding he was, how he seemed to think he could walk up to anyone and begin interrogating them.

'You tell me yours and I'll tell you mine,' she said, enjoying the way his features briefly reflected surprise.

'You don't know who I am?'

'Should I?' She batted her lashes then sipped the champagne, enjoying the rush of ice-cold bubbles as they filled her mouth and then flooded her body.

He frowned. 'I suppose not.'

'Are you famous?' she pushed, enjoying teasing him.

'No.'

'Then why would I know who you are? Or have we perhaps met?'

His laugh then was a gruff sound of genuine amusement. 'I think we'd both remember.'

'You're certainly not lacking in confidence, are you—?' She used his intonation, inflecting a slight question at the end of her words.

'Zeus,' he responded, almost brushing aside his name. 'And I think you'll find I'm not lacking in lots of things.'

Her own laugh was—to her chagrin and surprise—also genuine. 'Does this usually work for you?' she purred, taking another sip of champagne before placing the glass down and putting her elbow on the bar, propping her chin in her palm so she could lean a little closer to him.

He scanned her face. 'Are you saying you're not interested?'

Careful, Jane.

She wanted to push him, without pushing him away. 'Hmm,' she murmured, reaching for her hair and stroking it. 'I'm not saying that, exactly,' she said, after a pulse had throbbed between them. 'I did ask your name, after all.'

'That's true and promised your own in exchange.'

'Jane,' she said, wondering why it seemed as though the simple act of uttering her name was somehow akin to the throwing down of a gauntlet. Blood seemed to pound far too fast through her veins, so she was intimately familiar with the fragility of her body's construction, the paper-thin vascular walls that suddenly might not be able to contain the torrent of her body's pulse.

'Jane,' he repeated, and the same pulse she'd been worried about seconds earlier seemed to rush even faster. He said it like a promise; he said it like a curse. 'It doesn't suit you,' he said, tilting his head a little.

Her stomach dropped to her toes. Only Charlotte knew that Jane had, in fact, been christened Boudica Jane—a glimpse into her parents' aspirations for her. To save the world, by following in their footsteps. If only they'd held her hand and allowed her to walk a little more closely.

'Disappointed?' she deflected, in no way interested in revealing her true name to this man. She had dropped the Boudica in the third grade, when a girl in her class had taken to calling her 'booger digger'—naturally, it had caught on and she'd lived with the moniker for years.

'No. I'm sure I can think of something else to call you.'

His tone was undeniably intimate, husky with promise. She glanced away, cheeks flushing at the imagery his nearness and voice were provoking, so her eyes landed on one of the two men down the bar who'd offered to buy her a drink earlier. Zeus hadn't offered, she realised, so much as bought the drink and walked over as though that were his God-given right. The difference between him and mere mortals, she thought with a hint of a sneer.

The man down the bar winked at her.

'Friends of yours?'

She turned back to Zeus. 'No.'

'Though they wish they were?'

She lifted a shoulder. 'I can't say.'

'Why do I get the feeling I'm dealing with someone who's left a trail of broken hearts behind her?'

'Why do I get the feeling I'm dealing with someone who doesn't believe in a heart's function?'

He laughed again and she ignored the whisper of delight that breathed through her at that, at how much she liked hearing his spontaneous humour.

'*Touché*,' he said, reaching not for the empty champagne flute and topping it up, but rather lifting hers and taking a sip from it, whilst holding her gaze. Her pulse went into dangerous territory now. 'What if you're wrong?'

'I don't think I am.'

'I thought you didn't know who I am?'

'I've known men like you before.'

'I doubt that.'

'Arrogant, handsome, successful,' she enumerated, but with a slow smile to show that she was teasing. Flirting. Baiting… 'Tell me I'm wrong.'

'Why tell you, when showing you would be so much more fun?'

Her heart galloped along. 'How do you suggest doing that?'

'Well,' he said, leaning closer, holding her champagne flute. 'Let's start with a drink and go from there.'

The promise in the latter part of that sentence was exactly what she both dreaded and needed. A promise for more, because that was how she was going to hook Lottie's nemesis and keep him distracted, but also, now that she was face-to-face with Zeus Papandreo, she freely admitted that it was going to be harder to control this thing than she'd initially anticipated.

Jane had considered her heart—and libido—to have been iced over six years earlier, with that awful heartbreak in her final year of school, but in fact, she was learning, on this night of all nights, that there was at least one man who was capable of reviving the latter. For there was no denying the heat flooding her body was pooling between her legs, and that if he were to glance down, she suspected he'd notice the way her nipples had grown taut beneath the flimsy material of her bra.

'A drink,' she heard herself purr, glad that love and loyalty to Lottie had reasserted itself. 'And after that, we'll see…'

CHAPTER TWO

AT FIRST GLANCE, THE BAR had appeared to be a rectangular room with timber walls and windows on one side that looked out onto a busy, restaurant precinct street. But with Jane's acceptance of sharing a drink with him, Zeus had nodded swiftly, put a hand in the small of her back and guided her away from the bar and through the crowd, towards a wide set of doors she hadn't initially noticed.

'It's more private in here,' he said, leaning down closer to her ear when he spoke, because it was loud, and the warmth of his breath made her whole-body tingle. She forced herself to focus, to regain control of her wayward senses.

'All the better to hear me with?'

'Hear you, see you…'

'Blow my house down?' she couldn't resist volleying back.

'As you said, we'll see,' he promised, and the words were so unmistakably sensual that her whole body seemed to catch fire. The hand in the small of her back was warm and he moved it a little upwards. She glanced at him then, at the exact moment his eyes dropped to her lips, and she felt as though the world had stopped spinning.

They stood perfectly still, in the middle of the private area of the bar. Jane was dimly aware of a few other tables of guests, but she couldn't properly register them, nor hear anything other than a general din of noise. In the centre of her mind, and in every peripheral space as well, there was only Zeus.

'I—' She sought to fill the silence, to blot out the awareness that was humming through her, because this was supposed to be a ruse, and she was meant to be playing the part of someone like her mother. Beautiful, sophisticated, wealthy and with a casual attitude to sex and relationships. Instead, she found herself slipping back into her real self, into Jane Fisher, virtually orphaned, unloved, bullied as a child, broken-hearted at seventeen and afterwards, terrified of and turned off by sex. Those wounds had cut deep, and now, opposite Zeus, she felt a bundle of insecurities.

'Come and sit with me, Jane,' he said, but there was almost a hint of resignation in his tone. Of something that didn't, in fact, make sense. Until she remembered that if she were faux husband hunting, then he was doing the same: looking for a woman he could con into marriage.

Resignation, because he didn't want to marry.

Resignation, because he needed to flirt with someone until they couldn't say no to his charms and would agree to anything he proposed.

Resignation, because this was all fake—for him, absolutely—and he almost couldn't be bothered with it. But for the trillion-dollar empire he viewed solely as his birthright, what wouldn't he do?

Love for Lottie had Jane straightening her spine, and finally, she was in control again, able to tamp down on the fast-moving current of sexual attraction and focus on the end goal. Distract, distract, distract. Thwart, thwart, thwart.

This wasn't a big deal. Men like Zeus were so used to thinking they could take whatever they wanted, regardless of who got hurt. Well, it was past time for him to learn his lesson, and Jane would relish giving it to him.

'Where?' She made a show of blinking up at him, her own long lashes flicking against the softness of her cheeks.

He gestured towards a booth in the corner, dimly lit and private.

Her heart trembled despite her assertion moments ago that she was back in charge. But she didn't convey a hint of her doubt. Instead, she turned on her stiletto heel and walked steadily towards the booth, sliding all the way along, into the corner.

It was only when she sat down that she realised he hadn't brought their drinks with them, and her throat was parched and her nerves in desperate need of stilling.

No matter—almost seconds later, with a flick of his fingers, a bartender appeared.

'What will you have?'

'I—was fine with the champagne in there,' Jane pointed out.

'Champagne,' he said, then turned to face her, placing his elbow on the table and his other arm along the back of the banquette seat, so he effectively caged her in the breadth of his body. After Steven, Jane had been terrified of dominant men. She'd tried dating a few times, but had gravitated towards slim, slight cerebral types. Men who couldn't hurt her. Men she could defend herself against.

Zeus certainly didn't fit that mould, and yet she wasn't afraid. At least, she wasn't afraid of him. The fear that was trembling at the base of her spine had more to do with the force of want pulsating inside her.

She stared across at him, half wanting to back out of this—even when she knew she never could.

'You're buying another bottle?'

'You want more?'

'There's a bottle open on the bar in there.'

'Would you like me to go and get it?'

'It just seems a little wasteful.'

'I'm not bothered.'

She didn't act quickly enough to suppress her sneer. Yes, she'd known men like him before. So carelessly wealthy, so utterly taking their ridiculous bank balances for granted. They never realised what a difference that money could make to the less fortunate.

The waiter returned with a champagne bottle and two glasses. When he went to open it in front of them, Zeus took the bottle and waved the server away in that manner of his that was pure 'I am king, hear me command.'

'Well, Zeus,' she drawled as he uncorked the champagne and poured two glasses. 'Tell me about yourself.'

He quirked a teasing expression in her direction, then lifted his glass in a silent salute. She reached for her own, clinking them together.

'To new friends,' he murmured.

'And old ones,' she added, thinking of Lottie like a touchstone now, aware that she had to focus on her loyalty to the other woman so as not to quit this hare-brained scheme.

He dipped his head once, apparently accepting her

amendment, then took a sip. 'What would you like to know?'

'Do you work near here?'

'Yes.'

Her lips flickered into a smile, then tightened when he glanced down, his eyes staring at her mouth in a way that made them tingle. The room was not warm, and yet Jane's body was. She felt awash with heat and sipped the ice-cold champagne gratefully.

'Where?'

'Two blocks away.'

Jane rolled her eyes at his vagueness. 'What do you do?'

'I'm in a family business.'

'How quaint,' she responded, intentionally goading him. 'Do you work with your parents?'

'My father retired five years ago,' he said. 'And my mother died in the spring.'

Jane's grip on her champagne flute almost faltered. She'd known that, though she'd temporarily forgotten. The way he said it pulled hard on her heart.

'I'm sorry.' The response was dragged from deep within her. She reached out and put a hand on his knee, surprising herself with the need to offer comfort. 'That must have been very hard.'

He nodded once, sipped his champagne, looking away, and Jane could have cursed. She wished she hadn't seen this side of him, this glimpse of humanity, because it would have been easier to ensure she didn't feel anything for Zeus as humanising as pity.

He was someone she had to bait into a fake relationship, and in order to achieve that, she had to continue to regard him as her best friend's nemesis and nothing more. That was easy when he was flirting like it was a professional sport, and looking at her in the same way those other men in the bar had. But when he said something so intimate, how could she not soften, just a little? Just for a moment?

'What brings you to Athens?'

The change of subject was swift and slightly disconcerting, because she was still wrapped up in sympathy and softness for him, whereas Zeus had regrouped alarmingly fast. She tried to keep up, but took a sip of champagne just to help settle those frustratingly discordant nerves.

'How do you know I don't live here?' she asked, stalling for time.

'You've never heard of me,' he pointed out.

'Okay, buster. Spill. You're obviously famous or something,' she said, glad to turn the tables and redirect conversation back to him.

'Not famous,' he disputed. 'But locally known.'

'Because you have the kind of eyes a woman could lose herself in?' She couldn't resist teasing, enjoying the way those dark eyes flashed to hers with speculation and heat.

His laugh was unsettling, though, because it shook her to her core right when she had thought she was back in control.

'Because my family has been based here for hundreds of years, run businesses out of Athens that are known all over the world.'

'You're Zeus Papandreo,' she said, glad she could at least get that out in the open, as it made her feel like less of a liar.

'Guilty as charged.'

'But you're not guilty,' she murmured. 'You're proud.'

'Yes.'

Anger fired inside her. Proud because he was a Papandreo. Proud because he belonged to that family. With no notion of the dark side of the moon, of what it had been like for Lottie to grow up shunned and hidden, with the ignominy of her conception and birth hanging over her head as though she were some dirty secret.

'I can understand why,' Jane muttered, wishing she were a slightly better liar, because she couldn't quite flatten the contempt from her tone, and Zeus was so perceptive, she was almost certain he caught it. She expelled a breath and forced a smile, trying again. 'Your family's success is remarkable.'

He shrugged. 'It's easy to be successful when you have a legacy like this behind you.'

More anger whipped inside her. Not only had this man grown up with everything at his fingertips that should have been Lottie's, he was also clearly moving the pieces in his life to marry, swiftly, to further deny Lottie what should now be hers.

Hell, if Jane hadn't already been committed to this, then she was doubly so now. She would move heaven and earth to secure Lottie's birthright, even just so Lottie could sit at the top of the tower and look down on Zeus and their father for a time. She'd earned that right, damn it.

'Modesty, Mr Papandreo?' she asked, pleased that she was able to continue acting flirtatious when she was feeling anything *but*. Except, that wasn't strictly true. Regardless of how much she hated and despised this man, because of what he'd had that Lottie should also have had, her body seemed to have its own ideas.

'Honesty. I'm secure enough in my achievements without needing to exaggerate them.'

She arched a brow, and out of nowhere, she imagined that if he was anyone else, she might actually have been halfway enjoying herself. He was such a consummate flirt; he made this easy.

'So, Jane, you're on holiday in Athens?' he prompted after a beat's silence.

'Yes,' she said, trying to remember the fib she and Lottie had concocted. They figured they needed three months to give Lottie enough time to find someone to marry and put everything in motion. Three months lined up with summer and, as luck would have it, the maternity contract Jane had been covering had finished two weeks earlier, so she was at a loose end for the next little while, anyway.

'For any reason in particular?'

'I've never been.' That, at least, was true.

'How is that possible?'

'Well, I hate to break it to you, but it's not actually the centre of the world.'

He pulled a fake wounded expression. 'But surely it's one of the most beautiful places.'

'I'll have to take your word for it,' she murmured. 'I only arrived this afternoon.'

His brows shot up. 'And you're wasting time in a bar, rather than exploring?'

'I was thirsty.'

He laughed. 'And hungry?'

'That depends. Are you asking me for dinner?'

His eyes bore into hers. 'Unfortunately, I have plans tonight.' Her heart dropped to her toes in an unexpectedly real response. Plans? She panicked. A date? With someone else? Another contender for his bride? Desperation made her lean a little closer, and she realised she still had her hand on his knee from earlier.

Go big, or go home, she thought, gliding it just an inch or so higher, as her eyes hooked to his and held.

His pants were soft to touch, but his leg muscle was tight and strong, so she couldn't help but imagine him without these pants. Imagine the way he'd be all tanned and hair roughened and... The image was making her insides swirl uncomfortably.

What are you doing? her inner Jane cried.

The inner Jane who'd kept her safe for six years by urging her to avoid men, and particularly men like Zeus. Not only was she flirting with him, baiting with him, she was also walking right into a fire, seemingly uncaring about getting burned.

'That's a shame,' she murmured as her glance fell on his lips. Her whole body tingled.

'Is it?'

'Well, for me,' she murmured, unconsciously moving closer. 'I would have liked to share dinner with a local. I'm sure you could tell me the best sights in town.'

'Like a tour guide?'

'Something like that.'

'Jane,' he said, moving then so their legs brushed beneath the table, and his much larger frame suddenly seemed not only to trap her but also to envelop her completely. In that instant, she was overwhelmed by her senses—his smell, his warmth, his closeness, the feeling of his trousers beneath her palm. But not fear. Again, she marvelled at that, because fear had seemed to be such an ingrained response in her, with so many men since Steven. Why not Zeus? 'I'd like to see you again.'

Her gut twisted. 'I thought we just agreed you'd be my tour guide.'

He nodded slowly. 'But we both know that's not what I'm talking about.'

Her heart stammered hard into her ribs. 'Isn't it?'

He arched a brow. 'Unless I'm mistaken…' And then, he mirrored her gesture, putting his hand on her bare leg just above the knee and moving a little higher. The contact was both completely welcome and utterly shocking—shocking because of how her senses screamed in immediate recognition and want. Need.

She blanked thoughts of Lottie then, trying not to imagine what her best friend would say if she knew how much Jane was enjoying this lothario's attentions. Jane! Who'd thought no man on earth could stir anything like interest in her any longer. She hadn't felt a rush of physical attraction for *anyone* since that awful night when she'd lost control—had it taken away from her—and been truly terrified. It was as though her whole body had been put into stasis, yet now it was waking up, and waking up fast.

He moved his hand higher, slowly, eyes watching her the whole time, silently inviting her to stop him, to ask him to stop, but she didn't. Just knowing that he was watching for that relaxed her enough to enjoy this. She felt *safe*. Her lips parted and she moved a little closer, dropping her head near the curve of his neck.

His fingers crept towards her inner thigh, to the expanse of flesh revealed by the very short skirt she wore, and higher still. 'Tell me to stop,' he said, inviting her to pause this madness, his voice low and throaty.

'We're in a bar,' was all she said, but it was hardly an answer, or a problem, because they were hidden away in a corner of the bar, and his frame was large enough to hide her entirely from view.

'So we are,' he agreed, before dropping his head and finding her lips, kissing her as though it was what he'd been born to do, kissing her so that her breath burned in her lungs and her whole body exploded in an electric, binding flash of light. Kissing her at the same moment his fingers brushed the silk of her underpants and found her most sensitive cluster of nerves, teasing her there through the fabric; teasing her until she was moaning into their kiss, and her body was awash with a strange, overwhelmingly heady rush of adrenaline.

The fact they were in a bar no longer mattered—Jane couldn't have said *where* she was in space, time or life. She knew only that if he stopped touching her, she might scream. Fortunately, he didn't stop touching her, nor kissing her. She writhed her hips, eager for more, wanting him to really touch her, no longer conscious of who she was, who he was, nor what she was supposed to be doing. He moved his kiss lower, to her neck, and then held her tight against him as his fingers began to brush faster. The waves that had been building inside her hit a peak and crescendoed, and then, because she'd lost all sense of time and place, she moaned loudly, so he kissed her again to swallow the sound, kissed her as she moaned into his mouth, as sanity and pleasure seemed to burst apart, forming a thousand droplets inside her. Making her whimper, making her weak, when she'd sworn she'd never be weak again.

She pulled away from him quickly, staring at him with a look of absolute shock.

He couldn't blame her.

When was the last time he'd done anything like that? Years. Years and years. Maybe as a younger man, he might have given in to the temptations of his body and found a woman who was as driven by a need for pleasure as he was, enough to throw caution—and geography—to the wind, but Zeus was thirty-three now, and in far greater control of himself.

Or so he'd thought.

But one look at Jane…hell, he didn't even know her last name. No matter. One look at her across the room and something had slipped into place inside him; and it didn't take a genius to work out why.

The marriage ultimatum.

Zeus was not a man who enjoyed ultimatums, nor did he relish the prospect of marriage, particularly not with the woman—or the sort of woman—he had in mind. So Jane, whoever she was, was simply an act of rebellion, of acting out while he was still free to do so. A last hurrah, so to speak, before he turned his mind to what he absolutely had to do.

'Give me your number,' he demanded, pulling his phone from his pocket and putting it on the tabletop. Her cheeks were flushed, and her fingers shook. She glanced around uncertainly. Shy. Like a sweet little innocent, when he suspected the opposite was true.

But she nodded then and quickly tapped something

into his phone. He took it and for good measure, pressed the call button. He heard hers begin to trill and hung up, satisfied that he would see her again.

'I—that—I don't—'

He pressed a finger to her lips, the same finger that had just been so achingly close to her sex. 'Don't explain. I felt it, too.'

Her eyes widened and her tongue darted out to lick her lips but instead connected with his finger. His gut felt as though it were filled with stones. Suddenly, the date he'd organised in response to his father's revelation was the very last thing he wanted to do.

'It's just not—'

'No explanations,' he insisted. 'I'll call you.' And because he suspected that if he were to remain for even five more seconds, he would lose the willpower to walk away altogether, he stood and left in one swift motion, refusing to look back even when he desperately wanted to.

He had more important things to consider than indulging his suddenly voracious libido. Like getting married just as soon as he could possibly arrange it.

CHAPTER THREE

Right up until an hour ago, Zeus had decided that Philomena was the perfect contender to be his bride. She was smart, incredibly ambitious, and they'd known one another for more than ten years, so he knew he could trust her. She had dated a couple of men, for around a year each, but as far as he knew, had never been seriously involved with anyone, which made him wonder if she was as averse to commitment as he was.

Most importantly, she was available and, going by her dress, interested enough to want to impress him. Which made it impossibly frustrating that he couldn't get Jane out of his mind.

Even here, sitting across from Philomena, listening to her talk about her work at a law firm a few blocks away, he could barely focus on what she was saying—and a lack of focus was *not* something Zeus generally experienced any issues with. On the contrary, he had a laser-like intensity when he turned his mind to something. And what he'd decided to turn his mind to was the imperative to marry, and fast.

Jane was a tourist. Someone he didn't know the last thing about—including her surname. So what if one look at her made his whole body aflame with desire? He'd had great sex before. Surely, he wasn't going to be led around by a certain part of his anatomy that should have known better. Not now, when the stakes were so high.

He couldn't afford to get distracted. He couldn't afford to be seen around town with Jane, if he wanted someone like Philomena to take him seriously. Which meant he should do the smart thing and delete her number off his phone. As in, an hour ago. He should have deleted it as soon as he walked out of the bar, not stared at it the entire car ride over here, as if willing *her* to call *him*.

And what if she had? Would he have ditched Philomena and the carefully laid plans for his future, all to spend one night with Jane?

He was at a juncture in his life, a turning point. Everything he had grown up to believe was his by rights was now in jeopardy. The business wasn't just a business to him, but rather, a home.

When he was nine years old and his mother received her first cancer diagnosis, he'd gone to the office with his grandfather, sat opposite him while he worked. When he was thirteen and the cancer came back, it was his father he shadowed in the holidays, learning, focusing on the business, understanding every aspect of it because it was better than thinking about his pale, slim mother and the light that was fading from her. When he was eighteen, and his mother had been in a brief period of remission, it was Zeus who took over the company for six months, while his parents went on holiday together. At twenty-one, when a new diagnosis had come, he did the same thing, allowing his father to support her through the frequent hospitalisations. The business was his sanctuary; it was *his*. Watching his mother's illness return time and time again had left him with an unshakable sense that human relationships were frail and untrustworthy, that the greatest love of all could be taken away at any point.

And yet, in the midst of that, he had known he would always have the company. He would always be the sole Papandreo heir. Ensuring that remained the case was what he should have been focused on, and only that. Not Jane.

He closed his eyes for a moment, and he saw her as she'd been at the bar. He'd been drawn to her almost the moment he'd stepped across the threshold. And who could blame him? She had the kind of beauty men went to war for, with that tumbling, lustrous blond hair and wide, curved mouth, full lips that had been painted a seductive red, wide, pretty blue eyes, high cheekbones and deep dimples when she smiled. As for her figure—

'Zeus?' Philomena reached over and put a hand on his. 'Are you well?'

He stared down at Philomena's hand and forced himself to concentrate. Too much was riding on him getting married quickly to be distracted now.

'I'm fine,' he responded, a little sharply. 'Go on.'

She frowned, but did continue speaking, much to his relief. Now, if only he could control the direction of his thoughts, because without his consent they were obsessing over Jane, so that, as the night wore on, he found his nerves were stretched well beyond breaking point.

Jane had just stepped out of the shower and was pulling on one of the fluffy hotel robes when her phone began to buzz and her pulse immediately leapt into her throat as she imagined that it might be Zeus. It was almost midnight, though. Surely, he wouldn't call this late? Only… after what had happened in the bar, could she blame him if he thought she might be up for a literal one-night stand?

Heat flushed her cheeks when she recalled the way she'd responded to his touch. No, the way she'd practically *begged* him to touch her.

And it hadn't even been about Lottie, but rather Jane's needs.

How had that happened? That night with Steven had terrified her. Up until then, they'd messed around, and she'd fallen in love with him—or thought she had. She trusted him, and she thought he'd been happy to wait, just like she'd asked. Instead, he'd plied her with alcohol and slept with her—her first and only time with a man—when she was too out of it to know what she was doing. She only remembered some of it, because of the fog of alcohol. But she knew that it had hurt, and that it had been fast and that he'd laughed off her upset afterwards. It had been a betrayal from which she could never return. Afterwards, any man's touch had left her cold at first. It had taken years before she was willing to date anyone, and she'd kissed some men, perfunctorily, and hadn't hated it, but she'd always been terrified of anything more intimate because…what if? What if they promised her something and then broke that promise?

She reached for her phone, snatching it out of her bag, face pale now, and flicked it over to see the screen. Lottie's smiling face looked back at her, the photo taken about a year earlier when they were on holiday together in Scotland. Lottie was wearing one of the telltale scarves from the Harry Potter movies—a firm favourite of both of theirs for as long as Jane could remember. She expelled a calming breath, glad to see it was Lottie and no one else.

'Hi,' she answered.

'Oh! You're there. I was about to hang up.'

'I was in the shower. Is everything okay?'

'Yeah, why?'

'It's just…late,' Jane finished with a shrug.

'Oh, shoot. I forgot the time difference. Sorry.'

'It's fine. I'm up.'

'I just wanted to check in.'

'See if I've made any progress?'

'Well, I mean, not to put too fine a point on it, but our future plans for global domination are kind of riding on it…'

Jane smiled, collapsing down onto the sofa, wondering at the strange sense of disloyalty that was filling her mouth with acid. 'I met him,' she answered, fingers pulling at some fluff on her robe.

Lottie let out a low whistle. 'You only flew in today. That was fast.'

'I went to that bar.'

'And he was there?'

'Yep.'

'Let me guess… He fell at your feet and begged to kiss them?'

Jane rolled her eyes, but the gesture lacked acerbity, because her pulse was throbbing, and her insides were squirming. One touch had ignited her, body and soul. 'No, sadly,' she said, the words sounding foreign to her own ears.

But Lottie didn't appear to notice. 'So, what's the plan?'

'Plan?'

'I presume you have one?'

'Well, he has my number,' she said, and then, sitting a little straighter, 'and I have his.'

'Excellent. You're a genius.'

'Well, we'll see. I get the feeling I'm biting off way more than I can chew.'

'In what way?'

Something twisted in her abdomen. She stood up, pacing, a strange energy making it impossible to sit still. 'He's every bit the practiced flirt, just like we thought.'

'No kidding. You saw the same photos I did, right? A different woman every week?'

'At least,' Jane snorted. 'Maybe even every night. He seemed pretty well known at the bar.'

'I'll just bet he did.' The condemnation in Lottie's voice was pronounced. 'What else?'

'What do you want to know?' Jane asked, ignoring the sense of guilt and focusing on her best friend.

'Nothing,' Lottie responded then with a sigh. 'And everything. He's my half-brother. Does he look like me?'

'No. You know that—you've seen as many pictures as I have. You're the spitting image of your mother. Apart from your love of coffee and history, I can't imagine you as being half Greek.'

'I like ouzo, too,' Lottie said with a laugh, reminding Jane of the first night they'd gotten properly drunk. That time, they'd broken into the groundskeepers' hut and swiped what they thought was vodka and turned out to be the aniseed Greek spirit. After the first awful taste, they had been undeterred.

'How's your Operation Find a Husband going?' Jane changed the subject with relief and settled back on the couch to listen as Lottie recounted what could only be described as the first date from hell, all the while her naughty imagination kept trying to draw her back to the bar, to Zeus Papandreo and the magic of his touch…

At first, she didn't hear the ringing of her phone, because she was in the middle of a huge crowd of summer tourists, all marvelling at the ancient beauty that was the Acropolis. Beside her, an American family had been debating the architectural merits. Their teenage son had seemed to have a lot to say on the subject, and his parents had been content to let him drone on, and on and on, while their youngest child, a little girl of about seven or eight, devoured a huge ice lolly.

Hot and a little sweaty, Jane was looking at the nearly finished treat with undisguised jealousy when the girl reached out and pointed towards Jane's bag. 'You're ringing,' she said in a broad accent.

Jane blinked, tearing her gaze from the little girl's ice lolly to her face, which was smiling sweetly.

'Oh, right.' She looked across to find that even the teenager had stopped talking, and the parents were looking at her expectantly, too. She realised she was standing very close to their group, almost as if she wanted to be adopted in by them.

She stepped back quickly, smiled curtly then turned away, diving into her bag to remove the phone. In a fit of irritation—self-directed, because she'd been thinking about Zeus and acting like a twit—she answered the phone. Only to hear his voice, coming down the line, dark and somehow every bit as hot as the summer day.

'Jane,' he drawled, the simple word almost indecent.

She quickly pulled away from the thrum of people, as much as she could, trying to find somewhere quiet to have this conversation.

'I'm sorry, who's this?' She couldn't resist teasing.

She could practically hear him smirk down the phone. 'We met last night, at the bar.'

'Right. Zoro?'

Now he laughed and she smiled, secure in the knowledge that he couldn't see her, so he wouldn't see how she sort of liked sparring with him.

'Are you free tonight?' he asked, barely a moment later.

She bit into her lower lip. For the sake of self-preservation, she should run a mile. She should tell him 'no,' that she was busy. That was exactly what Jane Fisher would have done, if left up to her own devices. But this was for Lottie. They had a plan, and it was up to Jane to play her part.

'I might be able to move some things in my busy holidaymaker schedule around, depending on what you're suggesting.'

'I'm glad to hear it,' he said, then softly, 'How does dinner sound?'

She expelled a breath of relief. Dinner was fine. Dinner was *out*. In public. No chance of him getting the wrong idea if they were seated across from one another in a busy restaurant.

'Great,' she rushed, trying to remember she should sound delighted and not as though she were heading to the gallows.

'Text me your address and I'll pick you up at eight.'

She bit into her lip. 'I'm at a hotel. I'll get a car to the restaurant.'

Silence. He didn't like being contradicted, she could tell. Well, tough. Jane intended to stay firmly in control of this situation, no matter what. Control was her defence against the dark ravages of her past; control was her salvation.

'What's the matter, Jane?' he asked, but his voice was teasing now, as though he was making fun of her. 'Are you afraid that if I come to your hotel we might decide *not* to go out, after all?'

That was precisely her fear, she admitted to herself. New fears of how much she wanted him, and old fears of being hurt and taken advantage of. Of sacrificing the control she'd fought so hard for.

'Of course not,' she muttered, looking around to make sure she was still alone, a little way off the beaten tourist track. 'But it's not the nineteen fifties. I'm more than capable of making my own way to you.'

She waited for him to argue and wondered how long she'd hold her steel for, but then he simply said, 'Okay. I'll text you the restaurant. See you at eight, Jane.'

She let out a breath of relief.

'And Jane?'

Her heart skipped a beat.

'I'm looking forward to seeing you again.' He disconnected the call, and Jane closed her eyes on a rush of awareness and a growing sense of panic.

She had about five hours to talk some sense into herself and retrain her body so that it wouldn't practically melt whenever he was nearby. Five hours to remind herself that the only reason she was seeing this man—this man she hated on behalf of her best friend and womankind everywhere—was because of the horribly old-fashioned term of inheritance. This meant the world to Lottie, and there was no way Jane was going to let her down. Not after everything she'd already been denied in her life. Jane had her back and always would. She just wished she could stop fantasising about Zeus!

Five minutes after eight, she strode into the restaurant in yet another dress she'd borrowed, this time from her mother's wardrobe. It was a couture dress from a few summers ago, meaning her mother had long since forgotten it existed and wouldn't miss it. A vibrant pink, with slender straps, it clung to the torso then flared at the hips in a skirt that fell to just beneath the knees in a classic prom dress silhouette. But there was something risqué about the dress and the way the back hung low, revealing the line of her spine to just above the curve of her bottom.

She'd teamed it with flats tonight. Even for Lottie and this scheme, she couldn't force her feet into another pair of high heels. Not after she'd walked all over Athens and was still recovering from a dose of pinch-toe-itis courtesy of the night before.

'This way, madam,' a waiter said with a deferential bow when she told him her name.

He led her through the restaurant, past the incredible windows that showed views towards the Acropolis, towards yet another room, this time small enough for one table, and with a sheer curtain hanging across the doorway.

Her heart plunged.

She'd been hoping to sit across from him in a crowded restaurant, not to be in yet another out of the way table like this, with the magic of Athens glittering in the background. They had their own private window, though she supposed, if it was any consolation, the view was hardly likely to get more than a second glance from Jane, given that Zeus was standing up to greet her.

'Jane,' he said, crossing towards her, ignoring the waiter, who faded into the background. She swallowed, but her mouth was inexplicably dry and there was nothing she could do to moisten it. He took her hands in his, held them for a moment then lifted one to his lips. Her stomach dropped to her toes; her insides squeezed with recognition.

'Zeus,' she said, trying to focus. Trying to remember how she needed to act—for Lottie—but also for herself.

'Thank you for meeting me.'

She arched a brow then gestured towards the window, glad to wrestle back control of her hand. 'You promised to show me the sights. You weren't lying.'

'I never lie,' he said, and guilt coloured Jane's face. She *wasn't* lying to him, though, just by omitting her connection with his family and her reason for being here. He hadn't asked; she was under no obligation to volunteer the information. He put a hand on her hip then, drawing her closer to him, and he kissed her cheek in a manner that was somehow so much more intimate than anything they'd done the night before. A shiver ran the length of her spine.

'I—' she whispered, voice husky. 'I need to tell you something,' she said, pulling away so she could see his face. And the importance of this moment slammed into her. The knowledge that what she told him might ruin Lottie's plan—but that it had to be done. She couldn't keep doing this without putting some guardrails in place; it was too dangerous for Jane. Too hard for her.

His eyes bore into hers and he nodded without making any effort to put some distance between them.

'Last night—what happened in the bar—'

'I thought we discussed this already.'

'No, you decreed I shouldn't explain, but that's not good enough. I have to.'

Amusement sculpted his lips and lifted his brows. 'I decreed?'

'Yes. You're very bossy, you know,' she said with a semi-apologetic grimace.

'I have been told that before.'

'I'm not surprised.'

'Not often so gently, either,' he added, and one side of her lips tugged upwards in a smile. 'Go on, Jane. Explain whatever it is you would like to say.' He pressed a finger beneath her chin, though, lifting her gaze to his. 'Though I do not consider anything requires an explanation. As I said last night, I felt it, too.'

'You felt what, exactly?'

His eyes flared for a moment and then he pulled her closer, holding her against his body, stroking the naked flesh of her back. 'Desire.'

Yes, desire. It had been a potent force between them, something she'd never really experienced. Not like that— a freight train, rushing headlong towards her. 'Be that as it may,' she said, the conversation becoming almost impossible to focus on when faced with the evidence of the attraction that was flaring between them, particularly from his growing hardness. She closed her eyes, praying for strength. She had to walk a fine line here to keep him interested without selling her soul to the devil. Lottie wouldn't want that, and it was a bridge too far for Jane.

This was not, and had never been, about sex. 'I need to be honest with you about my... What I want.'

'I would dearly like to hear all about what you want,' he said, dropping his mouth to the curve of her neck and kissing it, so she groaned and shifted her head to grant him more access. Did she really have to do this? Of course she did. A man like Zeus undoubtedly had relationships that included sex. A lot of sex. And after last night, he probably presumed she was like any of his other conquests; but Jane wasn't. This could only continue if he understood that she needed to go slow. To be in control. And yet, she angsted back and forth over the necessity of telling him, because a part of her wanted him to see her like any other woman, to kiss her and touch her and possibly even make love to her, because maybe then she could reclaim that part of herself that had been burned by Steven beyond—she'd always thought—repair.

'I'm celibate,' she blurted out, tired of the argument going on in her mind, placing a hand on his chest, needing some space, and sanity, to return.

'Celibate?' He arched a brow enquiringly, as though he'd never heard the word.

'I don't sleep with people.'

'You don't, or you haven't?'

'I haven't, for a very long time,' she admitted, pushing Steven out of her mind with difficulty. 'And I don't intend for that to change anytime soon.'

'I see,' he said when it was clear he didn't. 'Why?'

'I decided I would wait until I was in a committed relationship. With someone I love. And trust.' She lifted one bare shoulder. 'I don't necessarily mean I'm waiting until I get married, but at least...engaged,' she responded.

And the moment she told him that—which was the truth, from the bottom of her heart—she realised how a man in his situation might take it.

As an easy way to tick several boxes, all at once.

And her heart began to race at what she'd just unintentionally done.

If she were more Machiavellian, she might have seen it as a masterstroke, but for Jane, it felt as though she was being even more dishonest now. Devious and manipulative.

But he was listening to her with that intelligent, assessing dark gaze, studying her in a way that made her want to squeeze her eyes shut and run a mile, because she feared he saw so much more than she wanted him to.

'I just didn't want you to think, because of last night, that dinner would be a prelude to…you know. Me going home with you.' She took a step back with difficulty, her whole body flushing with cold at the absence of touch. 'If you want me to leave—'

'Leave?' he interrupted, frowning, as though she'd suggested she might grow another head from her hip. 'Why would I want you to leave?'

'Because I know what you're like. What men *like* you are like,' she amended quickly, because she wasn't supposed to know anything about Zeus. 'And I don't want to waste your time.'

'*Agape*, there is not a chance on earth of you doing that. Sit. Tell me more about yourself, starting with your last name.'

CHAPTER FOUR

It was the one thing she could have said to drive him to the breaking point. If there was one thing Zeus loved as much as he hated an ultimatum, it was a challenge, and here was the most beautiful, sensual woman Zeus had ever met, a woman who had had the rare power of keeping him from sleep the night before, so tormented had his dreams been, telling him that she was off-limits.

It was like a red rag to a bull.

But it was something more than that, too.

It's not like I'm waiting until I'm married...

Only, what if she did? What if she waited until she was married, and she just so happened to marry *him*?

He needed a wife. He needed a wife *quickly*, and if last night had proven anything, it was that things between them had the power to move swiftly—faster than either of them had really expected. He thought of Philomena and his insides were cold, despite the fact he knew she was the smart choice.

Jane wasn't marriage material.

No, that wasn't accurate.

He couldn't marry someone like Jane. She was dangerous. Threatening. Because with Jane, there was a risk he might come to want more—that he might actually care about her more than in a sensible, rational, platonic way. Even the way her lip had trembled a little as she'd confessed her celibacy had triggered a long-suppressed protective instinct, reminding him of how he'd felt as a young boy who'd desperately wanted to fix his mother, but couldn't.

Zeus had grappled with that impotence and decided the only antidote to it was strength. Control. Making sure he was in charge of every element of his life. With Philomena, he could imagine that. It was easy. He liked and respected her, she was intelligent and interesting, but he could never imagine becoming addicted to her.

Whereas Jane... His eyes shifted to her face just as she pursed her lips together, almost as if she were nervous, and his stomach twisted.

'What do you do, Jane?'

'Do?'

'For work.'

'Right.' She blinked those wide-set blue eyes, as if he'd dragged her back into the present from some absorbing thought or other. 'I'm a lawyer.'

He tilted his head, thoughtfully.

'That is to say, I have my law degree and was admitted to the bar, but I actually work in the not-for-profit sector.'

'Charities?' he asked, for some reason not surprised. Despite her almost excessive beauty and confidence, there was something vulnerable and sweet about her, too. He could imagine her caring a little too much—the opposite of him, then.

She nodded, and her blond hair, which she'd styled in loose, voluminous waves, bobbed around her face, so he itched to reach out and touch it. To touch her. *I'm celi-*

bate. The words chased around and around in his mind, making him wonder *why*. Clearly, it wasn't a lack of sensual need and desire—he'd felt that flare between them the night before, and her attraction to him had been as unmistakable as his own.

'Which sector?'

'Mostly, I deal with homelessness, though I've just come off a maternity contract working for people leaving domestic violence. We helped get them set up in shelters and whatever else was needed. Oftentimes, these people are leaving with absolutely nothing, so it involves sourcing clothes, computers, new phones and phone numbers so they can apply for jobs, everything.'

He leaned closer, focusing on her with razor-sharp intensity. 'Did you always want to work in charities?'

She tilted her head to the side thoughtfully. 'I guess so.'

'And the law degree was the best way to do that?'

'Actually, I tend to work on the legal side of these foundations, so yes.' She nodded. 'But also—'

He waited for her to continue, wondering at the slight pause, the flushing of her cheeks. She sipped her champagne then leaned forward, mirroring his body language. And when she shifted, her legs moved, too, so her knees brushed against his and he felt a tightening in every cell of his body.

I'm celibate.

'I guess you could say I'm also in the family business.'

'Your parents are lawyers?'

'My father is,' she said with a wave of her delicate, fine-boned hand. Her skin was so flawless, like honey and caramel all melted together.

'In the same sector?'

'Human rights. Edward Fisher. You might have heard of him.'

'Edward Fisher is your father?'

She nodded once.

'Impressive. He's achieved a lot.'

Her smile was tight. 'Yes.'

'You must be very proud.'

'Must I?' She sighed then. 'Sorry, we're not close, but yes, I'm proud of the work he's done.'

Fascinating. Dangerous. Zeus knew he should walk away. Make up an excuse, leave, just like he'd done the night before, then delete her number. Change his if he had to. Because Jane was the last woman he should be spending time with at this point of his life. Right now, when it was imperative that he make the smart decision and marry someone who would be right for him, he couldn't afford to waste time with a woman who had the potential to scuttle all his plans.

Except…it was just dinner. He could spend some time with Jane, see where it went. Philomena had been his friend for a long time; she wasn't going anywhere. If he decided to suggest marriage to her, he could do that in a week, a fortnight, a month. In the meantime, he was free to do what he wanted, just as he always had.

But the sooner you're married, the better, a voice in his head chided him. Then, he could set aside the worry about inheriting the company. He could formalise his ownership, and his father's indiscretion would lose any power to hurt him.

A muscle throbbed in his jaw as he contemplated the deep betrayal of his father's affair, the shifting of the man from the pedestal upon which Zeus had held him.

He'd thought they were united in their desire to protect Anna Maria Papandreo. To love her and keep her safe and happy. But all the while, Aristotle had been sleeping around behind her back.

Anger flooded Zeus, so for a moment he almost forgot where he was.

'Zeus?' Jane reached across the table and put her hand on his. 'Are you okay?'

He laughed, but it was a forced, brittle sound. 'I'm fine.'

'Look, if you want to go,' she said with a lift of one of those delightful, bare shoulders, 'I'll understand. I know I'm not what I seem.'

He considered that carefully. 'What do you think you seem like?'

She gestured to her hair first. 'I think guys see the blond hair, my figure, and decide I'm some kind of sex kitten, ready to leap into bed.'

'You're very beautiful,' he said, rather than admit that his first thought upon seeing her had been wondering how quickly he could get her from the bar to his home and naked on his sheets.

Unlike a lot of women he knew, she didn't seem flattered by that. If anything, her expression tightened to one of disappointment and when she said, 'thank you,' it was through gritted teeth. There was more here than she was telling him. More he wanted to understand, because understanding things was one of Zeus's core business strategies. Whenever they'd taken over another company, he'd spent the first month simply observing. Seeing how it ran. Where were the problems? What were the strengths? While it would have been easy to rush in like a bull at a gate with his own ideas and thoughts, he'd have risked missing something important.

'Tell me what happened,' he invited, leaning back in his chair but kicking his legs forward, so they were placed on either side of hers. Jane's eyes widened and heat flared in his gaze; he felt it, too. Desire. A rush of it, wrapping around them like a cocoon, but nothing so comfortable or soporific. No, this was a wild, flagrant cataclysm of animalistic wants, which made it all the more imperative for him to understand why she needed to fight this.

'With my father?' she asked, and he suspected she was deliberately misunderstanding him.

'With your celibacy.'

'Oh.' She glanced down at her drink, and at that moment, the curtain swished open and a waiter walked in. Zeus could have strangled the man, though of course, the intrusion wasn't exactly his fault. Nor was it unexpected. They were at a restaurant; they had to order food. That was how it worked.

'Good evening. Do you have any questions about the menu?'

'I haven't even looked,' Jane murmured.

Zeus fixed the waiter with a stare. 'What does the chef recommend?'

The waiter reeled off a few dishes; Zeus turned to Jane. 'Any problems with that?'

She shook her head and this time, when her blond hair bounced around her angelic face, it released a hint of her fragrance, vanilla and cherries, so his gut clenched. He turned to the waiter to tell him to bring the chef's recommendations and caught the look of undisguised admiration on the other man's face as he also stared at Jane.

Something twisted sharply in Zeus's gut, and not just at the waiter's lack of professionalism. Jealousy. Protectiveness. Emotions that should have made him run a mile, rather than sitting there, waiting impatiently for them to be left alone.

'That's all.' He dismissed the waiter curtly and caught the other man's cheeks darken with a hint of embarrassment. Zeus turned back to Jane.

When they were alone again, she arched a brow and smiled at him. That smile that seemed to filter all the light from all the world and beam it across the room.

'You sound cross.'

He shook his head once. 'I'm not.'

'Not with me,' she said, then lifted her shoulders again. 'Or jealous?'

Was he that transparent? And how bad was that? The fact that he was being so exposed to this woman, when usually he was a closed book. Warning sirens were blaring but he didn't seem capable of heeding them.

'You just told me you don't like being objectified and then he walked in and couldn't stop staring.'

'Isn't that a little like the pot calling the kettle black?'

He didn't like it, but she was right. The night before, he'd seen little beyond her obvious physical beauty. Just like the other men at the bar who'd been ogling her.

'It's fine,' she said, shaking her head. 'I went through a phase where I tried very hard to escape notice, but I got sick of it. It's not my problem if the world views me a certain way. But in terms of men, it's important to be honest. I wouldn't want to lead you on...'

'So, you do date?'

She paled visibly. 'I—'

It would have been kind to let her off the hook. To change the subject to something less important and personal. But Zeus was driven by a selfish need to understand her better, and so he sat silently, staring at her, waiting.

'Yes, I've dated,' she said, biting into that full, lower lip. 'But not seriously. Not since— Not in a while.'

'Something happened,' he said, sure now that he was right, 'to cause you to avoid men.'

She swallowed, her throat shifting visibly. 'Yes.' She toyed with the stem of her champagne flute, then glanced across at him uncertainly. 'I—had what you could call a bad experience. I decided to be very careful after that.'

'You weren't careful before?'

'I was naive,' she muttered. 'And far too trusting.'

He resisted the urge to point out that trusting anyone was a fool's mistake; she didn't seem to need to hear that from him. 'And someone hurt you.'

She flinched, glancing down at her drink. Until that moment, he'd presumed she meant emotionally, but there was something about the strength of her reaction that thundered all the breath from his body, as he imagined that the hurt she was referencing might, in fact, have been physical.

'Jane...' He chose his words with care, ignoring his own self-preservation instincts, which were still imploring him to run a mile from this woman. 'You don't have to answer this...' He reached out and put his hand on hers lightly, stroking the back of it. 'Are we talking about an abusive relationship?'

Her eyes were saucer-wide when they met his, and to Zeus's relief, she shook her head, hair cascading around her shoulders. But then she looked down at the table once more and it felt as though a noose were tightening about his neck. Because she was hiding something. Lying to him. He knew it. He could tell. Something very bad had happened to her, and just the thought of that made Zeus's blood boil. He stood then, every cell in his body reverberating in rejection of what he was contemplating, as he came to crouch at her side so he could be closer to her, closer to her eye level.

'Listen to me,' he said, one hand on her thigh. She stared at him, eyes wide, lips parted. 'I am not going to pressure you. Not to tell me what you don't want to tell me, and not to do anything you're not comfortable with.' He stroked her thigh gently, saw the moment her pupils dilated, and heat flushed her cheeks. 'But sex, between two consenting adults, is a beautiful, special thing. Not to mention a hell of a lot of fun.' He knelt so he could brush his lips over hers. 'If you've had a traumatic experience in the past, it's natural that you'd want to run from it, that you'd want to avoid situations that might be a repeat of that.' He stroked her cheek, wondering at this strong protective instinct, at the way this woman he'd just met seemed to be the centre of his universe all of a sudden. 'I will never hurt you. I will never push you to do something you're not comfortable with. And I will always, always listen to you. You're in charge.'

Her eyes widened and she nodded, but it was a jerk, a pulse of her head, and he had no idea whether she believed him, or what he was promising. The morning before, he'd woken up with a clear objective, front and centre.

Get married.

To a woman he liked but would never love. To a woman

he found attractive but wasn't attracted to. To a woman that couldn't possibly threaten the silo of independence he'd created, very intentionally, around himself.

And instead, he was tumbling headlong, in a way he couldn't fight, into a situation with a woman who had the potential to occupy every single bit of his brain space.

But only if he let her.

Only if he let *this*. Desire, sexual chemistry, these were just part and parcel of being humans in the world. Couldn't he enjoy the physical side of this without letting her get under his skin? She didn't have to threaten anything. He was in control, just like always. Except when it came to sex, because he had an unshakable sense that in that regard, she needed to call the shots. To heal and recover. And he was more than willing to let her use him to get over whatever had happened in her past. After that, he'd get married. To someone else. Someone safe. And the company that meant more than anything to him in the entire world would be, indisputably and irrevocably, his.

Jane's knees were shaking for an entirely different reason now, as she pushed into the ladies' room. Not because she needed to avail herself of the facilities, but because she needed, desperately, space. Having sat opposite Zeus for an entire dinner, legs touching but nothing else, she felt as though her nerves were stretched tighter than a high wire. Her pulse was throbbing and her palms wouldn't stop sweating.

I will never hurt you.

Five words that no man had ever known she needed to hear, an assurance that for some reason, with Zeus, she hadn't needed him to say because she'd *felt* that truth in him, right from the start. The fear she usually felt with the other sex hadn't been there. Not even a little, despite his far greater size and obvious habit of being in command.

With Jane, he was willing to take a backseat. He was willing to let *her* dominate. Because a man with a genuinely strong sense of self wouldn't be intimidated by that. His ego wasn't so fragile that he had to push his will on hers.

But this was all a *disaster*. She wasn't here to be swept away by an attraction to Zeus Papandreo. She was here to tease and tempt him just long enough to stop him from getting married before Lottie could.

What a stupid, stupid idea that had been, she thought with a grimace, staring at her reflection in the mirror. Absent-mindedly, she reached into her purse for some lipstick then carefully reapplied it. How exactly had she thought she'd keep a guy like Zeus interested without sex coming up between them? With witty conversation?

It was not, in the end, a particularly well-thought-out plan. Or maybe the plan had been fine, but meeting Zeus had been her undoing, because she was starting to think he was nothing like she'd suspected.

Had he hurt Lottie? Inadvertently, yes. By being the acknowledged child and heir, the man who'd been raised as a proud Papandreo, he *was* an instrument of pain to Lottie. But it was their shared father, Aristotle, who'd truly wounded Jane's best friend. Zeus wasn't responsible for the choices his father made when he, Zeus, was still just a boy.

Which meant what, exactly? That she was free to flirt with him, after all? To kiss him, touch him, have sex with him? It would achieve the same thing for Lottie.

But what about Zeus? Didn't he deserve better than to be used like that?

She dropped her head forward, panic tightening inside her, alongside a growing feeling that she was already in deep, deep water. But maybe the situation with Lottie didn't even have to come into this. She was capable of helping her friend without even having to actively engage in a scheme at all. What was happening with Zeus had morphed into something *genuine*, so it wasn't like she was lying to him, either. She was just…letting this play out. And eventually, she'd go back to the UK, pick up the threads of her own life and Zeus would just be someone in her rear-vision mirror. He'd never need to know her connection to Lottie, and Lottie wouldn't need to know that, far from hating Zeus Papandreo as a loyal best friend should, Jane had actually started to wonder if he mightn't be a genuinely decent person, after all.

CHAPTER FIVE

THE WHOLE DRIVE back to Jane's hotel, neither of them spoke. They sat on opposite sides of the backseat of his car, both very careful to keep a full seat of space between them. But the silence only made Jane more aware. Of his breathing. Of the rustle of his clothes as he shifted in his seat. Of the size of his legs, spread wide, strong and muscular. Athletic.

Athens passed in a blur, the Acropolis a golden beacon visible through the front windscreen, but Jane barely noticed the beauty of the backdrop. Every single atom of her was focused on Zeus. When they'd left the restaurant, he'd offered his driver to take her back to the hotel. Solo. Without him.

Because he'd promised to respect her boundaries, and he was showing her that he meant it. But Jane had demurred, saying that it was silly for the driver to drop her while he caught a cab. 'Can't you just drop me off first?' Their eyes had met and something had fizzed between them, a spark had ignited, and it was still burning.

But Jane knew that it was her decision how long she let it go for. If she wanted, at the hotel, she could turn to Zeus and say good-night and send him on his way. He wouldn't question it—that was their deal. And that was what she should do, she knew. If only to test him, to make sure he was being honest, when he promised that she was in charge.

It was an assurance, though, she found she didn't need, because for some reason she couldn't explain, Jane trusted him. At least, she trusted him as much as it was possible for her to trust someone. Naturally, there was still a wariness because of what Steven had done to her, and after how much she'd loved and cared for him, but this was different. Zeus was different.

You don't know that, a voice chided.

Was she being just as naive as she'd been back then?

The car pulled to a stop in front of her hotel, and she turned to face him, to find an expression on his face that made her stomach somersault.

'I enjoyed spending time with you, Jane.'

He made no effort to move. True to his word, she thought, heart lifting.

Say good-night and go upstairs.

She glanced at the seat between them, where his tanned hand rested, and bit into her lower lip.

'I did, too,' she half whispered.

'I'd like to see you again.'

She swallowed, her throat dry. 'I—' *Say good-night. Leave. Get out of the car.* 'Would you like to come up for coffee?'

Good Lord. The words tumbled out of her mouth without a skerrick of forethought, almost as if her body had ideas that her brain definitely didn't condone.

'We had coffee at the restaurant,' he pointed out with a wry smile. 'But I'd like to come up, regardless.'

Their eyes met and the spark that had been burning

tilted dangerously close to a full-blown explosion. Uncertainty thickened in her gut, but so did desire, and it was not a fair fight. After so long of subduing her sensual needs, the temptation of Zeus was impossible to ignore. He'd stirred something to life inside her just by his presence, and she felt as though it was impossible to fight it.

'Okay,' she said, and nodded slowly, because it was an agreement to so much more than heading upstairs. 'Let's go.'

She'd never noticed how small elevators were before. And it wasn't like the elevators in this fancy five-star hotel were even that small, but with Zeus right beside her, she felt his proximity and heat like a magnet. She glanced up at him as the doors swished closed and he turned, slowly, to regard her with eyes that were shiny dark and mesmerisingly intense. 'Remember, Jane, you're in charge,' he said, voice a low rumble.

'Why do I think you're not used to handing over control?' she asked, her voice strangely airy.

He arched a brow in a way that made her stomach loop in on itself. 'Which floor?'

'Oh, right, the key,' she muttered, reaching into her clutch purse and fumbling a little, because her fingers wouldn't cooperate. He waited patiently, but the longer he waited, the harder it got, because he was so close, and all she could think about was the way they'd kissed the night before, and wondering if they'd kiss again, and wanting, more than anything, for that to be the case.

But what if he did hurt her?

What if she couldn't trust him?

Steven had seemed trustworthy. Steven had always said all the right things, and then he'd treated her like a piece of meat. He'd grown tired of waiting for her to be ready to sleep with him, so he'd made sure it had happened.

What if—?

'Would you like me to do it?' he asked, and she realised she'd stopped fumbling and was staring at the breadth of his chest.

She nodded slowly, holding her clutch out to him. He didn't take the bag but rather reached inside and easily fished out the key card from the side pocket, then took her hand in his and upended it, so he could place the key card there. Rather than letting go, though, he came to stand beside her, his body pressed to hers, and he held her hand still as he guided it towards the pad on the elevator panel and swiped it. Her floor lit up immediately. She expelled a breath of relief—a sense of relief that only seemed to grow when he stayed right there, behind her, one hand wrapped around her wrist, his thumb brushing over her flesh gently.

She wasn't just aware of the sound of his husky breathing now, but of the feel of it, as his chest moved with each exhalation, and the air in the elevator seemed to grow thick and warm. Her whole body was throbbing, like her pulse had become overlarge and was taking over every organ. She wanted to turn around, to be standing *this* close to him, but toe to toe, to feel him, to see him. But she stayed as she was, because she had a feeling they were both out of their depths a little—even Zeus—and she knew that one wrong move would explode the whole situation.

And if it got really out of hand? Would she have any choice but to run a mile from this?

She swallowed past a lump in her throat, and when the doors opened to reveal the plushly carpeted corridor of her hotel level, she released a breath. Of relief, and gratitude.

'This is me,' she said, reluctant to move.

'So I gathered.'

He moved then, extending a hand to keep the doors open, his eyes on her with an emotion she couldn't fathom. 'After you.'

She nodded once, tried to make her legs move, but there was a lack of synergy between her brain and body. Or maybe it was that she was right where she wanted to be—close to Zeus—and so she found herself stuck there.

He held out his other hand to her then, broad and tanned, inviting her to put her own in his. More than a gesture, it was a sign of trust. Of him asking her to trust him, and when she placed her hand in his palm, and he closed his fingers over hers, it was as though she'd agreed.

She hoped she wasn't wrong, that this wasn't all an awful mistake.

They stepped off the elevator together. 'Which way?'

She gestured to the left and they began to walk, hand in hand, towards her door. She paused outside the front of it, then swiped her key, which she was still holding in her other hand.

The door clicked to show that it had unlocked, and Zeus pushed it open, standing where he was but holding it back against the wall, so Jane could enter first. She took a step, then realised he wasn't following.

'I can leave, Jane,' he said, misreading her hesitation. Because she wanted him to come in. She wanted everything to happen between them that the flame and flares seemed to promise *would* happen. But she just didn't know *how* to give in to that. She'd spent so long fighting this part of herself, forcing it down. Or maybe it just hadn't even been an issue, because she'd never met anyone since Steven who'd made her want to try this again. With Zeus, it didn't even feel like a choice.

'No,' she demurred, the word thick with urgency. 'I really do want you to come in. It's just—'

He waited, looking at her in that inquisitive way he had.

'I don't know what happens next,' she said, honestly, shrugging her shoulders. 'It's been a long time, and I'm—'

He reached forward and pressed a finger to her lips. 'We're not sleeping together tonight.'

Her heart sank to her toes and her brows drew inwards as she tried to process that. 'Oh.'

'Not because I don't want to,' he assured her quickly, as though he understood the doubt and uncertainties that had instantly plagued her. 'But because I think you need time to get used to the idea. To make sure it's what you really want.'

Her pulse ratcheted up. 'What if I already know it's what I want?'

His eyes widened and then swept shut, and she somehow just knew that he was fighting a battle of his own—between what he wanted and what he knew he should be doing.

'Then you'll still want it tomorrow night. Or the night after that. We don't have to rush this.'

Which was exactly what *she* should have been saying. Because this was about distracting him from getting engaged—except it wasn't. When she was alone with Zeus, it was about this and only this. Desire, need, want, pleasure. Lottie's plans were the furthest thing from her mind.

She nodded slowly, and only then did he step inside the hotel room. The door clicked shut between them and there they stood, toe to toe, just as she'd wanted to be in the elevator.

Her own breathing was rushed, her chest moving rapidly, so she was aware of the way her dress tightened across her breasts.

'This dress,' he muttered, reaching behind her and pressing a finger to her exposed back, 'should be illegal.'

She laughed softly, pleasure trilling in her veins. 'You like it?'

He grimaced. 'A little too much.'

'That's a shame. I was thinking of getting changed out of it.'

'Jane,' his voice held a warning.

She held one hand up between them, to reassure him. 'It's a beautiful dress. It's just not that comfortable.' She met and held his gaze. 'I want to take it slowly, too, Zeus. I need that. I just—still want to—' She tapered off, not sure how to express what she was feeling.

'Do something?' he prompted, putting his hands on her hips and holding her there. She shivered from desire, and in the back of her mind, she marvelled at how calm she felt. Where usually being alone with a man who was attracted to her flooded her veins with fear, she felt nothing like that now.

She nodded. 'So, maybe you could help me get changed?' she prompted, knowing that she was inviting them both to play with fire, and not caring.

His eyes flared and then he moved his hands lower, gliding them over the swell of her hips to her thighs, bunching the delicate fabric as he went. 'I did say you were in charge, didn't I?' he murmured, reaching the hem and holding it in his fists.

Pulse in her throat, she nodded again.

Slowly, oh, so painstakingly slowly, he lifted the dress upwards. Past her thighs, over her bottom to her waist, where he paused, eyes on hers the whole time, as if reading her, wanting reassurance that she was still okay with this. He was taking his promise very, very seriously, and the proof of that exploded the last vestiges of her doubt.

Zeus wasn't Steven.

Zeus was a man who could have any woman he wanted; he didn't need to force himself on some drunk teenager. He had principles and confidence; he was different to Steven in every way.

She lifted her hands over her head in a silent invitation—and insistence—that he keep going. He did. Slowly, though, so slowly she wanted to scream, his fingers brushing her sides as he pushed the dress towards her breasts and then over them. The contrast between the warmth of his touch and the cool of the air around them made the hair on her arms stand on end. The fabric was soft and it rustled against her ears when he finally pulled it over her head, then dropped it to the floor at their sides with a hiss from between his teeth.

'Holy mother of God,' he groaned, stepping forward and pressing their bodies together, hers naked except for a flimsy pair of lace briefs. 'You are exquisite.'

But she didn't want to hear that. She didn't care about

physical beauty, and she didn't particularly want it to be what he saw in her, either.

She lifted up onto the tips of her toes and her eyes held his as she slowly, hungrily, sought his mouth with her own. And groaned. In the bar, he'd kissed her as though she were a woman he desired, but here, alone in her hotel room, with her virtually naked, he kissed her as though she were an *objet d'art* that he desperately wanted to explore. His lips separated hers, his tongue danced against hers, his mouth was warm, like his fingers, and yet he was careful not to overwhelm her. Even when she wanted to be overwhelmed.

Frustration stretched inside her. She didn't want him to treat her like a fragile vase; she wanted to be treated like a red-blooded woman, thick with desire and needs that only he could assuage.

'Touch me,' she demanded, remembering the skill he'd shown in the bar the previous night. Before he'd known that she'd been hurt, that she was, in so many ways, fragile and vulnerable. 'Show me what I've been missing.'

He groaned into her mouth and she felt it again—that duality of Zeus. What he wanted, and what he thought he should be. Well, she was giving him permission to go with the former. He knew she had boundaries. He was the one who'd acknowledged those boundaries by laying it out: they weren't going to have sex tonight. But that didn't mean they couldn't do other things.

'I'm begging you,' she said against his mouth. 'Touch me. Make me feel like you did last night. Please.'

And on that last, desperate plea, his body shuddered and something inside him seemed to snap, because he dropped to his knees then, his hands on her hips shifting to the lace of her panties and loosening them, pulling them down her legs, so she could step out of them. At the same time she kicked her shoes off and stood before him completely undressed.

One of his hands came behind her and clasped over her rear, holding her where she was as his mouth teased the sensitive flesh at the top of her legs, flicking her inner thigh until she was trembling and flushed with heat, and then he was pushing her backwards, towards the wall, as if he somehow understood that she needed more support. One of his hands came between her legs, spreading them wider, and then his mouth was on her sex, his tongue flicking her, teasing her, making her cry out because she'd never been kissed like this before. She knew oral sex was a thing, but it was not something she'd ever imagined she would want to have done to her, nor that it could feel this good.

In fact, she hadn't known *anything* could feel this good. Her hands tore through his hair as madness seemed to saturate her soul, and then his fingers were there, too, pressing against her clitoris, moving faster, while his mouth shifted to the flatness of her stomach, kissing, tasting, and then his fingers were inside her and her hips were bucking hard as the waves of pleasure he'd built became almost too much to bear.

'Zeus,' she cried his name, then swore in an uncharacteristic gesture, because she was completely overwhelmed. He glanced up at her with a question in his eyes and she nodded her reassurance. 'Please, don't stop,' she groaned, half laughed, then cried out again as he returned his mouth to her, his fingers still buried in her depths, so the sensory overload was immense.

'I'm—I feel—I'm—' But she couldn't explain what was happening to her; she only knew that it was the best feeling in the world. Her whole body trembled and tingled, her nipples seemed to throb and ache, her knees were weak, her body was sheened in perspiration, and just the sight of him, between her legs, was sending her tumbling down a rabbit hole that she wondered if she'd ever find her way out of. Her body exploded with an all-consuming ferocity, a feeling she wanted to bottle and keep forever. Waves of it kept washing over her until she couldn't think straight, and her breathing was rushed and her voice hoarse. She stood there, grateful beyond words for the support of the wall, and the way his hand was clamped at her hip to stop her from sliding sideways. Her breathing was rushed, as though she'd run a marathon.

He stood, and before she could regain her breath, he was kissing her. Not slowly and inquisitively this time, not as though she were something fragile he was afraid of breaking, but with all the hunger and passion he'd just stirred. Kissing her as though she were the meaning to everything on this earth. Lifting her as though she weighed nothing, cradling her against his chest, kissing her still as he strode, long and confident, through the hotel room corridor and deeper into her suite. The bedroom was to the right; he found it easily and placed her on the bed but didn't leave.

Oh, no.

He came down on top of her, kissing her, so his weight was on her and for a moment, a moment that shocked her because it had no place here, with them, an old feeling of suffocating and being helpless and afraid, came back, so she froze. He must have perceived her stillness, because he stopped kissing her immediately and pushed up onto his elbows, relieving her of his weight.

Disappointment was sharper than relief, because Zeus wasn't Steven, and this was not that night.

He stroked her cheek, and her heart twisted. 'Okay?'

She nodded.

He arched a brow, as if he didn't believe her.

'Really,' she promised. She pushed up onto her elbows, so she could kiss him again, and this time, when he relaxed down on top of her, she was capable only of enjoying the pleasure of their bodies being melded together like this, the heat of him, the strength of him. Her hands roamed his back, the curve of his toned bottom, her nails digging in there, before she crept her hands higher and pulled his shirt from his waistband so that her fingertips could connect with the bare flesh of his back.

He hissed again and pushed away from her, this time fully off the bed, jackknifing away from Jane as though she'd detonated a bomb between them.

'What is it?' she asked, on her elbows once more so she could see him better. And she could *see*, very clearly, how turned on he was by what they'd been doing.

'Don't do that.'

'What?' Her eyes widened in surprise. Had she done something wrong?

'I'm holding on by a thread,' he muttered apologetically. 'When you touch me…'

'Oh.' Pleasure made her smile. 'I'm glad to hear I'm not alone in that department.'

He grimaced. 'You said you wanted coffee?'

'Coffee?' She pulled a face. 'Believe me, that's the last thing on my mind.'

'A cold shower?'

She laughed. 'Nope.'

'Jane—'

'Come here.' She patted the bed beside her, but he stayed where he was. 'What if,' she said, thinking aloud, 'I promise not to touch you?'

His eyes flared.

'But you can touch me,' she said slowly, seductively. 'Anywhere, any way you want to.'

His Adam's apple throbbed.

'No sex,' she reiterated, because he was right: that was a step she wanted to think about. And be completely sober for. Even though she'd only had two glasses of bubbles with dinner, her experience with Steven had been traumatising enough to know she would only ever make that choice when she could 100 percent trust her judgement.

'I've never met anyone like you,' he said, but to her immense relief he began to stride back towards the bed—and her.

'I think that might be mutual,' she confessed, swallowing a sigh as he sat beside her and then kissed her hard, fast and hungrily, just how she wanted him to be with her.

CHAPTER SIX

FOR THE SECOND night in a row, Zeus couldn't sleep. It had been hard enough the night before, when they'd kissed in the bar, but after everything that had happened between them in her hotel—and what specifically *hadn't* happened—he had a raging hard-on and an insatiable need for a woman he hadn't even known for seventy-two hours.

Right when he needed to be his most pragmatic self, it was like the universe, or fates, had conspired to send him a vixen—a woman who pushed *all* of his buttons. Sexy, beautiful, intelligent and vulnerable, so that he felt those warrior instincts he'd honed during his mother's cancer fight burst back to life. Even when he'd told himself he'd never care enough about another human to want to fight their battles for them. Even when he knew the cost of caring too deeply for anyone.

As the sun began to creep towards the cityscape, Zeus gave up on even attempting to sleep, slipped into a pair of shorts, a T-shirt and some joggers and let himself out of his mansion. Running had long been a balm to his busy mind, a way to not only calm his thoughts but, more importantly, to also bring order to them.

It wasn't like being attracted to a woman was new. Zeus had made an artform out of the three-night stand.

One night was too short—he liked to get to know the women he slept with. Anything more than three nights was way too long, because he didn't like to risk caring too much about them.

Until Jane, he'd never found it hard to live by that creed.

He supposed he bored easily. Or perhaps the women he'd been dating had been wrong for him, in terms of being able to hold his attention. Except, wasn't that exactly what he'd been aiming for? To be able to enjoy a woman's company for a brief while, then walk away without a backwards glance?

Something crept up his spine and left the hairs on the back of his neck standing on end, because when he imagined walking away from Jane, he didn't feel as though it would be easy, and he didn't feel as though he'd be prepared to do it in two nights' time. Which surely gave him all the more reason to do precisely that.

She was dangerous to him—he'd thought that before. He'd known it from their first meeting. She was *too* beautiful, too sexy, too alluring, too vulnerable, too everything, and suddenly, all of Zeus's carefully laid boundaries were being pulled at and weakened by a woman he knew virtually nothing about.

Except, he did know that she wasn't planning to be in Athens long-term. He did know that she was as committed to her career as he was to his. And he did know that getting married was as imperative now as it had been since his father told him about his half-sister.

Every day without a marriage licence being procured was a day closer to the risk of losing the company. Was he seriously willing to take the chance of waking up one day to find that he was no longer in the box seat to inherit the Papandreo Group? Of course not. The business was so much more than just a business to Zeus; it had to remain his.

Unless there was a way he could meet his half-sister, he thought, pausing midstride and standing still, hands on hips, breath rushed, as he stared out at the dawn-lit city.

He didn't *want* to meet her. He didn't want to come face-to-face with the evidence of his father's failings. But maybe he could offer her something to get rid of the threat altogether. Money. Enough money to make her realise that the company itself wouldn't be worth fighting for.

Except, what fool would take a lump sum, rather than the ongoing cash cow of the Papandreo Group? Was it worth making the offer, on the basis she *might* accept? Or did it risk exposing to her how badly he wanted to retain his position? And once she knew that, might she fight harder to secure the windfall she'd only just learned about?

He made a gruff sound of irritation, wishing he knew *something* about the woman his father had conceived behind his mother's back and realising, belatedly, that he *could* find out a little more about her. His skin slicked with something like distaste. He was not a man who would ordinarily engage the services of a private investigator, but surely, this was a time for desperate measures. To protect his business, his family's legacy and empire, to do the right thing for people who couldn't see clearly enough to do it for themselves, he thought, breaking into a run once more.

Yes, he committed to the idea, as he turned the corner towards his home, five miles later. He would hire a detective, he would find out more about what he was dealing with and then, if necessary, he'd explain the situation to Philomena and ask if she'd be willing to be his wife of convenience.

Jane would be, by then, a moot point, because she would have to be. Unlike his father, Zeus intended to take his marriage vows seriously, even if that meant turning his back on a woman who had very quickly become the sum total of what he wanted in his day.

Though she felt exhausted, Jane woke early the next morning. There was a restlessness inside her, a sense of impatience, and despite the way Zeus had worshipped her body the night before, Jane had woken up in the early hours wanting *more*. So. Much. More.

Snatches of memories filtered through her mind as she showered, lathering her still-too-sensitive body with a loofah and soap, revelling in the feeling of the water cascading over her head. Afterwards, she contemplated ordering room service—she was also famished—but decided instead to set out on foot and explore more of this city.

To walk.

To burn off her abundance of energy and try to put Zeus out of her mind.

She dressed in a pair of shorts and a singlet top, in preparation for a day that promised to be hot and grabbed a cap on her way out of the hotel room—she had no idea how long she'd be gone for, and her skin had a tendency to fry.

Not two blocks from the hotel, she stopped at a quaint little *kafenio*, with white chairs spilling out onto the street.

She ordered her usual oat latte and added a toasted flatbread with saganaki, spinach and eggplant. It arrived steaming hot, and she sat down to enjoy it, content to watch the world pass her by.

It was a sense of contentment that didn't last long.

Last night, in a fog of sensual need, of white-hot lust, she'd thrown herself headlong into the maddening rush of desire. She hadn't allowed herself to dwell on the consequences nor the complications of what they were doing. But as the sun rose and bathed Athens in a glorious golden hue—a colour that somehow seemed to echo the vagaries of time, imprinting this city's ancient presence on Jane—she was forced to see what had happened with all the shock that broad daylight could bring.

She bit into the flatbread, the gooey, melted cheese perfectly salty and dribbling a little from the edge. She wiped it absent-mindedly with her finger, focusing on a man across the street who was stacking newspapers into a vending machine.

After that night with Steven, she'd awoken groggy, hungover and sore all over. Muscles she'd never used before had screamed their complaint as she'd pushed out of the unfamiliar bed and looked around, trying desperately to get her bearings. Bruises across her torso, hickeys on her thigh, only very briefly preceded the onslaught of memories. Awful, awful memories. A feeling of having been totally out of control, unable to properly express what she was feeling and what she wanted—for it to stop.

This was different.

This morning Jane had woken with clarity and recollection. She didn't regret what had happened between her and Zeus, and she wanted *more* of it, and him. But she also needed a clear path forward. A way to do this without betraying her own sense of right and wrong, with regards to her promise to Lottie.

She closed her eyes and inhaled the fragrance of her coffee, wishing that it could somehow, magically, give her the guidance she sought.

Three days ago, she would have sworn that nothing and nobody would ever change what she owed Lottie and what Lottie meant to her. And the same was true this morning, she swore. But entering into an intentionally manipulative flirtation with Zeus Papandreo was so much more complicated now she knew him.

And liked him.

She dropped her head in shame, and her heart began to trot in a rhythm all its own.

Yes, she liked him.

He was nothing like she'd expected. At least, not in the ways that mattered. While he was confident, he wasn't arrogant. He was proud, but not unreasonably so, and he was so much more courteous and considerate than his reputation foreshadowed.

She took another bite of the sandwich, her features a study in misery.

If she told Lottie what was happening, would Lottie understand and perhaps tell her to come home? And then what? Would she just fly away from Zeus without giving him an explanation? And could she even bear to do that? Did she *want* to leave him?

No.

She wanted to stay and explore this to its fullest.

Last night she'd told herself this would be like killing two birds with one stone, only so much happier than killing. She could explore this with Zeus and get Lottie what Lottie wanted, and no one ever had to know how disastrously conflicted she'd felt about it all.

But what about Zeus? What about the business he obviously loved? Could she really live with being an instrument in his losing that? And if not, what did that mean for Lottie? She knew what this meant to her best friend—what it was supposed to mean to both of them.

She groaned, placing the sandwich back on the cardboard tray and gingerly wiping her fingertips together. There was no way to extricate herself from this situation without hurting someone. Lottie or Zeus. Lottie, her best friend of more than a decade, a woman who was more like a sister to her than anything else, clearly should have the biggest stake on her heart. And on her heart, she did. But her obligations? Her conscience?

She picked up her takeaway coffee cup and began to walk, frowning deeply, so she missed the hue of peach and pink that lit the sky as the sun grew higher, missed the purples, too, that reached out like long, magical fingers, directly across the horizon. She walked a long way, down a wide, straight street lined with large, verdant trees. She walked until her body was sheened in perspiration and then pulled her phone out to check the time, only to see several text messages on the front screen.

Lottie's required her attention first. I miss you! X

Guilt brightened the flush in her cheeks. The next message was from her mother.

Are you coming to the races next weekend? We have a box.

Jane rolled her eyes. For a long time, Jane had held little value to her parents, but now, an intelligent graduate who had morphed into a doppelgänger of the elegant Mrs Fisher, Jane was suddenly a worthwhile accessory for certain society events. She clicked out of that message and then, with a fluttering in her chest, tapped into Zeus's.

Can I see you tonight?

Her heart went from fluttering to exploding and she stepped sideways so she could lean against a building for support. Never mind that it was covered in years of dust and grime and Jane was wearing pale clothes. In that moment, she needed help just to stay standing.

She thought about what to respond with. Could he see her? There was nothing she wanted more.

And *that* was the problem.

It was all happening too fast, getting too intense, starting to *mean* too much. They needed to put the brakes on, slow it all right down, make it more casual, more fun. Maybe then she'd be able to live with herself for intentionally plotting his professional downfall.

She groaned and shook her head, hating what she'd agreed to suddenly.

She clicked out of his text and into Lottie's.

We need to talk. Call me when you're free.

She began to walk once more, her stride long and intent. Coffee finished, she discarded the cup in a nearby wastebin, then turned and looked around, realising that she'd wandered without paying attention and had no idea how to get back to the hotel. She lifted her phone from her pocket and saw another text from Zeus.

No pressure.

Her heart rolled over in her chest.

If only he knew how untrue that was! Jane was under the kind of pressure that could fell a person. She needed to speak to Lottie. She loaded a map up and began to walk towards her hotel, willing her phone to ring, and for it to be her best friend on the other end. Wishing, more than anything, that in speaking to Lottie, she'd somehow know exactly how to proceed.

Zeus was getting used to 'firsts' with Jane, and that afternoon he recognised another one.

It was the first time he'd messaged a woman and not heard back almost instantly. The first time he'd sent *multiple* messages and had them be ignored.

He vacillated between irritation and concern for the better part of the day. Irritation with himself, and with her. Irritation that he felt completely unlike normal and desperately didn't like it. Irritation with her for the power she somehow wielded over him.

Concern, because last night had been intense. True, they hadn't slept together, but he'd enjoyed stirring her to a fever pitch. He'd revelled in the power he held in that moment over her, to make her whimper and thrash, to make her body explode, and he'd driven her wild again, and again and again, until she was so exhausted she could hardly keep her eyes open. Then, he'd lifted her higher into the bed, covered her with the blankets and kissed her forehead before letting himself, and his rock-hard arousal, out.

Only a promise to himself that he'd see her again soon had allowed him to leave at all. He'd sized up the sofa and considered sleeping there, just so he'd be able to pick up where they'd left off in the morning.

Maybe it was because he was on the brink of making a commitment to someone else. It was possible that the knowledge a marriage was imminent for Zeus was making his brain and body perceive Jane as more special somehow than she really was. But even as he thought that Hail Mary, he knew it was a false hope, because the way he felt for Jane had everything to do with her, and nothing to do with the arcane inheritance surrounding the company.

He stood from his desk angrily and strode across the expansive office, staring out at the landscape of Athens' central business district. It was a view that usually puffed his chest with pride. He loved this city; he loved his family's contributions to both it and the broader landscape of Greece. He was a Papandreo, and in taking over the running of the company, Zeus was carrying on a proud, important tradition.

Not once had he questioned the righteousness of that.

But his father's stupidity and weakness had put everything in jeopardy. Now guilt was making the older man weak in an even worse way than infidelity: he was being reckless with the business. He was willing to bring in an outsider to run it, never mind her lack of experience and the fact she was his bastard daughter with God only knew who.

Zeus's entire world was shattering, just like it had

again and again as a boy, a teenager and finally, for good when his mother had died. Though by then, he'd hardened his heart to her loss, knowing that it was coming, accepting that he was powerless to save her, and that he would not make her pain worse by showing his grief. He wouldn't burden her with that; he was brave, to the end.

Breathing in deeply, so his chest stretched and flooded with air, he turned his back on the view and stalked back to his desk, reaching for his phone. No replies, still.

Grinding his teeth, he picked up his phone to make a call, but not to Jane. If only to prove to himself that he was still in control of his life, that he wasn't as utterly and completely at her beck and call as he feared he might be.

'Finally,' Jane groaned down the line, sinking into the sumptuous sofa of her hotel suite and staring out at the windows. 'I've been waiting for you to ring.'

'Sorry, I was on a flight.'

'To where?'

'That doesn't matter.' Lottie sounded harried, though. 'Is everything okay?'

'Fine. What's up?'

Jane frowned. 'I—' But now that it came to it, she struggled to find the words. How could she tell her best friend that the man they'd always, always hated was the most deliciously sexy person on earth? And that he also happened to be kind and interesting...? It felt like a betrayal of the highest order, and so she cast about for how to begin.

'Is it Zeus?' Lottie demanded. 'Are you okay?'

'I'm... Yes. Of course. Why?'

Lottie expelled a long breath. 'I just— I've been worrying that maybe I sent you on a quest to the lion's den. I couldn't live with myself if he hurt you, too, Jane.'

Jane squeezed her eyes shut, unsure how to confess that she feared she was the one who would be hurting *everyone* if she wasn't very careful.

'He's not going to hurt me,' she promised, and found the words were spoken with confidence.

'God, I hope not. I wouldn't trust him as far as I could throw him.'

'He's not like we thought, Lottie.'

Silence sparked. A silence that Jane perceived, because she knew Lottie as well as she did herself, was loaded and important.

'Oh?'

Jane bit back a groan. 'He's actually quite…nice.'

Nice! What a weak, watery word to describe Zeus Papandreo.

'At least, he's not the complete piece of work we'd always presumed.'

'I beg your pardon. No one who goes through women like that is *nice*.'

Jane chewed on her lower lip. 'I'm not saying he's perfect—'

'You hardly know him,' Lottie pointed out. 'You've only been in Athens a few nights.'

'I know,' she said, wondering why inwardly she rebelled against that as a concept. Hardly knew him? It didn't seem to come close to describing their relationship. 'I guess I just have a sense for…'

'Listen,' Lottie interrupted. 'Nice or not, he's my sworn enemy, and you're my bestest friend.' Her tone was joking, but Jane didn't smile. 'I want that company, and his father—Aristotle—has given me the perfect way to get it. To rip it out from *both* of them. It's not about Zeus. It's about my mother, what they took from her, took from me. It's about payback. It's about what I deserve.'

A single tear slid down Jane's cheek, because Lottie wasn't wrong, either. Jane knew what the secret affair had done to Lottie's mother, who'd never stopped loving Aristotle, even though she did her best to hide it. 'I know,' she whispered.

'Oh, God, Jane. You're crying. What's happened? Please tell me… I can't bear for you to get hurt.'

'It's just— I want you to have everything you want, Lottie, you know that. But…'

'You don't want to hurt him.'

She squeezed her eyes shut.

'You're too kind,' Lottie groaned. 'Look, he'll get over it. He'll get over you.'

'But not losing the business,' she said, remembering the pride in his features when he spoke of his place in the Papandreo legacy. Only that night, she'd hated him for his pride, because it had been stolen from Lottie. Now? It was intrinsic to him.

She toyed with the fabric hem of her shorts.

'He'll still be worth a stinking fortune,' Lottie pointed out. 'He can rebuild, do something else. He can use the same damned name for all I care.'

Jane swallowed past a bitter lump in her throat. Loyalty to Lottie was her principal duty, but only just.

'Let me put it this way,' Lottie continued. 'What do you think he'll do if he gets married before me?'

Jane stared across the room in silence.

'Do you think he'll give one iota of thought about me?'

Jane scrunched her eyes closed.

'Of course he won't. He'll take his triumph, his ownership of all things Papandreo, and that will be the end of it.' Lottie's voice stung, and Jane understood why. This was about so much more than the company. Lottie had been wronged her whole life by these people, even though Jane couldn't have said with certainty if Zeus had even known about her. The effect was the same. Lottie had grown up believing herself to be a shameful secret, seeing hurt in her mother's face and heart, knowing herself to be, in some way, an instrument of that. And if, or rather when, Zeus married, he would, Jane had no doubt, shut down any legal recourse Lottie had to staking a claim on the business.

'I'll stay for a week,' she said on a soft, tortured sigh. 'One week, to give you a head start. After that, I'm leaving Athens, and Zeus, and I don't ever want to hear his name again, okay?'

'A week?' Lottie groaned but quickly cut herself off. 'A week,' she repeated with much more strength. 'Okay, okay. I can work with that.'

Jane grimaced. 'Lottie…maybe there's a way you can have some of the company, but not all.'

'Are you actually suggesting I compromise with those bastards?'

Jane sighed softly. She had been, but she should have known better. She'd witnessed the hatred Lottie felt for them—up until very recently, Jane had felt it, too.

'No.'

'Look, take care of yourself,' Lottie begged. 'I know I've asked you to do a lot. I know how hard it is for someone like you to be, I guess, kind of ruthless, but for me, can you just *try*?'

She nodded unevenly, then remembered Lottie couldn't see her. 'One week,' she promised, and disconnected the call with a thud in the region of her chest.

One week was a slight head start to Lottie, but not a huge disadvantage to Zeus, either. And it did give her the safety to see him again, without worrying about how to extricate herself. She flicked her phone screen to life and loaded up Zeus's text messages.

How about dinner tonight? I can come to you...

CHAPTER SEVEN

HE'D CHOSEN ANOTHER glamorous restaurant, absolutely packed to the rafters with stunning A-listers, and it was clear that Zeus was well known here. Not because he was Zeus Papandreo, but because he was a regular at places like this, in this scene.

Jane regarded him across their small table, her head tilted slightly to the side, her heart in her throat. Maybe Lottie had been right. Maybe Zeus was just like they'd always thought, and it was Jane who was layering more humanity and decency over him than he actually possessed. But the way he'd kissed her forehead the night before and crept out, rather than trying to push his advantage and hop into bed with her, had been nothing if not chivalrous. Not to mention the way he'd made her feel...

'I have to tell you something,' she blurted out. He leaned closer, eyes boring into hers, making every part of her feel seen and exposed.

'That sounds ominous.' His voice, though, was relaxed. Casual. Easy-going. As though he didn't care, one way or another. About her, or whatever she was about to say. Jane frowned. Was it possible she'd been wrong about the intensity of this? She'd slept with one man, once. She'd been celibate ever since. Suddenly, she'd met someone who made her feel as though her knickers had caught fire; maybe it was the most natural thing in the world that she'd overlay those feelings with something more.

Something more than just casual attraction.

'Oh, it's no big deal.' She tried to mirror his tone. 'I've just had a change of plans. I'm heading home next week.'

Something flashed in his eyes. Something that she could have sworn was an emotion, but what? It didn't last long enough to even try to analyse it; a moment later, he was all suave and in control once more. 'What changed?' Casual enquiry, nothing more.

'A job,' she lied. 'I got an email today, so I'm heading back.'

'Another charity?'

She thought quickly. 'One I've worked at before.' God, she hated lying to him, though. In fact, she hated lying in general, but to Zeus, it felt like an awful betrayal. Still, this was how it had to be. She needed to put an end to this without letting Lottie down completely. A week was the best compromise she could offer.

'Okay,' he replied, nodding. But then his eyes sparked when they met hers, and he leaned across the table. 'Do you get seasick?'

She stared at him, the question coming completely out of left field. 'Erm, not that I know of.'

'What do you say about a week on my yacht, then?'

Her eyes widened. 'What?'

'We can explore the Med, all the little islands to the south. And more importantly, we can explore each other.'

Her whole body was screaming at her to say yes. It was more tempting than she could put into words. But her brain was kicking and shouting, because a week on his yacht was just the kind of vulnerability that she'd learned to avoid like the plague. She would be completely at his whim, completely at his command. If she was wrong about him, and he wasn't trustworthy and decent, then what?

Only, she wasn't wrong.

She knew that.

In a way she'd never felt about Steven, she fundamentally understood Zeus, and knew that, just as he'd said, he'd never hurt her.

A week on his yacht. A week away from Athens. Away from his business. A week where she could pretend it was just him, and her, and all the reasons she had for meeting him in the first place didn't exist. A sneaky little cheat, a bubble, a break from agonising over what she should do. Because a week on his yacht had a definitive beginning, a middle and an end, and when that end came, he would drop her back in a port, she'd get to a plane and go home, away from him, and the most beautifully complicated, utterly addictive man and situation she'd ever known.

'I say yes,' she whispered, and then she smiled, because in the midst of her angsting a solution had come that just made sense. 'Yes, yes, yes.' And they both laughed as though neither had a care in the world.

Another first, he thought, as later that night his driver deposited them at the marina. Having been to her hotel, waiting for Jane to pack up her things, his patience was at an all-time low. He wanted to be alone with her, more than he could say.

It wasn't like they'd be completely alone on the yacht—there was a full-time captain, a cook and a housekeeper, but it was more than big enough for the staff to have their own quarters, leaving Zeus and Jane free to explore one another, just as he'd promised.

Promised on a whim. Without any forethought or planning. Promised because she'd thrown a date at him that seemed too soon for how much he enjoyed her company. And yet, he'd felt relief, most of all. Because she was going, and when Jane left, everything in his life would be so much simpler. Without her here to crave, he would simply move on, refocus on Philomena, or someone like her. A sensible, easy-going wife who would be just as pragmatic about the union as he'd be, who would never threaten his independence or equilibrium. At some point, the matter of children would become an issue, but that was also a pragmatic decision, and he intended to foreshadow it with whomever he married.

Until then, he had a week with Jane, and he intended to enjoy every damned minute of that week, until she was out of his system once and for all. It wasn't normal to obsess over someone like this. It sure as hell wasn't normal for Zeus. But he wasn't worried. A week gave them time, and at the end of it, no matter what, he'd let her go and focus on the thing that mattered most to him in the world: securing his future as sole owner of the Papandreo Group. Jane was just a blip in his life, and after this week, he'd remember that.

It probably wasn't even really about Jane. At least, not completely. Three months ago, his mother had died. After more than a decade of preparing for it, of knowing it was coming, it had still fractured parts of him he hadn't realised could be touched any longer. Then, two weeks ago, his father had told him about his affair, about the daughter he'd fathered and financially supported all her life. And there'd been such longing in Aristotle's face, such regret, that Zeus had known that the older man wasn't going to let it go, either. As far as he was concerned, that was his daughter, as much as Zeus was his son. A muscle jerked in his jaw as angry defiance surged through him.

All the touchstones of his life were shaking—as if a large earthquake were persistently rumbling the foundations of his existence. And then there was Jane. A light in the dark. A distraction from everything. A reprieve.

After this week, he'd have to face reality. He'd have to get serious about shoring up his position in the company. He'd have to marry. For the first time, contemplating that brought an acrid taste to his mouth and he ground his teeth, wishing he could rebel against the provision of the company's founding documents.

Except...

Were it not for that provision, Aristotle's love child would have an even greater claim on all things Papandreo, wouldn't she? At least the provision gave a black-and-white requirement of ownership. He tried not to imagine her. He knew nothing about her yet—he was still waiting on information from the detective he'd hired—but he supposed it would not be difficult for anyone to propose a marriage like the one he was intending on offering to Philomena. Autonomy, independence, freedom, unimaginable wealth and, one day, a child, when the time was right. What if she'd already found someone willing to undertake marriage on those terms?

A bead of perspiration formed at the nape of his neck, but he refused to give in to that now.

He was here, with Jane, and he was going to damn

well enjoy the week. After that, he'd put everything in motion for the rest of his life. A life without Jane in it.

'Let me guess,' she murmured, looking at the boats in the marina, a fingertip pressed to her perfectly shaped lips, so the unpleasantness of his thoughts evaporated on a sharp wave of need. 'Yours is—' she scanned the line of craft '—that one.'

She pointed to a reasonably sized boat with a gleaming 'P' on the side. 'No, that's the Petrakises'.'

'Oh.' She frowned, went back to looking and then her eyes widened when they landed on a boat so much larger than the others that it almost didn't register at first. 'Not that one?'

He saw the amazement on her features and laughed. 'You'd prefer to bob around at sea in one of these?' He gestured to the small boats in front of them.

'I'm not complaining.' She winked, all beautifully confident and charming, so his gut twisted sharply as his cells seemed to tighten.

'I'm glad. I'd hate to disappoint you.'

'That seems unlikely.'

He grinned, reaching down and taking her hand. 'Shall we?'

Of course, the yacht wasn't just enormous, but also incredibly luxuriously appointed, from the gleaming white accents to the shining timber features, and walls of glass that showed the ocean to best advantage. The moon bounced off the marina and the other boats as the captain readied the Papandreo yacht for departure, and Zeus left Jane alone a moment to speak with his crew. The driver of his car had unpacked her bags—Zeus, she presumed, had his own things on board already, for he brought nothing. And then, while Zeus was still absent, the yacht began to move, pushing back carefully from the pontoon and drifting into the clear water behind the rows of yachts, executing a perfect manoeuvre that enabled them to be pointing towards the Saronic Gulf.

Overhead, stars glittered brightly against a sky that was all black velvet, and Jane sighed a happy, contented sigh as the boat seemed to glide atop the water with effortless ease.

She was so focused on the boat's journey that she didn't notice Zeus's approach. It was only when he came to stand behind her and slid his hands around her waist, eased her hair over one shoulder so he could press his lips to the sensitive flesh in the curve of her neck, and she shivered. Not from cold, but from a total bodily awareness of him. A need that was in overdrive. It was as though being here, on the open water, somehow freed her from all restraint. Not just of the conundrum of her deception, but of the hurts of her past. Finally, for the first time in years, she felt almost liberated from the shadow of what Steven had done to her, of how he'd made her feel.

She felt, simply, free.

She turned slowly, smiling, unaware of the way the silver light of the moon caught her face and made it shimmer, the way her eyes sparkled, and her hair seemed to glow. 'Tell me something,' she prompted, linking her hands behind his back.

'Anything.'

Her heart trembled with a rush of power. 'Anything? Hmm. Perhaps I'll change my question, then.'

His gaze roamed her face in a way that pulled at her stomach. 'What would you like to know, *agapiméni*?'

'Your name,' she said. 'It's kind of unique.'

He grinned. 'You don't think it suits me?'

'On the contrary, there is something kind of godlike about you,' she murmured, then laughed at his raised brows. 'You have this kind of…all-powerful vibe going on.'

'Do I?'

She nodded.

'In what way?'

'Fishing for compliments?'

'Curious as to how you see me.'

'Well, like the fact you're happy to let me call the shots with what happens between us, erm, physically.' She glanced over his shoulder, cheeks flushing with warmth. 'I think a lot of guys would have egos that were too fragile for that.'

'Maybe you haven't been involved with the right kind of men before,' he said gently, though, so her heart trembled. The boat glided out of the marina fully and into the bay. She leaned back against the railing, eyes hooked to Zeus's face.

'Well, that's definitely true.'

'Including the man who hurt you?' he prompted, his tone light, but she felt the push of his enquiry, his desire to know and understand her.

'Definitely him,' she murmured.

'And since him?'

She shook her head a little. 'No one serious.'

His eyes bore into hers like beams. 'Why not?'

She stilled. The feeling of freedom wavered a little.

Her throat tightened. She blinked away from Zeus, but he squeezed her waist. 'He can't hurt you anymore.'

She shook her head. 'It's not that.'

'You don't want to talk about it?'

She shook her head. 'I don't want to think about him,' she said, pulling a face. 'He's ruined enough of my life. I'm not going to let him ruin this, too.'

'Jane…' His hand moved over her hip gently. 'What did he do to you?'

She opened her mouth to tell him she *really* wanted to talk about something else, but then her eyes found his and something strange happened. Something powerful and altering. She looked at him and felt that bubble of freedom again, or rather, a bridge to freedom.

Maybe talking about it would help? Maybe talking about it was what she needed? Lottie was the only person she'd spoken to about it in the past, and even then she'd found it hard to give more than a cursory explanation as to what had happened. She'd lived with a sense of all-consuming shame and grief, rather than admit how awful it had all been.

'We were dating,' she said with a rise of her shoulders. A breeze lifted off the ocean, so her hair shifted around her face, and she smelled the salt of the sea and the sweetness of her conditioner. Zeus caught the blond hairs and tamed them behind one of her ears, his hand remaining at her shoulder. Warm, silently encouraging her to continue. 'I met him through a mutual friend, and I liked him straight away. I was seventeen, he was older, so naturally, I thought he was way, way cooler than me,' she said with a hint of self-deprecating humour, even though it wasn't remotely funny. 'A lot of my friends had started seeing guys, hooking up at parties. I kind of felt weird that I wasn't into hooking up or whatever.'

'You were only seventeen,' he pointed out.

She pulled a face. 'I somehow suspect you'd already notched up some experience by that age.'

His jaw tightened a little. 'Not as much as you'd think.'

'Really?'

'My mother wasn't well. It took a lot of my focus.'

'Oh, gosh. I'm sorry.'

He nodded once, dismissively. She felt his pain, though, and moved a little closer to him. He was so warm, so strong, being this close did something to her insides. Somehow, just his proximity flooded her with those qualities, too—warmth and strength—as though they were completely contagious.

'Anyway,' she continued. 'I met him and liked him. He was funny and handsome, smart, and I guess he gave me the one thing I'd been missing.'

Zeus waited quietly.

'Attention. He made me feel as though I was the centre of his world.' She shook her head with frustration at how stupid and trusting she'd been. 'I took everything at face value. I really thought he loved me.'

'He didn't?'

She shook her head. 'I doubt it.'

'Why?'

'After…that night,' she said on a soft exhalation, 'he was so…'

'What happened that night?' Zeus asked, and now his voice had a gruff urgency to it that pulled at her and made her whole body seem as though it were flying.

'It was another party. We'd all been drinking. A lot.

And I didn't really drink much at all, so you can imagine how a few glasses of champagne would have gone to my head, let alone the bottle or so I had. He kept bringing me drinks,' she muttered, back in time now, in that awful night. But somehow, the sting of it had faded, and talking to Zeus seemed to be taking away the last vestiges of power of that night to wound her. She marvelled at that, revelled in the sensation of freedom, even as she continued speaking. 'I'd told him I wasn't ready for—sex. I wasn't. I liked him. I thought I even loved him, but I didn't want to just have sex with him. I wasn't ready,' she repeated, as though Zeus understanding that was fundamentally important.

'Which was always your decision and right,' he said. Like he had a hotwire into her brain and knew *just* what to say.

'I started to feel a little sick. So much champagne,' she muttered. 'He said he'd find somewhere quiet for me to lie down.'

Zeus swore, darkness crossing his handsome features. 'Go on.' But the words were muted, as if uttered through gritted teeth, and she realised that this was hurting him, more than it was her.

'I'm okay, Zeus. It was a long time ago,' she assured him, softly.

'Go on,' he repeated as if he had braced himself for the rest and now needed to hear it.

She expelled a shaking breath. 'I don't remember a lot of it. The room was dark,' she said, voice trembling. 'His hands were rough.' She swallowed past a lump in her throat. 'I told him "no." I'm sure of it, though he disagreed the next day.'

Zeus nodded once, his lips held so tightly they were white rimmed. But his touch was gentle, his eyes sympathetic.

'I didn't want it to happen. I know that much. He was heavy on top of me. He smelt of beer and sweat. And it hurt. I think I passed out. I don't know.' And even though she felt somehow liberated from the memory, tears sparkled on her lashes now. She blinked away. 'So that was my first—and only—time.'

He was quiet and still for what seemed an age. The hum of the boat formed a background noise; the splashing of the waves against the sides of the craft occasionally flicked them with tiny droplets of salted water, but really, it was just the two of them, in the sort of bubble that was formed by the sharing of one's deepest secrets.

Then Zeus lifted his hands to her cheeks, cupped her face gently, holding her steady, his own body so powerful and large but not at all scary or intimidating. 'You were raped, Jane,' he said, stroking her cheek with his thumb. 'You were raped by someone you cared for, someone you trusted. It's the most natural thing in the world that you have carried that wound with you all these years.'

She opened her mouth to dispute what he'd said. *Rape* sounded so jarring, so violent, but of course, that was exactly what had happened to her. She hadn't consented to sleeping with Steven; she hadn't even been *able* to consent, given how drunk she'd been. He took what he wanted, regardless of how that impacted her.

A tear slid down her cheek. Not a tear of sadness, but rather relief, because she felt not only seen by Zeus, but also accepted. Understood. Valued.

'Have you spoken to someone?'

'Other than you?' she asked, the attempt at humour falling flat. Neither of them was in a humorous mood.

'A therapist. Someone qualified to help you.'

'No,' she whispered. 'It took me a long time to accept what had happened. Longer still to tell anyone—my best friend—about that night. I just couldn't... I felt...'

He waited, patiently.

'I blamed myself,' she whispered, shaking her head, squeezing her eyes shut.

'But you know now that you weren't to blame.' He said it as a statement, but she knew he was asking her.

She bit into her lower lip. 'I know that if the same thing had happened to my best friend, I would say exactly that to her. It's not your fault. It's just hard to look back on that night without regret. Why did I drink so much? Why did I go into a room with him? Why didn't I fight harder?'

'You shouldn't have had to fight. You trusted him. You loved him. He took advantage of your youth, your love, your inexperience, your drunkenness, your trust. It was a brutal betrayal. By every metric, this was his fault, not yours.'

She knew that. Of course she did. But understanding something academically didn't always equate to how one felt. She nodded slowly, anyway, because she couldn't fault his logic.

'I presume you didn't press charges?'

She shook her head. 'I wish I had, if only to stop him from doing the same thing to someone else,' she muttered. 'But it took me too long to process it all myself, let alone going to the police. And when I confronted him about it when we broke up, he made it clear that he would tell anyone a very different version of that night, paint me as someone who just regretted getting drunk and having sex, rather than what had actually happened.'

A muscle ticked in Zeus's jaw and the strength of his emotions seemed to barrage across at her.

'This man is not worthy of the title,' he spat after a pause. 'Your body is *your* body,' he said slowly, enunciating each word in his deep, husky voice. 'Yours to pleasure, yours to control, yours in every way. No man has the right to touch you if you do not want that.'

She nodded, a lump forming in her throat. These were all things she knew, but again, hearing Zeus say them was like treacle running over dry wood. It soaked in, softened everything.

'Afterwards, I just couldn't be with a man without feeling...scared,' she admitted. 'I tried. I dated. But any time a man would kiss me, I'd freeze up. I couldn't bear it,' she confessed, eyes latching to his. 'And then, I met you...' Her voice trailed off, because she couldn't explain what it was about Zeus that had somehow overcome those barriers. 'And I just felt...safe,' she finished huskily, not meeting his eyes, because revealing that to him somehow made a part of her seem too vulnerable.

'You are safe,' he promised, dropping his hands to her waist and pulling her against him, brushing her lips with his own. 'I promised you that, and I meant it.'

'I know.' She smiled then, a weak smile, but one that was filled with all the light of her soul. 'It's not just that you make me feel safe, though,' she continued her confession.

'No?'

'Honestly, I thought any sexual side of me died that night with Steven. I thought he'd killed the parts of me that were responsible for getting turned on. But then I met you, and everything screamed back to life. It's like you flicked a switch inside me and I feel…'

His eyes flared when they met hers. 'If nothing else,' he said, moving his hands to her back and bunching the fabric of her dress there, 'let me give you that, this week. Let me give you all the pleasure, all the knowledge, all the awakenings you have missed out on.'

She blinked up at him, something like awe building inside her. And more than that, she had the strangest sense of fate winding around them, as if each star was flicking a single piece of thread towards them, and as the boat cut through the dark waters of the gulf, those threads landed on Jane, and Zeus, and tangled together, wrapping them up, cocooning them in this place, this time, but somehow, also for all time. No matter what happened, this week would always be solely, completely, theirs, like an imprint of a moment that simply couldn't fade.

She nodded slowly, though it hadn't been a question so much as a pledge. She nodded because with all of her heart, with all of her soul, she agreed with him.

CHAPTER EIGHT

THE LAST THING Zeus felt like employing was restraint. From the moment he'd first seen Jane Fisher, he'd wanted her. He'd imagined her naked in his bed, utterly at his command. But even that night in the bar, he'd sensed a fragility to her. Despite her over-the-top beauty, her apparent confidence, something about her had urged him to be cautious. Careful. As though he might break her; as though she'd been broken before.

And she had been.

She'd been broken, and no one had helped put her back together again. She'd done that all herself, and even though she was strong and living her life, she wasn't fully embracing all of herself, nor all aspects of her life.

For that, she wanted him, and showing her what sex *should* be like would be one of the greatest privileges of his life.

So long as he could be true to his word and slow everything down. The last thing he wanted to do was overwhelm her with his own needs.

This wasn't about Zeus, but Jane.

He pulled her against his chest and kissed her. Slowly. Gently. His mouth probing hers. Tasting, teasing, tempting, until she was moaning against him, the softness of her body, the way her curves pressed to his chest, the warmth of her skin, her fragrance. It all hummed and buzzed and made him feel as though he were walking on a tightrope with a death-defying fall in both directions.

She said his name, a groan, a plea, a curse, and he felt it. He felt it deep in his soul; her tone matched his own.

Her hands pushed at his shirt, lifting it, her fingertips brushing his bare skin, pushing the shirt until it lifted higher, her palms flat against his hair-roughened chest, his nipples, so he bit back a curse in reflexive shock at how damned great that felt.

'Jane.' His voice held a warning, because he was not actually a god, and maintaining control when she touched him like that would take every ounce of his strength. But then he looked at her and realised: it didn't matter. It didn't matter how much it cost him; he would do this for her. She could touch. She could explore. She could feel. Be curious, taste, touch, and he would let her, even when he was holding on by a single thread, because she deserved that. Because he'd promised it to her.

So, he stood still as granite, as she pushed the shirt higher. 'Arms, please,' she murmured, eyes flicking to his with a mix of uncertainty and passion.

He lifted them, and she guided the shirt off his body completely, dropping it to the deck at their sides. More uncertainty in the depths of her gaze as she glanced at him and then leaned forward, pressing those perfectly shaped lips to his pec, flicking him with her tongue, expelling a long, shaky breath that covered him in warmth, before moving her mouth lower, towards his nipple. She rolled her tongue over it first, then her whole mouth, sucking there for a moment before moving to the other, and her hands drew invisible circles over his sides, her fingers light enough to raise his skin in goosebumps.

'You're beautiful,' she said after a moment, moving her kiss to his shoulder, nipping him with her teeth. 'God-like,' she added, her smile teasing now.

He was only capable of making a grunting sound in response.

'May I?' She reached for his pants, but he shook his head once, aware that the closer he got to naked, the harder this was going to be.

'You first,' he suggested, but carefully, gently, in case he was rushing her.

Their eyes met, her cheeks flushed pink, and he tilted her chin with his finger, demanding her eyes hold his. 'If you want. Only ever if you want.'

She nodded once. 'I know that. You don't need to say it.'

'I do. I need to say it each and every time, so you understand…'

'You're not him,' she said, simply. 'I know you'd never do what he did. I trust you.'

Trust. She trusted him.

Zeus closed his eyes for a moment, because it was such a monumental gift. Zeus knew that more than anyone. He'd spent his entire adult life walking alongside a deep sense of mistrust. Not of people, but of life in general. Of getting close to anyone, because of the unreliability of the future. Trust was not something he gave easily, so he appreciated Jane offering it to him now, and in the back of his mind, he wondered if maybe she might just be the one person who could make him reciprocate that. To trust her.

He'd frozen, but Jane hadn't. Her hands were reaching for the hem of her skirt, lifting it up her body, revealing another pair of silky panties and this time, a matching bra, so he was sucked right back into the moment by the sight of her on the deck of his boat dressed in only underwear and heels, her blond hair whipping around her face in a magnificently sensual display of the elements.

And all the power of thought dissipated, leaving him to act purely on instincts. The instinct to pleasure, to worship, to protect, all bound up together, guiding each and every one of his actions.

He lifted her easily and carried her, cradled to his bare chest, across the deck to one of the large, square sun lounges. The mattress was soft, a pale grey, and he placed Jane down on it reverently, before standing to look at her, committing this sight to memory.

Because trust was overrated, and the one thing he knew for certain was that they had this one week together. After that, she would be gone from his life, and he was okay with that. Much safer to accept her time constraints than start wanting more. So long as he could always remember just how perfect she'd been.

He brought his body over hers, careful to support his weight on his knees and elbows, kissing her with all the softness he'd used before, gently, so that it was Jane who deepened the kiss, pushing up onto her elbows to claim more of him, to encourage him to take more of her, too. And so he did. He kissed her back with the same intensity, until they were both panting, and her hands were roaming his body frantically, their hands moving in unison to remove first her bra and then her panties, her desperate longing sending arrows of need shooting through every part of his body.

He moved his kiss to the curve of her neck, teasing her sensitive pulse point there, then lower, to worship her beautiful round breasts, first with his mouth, until she was whimpering and arching her back in an ancient, primal sign of need, then his hands, which cupped their fullness, teased her taut nipples, while his mouth moved lower to the apex of her thighs. She screamed his name as her whole body tightened with the approach of her orgasm and he grinned against her, but didn't stop, because hot on the heels of his name came her plea for more. More, more, over and over, and her hands pushed through his hair, tussling in its length, as if that could save her from the inevitable tumble. Then, with a push of her feet into the soft mattress, she was lifting her pelvis, a guttural cry spilling from her lips as her whole body was racked by the release of her pleasure.

'Zeus,' she groaned moments later, while her breath was still coming in fits. 'That's... I... You're...'

He propped his chin on her abdomen, eyes holding hers with a mixture of need and amusement. 'Lost for words, Jane?'

She flicked his shoulder and collapsed back against the mattress. 'You know you definitely live up to your name in this department, right?' she demanded, pushing up onto her elbows so she could see him better.

'All positive feedback gratefully received.'

She laughed softly, but then she was quiet, and he felt the mood shift inside her.

'What is it?'

'I want to see you,' she said, simply. 'I haven't even... You're always dressed.'

'Ah,' he said with a mock-sombre nod. 'With good reason. I'm a ticking time bomb, and you, *agapaméni*, hold the fuse.'

'Why can't we light it?'

'Because we're not ready.'

'We're not?'

He shook his head, pushing up her body.

'I feel ready,' she disputed.

He hesitated, because wasn't that sort of the point? That this was up to Jane, to call the shots? He didn't want to disregard her wishes, but he needed to be sure. She'd said she trusted him; he wasn't going to abuse that trust.

'And you'll still feel ready tomorrow,' he promised. He kissed her lips and pulled her against his side, her naked body so utterly perfect and tempting that he honestly thought he deserved some kind of medal for holding back. Again.

'Tell me a story,' she murmured, head resting on his chest.

He thought about that for a moment. 'What would you like to hear?'

'Tell me about you,' she said. 'Tell me what it was like growing up as Zeus Papandreo.' She stifled a yawn as he began to slowly stroke her back, drawing lines along the edge of her spine.

'One of my earliest memories,' he began, 'was out on the water.'

Another yawn.

'My *yaya* was from an old fishing village, and when she married my grandfather, she stepped into a world of unimaginable wealth and comfort. Though theirs was, I have to say, a very traditional arranged marriage.'

'Arranged?' She shifted slightly so she could look up at him.

He made a noise of agreement. 'Our family business is bound up in a conservative clause that requires whoever is at the helm to have married before taking ownership. It's been that way for hundreds of years.'

Jane's skin paled slightly and he half laughed.

'Don't worry, Jane. I'm not building up to a proposal.'

She glanced away quickly, her eyes impossible to read when they were focused anywhere but him.

'I didn't mean—'

'Nor did I,' he assured her. 'Anyway, my grandfather proposed when he was twenty years old, and my *yaya* was only eighteen,' he said with a shake of his head. 'She went from living a modest life in a salty old village to suddenly being at the front and centre of Greek's elite.'

'That must have been a huge adjustment,' Jane murmured, though there was something in her voice that still spoke of hesitation.

'She took it in her stride, apparently,' Zeus said. 'But she never forgot her roots, and my grandfather didn't want her to. They came out onto the bay often. Not in a boat like this—*yaya* would turn over in her grave,' he admitted with a throaty laugh. 'This is not her idea of a boat. For her, you had to be able to feel the movements, touch the sea, to know that the ocean is a living beast, requiring respect and fear, awe.'

Jane sighed. 'That sounds so romantic.'

'It might sound romantic. In reality, I spent a lot of

the time that first year hanging over the edge, losing my lunch to seasickness.'

She laughed at that. 'Less romantic.'

'A lot less.' He flashed her a grin. 'But she was determined to turn me into a fisherman, of sorts.'

'What about your father?'

'It was never his thing.'

'And you?'

'I loved it. After I got over the shock of the open waters in a boat not much bigger than a car,' he laughed. 'I swear she did it just to throw me in at the deep end. But it worked. There was something so thrilling about being out there with them, feeling the turn and churn of the waves, knowing that I had to keep my wits about me and rely on the people I was with.' His voice took on a slightly harder edge then, because he'd often reflected on how false the message had been that his grandparents had taught him.

To rely on your shipmates, and everything would be fine.

Even when it simply wasn't possible to give such a guarantee in this life.

Zeus's expression tightened but he quickly dispelled the thought, because Jane's breathing was growing slow and rhythmic, her head heavy against his chest. He reached down beside him to a basket that held several rolled-up blankets and unfurled one over her. Anything to keep her just like this.

'What else?' she murmured groggily, so he resumed the gentle rubbing of her back, even as her eyes drifted shut.

He began to speak then of the time their boat had almost capsized, but he kept his voice soft and low, and after a few minutes she was fast asleep, and he was glad. He rested his head back into the pillows and tried not to think about his childhood anymore. Not about those halcyon days, when the sun had shone, and the water had been cool and reassuring and everything had seemed impossibly perfect. Not about the way his mother's diagnosis had dislodged every bit of his certainty and overpowered him with anger and doubt. Not about the way her death had changed him, permanently. He tried to focus purely on the here and now, on how good Jane felt pressed to his side, and as he drifted off to sleep, whilst his brain was occupying that liminal space between waking and not, he let himself imagine that she was the woman he proposed to, after all, and that rather than a cold, practical marriage of convenience, he ended up with someone warm and perfect, in all the ways he'd long ago learned to mistrust…

The lightest breeze rustled her hair, brushing it over her shoulders and face, making her reach up and scratch her nose, and then, when her hand fell back down, it connected with a warm, bare chest, and her eyes flared open in confusion for a moment. She was disoriented. One part of her was in her flat in London, one part in the hotel in Athens. Then she remembered, and she blinked her eyes around them, smiling a little to realise they'd fallen asleep on the deck of the boat. It had continued to travel through the night; the mainland was now in the far, far distance. She sighed; the sense of freedom she'd begun to enjoy the night before exploding through her in waves now.

It was barely morning. The sky was a hue of pale silver with touches of peach and orange, and the water had a steely grey colour. The moon was still overhead, shimmering like a splotch of white paint. She angled her face, studying Zeus still asleep, and something in her chest twisted hard and plummeted all the way down to her toes.

She didn't want to think about the future. She didn't want to think about Lottie, about the marriage clause in the family business's contracts; she didn't want to think about anything outside of this bubble. Maybe it was naive of her, but she needed to believe they could enjoy this week without any of those complications having an impact.

And more than that, she simply needed him.

Her cheeks flushed as she remembered her dreams and how they'd been flooded by wild, and very *not* PG images of Zeus. Partly memories, partly fantasies. She moved her finger over his chest, idly drawing circles around his nipples, before she smiled again, this time a smile of pure impishness, and moved her naked body over him, straddling him, before quickly leaning down and kissing his lips. He moaned, his hands instinctively coming to rest at her hips, his fingers pressing into the top of her bottom, so she dropped her waist, her sex connecting with his still-clothed erection, and she smiled against his mouth at the proof of how much he wanted this. Despite his patience. Maybe because of it?

'Jane,' he said, eyes bursting open and landing on hers.

'You said I'd still be ready today, and you were right.' She dragged his lower lip between her teeth, then deepened their kiss. 'I'm so, so ready, Zeus.'

His hands began to stroke her naked back, her bottom, her thighs, touching her all over, both gentle and demanding, the perfect combination; she pressed herself hard against his arousal, finding her sensitive cluster of nerves and shamelessly using him to stimulate that pleasure centre until it was almost impossible to breathe, and her eyes were filled with stars. His hands brushed over her breasts, and she cried out, because every part of her was so overly sensitive. It was like she was a forest of dry wood, and he'd struck a match, so bit by bit, she was burning up, and all she could do was admire the ferocity of the fire.

'Please,' she said, simply. 'I want you.'

He stilled, staring up into her face and then, to Jane's relief, he nodded once, kissing her as he began to remove his trousers, kicking them off before reaching for them as an afterthought and removing a condom from one of the pockets.

'You came prepared,' she said with relief.

'Naturally.'

Her cheeks flushed pink, because she hadn't even thought of that.

He placed the condom on the edge of the mattress and went back to kissing her, but with Jane on top, she felt so powerful, so in control of where she was touching him, of how fast they were going, and that control was addictive. His trousers were removed, but his boxers were still in place, and suddenly, she wanted, more than anything, to see *him*. To touch him. Her hands caught at the waistband of his shorts, and she began to push them down, but he stilled her to say, 'Jane, I should warn you—'

She glanced up at him.

'I'm big.'

Her brows shot up.

'I promise I won't hurt you.'

Curiosity now had her moving faster, pulling his shorts down just low enough to see that he was not exaggerating, even a little bit. He was huge. Long, wide and rock, rock-hard.

Her jaw dropped.

'I—see what you mean.'

'We'll take it slow,' he promised.

She couldn't look away from him.

'If you keep staring at me like that, Jane, this really isn't going to last very long.'

Reluctantly, her gaze travelled the length of his body.

'I'm— To be fair, I haven't seen a man's body in a very long time—'

His expression darkened then, and she knew why. Neither of them wanted to contemplate Steven in the context of this. He moved then, catching her and flipping her onto her back, bringing his body over hers.

'Remember, *agapaméni*, you are in charge. Always.'

She nodded, her heart soaring towards her throat as he unfurled the condom over his length. But rather than separating her thighs and taking her, instead, he returned to kissing her, then her breasts, then her sex, until she was incandescent once more and so wet for him, she could feel it between her legs. 'God, Zeus,' she cried out, and only then did he nudge her legs apart and press himself to her sex, holding there a moment as he wrapped her into a hug and pressed her to his chest, whispering Greek words in her ear. She stared above them at the dawn sky, painted the kind of palette she would never forget, even if it weren't the backdrop to such a moment, and slowly, gently, he pressed into her.

It had been so long for Jane, and she'd built it up to be such a terrifying event, she'd been so worried she might never have sex with anyone ever again. But in the end, in Zeus's arms, it neither hurt nor terrified her. It simply felt…perfect.

He *was* big, and at first, she experienced discomfort to accommodate him, but only at first. He gave her space to get used to his strength and size before he began to move, and all the while, he alternated between whispering in her ear in his native language and kissing her throat, her lips, her earlobe; and his hands—those awesome, talented hands—roamed her body, enslaving her breasts before one moved to her sex and began to brush over her there, in the same tempo as his movements, so whatever his arousal had been stirring within her, it was no longer possible to take it slowly. She was tumbling headfirst into a star-filled abyss, flooded with light and sparkle, magic and warmth, and she revelled in the cataclysmic explosion, with the fading stars above, the pale moon, the peachy-pink sky the witness to the most sublimely blissful event in Jane Fisher's entire twenty-four years.

CHAPTER NINE

THE FIRST PORT the boat stopped in was on Crete, at the ancient city of Heraklion, which they explored on foot. Jane was in awe of the history, transfixed by the beauty and so captivated that she hardly had time to think about what had happened that morning. When she *did* think about it, her cheeks flushed and her lips twisted into a smile, because it had been perfect. Not just what had happened between them on the deck, but afterwards, too. When he'd walked with her, hand in hand, into the yacht to a palatial bathroom, so she could shower. He'd offered her space, but she'd shaken her head because she didn't *want* space. She'd wanted him. More touching. More feeling. More kissing.

He'd stirred something to life inside her and it was turning out to be quite insatiable.

They'd showered together, loofah-ing one another with sudsy bubbles, kissing, laughing, worshipping some more, and when they were finished, he wrapped her in a towel and gave her a brief tour of a small section of the boat—ending in his bedroom. They'd stayed there, in bed, until the boat had stopped moving and Zeus had glanced through the windows and commented, 'We're in port. Fancy some exploring?'

She'd been reluctant to leave the boat, which had been obvious to Zeus. He laughed. 'Just for a few hours, *agapaméni*. We'll be back soon.'

In the end, she was glad she'd agreed, because Heraklion was incredible. Not just beautiful, though it was that; the city was charged with a strange energy. As though all the layers of its history were still here, somehow, caught between the wide streets and stone buildings.

'Hungry?'

She hadn't realised it until now, but she was famished. 'Definitely.'

'I know a place.' He gestured with his hand, then caught hers in his, and glanced down at her. Jane's eyes met his and she almost lost her footing, so powerful was the sense of something flashing between them. She smiled quickly and out of nowhere, thought of Lottie and her duty to her best friend, and her whole body seemed to weaken.

'Here.' He gestured again to a charming little restaurant. The glass-panelled door was painted a bright blue, the awnings above the windows were blue-and-white-striped and the chairs on the sidewalk were white wrought iron. At each table, there was a small vase with a single carnation placed inside. It was quaint and charming, rustic and old-fashioned, everything Jane adored, but she felt slightly off-kilter in that moment, with the mental reminder of how duplicitous this all was.

Except it wasn't, she reminded herself forcibly. She was here with Zeus for one week. That was all. It didn't matter that she'd been sent by Lottie with a ploy to delay his ability to propose to anyone else. It didn't matter that meeting him hadn't been fate or an accident, but rather part of Lottie's scheme. It didn't even matter that if she ever had to make a choice between Lottie and Zeus, she would choose Lottie—of course she would, because they had been best friends for over a decade, and each woman meant the world to the other. She'd never have to make that choice, though, because Zeus would never know about Jane's connection to Lottie. This week was safe from all of that.

She exhaled as they were shown to a table by the window, and Jane was glad to be sitting inside, in the air-conditioning, rather than at the tables on the sidewalk. As charming as they were, the afternoon sun was beating down and she suspected it would be unbearably hot to sit there and eat.

They ordered calamari and a salad and a glass each of white wine, and while they ate, Zeus mostly talked about the island. Lottie had a very soft recollection of its history, courtesy of school classes, but nothing had really sunk in. Zeus, she discovered, was somewhat of an expert.

'How do you know all this?' Jane asked as coffee was delivered, along with a single enormous slice of *ketaifi*.

Zeus seemed to hesitate. 'My mother loved history. When she was unwell, I would read her books—histories, historical accounts, myths. She loved it all. She was incredibly proud to be Greek,' he said, one side of his lips twisting in what might have been described as a smile by someone who'd never seen his *actual* smile. Something heavy thudded in her stomach. Guilt.

Because Zeus's mother had died only recently, and yet he was carrying on as though everything was fine and normal. But surely, he was still grieving her?

'You said she was sick?'

His lips tightened, outlined by white. 'Yes.'

Which was shorthand for, 'can we not talk about it'?

But if they were to know one another only for the rest of this week, then Jane wanted to *really* know him. To leave no stone unturned. It wasn't as though she'd be able to pick up the phone in a month's time and ask him whatever she'd forgotten to ask now. Leaving Zeus would be a one-way trip.

'And you helped care for her?'

He flinched slightly, looked towards the window. Walling himself off from her. Beneath the table, she pushed one foot forward so she could stroke his ankle.

'We had nurses,' he answered, reluctantly. Slowly. 'Around-the-clock care, in the end.'

Jane nodded, but he wasn't looking at her.

'My father preferred to stay by her side. I took over the business at her lowest points, when he couldn't bear to leave.'

He painted a bleak picture, though he spoke of it with such sparing words. 'It went on for a while?'

Zeus turned to face her then, held her gaze for several beats before reaching for his coffee—thick and dark. Again, she thought of Lottie with a pang in her chest.

'Her first diagnosis was when I was nine years old.'

Jane closed her eyes against the pain of that.

'It became normal,' he said, stiffly. Coldly. In a way that was rehearsed. Like he'd said this before, or at least thought it. 'She was sick, and then she wasn't. Periods of remission were, at first, like the sun, breaking through after a fierce storm. The sheer sense of relief was almost crippling. But then she became sick again. Then better, then sick. I stopped expecting recovery—or even for her periods of wellness to last. Every day she felt good was a gift, but I knew, I always knew, it was temporary.'

Jane shook her head, trying to stem the tears that were making her eyes sting. She didn't know what to say. She personally knew people who *had* recovered from cancer. Who'd gone into remission and stayed there. What Zeus's mother had experienced sounded like an unbearably aggressive and harrowing form of the disease.

'I'm so sorry,' was all she could say, the words slightly tremulous.

'It's life,' he said, and for all that her voice had been rich with emotion, his was utterly devoid of it. Even his eyes were cold when they met hers. Cold in a way she'd never expected to see in Zeus. Ruthlessly blanked of feeling, of sentiment. 'It's unpredictable and cruel.'

'Not always.'

'No?'

She shook her head. 'Most of the time, life is wonderful. And the unpredictable is part of what makes it so.'

He stared at her for several beats and then glanced back towards the window. 'We'll have to agree to disagree, *agapaméni*.'

But she didn't want that. She didn't want him to be so burdened by his pain, by the unpredictability of his mother's illness, by the impact that had clearly had on him. They had one week together, and she couldn't bear to think of him living with such a dim view of the world.

'How is your father?' she asked, to draw his attention back to her and, obliquely, their conversation.

Zeus continued to stare out at the street, one of his large hands holding the small coffee cup in a way that, in other circumstances, she would have found amusing.

'In reference to my mother's death?'

'Yes.'

'It's complicated.'

Jane frowned. 'Why?'

Zeus turned to face her then, scanning her features as though he'd forgotten who she was, and Jane's heart went cold. After what they'd shared that morning, she didn't *ever* want him to look at her like that. She blinked away, tears stinging her eyes for another reason now.

'He loved her very much,' Zeus said, finally. 'They married young, essentially grew up together in many ways. She was his partner in every way. He is…bereft.'

Jane glanced back at him in time to catch an expression on his features that spoke of resentment. Anger. She frowned a little. There was more here than Zeus was telling her.

'And you?' she pushed, aware that he didn't want to be having this conversation but continuing regardless. 'You must also be bereft?'

'I was prepared for it.'

She flinched. 'Does that make a difference in the end?'

'It must.'

She shook her head, frustrated. Because he was stonewalling her. He was hiding his feelings rather than admit them. She *knew* Zeus now. She knew his emotions ran deep, and that he must still be feeling an enormous black hole of grief for the mother he'd only recently lost. Or was he so determined to conquer grief, to be strong over it, that he refused to accept it, even to himself?

'I knew it was coming, Jane. From when I was just a teenager, I had prepared myself for it. As I said, every day she was well was a gift, when she wasn't, it was…

my baseline. I braced for her death, and in the end, she was in so much pain, barely lucid. It was a release for her. I know it was.'

A tear slid down Jane's cheek. He spoke so calmly, so sensibly, but Jane couldn't hear his description without feeling all the pain of what he was describing.

'Don't cry, please,' he insisted, reaching for a napkin so he could lean over the table and wipe her cheek gently.

'It's just… I'm so sad for you.'

'Don't be. Do I look sad?'

She looked at him and shook her head, but not to disagree, rather out of confusion. She couldn't fathom his feelings, and it bothered her. It was like he'd hardened his heart intentionally, because he knew that without taking that precaution, her death would hurt too, too much. She supposed it made a sort of sense. To pre-emptively cope with a wound that might otherwise have the power to cut you off at the knees. So, he'd emotionally withdrawn from the situation, while still supporting his father and mother.

But had he pulled all of his emotions back? Did that explain his string of short-term affairs and no serious girlfriends?

'Shall we get moving?' His voice was light, as though that conversation hadn't just taken place. Her eyes held his as her mind continued to ruminate, but she nodded.

'Sure, let's go.'

She knew, though, that no matter where they went, she wouldn't let the conversation drop completely. She'd started to see more of Zeus, had begun to understand him, and she wouldn't rest until that was complete. She had one week—she intended to use it fully.

* * *

The sunset was particularly beautiful, observed from the deck of the boat, which was moored in a cove on the other side of Crete, in the Gulf of Mesara. But it was not the most spectacular thing in Zeus's vision. No. That would be Jane, swimming in the crystal-clear waters just off the boat, as though she'd recently discovered she was, in fact, half mermaid.

She ducked and dived beneath the surface, spun pirouettes, then emerged for air, her big blue eyes surrounded by dark lashes courtesy of the water, her hair plastered to her head.

He'd heard the expression *breathtaking* without really understanding that it could describe an actual physical phenomenon. Right now, looking at her, it felt as though his breath had been squeezed from his lungs. And not in the way he'd felt when his mother had died. That had winded him, had made him feel as though his own body was losing life.

He'd braced for it, yes. Or thought he had. But how could one really brace for that sort of loss? Months later, he still found it almost impossible to believe he was living in a world that was absent his mother. In a way, her having been sick for as long as she was had made that a new kind of normal. He was used to going to his parents' place and taking up a book from the shelves, taking it to her and picking up wherever they'd left off. Or sometimes, she'd have something particular she wanted to hear about, and then she'd make a request of him, which he was always happy to oblige.

It had been three months, but the sense of being winded hadn't really eased.

His father's revelation about his affair and love child had been proverbial salt in the wound. It had hurt like the devil. To imagine his father sleeping with some other woman, while his mother suffered. While his mother faced what must have been every parent's worst nightmare: the idea of leaving behind a beloved small child.

'You're sure you don't want to swim?' she called up to him.

He'd initially demurred. He rarely swam in the ocean, though he couldn't really remember why. An old fear? A habit? A disinterest? There was a pool and spa on board. If he felt like swimming, he could use either of those.

But Jane's delight in the raw, elemental ocean was like a lightning bolt bursting through him. She looked so free and unburdened, and suddenly, an urge to dive into the ocean and let it wash away his grief—a grief he kept so firmly locked inside that no one, not even Jane, not even here, could know.

Before she could ask again, he was pushing out of his slides at the same time as removing his shirt.

Her delighted expression was the hammer in the nail of his decision. What wouldn't he give to see her features shine like that?

He took the steps down to the pontoon at the rear of the yacht, strode to the edge then dived in, surfacing right beside her. She spun to him and laughed, treading water easily, as though she swam often.

'You're like some kind of mermaid,' he observed, kissing her softly, because he couldn't resist.

'I like the water. Always have.'

He caught her around the waist and held her close, his

legs taking over the work of keeping them afloat. 'Do you swim often?'

'I was on the team at school,' she replied. 'It was a lot of early starts.'

'And now?'

'Now I prefer to swim for pleasure. There's a Lido not far from my place. I go there a few times a week.' She looked around, her expression serene. 'It doesn't really compare to this, though.'

'No?'

She shook her head. 'You must love coming out here.'

He considered her, felt something churn in his chest. Her vivacity and love of life were just so palpable. Even after the betrayal she'd endured, the hurt she'd lived with, Jane had still managed to hold on to something rare and precious: positivity.

'Yes,' he agreed, simply, because she was right. He did love being on the water. It made him feel elemental and powerful again, but also human, because it was a stark reminder of how much more powerful the ocean was. 'Though I tend to swim on the boat.'

Her brows lifted skyward. 'There's a pool on the boat?'

He laughed. 'And a spa.'

She let out a low whistle. 'I mean, it's obviously fancy. I just didn't expect...' She trailed off and shrugged. 'I get the impression you work a lot,' she said after a beat. 'Does that leave much time for this?' She gestured towards the boat and then the sunset.

His eyes roamed her face, and he was transfixed. Not just by her beauty, but by the ability she had to ask the kinds of questions he usually sidestepped with ease, in just such a way that made him want to bare his soul to her.

It had to be because she was leaving within a week. There was a security that came from that, a certainty that no matter what happened between them, it wouldn't change either of their futures. He was destined for a pragmatic, sensible marriage, to jump through the hoops so he could inherit the company he'd always considered his by right. And she... He frowned reflexively. What did Jane's future hold?

She'd come into his life as a woman still carrying the wounds of her past, and in many ways, those wounds had broken her. But she was stirring back to life, becoming whole again; he could see that happening before his eyes. So, what did that mean? That she'd go home and instead of being repulsed when another man kissed her, might she lean into it? Start to enjoy the promise of flirtation and the spectre of sex?

He pulled away from her quickly, so she said his name on a short breath of surprise. 'What is it?'

'Nothing,' he lied. 'Let's swim.' He smiled, but it felt like a facsimile of the real deal, and he knew she saw that, because her face showed concern. He ignored it. He didn't want her concern, and he didn't want to contemplate what came next. Suddenly, the idea of Jane moving on from him sat like a rock in his gut.

They raced around the yacht until Jane's arms were like jelly and her legs were sore, as the sun slipped lower and lower towards the horizon, and then, as they passed the pontoon on the back, she stopped swimming and grabbed hold of the rails.

'I think I'm done,' she said, trying to keep her tone light, when there was something dark stirring inside her.

A frustration, with the way he shut her down whenever she took the conversation in a direction he didn't want to go.

It *hurt*.

It hurt, after she'd told him about Steven. It hurt, because she'd trusted him.

But at the same time, it wasn't as though she didn't have secrets of her own. Like Lottie.

They didn't have to tell each other *everything*. Except, her friendship with Lottie was somewhat irrelevant to all of this. It might have been the catalyst for their meeting, but their relationship now existed in a way that was totally outside the bounds of the plan Lottie and she had discussed before Jane had met Zeus.

Anything important about her, she'd told him. She'd shared herself with him. And yet, he seemed determined to keep parts of himself closed off, even from her.

Was it possible that she was mistaking their physical intimacy for something more?

Lottie always said Jane was messed up because of the way her parents had treated her, and she knew her best friend was right. All her life, she'd known that her parents didn't love her like parents should love their child. They'd sent her away to boarding school at five years old, and from then on, she'd seen them only briefly during holidays, and sometimes, not even then. When Jane had started dating Steven and professed herself in love with him, Lottie had laughed and shaken her head. 'You want to be in love with him, because you want him to love you back. No one is going to fill that hole in here, though, that your parents dug, except for you. You have to love and accept yourself before anyone else can.'

Well, she'd been right about Steven, and she'd probably been right about all of it.

Now Jane was looking at Zeus as though he were in some way a mythical piece of her that had been missing all this time. Whereas she was probably just trying to fill that same awful, painful void. Not with love, but with intimacy and trust. Yes, the kind of trust she'd never known, because she sure as hell couldn't have said she felt that for her parents. And the fact he wouldn't open up to her showed that he didn't trust her, even after all she'd shared with him.

It hurt.

It hurt way more than a casual week-long fling should be able to hurt her. But Jane found, as she showered alone, that there was nothing she could do to change that. She wanted more from Zeus than he seemed willing to give, and she had two choices: accept it, or leave early. She didn't like either alternative.

CHAPTER TEN

'YOU'RE QUIET,' HE SAID as their dinner plates were cleared away. He'd sat through the meal, watching Jane push her quinoa salad around on her plate and take minuscule bites of the chargrilled fish, occasional sips of wine. It wasn't like she'd been sulking. Nor ignoring him. She'd asked questions about his grandparents, as well as the history of the area, but there was a tension in her that was very, very obvious. In complete contrast to the way she'd been in the water that very afternoon.

Before he'd joined her and shut down her line of questioning.

Because she asked too much. No, she *saw* too much. Other women had asked him personal questions, and he'd never found it hard to sidestep them. With Jane, he felt a pull towards full disclosure, and it made him uncomfortable. Hell, it made him want to break out in a cold sweat. His one rule in life was not to trust *anyone*. Or anything. He dealt in facts, figures, the tangible certainty of black-and-white numbers. When it came to people, he expected to be disappointed. To get hurt.

'I'm tired,' she said, pulling her lips to the side. Lying. She was upset. Uncertain.

'Jane,' he said on a tight sigh, because he knew why she was upset now; he just wasn't sure how to broach it.

He didn't have to worry about that.

'Zeus, I've never done anything like this before,' she said after a beat, her voice a little uneven. 'As you know.' Those words were slightly acerbic. 'I don't really know how it's meant to work.'

He stared at her. 'Work?'

'Yeah. Like, is it just sex? Is that the main thing we're doing?'

His gut churned. Wasn't that his stock in trade? How he usually had relationships? Sure, there was the polite dinner beforehand, a bit of surface-level conversation, but ultimately, he preferred to keep things easy. Casual. Enjoyable.

'You're upset.'

'I'm trying to understand,' she corrected with a defiant tilt of her chin, 'how you expect me to be.'

'I just want you to be yourself,' he muttered, recognising the hypocrisy of that. As did she, evidently, because she sat back in her chair and crossed her arms, one brow arching upwards.

'Are you sure? Because when I'm myself, and I try to ask you questions, you shut me down.'

She had a point, but she was also being a little unreasonable.

'I spoke to you about my mother today.'

'And it was like pulling teeth.'

'What do you want? A therapy session? Would you like me to bare my soul to you?'

'Not if you don't want to,' she snapped, reaching for her wine and taking a sip before replacing it on the table with enough force to slosh the liquid against the edges of the glass like a roiling ocean.

'I don't want to,' he said, wishing the words sounded slightly less accusatory.

'Fine, then. So, it's just sex.'

But that characterisation sat ill in his gut. 'Jane—'

'No, it's fine. It's just good for me to know, so I can personally do a little less of the soul baring.'

He ground his teeth. 'I didn't mean that.'

'This is my problem, not yours.'

'What problem?'

'Nothing.'

'Jane—'

'It doesn't matter.' She stood up and paced towards the railing, turning her rigid, straight back to him, staring out in the direction of Crete. He looked at her for several beats before pushing back his own chair and striding in her direction.

She whirled around as he approached. 'I don't want to talk about it.'

She was hurting. He'd hurt her. He shook his head, unable to accept that. 'I'm sorry.'

She glanced away. 'Don't.'

'This is different. Everything's different with you. I don't know what I'm doing, either.'

That had her eyes slamming back to his with a ferocity that almost knocked him backwards.

'What do you mean?'

'You've been making conversation, asking questions about me, my life. That's fine. You're not the first woman to be curious.' Her cheeks flushed pink. 'But you are the first woman I've ever felt like I wanted to be honest with.

To actually *talk* to. Not as a means to an end, but because there's something addictive about you. And that scares the hell out of me, Jane.'

'Scares you?' she repeated, her eyes on him like he was a puzzle she desperately wanted to break.

'I don't like things in my personal life to be unpredictable.'

She frowned, her features shifting, softening. 'Because of your mother?'

His first instinct was to deny it. He *hated* to discuss any of it. He'd built walls around his pain, and he liked having those walls there. They kept him safe, secure, able to function in the world. Because deep down, he knew that nine-year-old he'd once been was still a part of him, reeling from the very idea that his mother, the woman he loved more than anyone on earth, could possibly be so sick.

How could he deny it to Jane, though? Because it wasn't just his mother. His father had further pulled the rug out from under him with the revelation of his infidelity and secret child. The sense of betrayal was immense.

'I don't trust easily,' he said after a beat. 'And yet, I find myself wanting to trust you, Jane. Why is that?'

Her eyes widened and her skin paled, almost as if it was the last thing she expected—or wanted—him to say. 'I don't know.' A whisper, and then she reached for his hand. 'But it's something we have in common. I mean, after Steven, trusting anyone has been almost impossible for me, but with you…'

His eyes closed on a wave of acceptance. So, it was different, for both of them.

'I get that you find it hard to open up to people, but

you just lost your mother, Zeus. That's got to bring up some issues. I'm just saying I'm here.'

For the next week, anyway. 'I know,' he said with a single nod. 'And thank you.'

Jane wasn't sure he should be thanking her. Not after she'd lost her temper, all because of his perfectly reasonable desire to maintain some personal distance between them. She'd felt lost, though, confused, worried that she was yet again feeling more for someone than she should. And wasn't she?

I don't trust easily, and yet I find myself wanting to trust you, Jane.

In the middle of the night, with Zeus fast asleep beside her, she slipped out of bed and moved from their room, out onto the deck. It was an inky-black night with low cloud cover, meaning the stars were covered and those that weren't were dimmed by the light pollution of Crete. Nonetheless, she settled back onto the large pool lounger they'd shared that first night and stared upwards, as though answers would come to her if only she looked long enough. Except they didn't, perhaps because there was no satisfying answer.

Instead, she lifted her phone and tapped out a message to Lottie.

How's it going?

'Couldn't sleep?' Zeus's voice was a deep rumble and Jane jumped, guilty at having been sending a message to Lottie—the woman who single-handedly wanted to bring about Zeus's removal from his family business.

'Nope.'

'Funny, I thought you'd have been worn out,' he teased, coming to sit beside her, sliding an arm around her and drawing her to his chest. She nuzzled in there, sighing at how right it felt to be this close to him, how much she loved it here.

'Oh, you're doing an excellent job in that department. Don't worry, Mr Papandreo.'

'Are you still upset?' he asked after a slight pause.

She glanced up at his face, her heart turning over in her chest. She shook her head.

'What did you mean earlier, when you said this is your problem, not mine?'

Jane's stomach clenched. 'Oh. It doesn't matter.'

'Now who's avoiding the difficult questions?' he asked, squeezing her shoulder lightly.

Her smile was half-hearted but then she sighed, resting in closer to his side, her hand absent-mindedly drawing spirals around his hip area. 'I'm not close to my parents,' she said, and if he thought it was a strange comment, he didn't say anything. 'Not like it sounds as though you were with your mother and are with your father.'

She felt him shift a little, and sympathy tightened in her gut. Did he know about his father's affair? Or was it multiple affairs? There was so much Jane didn't know, and yet the small amount of information she had about the other man made her angry. On behalf of Lottie, yes, but now also on behalf of Zeus.

'*Are* you close with your father?' she asked, tilting her face to his.

'It's complicated.' He'd said that earlier today, too, when she'd asked about his relationship with Aristotle.

'In what way?'

But he stiffened perceptibly. 'We were talking about your parents,' he reminded her, and a familiar sense of irritation sparked inside her chest. She didn't push it, though. She'd told him how she felt, and now it was up to Zeus to change, or not. She knew that this was new for him, though, that he was grappling with the new experience of how much he wanted to confide in her, and that had to be enough.

'When I say we're not close, I mean... I barely have a relationship with them.'

He was very quiet, but his eyes were intensely focused on her face.

'I was sent away to boarding school when I was very young, and I spent most of my time there. In the holidays, I would go home, and sometimes my parents were there, sometimes they weren't. Usually, it was a nanny who had the most to do with me.'

He spoke soft and low, 'I see.'

'My father's job required him to travel a lot. My mother went with him. They never planned to have children. I was a mistake.'

'An accident,' he corrected, as though the semantics of that might save her from the pain of knowing how unwanted she'd been.

'I think my mother did her best for a few years, but she grew tired of it all. Hence, boarding school.'

He shook his head a little. 'Were you at least happy there?'

She laughed, but a sound without humour. 'I hated it. I was teased mercilessly in primary school.'

'What about?' he demanded with a sense of outrage that softened parts of her she hadn't known needed it.

'Promise you won't laugh?'

He nodded gravely.

'My name.'

'Jane?'

'My name is actually Boudica,' she muttered. 'My parents, it turns out, decided to burden me with that, too. It wasn't enough for me to know I wasn't wanted, why not throw a truly unusual name into the mix?'

'I like it,' he said, and her heart turned over in her chest. 'It's beautiful.'

'I hated it.' She didn't go into the nicknames. 'And it was different. Too different for the children at school to understand.'

'It's just a name.'

'You know what kids are like. Once they got it into their heads to tease me about that, and saw they could get a reaction, they found other things.' She glanced downwards, self-conscious at revealing this to him. 'Anyway, thank God when I changed schools, they actually moved me back down, closer to London. I didn't know anyone. It was a proper fresh start. And on the first day, I met my best friend, Lottie, and that changed everything.' She realised, only after she'd finished talking, that she'd probably revealed way too much. What if he knew his half-sister's name was Lottie? What if he knew she'd gone to a boarding school on the outskirts of London?

But there was no recognition on his face, only a mix of sympathy and curiosity. 'How?'

She expelled a shaking breath of relief. 'Lottie was just like me, in lots of ways. Her own childhood was pretty messed up. She wasn't super close to her mother or father. We just got each other. But she's different to me in one vital way.'

'Oh?'

'She's as tough as nails. Lottie's a fighter. She was just born that way. Or maybe life turned her into one? I don't know. But all the things that had happened to me and made me kind of timid and nervous had made her angry, determined to change the world. Lottie can't help but see a problem and want to fix it.'

'And you were something she wanted to fix?'

'She would say I didn't need fixing, that I just needed to understand myself better.'

Zeus's features shifted with admiration. 'Smart woman.'

Jane's chest spasmed. If only he *knew* that they were discussing his half-sister! Who was smart, and kind and just generally wonderful!

'Oh, yes, and my biggest champion. She just had a way of making me see sense.' Jane moved her hand to his, lacing their fingers together. 'So, when I started dating Steven, and told Lottie I was in love, she took it with a grain of salt. She understood what I definitely wasn't able to—that I was looking for the kind of love and acceptance I'd always wanted and never got. My being needy didn't make Steven any more likely to love nor deserve me.' Another sigh. 'I wish I'd listened to her. Lottie would have never trusted a guy like him.'

'You weren't to blame,' he said firmly, as if it was the most important thing in the world that she understands that.

'I know. But at the same time, Lottie is just so much better at this stuff.'

'Despite what you think, Jane, you're trusting. That's not a weakness. Even after your parents' neglect, you see the best in people.'

Her lips pulled to the side as she considered that. 'Why can't you do that?'

He stared down at her, surprised by her having turned it back on him.

'You have seen your mother suffer for a long time—it's impacted you. I do understand that. But why can't you accept that grief is a part of life, in the same way joy is, and that you can't have one without the other?'

A muscle jerked low in his jaw; he didn't answer.

Jane settled back against his chest. 'Tell me about her,' she said quietly, because in asking about his mother, she wasn't asking him to recount his experiences of her illness, or her death, but rather her life. And she listened as he—reluctantly at first, and then more willingly—began to describe her. Her likes, her hobbies, her passions, the food she'd made for him when he came home from school, all of it. At some point, they drifted off to sleep like that, her head on his chest, her mind and heart filled with his words, the spectre of his mother over them, like an angel of destiny.

The next day, the boat moved to a different island, this one smaller and covered in greenery, so they walked a nature path from one side to the other and stopped for lunch at a small, beachfront taverna that served the crispiest, saltiest potatoes Jane had ever eaten. They drank ice-cold beer, then walked back towards the boat, and whatever frustrations Jane had felt the day before, about the parts of himself that Zeus kept walled off, seemed to have ebbed away like the waves in the ocean. Perhaps because he *had* started to talk to her the night before. Or perhaps because he'd acknowledged his shortcomings and the reasons for them. Or maybe because he'd told her that she was different, special, and she was still, deep down, that same seventeen-year-old, wanting to be loved.

Her step faltered slightly as that idea burst into her mind.

Loved?

It wasn't about love. Not with Zeus. Making love, sure. Passion. Pleasure. Respect. She enjoyed his company.

But she couldn't—wouldn't—love him.

How impossibly complicated, not to mention outrageously stupid, would that be? This was the man who'd been—admittedly unwittingly—an instrument of Lottie's pain all her life. How often had they stared daggers at him, whenever there'd been a photo of Zeus and Aristotle attending an event together? Lottie, glutton for punishment that she was, had set up a news alert on her phone and got emailed any time Aristotle or Zeus were mentioned, so there was never a shortage of information to devour and despise.

Like a good best friend, or an excellent foot soldier dragooned into a war out of loyalty alone, she'd hated Zeus, too. She'd hated Aristotle more, because his choices had wounded both Lottie and her mother, Mariah, but Zeus had committed the unforgivable crime of having held the place in life that should have been Lottie's. Whereas Lottie had had to live with the ignominy of knowing that her very existence was a burden and a regret, that she was so shameful to the Papandreos her mother had been paid millions of pounds to keep quiet.

Never mind that Aristotle had been the love of Mariah's life, and her heart had been broken beyond repair by his cruelty. Never mind that her heart had been too badly broken to properly accept her daughter into it.

It was just such an awful mess.

Even knowing all that, though, Jane couldn't bring herself to hate Zeus like she once had. She couldn't bring herself to think of him with anything other than...*not love*. She couldn't be stupid enough to make that mistake again. It had been bad enough with Steven, but at least then she'd had the defences of youth and naivety on her side. Now what?

She'd come into this with her eyes wide open.

She knew more than enough about him, and his predilection for short-term, meaningless flings. And she knew all the emotional baggage—even if he didn't—that made any kind of real relationship between them impossible.

So why did she walk with him, hand in hand, on that small island in the south of Greece, and smile as though she was the happiest woman in the world? She smiled, she realised, like a woman in love—apparently, some parts of her just hadn't quite gotten the memo.

CHAPTER ELEVEN

Long, sun-drenched days bled into balmy, starlit nights, all of them spent either in the water, on ancient, stunning islands, or naked together on the boat. Of all the weeks in her life, Jane had never known one to go as swiftly as this one. It was as though time had been sped up, and they both sensed it. They slept sparingly, catching a few hours here or there, when they were too utterly exhausted to fight it any longer.

They ate the most beautiful food, whether on the islands they visited, or aboard the boat. Zeus's chef procured just-caught seafood, the ripest fruit and vegetables, and served it all simply, to showcase the delightful flavours.

And they talked. Not about Zeus's mother, or his father, or Jane's parents, but about their lives, their childhoods, their favourite movies, books, places they'd visited. They made each other laugh in a way that Jane knew she could become addicted to, if she weren't very, very careful.

So, she was careful.

Careful not to let her guard down completely. Careful not to let her heart be exposed more than it had been. Careful not to fantasise about falling in love with a man such as Zeus. Or Zeus himself, more specifically, because she doubted that there was another man like him.

But two days before she was due to leave, as they were walking along a deserted beach at sunset, he stopped walking all of a sudden and spun Jane around, so that she was looking out to sea. He pulled her back against his chest, held her there, so her breath grew rushed and hot.

'Do you see that mountain over there, in the distance?'

She squinted across the sea, to where a shape seemed to emerge from the middle of the ocean. 'Yeah?'

'That's Prásino Lófo,' he said.

She repeated the Greek words before tilting her face to his. 'What does it mean?'

'Very literally, it means Green Hill,' he said with a slow smile.

'Green Hill. Erm…very…er…creative.'

'The name came with the island.' He shrugged. 'My grandfather bought it, as a gift for my *yaya*.'

Her smile slipped and she refocused her attention on the island itself. She couldn't see much of it, but she tilted her face to his.

'It's your family's island?'

'When my parents married, my grandparents gave it to them as a wedding present.'

Jane nodded, but her mind was galloping ahead, even before he spoke the words.

'It has always been promised to me, when I marry,' he said. 'It's tradition.'

When he marries.

Someone else.

A reality that was far closer than Jane dared to think about. She couldn't. She wouldn't.

'Some wedding present,' she said, the words rushed

and a little high-pitched. 'I thought crystal bowls were the norm.'

'Or candlesticks,' he responded, squeezing her tighter around the waist.

'Or at least registering for gifts. And I don't think you could put a Greek island on your registry without people thinking you were a little touched in the head. Then again, perhaps in the circles you move in…' She let the sentence taper off because she had no way of finishing it. She didn't want to contemplate Zeus marrying, belonging—in the sense that any human could belong to another—to someone else. Coming home to her, holding her, kissing her, making love to her.

Jane squeezed her eyes shut, her back to him, before forcing the thoughts from her mind.

'What's it like?'

'I haven't been there in years,' he admitted. 'But I remember it as being quite beautiful.'

They began to walk once more.

'It's overgrown and lush, with forests from one side to the other, though my father did add a very nice home and a nine-hole golf course.'

'As one does,' Jane drawled, earning an indulgent smile from Zeus.

'He stopped going there, once my mother was too ill to travel.'

'It must have been so hard on you both,' she murmured.

And perhaps because their time together was drawing to a close, he glanced down at her and said, 'It was, at first. I didn't know how to handle it. Seeing her like that. She'd always been so vibrant, so alive. And then she got sick, and the treatments were worse than the cancer. She slept almost all the time. I couldn't go near her in case I had a cold or flu. It was almost impossible to understand, as a boy. All I wanted was to be able to click my fingers and make her well.'

'Oh, Zeus,' she said, shaking her head a little.

'I spent a lot of time with my grandparents. They were very good at trying to keep everything as normal as possible for me, but I knew. I knew how sick she was, and that there was nothing I could do to help her.'

She squeezed his hand.

'I hated it, *agapeméni*. I hated feeling as though I was powerless to do a damned thing. Seeing her in pain, my father heartbroken, my whole world slipped through my fingers. I could do nothing.'

She shook her head, tears threatening. 'That's not true. You were there, for your father, and your mother. You stepped in and helped with the business, you read her stories, you grew into the kind of man she must have desperately hoped you would be. She would have been so proud of you, Zeus. She got to see you become this.' She squeezed his hand again, in the hope it would show him how much she meant it.

'I think she would have liked to see me take a different path than this.'

'In what way?'

He was quiet for several long strides, and then, on a long exhalation, 'From a very young age, the company became my entire life. At first, it was an interest, a passion rather than anything else. But as she became more and more sick, it became a tangible distraction. Somewhere I could go and be useful. I had no power to heal my mother, but with the company, I was able to do *something*. I was good at it, too. I stepped into my father's shoes. I saw problems and I fixed them. I saw opportunities and took them. I became obsessed and gradually, it became my whole life.'

Something hard and sharp opened up inside Jane. A shape that was almost impossible to accommodate, and every step she took seemed to jag it against her ribcage.

'But it's just a business,' she said eventually, the words a little breathless. 'And isn't the point of business to make money? Clearly, you have enough money.' She sounded desperate to her own ears.

'Money is the last thing I care about,' he contradicted.

'Then why does it matter so much?' She couldn't meet his eyes. She couldn't look at him without the dark, all-consuming sense of betrayal rearing up and swallowing her alive. Lottie was going to take the business from him. She was going to move heaven and earth to achieve that—anyone who knew Lottie knew that she always, always achieved what she set her mind to. And Zeus was going to lose *everything*.

'Where do I begin?' he said with a lift of one shoulder. 'It gave me a sense of control. When things at home were spinning wildly away from me, and I could do nothing to help, in the business, I could pull levers to effect change. It was my sense of purpose when I needed one most. My mother's death hasn't changed that. If anything, it makes me more determined to build the Papandreo Group into the best it can be.'

Jane lifted a hand to her lips, pressing it there. The telltale gesture simply slipped out, but Zeus didn't appear to notice.

'When I took over as group CEO, I came up with a ten-year plan that would revolutionise our business model. I'm only five years in, but already we're tracking well ahead of schedule.'

'Your father must be very proud,' she murmured, simply to fill the silence, because he had told her something great about himself, and she needed to acknowledge it. But her head was spinning, her heart hurting, her chest heavy, as though bags of cement had been placed on her.

'My father…' He hesitated and she glanced up at him, seeing tension radiating from his handsome face. 'We're not in a good place right now.'

She could tell how hard it was for Zeus to admit that. It was the sharing of a secret, of a part of him that he instinctively wanted to keep hidden.

Everything she knew about Aristotle caused her to dislike the older man, but she kept her tone neutral as she asked, 'Why not?'

Zeus's eyes skimmed to her face then bounced away to the ocean. They were close to where his boat was moored, but she didn't want to leave this idyllic beach without finishing this conversation. She was worried that once they stepped onboard, he'd move on to something else. She slowed her step imperceptibly.

Zeus made a gruff sound, part sigh, part grimace. 'He's not the man I thought he was.'

Jane chewed into her lower lip. This was getting close to home, close to Lottie, she just knew.

'Last week he told me that he'd had an affair.'

Jane's footing stumbled a little and Zeus's arm shot out to wrap around her waist. Instinctively protective. Her heart sped up.

'Recently?' Her voice was hoarse to her own ears.

'Who knows? This affair was many years ago, but how can I trust it hasn't been going on longer? That there haven't been other women?'

'Why would he tell you about one but not others?' she pointed out, logically.

'Because in this instance, there's a complication.' He glanced down at her and Jane's heart skipped several beats in a row. 'A daughter.'

She gasped. Lottie. So, Zeus had only just found out about her. He hadn't known about Lottie and chosen to ignore her. He'd been as innocent in all of this as Lottie herself. Guilt, grief, pain and panic swirled inside Jane's gut.

'I see,' she whispered, because she *did* see. She saw all too much.

'She's twenty-three, and my father has been supporting her all these years. While my mother lay dying...'

'What would you have had him do, Zeus?' she felt compelled to say, in defence of her best friend. 'Leave her to fend for herself?'

A muscle jerked in Zeus's jaw.

'He took steps to make sure she was never discovered—for my mother's sake. It would have destroyed her to know he'd cheated.'

Jane's eyes filled with tears; she blinked quickly to dispel them.

'But now my mother's gone, and all of a sudden, he wants to acknowledge this woman. To bring her into the family,' Zeus spat, and now Jane found the simple act of walking beyond her.

'What?' Her voice was hoarse. Just a whisper.

Zeus was so wrapped up in his own thoughts that he evidently didn't notice how pale Jane had become, all the colour fading from her cheeks as she stared up at him.

'As if I have any interest in knowing her.'

'Why not?' Jane groaned, pressing a hand to his chest. This was *Lottie* they were talking about. Lottie, Jane's best friend. Lottie, who was smart and charming and sweet and kind. Lottie, who could light a room up just by walking into it.

'She is evidence of my father's failings.'

Jane's eyes swept shut. 'Zeus, it's not that simple.'

He was silent.

Jane tried again. 'She's a person, and none of this is her fault, just as it's not your fault. And maybe it's not your father's fault, either. He made a bad decision when your mother got sick. A terrible decision, but he was probably driven half-mad with grief and worry. People do silly things sometimes. They make mistakes. Surely, you have it in your heart to forgive him?'

'No.' He stared down at her now with eyes that were black with fierce determination, and she shivered; this was a side to him Jane hadn't seen. 'Betrayal is the one thing I cannot forgive, not from someone I trust.'

Jane's heart turned to ice and her skin stung all over. Panic flared through her.

'The worst of it is because of the way our company is structured, she has it in her power to take it away from me. All of it.' The words were clipped, his tone short. A lump formed in Jane's throat. 'I can't let that happen.'

She wanted to agree with him. If she didn't know Lottie, she would have readily nodded and told him that of course he couldn't. She knew what the company meant to Zeus; she understood why it was so special to him.

'Surely, you can work out a way to incorporate her into your life, your company...' Though she doubted Lottie would want that. It was all so useless.

'You cannot be serious?' His face held that same expression, that ruthless, bitter anger, so Jane flinched a little.

He softened immediately, lifting a hand to her cheek.

'You see goodness in everyone. I see only the risk of what could go wrong by involving the wrong person. Just because my father had an affair over two decades ago doesn't mean I have any interest in bonding with the woman he insists on calling my *sister*. As for the business, it is mine, Jane, and I will do whatever I can to ensure it stays that way.'

Jane spun away from him before he could see the heartbreak on her face, because she knew what it would take for him to secure the business. As soon as she left, he'd find someone to propose to and would marry as swiftly as the laws would allow. He would be someone else's husband, and Jane would be alone, licking her wounds, having failed Zeus and her best friend.

Only, later that night, back on the boat, Jane realised that maybe she could do something to fix this, after all. When she'd come to Greece, it had been with a simplistic and ill-thought-out plan to delay Zeus's marriage plans. To complicate things for him. She wasn't even sure *how* they'd thought she'd do that. It had been a knee-jerk reaction to the news Lottie had received about the company. Years and years of her hurt at having been hidden away by Aristotle Papandreo, paid off to stay silent, had culminated in a fierce, angry plan to make them pay.

But now Jane knew so much more. She'd seen behind the curtain, and she understood Zeus so much better. She understood his heart, his mind, his goodness and decency. What if she could convince Lottie to abandon her plans to take over the company, to force them into a meeting?

Zeus would never forgive her, Jane recognised. Her betrayal would make that impossible—he'd said as much, and she couldn't blame him. But so what? If it meant the two people she loved most—and she could no longer deny that she had fallen in love with him—could be made happy, could be united, then wasn't it worth sacrificing her own happiness?

Wasn't that her duty?

When you loved, you did what was right for the person you loved, even if it hurt.

And it would hurt, she recognised. It would hurt like the devil, but she would do it. Just as soon as this week was over, she'd fly to Lottie and she'd convince her— she'd use every last word in the dictionary until Lottie understood that Zeus was not the monster they'd always built him up to be. He was, in every way, the total opposite.

When the sun came up the next morning, there was a heaviness inside Jane. It was their last day together. After this, everything between them would change. As soon as she forced a meeting between the two half siblings— which she now knew she absolutely must move heaven and earth to accomplish—Zeus would know that she'd been lying to him all along and he would never again look at her with eyes that seemed to promise he'd climb into heaven and pick out the stars if she asked it of him.

She sat up groggily in the bed, looking towards the window to see a lot of trees on the shore of a sweet little cove. The boat must have moored here overnight; she could hardly keep track of all the islands they'd hopped to.

'I thought we could take a look up close,' he said. 'Start getting your land legs back.'

She glanced down at Zeus, who was awake, but reclined in the same pose he'd been in a moment ago, his bare chest exposed to her, his face so sharply angular and beautiful. She took a moment to commit this to memory and to fold the memory in a little space inside her brain.

'What is it?'

'Prásino Lófo.'

'Your family's island?'

He nodded.

'I'd love to see it,' she said, though the words were heavy, because she knew what the island meant to him and his family. If her plan to unite Lottie and Zeus didn't work, then the marriage wars would be back on, and this island would be Zeus's gift from his father. To enjoy with his new bride.

Bitterness soured her mouth.

'We'll have lunch there,' he said, his hand reaching out for her waist and pulling her towards him, oblivious to her inner turmoil. 'There's no need to rush—we have plenty of exploring we can do here first.' He kissed her as though he had not a care in the world. As though the walls weren't all coming crashing down around them. And, Jane supposed, for him, they weren't. This was still just a simple week-long fling. She surrendered to his touch, his kiss, to the feelings he could evoke, partly because they drove the guilt from her mind temporarily, but mostly because she simply couldn't—and didn't want to—resist him.

He was taunting himself, and he knew it. Bringing Jane to this island so he could always imagine her here. Jane, who might have been his perfect, ideal wife, in a parallel universe. In a universe where he could open himself up to the uncertainties of life, to the idea of loving someone who might leave him, who might hurt him.

In that world, she belonged here.

In this world, too, he thought, watching as she strolled onto the large timber balcony that hung, cantilevered from the house, over a cliff atop the ocean. 'It's so beautiful,' she said, shaking her head a little, so her blond hair, naturally wavy, he'd discovered this week, flew loose around her face, reminding him of gold.

'It was a labour of love for my parents,' Zeus admitted, remembering the way they'd pored over the plans when his mother was well enough. 'They would talk about coming here with their grandchildren.' His smile was grim. They'd all known his mother wouldn't live to see grandchildren, particularly when marriage had been the last thing on Zeus's mind. But it had given her pleasure to imagine, to hope.

'Hence the millions of bedrooms?' Her tone was teasing as she came to stand beside him. 'You'd better get busy, Zeus, because there's room here for at least ten children.'

He didn't laugh. The thought of marrying someone

else, of having children with them, was now like acid inside his throat all the time.

'Do you think you will?' She glanced up at him, the humour gone from her face, too.

He didn't follow. 'Have ten children?'

She waved a hand in the air, her features a little troubled. 'Marry.'

He shifted his body to face her, and the air between them seemed to grow heavy and thick all at once, making it difficult to breathe. In another world, if he were any other man, this might be where he'd say something like, *That depends if you'll agree to marry me.* But Zeus had been shaped by all that he'd seen and lost, by the fear and pain and anticipation of death that he'd been forced to live with almost his entire life. The thought of opening himself up to that again was the antithesis of his approach to life.

And yet, the thought of Jane hearing about his engagement in the papers in a week's time, maybe two weeks, depending on how quickly he acted, and not understanding his reasons for it...

'When I marry,' he said carefully, 'it will be a pragmatic marriage, not for love.'

She bit into her lip, her eyes showing a swirling current of emotion. 'Why?'

'Because I don't want that kind of marriage.'

She shook her head. 'That doesn't make sense.'

'Doesn't it?' He reached out and caught her hair, tucking it behind her ear. 'You know me, Jane.' Even to his own ears, his voice was deep and rumbly. 'After this week, I think you know me better than anyone. Can you really stand there and tell me you don't understand?'

Her lips parted on a quick expulsion of breath.

'The more I felt for someone,' he said, voice gruff, as though it had been dragged from his chest over hot coals, 'the less able I would be to have them in my life.' He stroked her cheek. 'I'd always rather let go on my terms, you see.'

Did she understand what he meant? What he wasn't saying? Did she know how much she'd come to mean to him?

A single tear slid down her cheek, and she turned her face into his palm, eyes sweeping shut. The afternoon sun dipped towards the ocean and cast her in a halo of gold, so she shimmered like an angel.

'I'll always be glad to have met you,' he said, and then, because he couldn't resist, he pulled her to his body and kissed her as though they'd just said their wedding vows, and this was the beginning of the rest of their lives together, rather than the beginning of the end—their last night.

CHAPTER TWELVE

ON THE MORNING of their final day together, Zeus woke early, despite the fact they'd barely slept. Urgency had overtaken them both, so they'd made love hard and fast and then long and slow, reaching for each other, memorising every inch of one another's bodies, remembering everything about this connection they shared.

But the morning broke and with it the reality that Jane would leave him today.

He'd known it was coming.

They'd faced that reality together a week ago, and here they now were, staring down the barrel of the End. He refused to let that hurt him. Or to admit how much it was hurting him?

He wanted to stay with her, in bed, but at the same time, he was possessed by a strange energy. An adrenaline that was pumping through his veins, making him jumpy and unsettled, so he stepped out of the bed with one last look at her sleeping frame, her hair over one shoulder, her lips parted in sleep, and his heart seemed to splinter into a thousand pieces.

Lips a grim line, he strode from the room towards the galley, where he began to brew a coffee, staring out at Prásino Lófo with a heavy heart. Jane had belonged here;

he wasn't imagining that. When she'd stepped onto the island the day before, he'd felt as though something in his chest had locked into place, and that feeling had only built and built until he couldn't help but imagine her there forever. His wife, his other half, his love.

He dropped his head and stared at the benchtop, his heart racing now, a fine bead of perspiration forming at the nape of his neck, because he could no longer pretend that he didn't love her. That he didn't trust her. That he didn't want her—not just out of a sense of transient limerence, but in a lasting, vital way.

It terrified him, because *nothing* was lasting. Nothing was certain.

He'd learned that lesson at a very, very young age. He'd lived alongside a permanent fear of waking up, every day, and having it be the last day in which he saw his mother. That uncertainty had damned near eaten him alive, and he'd seen it all but destroy his father.

How could Zeus possibly be stupid enough to have allowed himself to fall in love?

He had to let Jane go. He had to say goodbye, watch her walk away and never, ever think of her again. He had to employ every ounce of strength at his disposal. Only then would he be safe from those exact same feelings.

Waking up, not knowing if she would be safe, if she would be well. He couldn't do it again, not ever. Loving Jane would mean forever putting his heart on the line, making himself vulnerable and weak. He couldn't do it.

Except…

Would Jane's leaving solve anything? Whether or not he loved her was not an academic concept, but rather, he now accepted, reality. He did love her. She was a part of him, body and soul. So that vulnerability was there, whether she was in his life or not.

The foolish part of what he'd done was inviting her on the boat. He should have run a mile in the opposite direction from her that very first night, when he'd kissed her and felt as if the world's rotation had dramatically picked up speed.

That was when he'd seen the warning signs, heard the siren, had known she'd be trouble. Had known she'd threaten the parameters of his existence. He hadn't run, though, at least, not away from her. If anything, he'd barrelled headlong into this regardless, and now, a little more than a week later, he was in love with her.

He was *in love* with her.

He lifted his head, focusing once more on the island, his heart hammering into his ribcage as realisation began to unfurl through him. He *loved* her. And if she loved him, maybe he could have his cake and eat it, too? He needed to get married, and he'd been thinking of his female friends who might be open to a businesslike marriage arrangement, but somehow, he'd found an option that was so much better.

He could propose to Jane.

Marry her.

Bring her here, to this island, where his wife belonged. Where *she* belonged. He could kiss her every day, for all the days of her life, so that she would never again feel unsafe or afraid. He could love her with every fibre of his being, accepting that risks were inherent to that, but that the alternative was so, so much worse.

Losing her by choice was an action he would never forgive himself for—if he let her walk away without telling her how he felt, he'd always regret it.

His heart burst with lightness and *joy*, an emotion he couldn't remember feeling much of before meeting Jane. It was as though she'd woken him up from a terrible and protracted nightmare, and he was remembering who he was again.

He spun around, intending to stride back to his cabin and wake her up with the realisation he'd just had, but he stopped, because she'd been up almost all night as well, and he didn't want to break her sleep. Yet.

He could wait.

He could wait, to deliver the most important words of his life.

Adrenaline continued to pump through his veins, making him jumpy. Coffee probably wasn't necessary, but he poured a cup anyway and idly picked up his phone, opening his emails—a habit he'd been neglecting since being boat-bound with Jane.

He couldn't help but grin as he flicked through them. Not because of the content, but because he had the woman of his dreams on the boat, a woman he trusted and loved in equal measure, and this was going to be the beginning of the rest of their lives together.

Near the top of his emails, he recognised one had finally come through from the UK-based detective he'd hired. Amazingly, Jane had even managed to push almost all thoughts of his *sister* from his mind.

He clicked into the email, and read the text:

Dear Mr Papandreo,

An extensive background check of Charlotte Shaw has now been conducted. Please find the following information:

Up until then, he hadn't even known her last name. It went on to list her date of birth, residential address, educational qualifications, the fact that she worked in the not-for-profit sector, and was not currently in a relationship.

Also, please find attached some photographs of the subject.

Should you require any further information, do not hesitate to reach out.

Zeus scrolled down to where the photos had loaded into the email. His finger was shaking slightly; he had no idea what she'd look like. She was his half-sister; his father's blood ran in her veins as surely as it ran through his, so he suspected she might look something like him, but the first image that came up on his phone showed a slender redhead with green eyes and alabaster skin. Only her expression was somehow familiar to him. It was a yearbook photo, probably taken sometime earlier, and she was staring directly at the camera in a 'don't mess with me' kind of way that he felt in his bones.

He scrolled to the next photo. This was taken more recently, by a telephoto lens, he'd guess, courtesy of the detective. Charlotte Shaw was stepping out of a grocery store, carrying a paper bag. He could just see the top of a baguette and a bottle of wine.

He flicked down to the next photo and froze. Or perhaps he didn't. Perhaps it was the whole world that froze? It didn't make sense. Nothing about it computed. What was his half-sister doing in a photograph with Jane Fisher? What was Jane—*his* Jane—doing with her arm around Charlotte Shaw's shoulders? The picture was taken from a newspaper, and the detective had cropped enough to show the headline, 'Breaking Barriers for a Cause.'

Perhaps they'd met through work. Met once. Didn't know each other.

But they didn't *look* like two people who didn't know each other. They looked...like friends. His heart thudded and acid burned the back of his throat as he began to look at Jane, and their relationship, through a wholly different prism. From their first meeting, at a bar he had been photographed leaving many, many times. If one did an internet search for his name and clicked into the images, he knew there were pictures there, clearly showing him and the name of the establishment. How easy it would be to find him—and how easy to tempt him, with someone like Jane.

His blood thundered and roared through his body, deafeningly loud.

He loaded up a search browser and typed in Jane's name, as well as his half-sister's, and the full article was one of the first to appear. It had only been written six months earlier.

Childhood best friends making waves in the not-for-profit sector, was the subtitle.

Childhood best friends.

Charlotte Shaw, his half-sister, was Lottie. Jane's Lottie. The best friend he'd praised and been inwardly glad Jane had in his corner!

Nausea rolled through him. Disbelief was quickly followed by shock, then acceptance. And then, finally, fury.

Fury because he'd been played. But to what end? A part of him wanted to cling to the fanciful notion that this was all some big, silly coincidence. Something they could laugh about together. After all, Jane was the woman he loved. A part of him wanted to hold fast to the dreams he'd started to walk towards, to the future he'd envisaged only minutes ago.

But Zeus was not one to run and hide.

Jane had lied to him, and he had to know why. Boxing away the love he felt for her, telling himself it was based on falsity and pretence, he sat at the table and stared straight ahead, ordering his thoughts, making a plan and waiting. For when Jane woke up, they'd have this conversation, and he wouldn't rest until he knew everything.

'Good morning,' she said, trying to hide her ambivalence about whether or not the morning was, in fact, good or not. Ambivalence? She wished she felt ambivalent. The truth was she knew this was going to be one of the hardest days of her life. The only thing getting her through was the certainty that she was leaving Zeus to fly to Lottie, whom she would sit down and make see sense about this whole situation. Just imagining the truce she could bring about between the two of them was almost enough to ease her pain. Almost, but not quite.

And maybe, just maybe, when it was all out in the open, and things had calmed down, Zeus might even understand…

'Are you packed?'

His voice was strange. Dark and heavy. His eyes met hers, but they were ice-cold, utterly different to how he'd looked at her the night before, with something that had felt almost like love to her silly wishful heart.

Perhaps he was just finding the emotion of the day too

much, like she was? He was standing across the room, hips pressed to the kitchen counter, mug of coffee in hand, and he looked good enough to eat.

'I— Not yet.' She'd been putting it off, naturally. She wanted to eke out as much of this day together as she possibly could.

'I've organised for my helicopter to take you to Athens from the island. It will be ready in ten minutes.'

She gaped. 'Ten...minutes?'

He nodded once. 'Which should be just long enough for you to explain to me exactly how you know Charlotte Shaw, and exactly what the plan was in coming to Athens?'

Jane gasped, her eyes filling with stars, the world growing black, so for a fearsome moment she thought she might pass out. He was staring at her as though she were something disgusting on his shoe, as though he could barely stand to breathe the same air as her. 'How did you—?'

How he'd found out was hardly the most important thing to ask, but it was a reasonable question.

Nonetheless, his eyes flashed with fury that she'd immediately asked that, rather than something else.

'That's irrelevant. And I'll be the one posing the questions.'

She shuddered. He wasn't angry, she realised. She'd been wrong to perceive fury in his eyes. Disgust, yes, and coldness, which was somehow so, so much worse.

'You knew about the marriage clause of my family's business all along.'

She closed her eyes on a wave of panic. 'Zeus, let me explain—'

'Did you know about it?' he interrupted, staring her down, so when she blinked her eyes open, she was lanced by the intensity of his gaze.

'Yes.' A whispered admission; a death knell. His own eyes closed then, briefly, on a wave of acceptance, so she realised that up until that moment, he'd been holding out some form of hope that maybe she hadn't known. That maybe the marriage clause *wasn't* why she'd come to Athens.

'And you were supposed to, what? Tempt me into marriage then stand me up at the altar?'

'No.' She spat the word like a curse.

'I find that hard to believe.'

'It wasn't a particularly well-thought-out plan,' she whispered. 'Lottie—'

At the mention of Charlotte's abbreviated name, he cursed softly so she grimaced.

'She was upset. After your father told her about the arrangement, she...'

'Wanted the company, yes, that much I deduced for myself.'

'You see it as your birthright,' Jane murmured.

'It *is* my birthright. I was raised to do this.'

'But she is also a Papandreo.'

His nostrils flared.

Jane's loyalties were so incredibly torn. She had to make him see Lottie's side, even when she knew that would cost her everything with Zeus. Her throat hurt from the weight of unshed tears, but she continued.

'You don't know what it was like for her, Zeus.'

He made a gruff sound of disgust, but Jane continued regardless, her voice shaking a little. She felt tears splash down her cheeks, warm and fat, but she didn't bother to check them.

'All her life, Lottie has felt like someone people were ashamed of. Her mother—'

He swore again. 'Do *not* speak to me of that whore.'

'Zeus…' Jane was appalled. 'Mariah Shaw is *not* a whore, and I'll have you know she was head over heels in love with your father. She's loved him all this time, has never been with another man since. How can you possibly judge someone you've never met?'

A muscle jerked in his jaw as he continued to lance her with his dark stare.

'She didn't want to make things harder for him—'

'How generous of her.'

'Or your mother,' Jane added softly.

'And I'm sure the ten million pounds my father paid her, not to mention ongoing child support, had nothing to do with that.'

Jane flinched on behalf of Lottie and her mother. 'You don't think Lottie was entitled to be raised in a lifestyle akin to yours? Would you have preferred it if your father had left Mariah to struggle, as a poor single mother?'

Zeus's face paled beneath his tan. At least on that front she was sure she'd gotten through to him.

'Five minutes,' he said, voice cold, so even if she had felt like she'd made some headway, she realised very quickly that it wasn't enough.

Jane closed her eyes, her heart hurting more than it had ever hurt in her life. 'What else do you want to know?'

'The plan. All of it.'

'There was no plan,' she said, but he made a scoffing noise to dispute that. 'Not a very good one, anyway.'

He stared at her, waiting for her to continue.

'Lottie wanted me to distract you,' she said, biting into her lip.

'To make me want you,' he murmured. 'So that I wouldn't propose to anyone else?'

Jane squeezed her eyes shut and nodded once, a tiny shift of her head.

'And in the meantime, she'd be looking for someone to get married to, so that she could take the business away from me?'

It all sounded so incredibly awful said like that. But what could she do? There was no sense denying it.

'Is that correct, Jane?'

She bit into her lip. 'You need to understand—'

His nostrils flared. 'I understand perfectly,' he cut her off. 'All this time, when you were imploring me to bare my soul to you, you already knew so much about me. You have *lied* to me, every step of the way, haven't you? From that first night in the bar, until this morning, you have hidden your true self from me.'

She shook her head, her stomach churning. 'No, Zeus, that's not true.' She strode across the room then, curling her hand around his arm, shaking him. She needed him to understand. 'Everything between us has been real. *This* is real.'

His only response was to angle his head and stare at her hand as though it were something vile and disgusting. 'Do not touch me, Jane.'

She dropped her hand like she'd been burned, quickly wiping away her tears, only for more to take their place.

'Zeus,' her voice trembled.

'You did so well,' he drawled. 'What excellent bait

you proved to be. Though you didn't need to go so far as making up sob stories about your romantic past. I wouldn't have cared if you'd slept with every man in Britain—I still would have wanted you with the force of a thousand suns.'

'I didn't make that up,' she whispered, her chest cleaving apart at the very idea of lying about something so intimate. It had been such a huge deal for Jane to disclose the truth to him. She swallowed, but her throat was constricted. Her head ached.

'You'll forgive me if I don't believe you. You have no credibility with me, and with good reason, wouldn't you say?'

She was shaking like a leaf. She reached behind her for a chair, sitting down with a dull sense of aching bones.

'Unfortunately for you and your friend, your plan failed.'

Jane blinked up at him, eyes wide.

'I'm getting married, you see,' he said, and her heart stammered as her legs began to tremble.

'What?'

'Mmm-hmm. I proposed to a friend of mine the night I met you. You'll remember I had a dinner?'

Jane's lips parted.

'It was one of the reasons I had to bring you onto the boat. I could hardly risk the press getting wind of the fact I was sleeping with you, when my fiancée was off buying wedding clothes.'

'I don't believe you,' Jane whispered, shaking her head.

'Only one of us is a liar here, Jane.' The indictment was like a slap; she flinched at the depth of hatred in his voice. The ice. The rejection.

Every part of her hurt. Every cell, every drop of blood, every atom of her being.

'You think I haven't hated lying to you, Zeus?'

'You haven't exactly seemed conflicted.'

'Yeah, well, I have been,' she shouted, then sobbed, because it was all so awful, so devastatingly bad. 'Do you want to know what I was planning to do today?'

He stared back at her without asking the question.

'I was going to go to Lottie, to tell her about how wonderful you are, how much she'd love you if she got to know you. I was going to beg her to put off whatever plan she'd concocted and focus on meeting her half-brother, on meeting the man that I love.' Her voice stammered over the last word and her cheeks flushed with pink at what she was admitting to him. But he needed to know how real this was for her; how incredibly special it had all been.

'You don't love me,' he responded, rejecting her admission.

'How can you say that?'

'Because you have been lying to me this whole week,' he reminded her, voice deathly quiet.

She sobbed once more.

'I wanted to tell you the truth, but it's not my truth to tell. I needed Lottie…'

'You listened to me describe what that business means to me, all the while knowing that every moment we spent on this boat was a moment closer to your best friend triumphing over me, taking it all away.'

'I would have done everything in my power to stop that, I promise.'

'Your promises aren't worth a damned thing,' he

snapped. 'Time's up.' He straightened, crossing his arms over his chest. 'I have a wedding to prepare for.'

She flinched, standing, moving to him, reaching out but he stepped away.

'Don't,' he insisted, firmly.

She could hardly speak for how hard she was crying. Her soul was shattered. Every part of her life had been distilled to this moment; she was falling apart.

'Please don't marry her,' she whispered.

He glared through her. 'You're trying to succeed in your plan, even now?'

She shook her head. 'I don't care about anything but this.' She pushed her hand into her chest then gestured to him. 'You and I—'

'Have been having sex,' he muttered.

'Don't do that.'

'Do what? Be honest? I'm sorry if that offends you.'

'Don't say we're just sex. You know this is so much more.'

'It's all a lie,' he spat. 'All of it.'

She wanted to scream at him, to make him understand how wrong he was, but what would the point be? He was clearly determined to think the worst. She sobbed and nodded, unable to think of a single thing she could say that might get through to him.

'I'm so sorry,' she whispered, because she was. From the very depths of her heart, she regretted having agreed to go along with this. And yet, if she hadn't, she never would have met Zeus, and she couldn't countenance that. 'And I do love you, Zeus. Whatever else you believe, I hope one day you'll at least accept that.'

And she turned and ran back to the room they'd been sharing, to throw her clothes into a bag so she could get off his boat before she collapsed into a heap.

CHAPTER THIRTEEN

FOR FORTY-EIGHT HOURS, Zeus did very little but drink Scotch, drift on the ocean in his yacht and contemplate every single word they'd spoken. Every emotion. Every barb. He'd accused her of lying—and she had—but he'd lied, too, in the end about his engagement. He was ashamed of himself for doing the one thing he'd promised them both he never would: he'd hurt her. And he'd done it deliberately. He'd wanted to dig the knife in, so to speak, because of how she'd made him feel.

So what? Didn't she deserve it?

Of course. She'd manipulated him for financial gain. She'd been sent by her best friend to destroy the one thing that mattered most to him. By every metric, she was an awful, awful person.

So why didn't he feel more relieved? Why was he drinking himself into a stupor rather than flying home and proposing to Philomena then and there?

Because he needed time to deal with this. Unlike his mother's death, he hadn't been braced for Jane's betrayal. He'd *trusted* her, he thought, angrily. He'd let his guard down with her, something he'd never done with another soul, and she'd promised him he could. That it was safe. She'd made him trust her. Because it wasn't enough just to screw with him? What kind of sick game had she wanted to play?

Disgust—at himself and her, at his father and Charlotte—flooded his body. He poured another measure of Scotch, held it close to his chest and tried to think clearly. To contemplate his next move. Marriage. To someone else. He knew it was vital, but just the thought of it turned his stomach.

He'd loved Jane, and despite her betrayal, there was a part of him that still did. At least, that loved the version of her she'd shown him.

This is real.

Liar.

He threw back the Scotch then slammed the glass down, wondering how the hell he could get her out of his head and heart.

Four days later, Zeus arrived at his office with no outward hint of what had happened on the boat. Dressed in a suit, he strode in, determined to take charge of his company, to work out a way to keep it in his name, telling himself that was still the most important thing in his life.

Only, within minutes of sitting behind his desk and drafting an email to his lawyer, one of his assistants buzzed his phone.

'I'm sorry to interrupt, sir, but there's a woman here to see you.'

Images of Jane filled his mind. Was it possible she was still here? That she'd come to see him? And so what if she had? His breath hitched in his throat. His gut shanked.

'I'm busy,' he replied, because it was important that he not see her again. Not yet. He wasn't prepared.

'She says it's urgent.'

He ground his teeth. 'Fine,' he said, standing. 'But tell her I only have five minutes.'

He prowled to his floor-to-ceiling window overlooking Athens and waited, every bone in his body feeling heavy and stiff. The door opened and he made an effort to turn slowly, to brace for the impact of seeing her.

It was not, however, Jane who'd come to his office, but rather the woman he'd spent weeks hating and despising. His half-sister, Charlotte Shaw.

'You,' he muttered, glaring at her, surprised that she was shorter in real life than he'd expected, and far slimmer, too.

'You,' she spat back at him, crossing her arms. 'Well, if I didn't hate you before, I sure as hell have a reason to now.'

He laughed darkly. 'Are you kidding me?'

'Nothing about this is remotely amusing.'

'You're telling me?' His eyes fell to her hand, and he saw on her ring finger a large emerald ring, so his stomach clenched—though, strangely, he'd been half expecting this, and he wasn't even sure he could raise the energy to care anymore. Ironic, given how focused he'd been a moment ago on securing the company. 'You're engaged?'

'And you're a Grade-A jackass,' she snapped.

His head reeled. 'You sent your best friend to Athens to seduce me so you could steal my company,' he said baldly. 'And I'm the jackass?'

She at least had the decency to look ashamed.

'Yeah, well, you sent her home utterly destroyed, so what are you going to do about it?'

His gut churned. Pain slashed through him. Jane, destroyed. Like she'd been on the boat, when she'd sobbed and pleaded with him to understand that she loved him. When she'd apologised and said she wanted to explain, and he'd cut her off, because on that morning, he'd truly felt as though no explanation would ever suffice.

'I'm sure she'll recover.'

'Are you? Well, that shows how well you know her, because I've *never* seen Jane like this. Not even after Steven.' It was the worst thing Lottie could have said to him. The truth of that plunged into him like a knife.

'And it's my fault,' she continued. 'I'm the one who begged her to do this. I'm the one who pushed past her objections, who pleaded with her, because I knew that she would never say no to me. I used her,' Charlotte continued, guilt-stricken, crossing her arms, 'and now I have to fix it.'

'Some things can't be fixed,' he said darkly, thinking of his love for Jane and how transformative it had been—and how devastating to recognise that it had also been based on a scam.

'You're not even going to try?'

'Why would I?' he demanded, blanking Jane from his mind with Herculean effort.

'So, you don't love her?'

He kept his expression neutral, but just barely. 'I can't see what business that is of yours.'

'I'm making it my business.'

He actually laughed, a deranged sort of sound, totally lacking humour. 'That's not your prerogative.'

'This makes it so.' She lifted her hand, so the ring sparkled visibly. 'You care about this company.'

His nostrils flared with an angry breath.

'You want to keep it?'

He thrust a hand onto his hip.

'Well, I will walk away, sign whatever I need to in order to give up my stake in it, if you promise to at least go and *talk* to her.'

The bottom seemed to be tilting out of his world.

'I thought you wanted the company badly enough to do anything?'

'I want my best friend to be happy more,' she said with a withering and derisive scowl. 'I would give up anything for her, as she would for me. Did you even know that's what she was planning to do?'

He didn't move.

'She was coming home to tell me that she loved you, that she thought I'd love you, too, that she wanted us to be friends. She knew it might mean losing you, but she was going to put you and me first, because that's the kind of person she is. And if you truly don't see that,' she said, stalking back towards the door and wrenching it inwards, 'then you don't deserve her.' She left without a backwards glance and Zeus had the unfamiliar and unwelcome experience of having been hit by a tornado.

For the first time in a week, Jane left the flat. She didn't feel like it. In fact, she desperately wanted to stay buried under her mountain of duvets and keep crying, but there was also a restlessness to her grief, or perhaps to her cravings for Zeus, that had her yearning to move her body. To feel blood rushing through her, to feel *alive* once more. So, she pulled on yoga pants and a loose shirt and set out for a run, targeting her favourite route through the Heath, uncaring that the day was hot and the breeze non-existent. It felt good to sweat. It felt good to be so hot it was almost a form of torture. It felt good to fill her lungs with air and expel it so hard and fast everything burned.

At least now she knew she was alive. She ran for almost an hour before turning back towards her flat, and when she reached her street, she was so focused on the harsh ache in her lungs that she didn't notice the sleek black car parked in the narrow road, right outside her front door. As she got near it, though, the driver's door opened, and the sound caught her attention. She glanced across and stumbled, gasped, because there was Zeus Papandreo, looking intimidating and perfectly unbreakable, looking just as he had in her dreams, looking right back at her, and she stopped walking, with no idea what she could say, nor why he was here, but just knowing that she wasn't ready.

She couldn't face him.

'I'm— I need—' She pressed her fingers to her lips and took a step backwards, her face pale.

'Can we talk?'

She shook her head instinctively. On the one hand, she was desperate to talk to him some more, to do anything to spend time with him, but on the other, their last encounter had left her so badly bruised, she couldn't go through it again.

'I can't,' she whispered, dropping her head and staring at her feet. 'I want to, and I probably owe it to you, but I can't go through any more of that.' Her voice was barely above a mumble. 'I can't fight with you again.'

'I don't want to fight with you.'

A tear slid down her cheek. She flicked a glance at him. 'I don't believe you.'

His eyes slammed shut on a wave of emotions she

couldn't interpret. 'I don't blame you.' He sighed. 'Listen, Jane, I was very angry that morning. I should have taken some time to get more facts, but I didn't. I took it out on you. I'm sorry.'

She shook her head quickly. 'More facts wouldn't have changed your mind. I did everything you accused me of.'

'You didn't lie to me,' he said, stepping closer towards her. 'Not about us. Everything we shared was real, and true, just like you said.'

She shook her head again. It was all too much. She didn't want to hear this, only to have him walk away and marry someone else. Did he have any notion how that idea had tortured her? The thought that he'd been engaged to someone else the whole time they'd been together? Having sex, as he'd so crudely put it. She took another step backwards, as if to repel that idea, and his features sharpened into a look of regret.

'Oh, Jane,' he sighed softly. 'If I could take back that morning—' he held his hands up, palms towards her, in a gesture of conciliation '—believe me, I would.'

She bit into her lower lip, heart popping like fizzing candy. She wanted to believe him, but how could she?

'The idea of having been lied to by *you*, the idea that I had been so damned foolish and mistaken what we were for something else entirely, it just made me feel so stupid. So angry. So hurt. And I took all of that out on you, instead of letting you explain. Instead of *hearing* what you were saying.'

'You did—'

'No, I mean really hearing you. Hearing you when you spoke about Charlotte's life, and how my father's choice to shield her from the world was a daily abandonment she has had to live with. How you saw that and moved in to mop up the pieces again and again, because even though she is strong and courageous, you see the same vulnerabilities in her that you feel in yourself. I wish I'd listened to you when you'd explained that she's your best friend, that you felt obligated to help her, even when you questioned the wisdom of her plan. And mostly, I wish I'd believed you when you said you wanted to change her mind, that you were planning to tell her that this was all wrong.'

Jane's eyes widened with shock and surprise. 'How did you—'

'Charlotte,' he said, dragging a hand through his hair. 'You got your wish. We ended up meeting, spending some time together these last couple of days. She made me see what a monumental ass I'd been. Which is why I'm here.' His brow furrowed. 'Actually, I don't know if that's true. I suspect that even without Charlotte, I would have come to my senses eventually. She just dragged me there ahead of schedule.'

Jane blinked at him, her gut throbbing.

'I was never engaged to anyone else, Jane. I said that because I was lashing out. It is one of the biggest mistakes of my life. To know that I hurt you, that I inflicted that wound on you, because of my own pain, is something I will always be unbearably ashamed of.'

She groaned, dropping her head forward, because he *had* hurt her. Those words had tortured and tormented her every minute since. The prospect of him marrying— even when she'd contemplated that before.

'I didn't come here expecting that we could just get past this. I know it will take time. But I wanted to come to apologise first, and then to ask if you would even consider giving me another chance?'

Her head lifted of its own accord, her eyes locking to his.

And she felt all the uncertainty there—an uncharacteristic emotion for a man like Zeus—the sense that he was putting himself so far out on a limb for her. But Jane's heart was so battered, and her doubts so huge. Not about whether or not she loved him, but about what they could do next. For as much as he was begging for forgiveness, didn't she owe him the same?

'I wish I'd never agreed to do it,' she said softly, twisting her hands in front of her. 'But Charlotte was so sure—'

'And she's hard to say no to. I've seen it, believe me.'

A half smile lifted one side of Jane's mouth before dropping abruptly.

'If you hadn't agreed to it, we never would have met.' He closed the distance between them and this time, Jane held her ground, knowing he was going to touch her, and welcoming that. Needing it.

Slowly, so slowly she had time to avoid him if she wished it, he reached down and added his hand to hers, where they were still knotting at her front. 'From the moment we met, it was never about your promise to Charlotte, was it?'

Her eyes were round as they flew to his face, and she shook her head quickly. 'It was always about you.'

'And you,' he murmured, eyes dropping to her lips. 'And the kind of love that's rare and special and deserves to be fought for.'

Her breath rushed out of her lungs. 'Love?'

'Love. Obsession. Desire. Need.'

She laughed then, a laugh that was filled with the levity of a heart that was starting to glow with warmth once more. 'All that, huh?'

'And so much more. The kind of love that lasts a lifetime,' he promised, squeezing her hand then growing serious. 'Jane, before I found out about your connection to Charlotte, I felt as though I was walking on air, because I'd finally realised how I felt about you. I knew I'd met the love of my life, and that the kind of future I'd never allowed myself to hope for was suddenly all I could focus on. I had every intention of proposing to you that very morning, my *agapeméni*, in the shadows of the island that will soon be ours.'

Stars filled her vision, and she moved then, wrapping her arms around his waist and pulling him closer to her body. 'Is that your way of asking me to marry you, Zeus?'

'It's my way of *begging* you to relieve this enormous, crippling pain I've felt since you walked out of my life. How ever you can be in my world, whatever role you're willing to play, I want you there. I love you, and I am, and always will be, completely and utterly yours.'

A tear slid down her cheek, but for the first time since the yacht, this was a tear of joy, of giddy, blinding happiness and contentment. 'Well, then,' she murmured. 'I don't know how I could refuse,' she said, kissing him until her breath was burning in her lungs, a kiss that grew steadily more and more intense and passionate, so it was Zeus who pulled away, breathlessly, to suggest they move inside her flat rather than continue giving Hampstead a show.

And those were the last coherent words either of them spoke for several hours.

Afterwards, though, Jane realised there was one question she hadn't brought up. 'What will happen with the company?' Something heavy pressed against her chest, a weight that threatened to jeopardise the sheer joy she felt. 'I know it's yours, but at the same time, if our wedding meant Lottie couldn't be a part of it...'

'My father is having documents drawn as we speak. We cannot change the contracts of ownership, but we can redesign the organisational structure. I haven't discussed it with Charlotte yet, but my hope is that she'll agree to come on board with the Foundation, in the first instance. It seems like a natural fit.'

'Foundation?'

'I'm surprised I didn't mention it,' he said, his shoulder nudging hers. 'We run a large charity as part of our business, though I'm not surprised you're unaware. Silent philanthropy has always been important to my father, as it is to me. The charity is active in the US and much of Europe. As luck would have it, we're on the lookout for a director of operations. I think Charlotte would be perfect for the job.'

Jane's heart soared. 'Oh, she would be.'

'As would you,' he said, eyes roaming her face. 'There are other roles...'

She reached for his hand and squeezed it. 'I'll find another job,' she said. 'When I'm ready. But for now, if I'm completely honest, I'd like to focus on this.' She gestured from herself to him. 'For the first time in my life, I feel happy, and I feel loved, and I feel as though when I'm with you, I'm right exactly where I'm meant to be.

I'd sort of like to just soak that up for a while. Does that sound weird?'

'*Agapaméni*, it sounds perfect.' And he reached down then, to the side of her bed, pulling his pants up and rifling through the pockets to remove a black velvet box. 'I didn't come here holding any hopes,' he promised. 'Well, maybe a very small hope, based on what a kind and forgiving, and generous-hearted angel you are. But if there was any chance that you might agree to marry me, I wanted to have this to give to you.'

He popped open the black velvet box to reveal an enormous diamond ring encircled by sapphires. 'It was my grandmother's,' he said, voice a little thick.

Her eyes were filled with moisture as she extended a shaking hand towards him, so that he could slip the ring in place. It fit like a glove.

'I have my mother's ring, too, but my father has asked that he be allowed to give that to you—to welcome you to the family.'

'The family,' she breathed out, and then fell back against Zeus's chest, a smile stretched from ear to ear. Yes, she was just perfectly, exactly where she wanted to be.

* * * * *

MILLS & BOON®

Coming next month

BUSINESS BETWEEN ENEMIES
Louise Fuller

My heart feels like a dead weight inside my chest.

I stare at the man standing with his back to me beside the window, panic slipping and sliding over my skin like suntan oil.

Only it's not just panic. It's something I can't, won't name, that flickers down my spine and over my skin, pulling everything so tight that it's suddenly hard to catch my breath. And I hate that even now he can do this to me. That he can make me shake, and on the inside too, before I even see his face.

My stomach clenches and unclenches, and my heart starts to pound painfully hard, and I can't stop either happening. This is his doing. Just being near him does things to my body, things I can't control. But I need to control them.

'What's he doing here?' I say hoarsely. Although I don't know why I ask that question, because I know the answer. But I can't accept it until I hear it said out loud.

'Mr. Valetti is the new co-CEO.'

Continue reading

BUSINESS BETWEEN ENEMIES
Louise Fuller

Available next month
millsandboon.co.uk

Copyright ©2025 Louise Fuller

COMING SOON!

We really hope you enjoyed reading this book.
If you're looking for more romance
be sure to head to the shops when
new books are available on

Thursday 23rd October

To see which titles are coming soon, please visit
millsandboon.co.uk/nextmonth

MILLS & BOON

MILLS & BOON TRUE LOVE IS HAVING A MAKEOVER!

Introducing

Love Always

Swoon-worthy romances, where love takes centre stage. Same heartwarming stories, stylish new look!

Look out for our brand new look

OUT NOW

MILLS & BOON

FOUR BRAND NEW BOOKS FROM
MILLS & BOON MODERN

Indulge in desire, drama, and breathtaking romance – where passion knows no bounds!

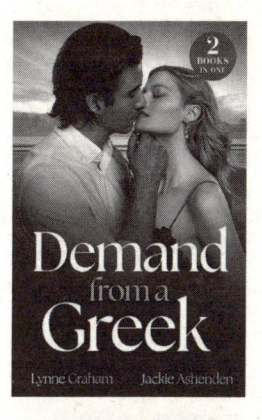

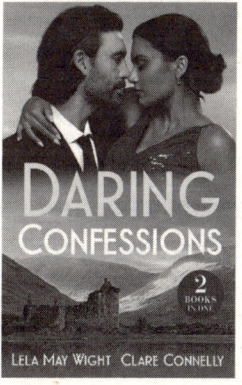

Demand from a Greek
Lynne Graham Jackie Ashenden

CRAVE ME
Michelle Smart Lorraine Hall

DARING CONFESSIONS
LELA MAY WIGHT CLARE CONNELLY

With his Ring...
Lucy King Millie Adams

OUT NOW

Eight Modern stories published every month, find them all at:
millsandboon.co.uk

afterglow BOOKS

Afterglow Books is a trend-led, trope-filled list of books with diverse, authentic and relatable characters, a wide array of voices and representations, plus real world trials and tribulations. Featuring all the tropes you could possibly want (think small-town settings, fake relationships, grumpy vs sunshine, enemies to lovers) and all with a generous dose of spice in every story.

♪ @millsandboonuk
◉ @millsandboonuk
afterglowbooks.co.uk
#AfterglowBooks

For all the latest book news, exclusive content and giveaways scan the QR code below to sign up to the Afterglow newsletter:

SCAN ME

afterglow BOOKS

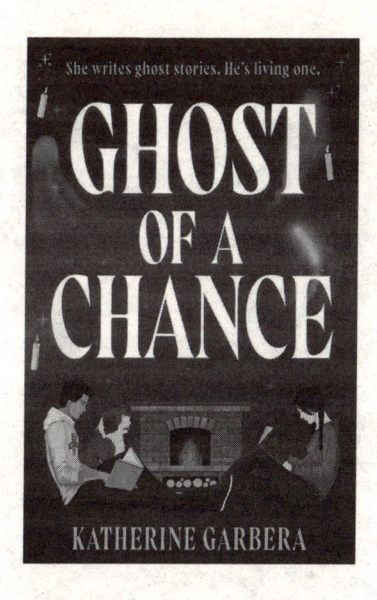

GHOST OF A CHANCE

She writes ghost stories. He's living one.

KATHERINE GARBERA

- 🛏 One night
- 💕 Second chance
- 🎭 Secret identity

OUT NOW

To discover more visit:
Afterglowbooks.co.uk

OUT NOW!

THE **TYCOON'S AFFAIR** COLLECTION

BUSINESS WITH PLEASURE

MAYA BLAKE

Available at
millsandboon.co.uk

MILLS & BOON

OUT NOW!

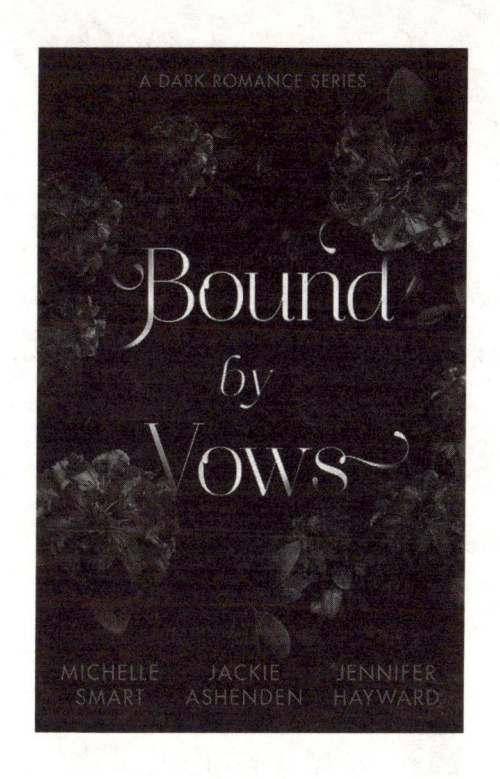

A DARK ROMANCE SERIES

Bound by Vows

MICHELLE SMART · JACKIE ASHENDEN · JENNIFER HAYWARD

Available at
millsandboon.co.uk

MILLS & BOON

LET'S TALK
Romance

For exclusive extracts, competitions and special offers, find us online:

- **f** MillsandBoon
- **X** @MillsandBoon
- **◉** @MillsandBoonUK
- **♪** @MillsandBoonUK

Get in touch on 01413 063 232

For all the latest titles coming soon, visit
millsandboon.co.uk/nextmonth